# The Falcon at the Portal

# Elizabeth Peters

·

## THE FALCON
## AT THE PORTAL

AN AMELIA PEABODY MYSTERY

AVON BOOKS, INC.
1350 Avenue of the Americas
New York, New York 10019

Copyright © 1999 by MPM Manor, Inc.
Interior design by Kellan Peck
ISBN: 0-380-97658-7

AVON TWILIGHT TRADEMARK REG. U.S. PAT. OFF. AND IN OTHER COUNTRIES, MARCA REGISTRADA, HECHO EN U.S.A.

Printed in the U.S.A.

www.avonbooks.com/twilight

**TO RAY**

A thousand of every good and pure thing...

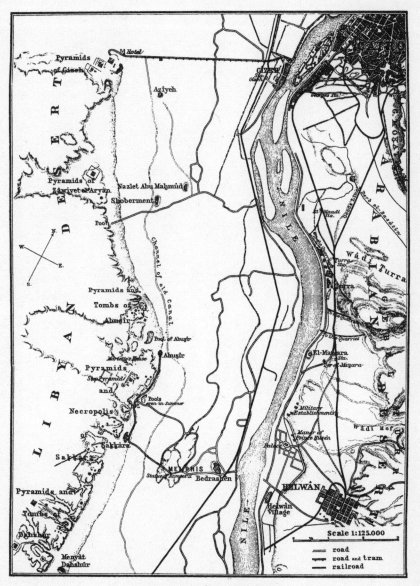

Cairo and environs in 1911

# The Falcon at the Portal

# Preface

The Reader will note that there is a gap of several years between the date of the last published volume of Mrs. Emerson's memoirs and the present book. Thus far the search for the missing manuscripts has proven vain, but the Editor has not abandoned hope of finding them. As in the previous volume, she has inserted sections of Manuscript H and letters from Collection B at appropriate intervals.

The quotations at the head of each chapter were taken from *A Captive of the Arabs*, by Percival Peabody, Esquire. (Privately printed, London, 1911.) We were fortunate to be able to obtain a copy of this exceedingly rare volume through the good offices of a friend in London who found it on a barrow in Covent Garden (price 50 p.). The text is an astonishing blend of the worst of two literary forms: the swashbuckling romances popular at the time and the memoirs of travelers and officials of the period. The views expressed by Mr. Peabody are no more bigoted and ignorant than those of many of his contemporaries; however, the parallels between his work and other memoirs are so exact as to suggest he borrowed freely and directly from them. The word plagiarism might be actionable, so this editor will not use it.

As always, I am indebted to friends in the Egyptology game for advice, suggestions, and hard-to-find material. Dennis Forbes (whose magnum opus, *Tombs. Treasures. Mummies.* is now available), George B. Johnson, W. Raymond Johnson, Director of Chicago House, Luxor, and especially Peter Dorman of the Oriental Institute, who read the entire bulky manuscript and corrected a number of errors.

I am also indebted to the genial, efficient, and enthusiastic group of people at Avon Books who have taken the Emersons under their collective wing: Mike Greenstein and Lou Aronica, President and Publisher; Joan Schulhafer and Linda Johns, super publicists; and especially my favorite editor of all time, Trish Grader. Thanks, guys. You could make Amelia reconsider her rude remarks about "publishing persons."

A note on the rendering of Arabic and ancient Egyptian words may be in order here. Both written languages omit the vowels, and certain consonants have no precise English equivalent, so transliterations into English may vary. A long *i* may be rendered as *i* or *ee*; the long *u* sound may be *u*, with or without a circumflex, or *oo*; the name of the pharaoh Zoser begins with a consonant that is sometimes written as Dj. This gives only a faint idea of the variants, which also changed with time. Mrs. Emerson is inclined to stick to the spelling current in her youth, but she also uses more modern variants of certain words, such as Dahshur and Giza. This is, the editor believes, a fairly common failing, so she is not about to apologize for inconsistencies.

**They attacked at dawn. I woke instantly at the sound of pounding hooves, for I knew what it meant. The Beduin were on the warpath!**

"What is it you find so amusing, my dear?" I inquired.

Nefret looked up from her book. "I am sorry if I disturbed you, Aunt Amelia, but I couldn't help laughing. Did you know that Beduins go on the warpath? Wearing feathered headdresses and waving tomahawks, no doubt!"

The library of our house in Kent is supposed to be my husband's private sanctum, but it is such a pleasant room that all the members of the family tend to congregate there, especially in fine weather. Except for my son Ramses we were all there that lovely autumn morning; a cool breeze wafted through the wide windows that opened onto the rose garden, and sunlight brightened Nefret's gold-red hair.

Reclining comfortably upon the sofa, Nefret wore a sensible divided skirt and shirtwaist instead of a proper frock. She had become as dear as a daughter to us since we rescued her from the remote oasis in the Nubian Desert where she had spent the first thirteen years of her life, but despite my best efforts I had been unable to eradicate all the peculiar notions she had acquired there. Emerson claims some of those peculiar notions have been acquired from me. I do not consider a dislike of corsets and a firm belief in the equality of the female sex peculiar, but I must admit that Nefret's habit of sleeping with a long knife under her pillow might strike some as unusual. I could not complain of this, however, since our family does seem to have a habit of encountering dangerous individuals.

Hunched over his desk, Emerson let out a grunt, like a sleepy bear that has been prodded by a stick. My distinguished husband, the greatest Egyptologist of all time, rather resembled a bear at that moment: his broad shoulders were covered by a hideous ill-fitting coat of prickly brown tweed (purchased one day when I was not with him) and his abundant sable locks were wildly disheveled. He was working on his report of our previous season's excavations and was in a surly mood for, as usual, he had put the job off until the last possible moment and was behind schedule.

"Is that Percy's cursed book you are reading?" he demanded. "I thought I threw the damned thing onto the fire."

"You did." Nefret gave him a cheeky smile. Emerson is known as the Father of Curses by his admiring Egyptian workmen; his fiery temper and Herculean frame have made him feared throughout the length and breadth of Egypt. (Mostly the former, since as all educated persons know, Egypt is a very long narrow country.) However, none of those who know him well are at all intimidated by his growls, and Nefret had always been able to wind him round her slim fingers.

"I ordered another copy from London," she said calmly. "Aren't you at all curious about what he writes? He is your own nephew, after all."

"He is not *my* nephew." Emerson leaned back in his chair. "His father is your Aunt Amelia's brother, not mine. James is a hypocritical, sanctimonious, mendacious moron and his son is even worse."

Nefret chuckled. "What a string of epithets! I don't see how Percy could be worse."

"Ha!" said Emerson.

Emerson's eyes are the brilliant blue of a sapphire, and they become even more brilliant when he is in a temper. Any mention of a member of my family generally does put him in a temper, but on this occasion I could tell he was not averse to being interrupted. He stroked his prominent chin, which is adorned with a particularly handsome dent, or dimple, and looked at me.

Or, as a writer more given to clichés might say, our eyes

locked. They often do, for my dear Emerson and I have shared one another's thoughts ever since that halcyon day when we agreed to join hearts, hands and lives in the pursuit of Egyptology. I seemed to see myself reflected in those sapphirine orbs, not (thank Heaven) as I really appear, but as Emerson sees me: my coarse black hair and steely gray eyes and rather too-rounded form transfigured by love into his ideal of female beauty. In addition to the affectionate admiration mirrored in his gaze, I saw as well a kind of appeal. He wanted *me* to be the one to sanction the interruption of his work.

I was not averse to being interrupted either. I had been busily scribbling for several hours, making lists of Things to Be Done and writing little messages to tradesmen. There were more things than usual to be done that particular year—not only the ordinary arrangements for our annual season of excavation in Egypt, but preparations for houseguests and for the forthcoming nuptials of two individuals near and dear to all of us. My fingers were cramped with writing, and if I must be entirely honest I will admit I had been somewhat annoyed with Emerson for burning Percy's book before I could have a look at it.

The only other one of the family present was David. Strictly speaking, he was not a member of the family, but he soon would be, for his marriage to my niece Lia would take place in a few weeks. That arrangement had caused quite a scandal when the announcement was first made. David was a purebred Egyptian, the grandson of our late, greatly lamented reis Abdullah; Lia was the daughter of Emerson's brother Walter, one of England's finest Egyptological scholars, and of my dear friend Evelyn, granddaughter of the Earl of Chalfont. The fact that David was a talented artist and a trained Egyptologist carried no weight with people who considered all members of the darker "races" inferior. Fortunately none of us gives a curse for the opinions of such people.

David was staring out the window, his long thick lashes veiling his eyes, his lips curved in a dreamy smile. He was a handsome young fellow, with finely cut features and a tall, sturdy frame, and in fact he was no darker in complexion than Ramses, whom he strongly (and coincidentally) resembled.

"Shall I read a bit aloud?" Nefret asked. "You have both been working so diligently, a hearty laugh will be good for you, and David isn't listening to a word I am saying. He is daydreaming about Lia."

The mention of his name roused David from his romantic reverie. "I am listening," he protested, blushing a little.

"Don't tease him, Nefret," I said, though I did not think he minded; they were as close as brother and sister, and she was Lia's greatest friend. "Read a little, if you like. My fingers are somewhat cramped."

"Hmph," said Emerson. Taking this for consent, which it was, Nefret cleared her throat and began.

"They attacked at dawn. I woke instantly at the sound of pounding hooves, for I knew what it meant. The Beduin were on the warpath!

"I had been warned that the tribes were restless. My affectionate aunt and uncle, whom I had been assisting that winter with their archaeological excavations, had attempted to dissuade me from braving alone the perils of the desert, but I was determined to seek a nobler, simpler life, far from the artificiality of civilization—"

"Good Gad," I exclaimed. "He was of no assistance whatever, and we could hardly wait to be rid of him!"

"He spent most of his time in the civilized artificiality of the cafés and clubs of Cairo," said Emerson. "And he was a bloody nuisance."

"Don't swear," I said. Not that I supposed the admonition would have the least effect. I have been trying for years to stop Emerson from using bad language, and with equally poor success to prevent the children from imitating him.

"Do you want me to go on?" Nefret inquired.

"I beg your pardon, my dear. Indignation overcame me."

"I'll skip over a few paragraphs," Nefret said. "He blathers on at some length about how he hated Cairo and yearned for the austere silences of the desert waste. Now back to the Beduin:

"Snatching up my pistol, which I kept ready by my cot, I ran out of the tent and fired point-blank at the dark shape rushing toward me. A piercing scream told me I had hit my target. I brought another down, but there were too many of them; sheer numbers overwhelmed me. Two men seized me and a third wrenched my pistol from my hand. In the strengthening light I saw the body of my faithful servant. The hilt of a great knife protruded from the torn, bloodstained breast of Ali's robe; poor boy, he had died trying to defend me. The leader, a swarthy, black-bearded villain, strode up to me.

" 'So, Inglizi,' he snarled. 'You have killed five of my men. You will pay for that.'

" 'Kill me, then,' I replied. 'Do not expect me to beg for mercy. That is not the way of the English.'

"An evil smile distorted his hideously scarred face. 'A quick death would be too good for you,' he sneered. 'Bring him along.' "

Emerson flung up his hands. "Stop! No more! Percy's prose is as paralyzing as his profound ignorance but not as bad as his appalling conceit. May I pitch that copy onto the fire, Nefret?"

Nefret chuckled and clutched the imperiled volume to her breast. "No, sir, it's mine and you cannot have it. I look forward to hearing what Ramses has to say about it."

"What do you have against Percy, sir?" David inquired. "Perhaps I should not call him that—"

"Call him anything you like," growled Emerson.

"Hasn't Ramses told you about his encounters with Percy?" I asked. I felt sure he had; David was my son's best friend and confidant.

"I saw several of them," David reminded me. "When—er—Percy was in Egypt three years ago. I could tell Ramses was not—er—overly fond of his cousin, but he didn't say much. You know how he is."

"Yes," I said. "I do. He keeps things too much to himself. He always has done. There has been bad blood between him and Percy since the summer Percy and his sister Violet spent several months with us. Percy was only ten years of age, but he was already a sneak and a liar, and 'little Violet' was not much better. They played a number of vicious tricks on Ramses, and they also blackmailed him. Even at that tender age, he was vulnerable to blackmail," I admitted. "He was usually doing something he didn't want his father and me to know about. His original sins were relatively harmless, however, compared with the things Percy did. A belief in the innocence of young children has never been one of my weaknesses, but I have never encountered a child as sly and unprincipled as Percy."

"But that was years ago," David said. "He was cordial enough when I met him."

"To the Professor and Aunt Amelia," Nefret corrected. "He was superciliously condescending to Ramses and barely civil to you, David. And he kept on proposing to me."

That got Emerson's complete attention. Rising from his chair, he flung his pen across the room. Ink speckled the marble countenance of Socrates—not the first time it had received such a baptism. "What?" he (Emerson, to be precise) bellowed. "Proposed marriage? Why didn't you tell me this before?"

"Because you would have lost your temper and done something painful to Percy" was the cool response.

I didn't doubt Emerson could have and would have. My spouse's magnificent physical endowments have not declined with the years, and his temper has not mellowed either.

"Now, Emerson, calm yourself," I said. "You can't defenestrate every man who proposes to Nefret."

"It would take too much of your time," David said, laughing. "They will do it, won't they, Nefret?"

Nefret's pretty lip curled. "I have a great deal of money and, thanks to the Professor, the power to dispose of it as I like. That is the explanation, I believe."

It wasn't the only explanation. She is a beautiful young woman, in the English style—cornflower-blue eyes, golden hair with just a hint of copper, and skin as fair . . . well, it would be as fair as a lily if she would consent to wear a hat when out-of-doors.

Nefret tossed the book aside and rose. "I am going for a ride before luncheon. Will you come, David?"

"I'll have a look at Percy's book, if you have finished with it."

"How lazy you are! Where is Ramses? Perhaps he'll go with me."

I am sure I need not say that *I* had not given my son that heathenish appellation. He had been named Walter, after his uncle, but no one ever called him that; when he was a young child his father had nicknamed him Ramses because he was as swarthy as an Egyptian and as arrogant as a pharaoh. Raising Ramses had put quite a strain on my nerves, but my arduous efforts had borne fruit; he was not so reckless or so outspoken as he once had been, and his natural talent for languages had developed to such an extent that despite his comparative youth he was widely regarded as an expert on ancient Egyptian linguistics. As David informed Nefret, he was presently in his room, working on the texts for a forthcoming volume on the temples of Karnak. "He told me to leave him be," David added emphatically. "You had better do the same."

"Bah," said Nefret. But she left the room by way of the window instead of going into the hall toward the stairs. David took up the book and settled himself in his chair. I returned to my lists and Emerson to his manuscript, but not for long. The next interruption came from our butler, Gargery, who entered to announce there was a person to see Emerson.

Emerson held out his hand. Gargery, rigid with disapproval, shook his head. "He did not have a card, sir. He wouldn't give me his name or say what he wanted, neither, except that it was about some antiquity. I'd have sent him about his business, sir, only . . . well, sir, he said you'd be sorry if you didn't see him."

"Sorry, eh?" Emerson's heavy black brows drew together. There is nothing that rouses my husband's formidable temper so much as a threat, explicit or veiled. "Where have you put him, Gargery? In the parlor?"

Gargery drew himself up to his full height and attempted to look superior. Since his height is only five and a half feet and a bit, and his snub-nosed face is not designed for sneering, the attempt was a failure. "I have stood him in the dining room, sir."

Amusement replaced Emerson's rising ire; his sapphire-blue eyes sparkled. Being completely without social snobbery himself, he is much diverted by Gargery's demonstrations thereof. "I suppose a 'person' without a calling card does not deserve to be offered a chair, but the dining room? Aren't you afraid he will make off with the plate?"

"Bob is outside the dining room door, sir."

"Good Gad. He must be a villainous-looking 'person.' You have whetted my curiosity, Gargery. Show him—no, I had better go to him, since he seems anxious to keep his identity a secret."

I went with Emerson, of course. He made a few feeble objections, which I brushed aside.

The dining room is not one of the most attractive apartments in the house. Low-ceilinged and limited as to windows, it has a somber air which is increased by the heavy, time-darkened Jacobean furniture and the mummy masks adorning the paneled walls. Hands clasped behind him, our visitor was examining one of these masks. Instead of the sinister individual Gargery had led me to expect, I saw a stooped, gray-haired man. His garments were shabby and his boots scuffed, but he looked respectable enough. And Emerson knew him.

"Renfrew! What the devil do you mean by this theatrical behavior? Why didn't you—"

"Hushhhhh!" The fellow put his finger to his lips. "I have my reasons, which you will approve when you hear them. Get rid of your butler. Is this your wife? Don't introduce me, I have no patience with such stuff. No use trying to get rid of her, I suppose, you'd tell her anyhow. That's up to you. Sit down, Mrs. Emerson, if you like. I will stand. I will not take refreshment. There is a train at noon I mean to catch. I can't waste any more time on this business. Wasted too much already. Wouldn't have done it except as a courtesy to you. Now."

The words came in short staccato bursts, with scarcely a pause for breath, and although he did not misplace his aitches or commit a grammatical error, there were traces of East London in his accent. His clothing and his boots were in need of brushing, and his face looked as if it were covered with a thin film of dust. One expected to see cobwebs festooning his ears. But the pale gray eyes under his dark gray brows were as sharp as knife points. I could see why Gargery had mislabeled him, but I did not commit the same error. Emerson had told me about him. A self-made, self-educated man, a misogynist and recluse, he collected Chinese and Egyptian antiquities, Persian miniatures and anything else that suited his eccentric fancy.

Emerson nodded. "Get to it, then. Some new purchase you want me to authenticate for you?"

Renfrew grinned. His teeth were the same grayish-brown color as his skin. "That's why I like you, Emerson. You don't beat around the bush either. Here."

Reaching into his pocket, he tossed an object carelessly onto the table, where it landed with a solid *thunk*.

It was a scarab, one of the largest I had ever seen, formed of the greenish-blue faience (a glassy paste) commonly used in ancient times. The back was rounded like the carapace of the beetle, with the stylized shapes of head and limbs.

The small scarabs were popular amulets, worn by the living and the dead to ensure good luck. The larger varieties, like the famous "marriage scarab" of Amenhotep III, were often used to record important events. This was obviously of the second type; when Emerson picked it up and turned it over, I saw rows of raised hieroglyphs covering the flat base.

"What does it say?" I asked.

Emerson fingered the cleft in his chin, as was his habit when perplexed or pensive. "As near as I can make out, this is an account of the circumnavigation of Africa in Year Twelve of Senusert the Third."

"What! This is a historical document of unique importance, Emerson."

"Hmmm," said Emerson. "Well, Renfrew?"

"Well, sir." Renfrew showed his stained teeth again. "I am going to let you have it at the price I paid. There will be no additional charge for my silence."

"Silence?" I repeated. There was something odd about his manner—and Emerson's. Alarm burgeoned. "What is he talking about, Emerson?"

"It's a fake," Emerson said curtly. "He knows it. Obviously he didn't know when he purchased it. Whom did you consult, Renfrew?"

From Renfrew's parted lips came a dry, rustling sound—his version of a laugh, I surmised. "I thought you'd spot it, Emerson. You are right, I had no idea it was a fake; I wanted an accurate translation, so I sent a tracing of the inscription to Mr. Frank Griffith. Next to your brother and your son he is the foremost translator of ancient Egyptian. His opinion was the same as yours."

"Ah." Emerson tossed the scarab onto the table. "Then you didn't need a second opinion."

"A sensible man always gets a second opinion. Do you want the scarab or don't you? I don't intend to be out of pocket by it. I'll sell it to someone else—without mentioning Griffith's opinion—and sooner or later someone will find out it isn't genuine, and they will trace it back to the seller as I did, and they will learn his name. I don't think you would want that to happen, Professor Emerson. You think well of the boy, don't you? I understand he is about to marry into your family. It would be embarrassing, to say the least, if he were caught forging antiquities."

"You dastardly old—old villain," I cried. "How dare you imply that David would do such a thing?"

"I am not implying anything, Mrs. Emerson. Go to the dealer from whom I got this, and ask him the name of the man who sold it to him."

**From Manuscript H**

Ramses spun round in his chair, dropped his pen, and swore.

"I did knock," David said, from the doorway. "You didn't hear?"

"I'm trying to finish this."

"It's almost teatime. You've been at it all day. And you haven't touched your luncheon tray."

"Don't you start, David. It's bad enough with Mother and Nefret badgering me all the time."

Frowning, he examined the meticulously traced hieroglyphic signs. The pen had slipped when David opened the door, turning an owl into a monster with a serpent's tail. He reached for a piece of blotting paper and decided he'd better wait until the ink had dried before trying to repair the damage.

"You were very ill." David came in and closed the door. "We were all worried."

"That was months ago. I'm perfectly fit now. I don't need to be reminded to eat my porridge and go early to bed, as if I were a child."

"Nefret is a medical doctor," David said mildly.

"She never finished her training." Ramses rubbed his eyes. "I'm sorry. I didn't mean that the way it sounded. Her perseverance in pursuing her medical training under the restrictions that women suffer is admirable. I only wish she wouldn't practice on me!" He picked up a glass from the tray, took a sip, and made a face. "The milk's turned."

David came in and closed the door. "What about beer instead? I just now took them out of the ice chest."

The brown bottles were sweating with cold. Ramses's stiff shoulders relaxed and he gave his friend an appreciative nod. "That was a happy thought. David, I apologize for what I said this morning."

"Friends need not always agree. It is unimportant."

"It's not that I disagree with your views. I just don't think—"

"I know. It doesn't matter, I tell you."

He offered Ramses a cigarette and lit it for him before lighting his own. It was like the old days, when they had sneaked away from Ramses's mother to indulge in the forbidden pleasures of smoking and drinking beer. Ramses wondered if David had deliberately set the scene.

They hadn't been as comfortable together since David had become involved in a cause Ramses considered both dangerous and futile. He sympathized with the desire of the new generation of Egyptians for independence, but he felt sure it had no chance of success at the present time. Egypt was a British protectorate in all but name, and with the political situation in the Middle East so unsettled, Britain could not risk losing control of a country close to the Suez Canal. The recent appointment of the redoubtable Kitchener of Khartoum to the post of consul general unquestionably signaled a hardening of policy toward the nationalist movement. David had a brilliant career and a happy marriage ahead of him. It would have been madness to risk them for exile or prison.

"I wondered if you had seen this." David pulled a slim volume from his coat pocket.

Ramses accepted the change of subject with relief. "Percy's masterpiece? I knew Nefret had it, but I haven't read it."

"Have a look at this chapter. You're a fast reader. It won't take you long."

He'd put a bit of paper in to mark the place. "It's a good thing you brought the beer," Ramses said, taking the book. "I suspect Percy's prose will require the numbing effect of alcohol."

I had been a prisoner for two weeks. Zaal visited me daily. In the beginning it was to threaten and sneer, but as time went on he developed a queer penchant for me. We spent many hours discussing the Koran and the teachings of the Prophet. "You have a brave heart, English," he said one day. "I hope your friends pay the ransom; it would sadden me to cut your throat."

Naturally I did not intend to wait until my unhappy father and affectionate friends could come to my rescue. After I had recovered from the injuries received during my capture, I spent several hours each day in such exercises as the limited confines of my dungeon cell permitted. Shadow-boxing, running in place, and vigorous calisthenics soon restored my strength. I concealed these activities from Zaal. When he entered my cell he always found me reclining on the divan. I hoped that my pretense at feebleness and his own natural arrogance would lead him to become overconfident. One day he would come alone, without his guards, and then—then he would be at my mercy!

I was awaiting his usual visit one afternoon when the door was flung open to disclose, not Zaal, but two of his thugs, supporting a third man between them. They had stripped him of his clothing except for a pair of loose drawers; his brown skin and unkempt black hair betrayed his race. His head was bowed and his bare feet dragged as they pulled him into the room and threw him onto the divan.

Zaal appeared in the doorway, grinning fiendishly. "You have your medicines, English. Use them. He is the son of my greatest enemy, and I don't want him to die too quickly."

The door slammed and I heard the rattle of bolts and chains.

I turned to look at my unexpected guest. He had slid from the divan and fallen onto his back. A black beard and mustache framed features of typical Arab form—thin lips, a prominent hawklike nose, and heavy dark brows. There were a few bruises on his chest and arms, but he was not seriously hurt. Most probably he had fainted from fear.

I brought him round, but when I lifted him to a sitting position and attempted to give him a sip of brandy he spat it out.

"It is forbidden," he said, in guttural Arabic, and then repeated the statement in stumbling English. He was younger than I had supposed, tall for an Arab but slightly built.

"I speak your tongue," I said. "Who are you, and why are you a prisoner?"

"My father is Sheikh Mohammed. I am Feisal, his eldest son. There is a blood feud between him and Zaal."

"It will not be a matter of ransom, then?"

The youth shuddered convulsively. "No. He will torture me and send my head—and other parts of my body—to my father."

"Then we must escape, and soon."

"We?" He stared at me in astonishment. "Why should you take the risk? Zaal will not harm you. Surely your friends will pay the ransom."

I did not bother to explain. Only an Englishman would have understood.

I planned to get him away that night, before Zaal could begin dismembering him, but unfortunately Zaal took it into his head to visit us again the same evening. He was somewhat the worse for drink, and looking for amusement. I cannot in decency repeat the vile proposal he made to my companion, nor the words in which Feisal (to his credit) refused. Remarking, "So, you prefer a beating?" Zaal ordered four of his men to seize the slight, shrinking form of the lad and hold him down.

It was not noblesse oblige alone that made me offer to take the beating in place of Feisal. My plan of escape would have been seriously jeopardized if I had to encumber myself with a companion who was unconscious or crippled—for of course it would have been unthinkable to abandon him. I knew I could withstand torture better than an Arab.

Zaal was too inflamed by passion, drink, and bloodlust to resist the temptation. It would have given the creature enormous pleasure to hear an Englishman beg for mercy. Naturally I had no intention of doing so. Feisal took a tentative step toward me. I called out to him not to resist and then pressed my lips tightly together, determined that not another sound should escape me. They tore off my shirt and threw me down upon the divan. Two of them gripped my ankles and two more twisted my wrists and held them. Zaal's stick crashed down across my back. I locked my teeth to endure the pain that lapped like flames across my back . . .

With his sleeve Ramses mopped up the puddle of spilled beer before it could stain the page on which he had spent the greater part of the day. He was still shaking with laughter when he tossed the book back to David. "Here, I've had all I can stand."

"You missed the best part," David said, turning over a few pages. "When you and he swear blood brotherhood before he delivers you safely to the tent of your father and rides off into the night alone."

"On his faithful white stallion, under the cold light of the distant desert stars, no doubt. He's certainly fond of banal adjectives, I . . ." Belatedly, the import of several pronouns sank in. He stopped laughing. "What are you talking about?"

David tossed the book onto the floor. "I may be a bit slow, Ramses, but I'm not stupid. Percy had gone prancing off into the desert and the rest of us were about to leave for England that spring when the Professor and Aunt Amelia got the ransom demand from Zaal. You had already made arrangements to spend the summer working with Reisner at Samaria. I didn't think anything of it when you decided to start a few days earlier than you had planned, but when Percy turned up, plump and swaggering and undamaged, not long after you left Cairo, I began to wonder. Now I know. Most of what he wrote is rubbish, but he couldn't have got away without help, and who else could the 'slight' little Arab prince have been but you? It certainly wasn't Feisal. He'll murder you when he finds out you took his name in vain."

"I'll tell him it was you."

David grinned, but shook his head. "I wouldn't have risked my neck for Percy. Why did you?"

"Damned if I know."

David looked exasperated. "How much of this—this nonsense is true?"

"Well . . ." Ramses finished the beer and wiped his mouth on his other sleeve. "Well, if you really want to know—not a lot."

Ramses had known what he must do as soon as the ransom note reached them. There could be no question of its authenticity; Percy had added a frenzied appeal in his own hand. Even his father admitted they couldn't take the chance of leaving Percy to the tender mercies of Zaal; he was a renegade and a drunkard, and God only knew what he might do when he was in one of his fits.

"Then," said Emerson gloomily, "Britain would feel obliged to avenge the bloody idiot and innocent people would be killed. Damnation! We will have to raise the money, I suppose."

"Uncle James will never repay you," Ramses said. "He'd swindle a starving charwoman out of her last halfpenny."

No one bothered to deny this, not even his mother. She knew her brother well, and detested him even more than Emerson did. Family honor demanded action, however, and the process was underway when Ramses set off for Palestine, a few days earlier than he had planned.

He knew where to find Zaal. He'd heard a lot about the fellow the year before, when he was excavating in Palestine with Reisner. Zaal was a bandit in the old style, preying on Arab and European alike, and retreating after each raid to the ruined castle he had made his headquarters. His followers were a scruffy lot, as cowardly and corrupt as Zaal himself, but a direct attack on the place would have been dangerous, owing to its location and remaining fortifications. The old Crusaders had known how to build a stronghold.

Ramses had no intention of attacking directly. It didn't take him long to make his arrangements; he had friends in a number of places. The small oasis he selected was not far from the castle. Imposingly bearded and robed, in imitation of a well-known local gentleman, he settled down to wait, certain that the word would soon get back to Zaal. A single traveler, richly attired and accompanied by a heavily laden camel, was an irresistible target.

He put up only a token resistance when the motley crowd of riders descended on him. Pinioned inefficiently by two of the men, he endured a few kicks and blows with traditional Arabic stoicism until a whoop of delight from the fellows investigating the camel's cargo distracted his tormentors. It didn't occur to the greedy swine to ask what misadventure had kept him there so long, or to wonder why the noble, pious Prince Feisal was squatting beside a camel loaded with whiskey.

They had emptied several bottles, passing them from hand to hand, before they hoisted him onto a horse and tied his feet to the stirrups. Ramses wished they would get on with it. One of the villains had claimed his elegant robes and leather boots, and the sun was scorching his bare skin. He was pleased but not surprised to see them unload the whiskey and distribute it amongst themselves before they mounted. Zaal's indifference to the laws of Islam was shared by his men, but they did not share the liquor he kept for himself and his favorites.

The ruined ramparts rose up against the sky as they approached, winding along a steep path between rocky outcroppings. At the hail of the man leading the procession, the gate swung open and Ramses took careful note of the internal arrangements. An open courtyard, a few crude structures to shelter men and horses, a weighted bar on the inside of the gate . . . No, it shouldn't be difficult, assuming Percy was ambulatory.

He was looking forward to meeting his cousin, but he had to face Zaal first. The encounter was not without its points of interest, and only a trifle more unpleasant than he had expected. Zaal must have attained his position of leadership through sheer viciousness, since his physical endowments were not impressive. Of middle height, his beard and hair streaked with gray, he was so fat he resembled the obese bow-legged Egyptian god Bes as he waddled toward his captive.

"So who is this peasant?" he demanded. "Why did you bring him here?"

"He is a person of importance," the leader of the gang insisted. "He wore garments of silk trimmed with gold . . ."

"Ah? Where are they, then?"

A heated discussion about the disposition of the garments followed. Ramses cut it short. Folding his arms across his chest, he looked down his nose at Zaal and announced his adopted identity.

"So." Zaal's piggy little eyes brightened. "The son of Sheikh Mohammed?"

"The eldest son," Ramses corrected, with appropriate hauteur.

"Soooo. He would pay a large price to get you back?"

"To get me back undamaged, yes."

He stressed the essential word. He had heard about certain of Zaal's habits, and he didn't much care for the look in those squinting eyes as they moved over his body.

Zaal grinned and scratched his side. "Of course. I would like to be on good terms with your honored father. Sit down and talk. Drink tea with me."

May as well stay in character, Ramses thought, particularly since it suits my own inclinations. "The son of my father does not sit down with renegades and bandits."

Zaal only grinned more broadly.

"That is not courteous, my young friend. Shakir, give him a lesson in manners."

Two of them held him while Shakir obliged. After a few blows he decided he had made his point, and went limp, a little too late; he was only vaguely aware of being dragged out of the room and up a flight of stairs. The chamber into which they propelled him did not resemble a prison cell; through half-closed eyes he saw sunlight and a carpeted floor—and his cousin, sprawled comfortably on a pile of cushions. Then his captors tossed him facedown across a divan and he concluded he might as well stay there.

It was a wise decision. The ensuing dialogue between Percy and Zaal was illuminating.

"Who the devil is that?" was his cousin's first question.

"A young man who will, I hope, become a great friend of mine."

"What about the ransom?" Percy demanded. "Have you heard?"

"No. It is early days. What are you complaining about? You are living like a pasha. Do you want more brandy? Hashish? A woman? You have only to ask."

"Yes, well . . ."

"Be kind to my new friend," Zaal purred. "Tell him how comfortable he can be if he is as cooperative as you."

After Zaal had gone out Percy paced and muttered for a while. Then Ramses heard liquid gurgle. He rolled over and sat up. Percy studied him sourly over the glass from which he was drinking.

"Brandy," he explained. "D'you want some?"

Ramses shook his head. "It is forbidden."

"Your loss." Percy tossed down the rest of the brandy.

It was obvious he had not recognized Ramses. The latter rose and went to the window, which was open and unbarred. It faced the courtyard, and six feet under it was the roof of another structure.

However, Percy did not respond enthusiastically to "Feisal's" plan for escape. "Why the devil should I take the chance? My loving relations will send the ransom."

"So will my father. But I do not mean to sit here like a girl or an infant till he does."

They were speaking English, of necessity, since Percy's Arabic was virtually non-existent. Percy hadn't even enough interest in his companion to ask where he had learned the language. He remained sullenly resistant to Ramses's suggestions, and the latter was beginning to believe he would have to knock Percy unconscious and carry him out when Fate, in the unpleasant person of Zaal, intervened.

It was getting dark. Percy had lit one of the lamps and was sitting on a pile of cushions, grumbling because they were late bringing his dinner. When the door opened, he looked up with a scowl.

Zaal rolled in. He was very drunk and in a very amorous mood, but he wasn't stupid enough to have come alone. Two of his sturdiest men were with him. When he put his interesting proposition to the prisoners, Percy let out a bleat of protest.

"Leave me alone! Oh, God—please—take him!" He flung out an arm to indicate his companion and retreated to the farthest corner of the room.

"With pleasure," said Zaal. "I included you only out of courtesy to a guest."

He held out his arms and sidled toward Ramses, weaving from side to side. Ramses eluded him without difficulty and shook his head. "No."

"No?" Zaal sounded rather pleased than otherwise. "Defiance becomes you, my dear, but it would not be wise to resist."

"Embrace one of your own kind," Ramses suggested, employing a more explicit verb. "Surely there are dogs around the dung heaps."

The guards converged on him, while Zaal sputtered and swayed. Glancing at his cousin, Ramses realized with disgust that he wasn't going to get any help from that quarter. If Percy had had the courage to fight back, the two of them could have dealt with the guards and Zaal, and the way to escape would have been open, with Zaal as their hostage.

The best he could do was to keep Zaal from damaging his cousin, and minimizing the damage to himself. The first part wasn't difficult; obviously Zaal had not been interested in Percy until the fascinating idea of an encounter à trois occurred to him. Noblesse oblige had its limits, however, and he had no intention of submitting to what Zaal had in mind. A carefully calibrated kick finished the job the liquor had started, and ensured that Zaal would be temporarily incapable of that particular activity. The beating Zaal's dutiful henchmen administered was somewhat perfunctory—and it was a damned sight better than the alternative. When, several hours later, he indicated it was time for them to go, Percy didn't resist.


"There was a flat roof just under Percy's window and an easy drop to the ground," Ramses finished. "He could have got out it almost anytime if he hadn't been such a—er—cautious soul. I knew Zaal's men would be roaring drunk that night, so we waited till the sounds of revelry died into snores, and proceeded on our way. The hardest part was trying not to trip over recumbent bodies."

"So it was you who took the beating."

Ramses shrugged. "I wanted to get away that same night, and I was afraid Percy would collapse completely if anyone touched him. It wasn't all that bad. Zaal was saving me for . . . Oh, the devil with it. You caught me fairly, but I hope you won't tell anyone else. Especially Percy."

"Why not? Humiliating him publicly would be a breach of form, I suppose, but what's wrong with making him feel thoroughly ashamed of himself?"

"Good God, David, are you really so naive about human nature? Percy has held a grudge against me since we were children. How do you suppose he'd feel if he learned I was the sole witness to his contemptible performance?" Ramses stood up and stretched stiffened muscles. "I'd better change my shirt before I go downstairs. I seem to have spilled quite a lot of beer on it."

David wasn't so easily put off. "What are you going to do about this?"

"About what? Oh—Percy's interesting fabrications. Nothing. And neither are you. If you breathe a word of this—"

"Not even to Nefret?"

"Especially to Nefret."

"There you go again," David exclaimed. "Why do you object to showing yourself in a favorable light to a girl you want to impress? You've been in love with her for years. Don't tell me you've stopped caring for her."

"Let's just say that I've decided to stop dashing my brains out against the stone wall of her indifference. If she hasn't learned to appreciate my sterling character and spectacular good looks by this time, it's not likely she will."

"But she is very—"

"Fond of me?" Ramses conquered a childish urge to throw his beer-stained shirt at David. "I know she is. That's precisely why you mustn't breathe a word of this to her. Even if you swore her to secrecy, one day that flaming temper of hers would get the better of her and she wouldn't be able to resist taunting Percy, or blurting out the truth to someone who had made a rude remark about me. Then the word would get back to Percy, and he'd resent me even more. I have enough enemies as it is."

"I can't argue with that." David picked up the despised volume and rose. "But what possible harm can your cousin do you? He's too much of a coward to attack you directly, and no English gentleman would knife an enemy in the back, would he?"

Ramses turned and began rummaging in the wardrobe. It was hard not to snap back when David jeered about proper form and noblesse oblige and conduct becoming an English gentleman. He despised that sort of snobbery as much as David did, and David knew it.

Conquering his irritation, he took out a clean shirt and faced his friend. "Tell Mother I'll be down shortly."

David gave Ramses a long, level look before going out. It was rather like seeing one's reflection in a mirror, Ramses thought. No close observer would have mistaken one for the other, but a superficial description would have fit either—height six feet, hair and eyes black, face long, skin olive, nose prominent, build . . . slight?

Smiling, he slipped into his shirt and began doing up the buttons. Percy was a joke—a bad joke, a braggart and coward and sneak. No, a knife between the ribs wasn't his style, but there were other ways of damaging an enemy—methods a decent man like David could never understand. Ramses's smile faded and a little shiver ran through him, as if someone had walked over the spot that would one day be his grave.

The rest of us were already at breakfast when Ramses entered the room. I had felt it necessary to give him a little lecture the previous night, about working too hard and not getting enough sleep, and I was pleased to observe that he had apparently taken it to heart—something I could not always count upon his doing— for the unmistakable (to a mother) signs of fatigue were not apparent. Like the Egyptians he so closely resembles, Ramses has black eyes and long thick lashes. When he is tired, drooping lids hood his orbs and dark circles underline them. He pretended not to notice my intent regard and began consuming eggs and bacon, toast and muffins.

The others had been arguing about who would go to meet our Egyptian friends, whose boat was due to dock in London that day. It would have been unthinkable to have the wedding without those members of David's family who were closest to him and to us. Now that dear Abdullah was gone, there were only three of them. Selim, Abdullah's youngest son, had replaced his father as our reis; Daoud, one of David's innumerable cousins, was deeply attached to Lia, and she to him; Fatima, who looked after our house in Egypt, had become a trusted friend.

Everyone wanted to go to meet them, including Gargery. Voices were raised. Emerson's language became increasingly intemperate. Rose, our devoted housekeeper, kept buttering muffins for Ramses and urging him to stay at home and have a nice rest. Really, I thought, in mounting exasperation, there never was a household in which so many people felt free to offer their unsolicited opinions! I am bound to confess that our relationship with certain of our servants is somewhat unusual, owing in part to the criminal encounters that have so often disturbed the even tenor of domestic life. A butler who wields a cudgel as handily as he carves a roast is entitled to certain privileges, and Rose had been Ramses's loyal defender since he was three years of age, her affection unshaken by the mummified mice, the explosions of various chemicals, and the square acres of mud he had tracked through the house.

"Rose is right, Ramses," I said, nodding at her. "The weather looks unsettled, and you should not risk catching a cold."

Ramses raised his eyes from his plate. "As you like, Mother."

"Now what are you up to?" I demanded.

"I cannot imagine," said my son, "why you should suppose that my ready agreement with your thoughtful suggestion should be taken as an indication of—"

"Quite right," said Emerson, who knew that Ramses was capable of continuing the sentence until subject and verb were buried under an avalanche of subordinate clauses. "I will go in your place."

I had been afraid he would say that. Emerson's accompanying the welcoming committee was one thing; Emerson driving the motorcar, which he would insist upon doing, was quite another. The locals had become used to him, and promptly cleared off the road whenever he took the automobile out. One could not count on the inhabitants of London being so obliging.

After I had let everyone express his or her opinion, which is the inalienable right of every citizen of a democracy, I informed them of my decision.

"Nefret must go; Fatima will be more comfortable with another female present. David must go, they are his kin. There won't be room in the automobile for anyone else. Daoud, you know, is a very large person. So, that is settled. You had better get off at once. Telephone if the boat is late in docking, or if you are otherwise delayed. Drive carefully. Wrap up well. Good-bye."

It began to rain late in the afternoon, and the cloudy skies produced an early twilight. Nefret had telephoned shortly after midday to say that the boat was late and would not dock for several hours. All was in readiness; I had ordered cheerful fires to be lit in every room, and welcoming lights shone through the dusk. I was standing at the drawing room window looking out when a voice made me start.

"They won't be here for at least another hour, Mother. You aren't worried, are you? David is an excellent driver."

"He won't be driving, Ramses. Nefret will insist on showing off, and he hasn't the gumption to prevent her." I turned from the window. He was close by me, though I had not heard him approach. I greatly dislike that noiseless cat-footed walk he affects, and when I saw that the shoulders of his coat were dark with moisture and that his hair sparkled with raindrops, irritability prompted me to remark, "You've been out in the wet without a hat again. How many times must I tell you—"

"Your concern is appreciated but needless, Mother. Why don't you sit down by the fire and let me ring for tea? Nefret said not to wait."

I could not deny the sense of this, so I took the chair he held for me. After he had rung the bell he leaned against the mantel. "I want to ask you about this," he began, reaching into his pocket.

I stared in surprise at the object he took out. It lay curled in the palm of his hand, blinking round blue eyes and twitching minuscule whiskers. So complete was its state of relaxation that it would have rolled off onto the floor if Ramses's long fingers had not enclosed its body. He appeared as surprised as I.

"It is a cat, my dear," I said, laughing. "A kitten, rather. So that is where you went, to the stable to inspect Hathor's new litter."

"I forgot it was there," Ramses said self-consciously. "It crawled in and went to sleep, so I—er—that's not what I wanted to show you, Mother."

The rattle of crockery presaged the arrival of Gargery and one of the maids with the tea trays. Close on their heels came Emerson, shirt wrinkled, hair becomingly disheveled, hands inkstained, face beaming.

"Not here yet?" he inquired, inspecting the room as if he thought Fatima might be hiding behind a chair and Daoud concealed by the draperies. "Ramses, why are you standing there holding a cat? Put it down, my boy, and take a chair. Hallo, Peabody, my dear. Hallo, Gargery. Hallo—er—who's this?"

"Sarah, sir," Gargery replied. "She came to us last week and is now, I believe, able to be trusted in the drawing room."

"Certainly. Hallo, Sarah." He advanced on the poor girl with the obvious intention of shaking hands.

Emerson has absolutely no notion of how to get on with servants. He treats them like social equals, which is extremely trying for them. Those who remain in our service eventually become accustomed to him, but the girl was young and rather pretty, and although Gargery must have warned her about Emerson, she let out a little squeak of alarm as he loomed over her with affable interest warming his handsome face.

Ramses came to the rescue, depositing the kitten onto Emerson's outstretched hand and relieving the housemaid of the heavy tray, which he placed on a nearby table. The girl's eyes followed him with doglike adoration. I let out an inaudible sigh. So it was to be Ramses with this one. All the new female servants fell in love with my husband or my son, or both. It was only a minor inconvenience, since Emerson never noticed and Ramses was too well-brought-up to misbehave—not in my house, at any rate!—but I did get tired of stumbling over misty-eyed females.

I told Gargery we would wait on ourselves, and he removed himself and Sarah. Emerson sat down with the kitten on his knee. Most of our current crop of cats were descendants of two Egyptian felines and they had bred true to type—brindled fawn-and-brown coats, large ears, and a high level of intelligence. How this small creature would turn out it was impossible to say, but her face bore a striking resemblance to that of her great—or possibly great-great-, I had lost count—grandmother Bastet, who had been Ramses's special companion. Now wide awake and curious, she swarmed up Emerson's shirtfront and perched on his shoulder.

Emerson chuckled. "Has it a name?"

"She is only six weeks old," Ramses replied. "Nefret hasn't chosen names for this litter yet. Father, I was about to ask Mother—"

"It's a good thing the Egyptian pantheon is so extensive," Emerson remarked. "We've used the obvious names—Hathor,

Horus, Anubis, Sekhmet—but there are plenty of obscure deities yet to be—catch her, Ramses, she's heading for the cream jug."

The creature had taken a flying leap from his shoulder onto the tea table. Ramses scooped her up and held her, despite her squeaks and scratches, while I poured cream into a saucer and put it on the floor. Emerson was vastly entertained by the kitten's attempts to drink and purr simultaneously. I was not so entertained at seeing the Persian rug spattered with cream.

"Mother," said Ramses, absently wiping his bleeding fingers on his shirtfront, "I was about to ask—"

"Don't do that," I exclaimed. "Use a serviette. Good gracious, you are as bad as your father; it is impossible to keep the two of you in clean shirts. What Rose will say—"

"Why are you in such a scolding mood, Peabody?" Emerson inquired. "Not having one of your famous premonitions, I hope. If you are, I don't want to hear about it."

His use of that name suggested that despite his mild complaint he was in an affable mood. When first we met, he had addressed me by my surname as he would have addressed a professional equal—a man, in other words—and over the years it had become a term of affection and approbation. I never employed his given name of Radcliffe, since he does not like it.

"Not at all, my dear," I said with a smile. "My concerns this evening are those of an affectionate friend and hostess. I do want everything to go well! I am not too worried about Selim, he has been in England before and fancies himself quite a man of the world, but this is Daoud's first trip abroad, and Fatima was for most of her life a conventional Moslem wife, veiled, illiterate, and subservient. I fear she will be completely overcome by the variety of new experiences she must face. And how will she get on with Rose?"

"I cannot imagine," said Emerson, "why Rose's opinion carries such weight with you. Curse it, Peabody, you are inventing difficulties where none exist. Fatima had the courage to come to you and ask for a position as housekeeper after her husband died; she had sufficient intelligence and initiative to learn to read and write, and to speak English. I'll wager she has relished every moment of the trip."

"Oh, very well, Emerson, I admit it! I am on edge. I don't like Nefret driving that vehicle at night, in rain and fog; I am worried about our friends' catching a chill—they aren't accustomed to our miserable damp weather. I worry about the wedding. What if they aren't happy?"

Emerson's face cleared. "Ah, so that's it. Women always get into this state before a wedding," he explained to Ramses. "Don't know why, they are frightfully keen on people getting married, but once the matter is settled they begin stewing and worrying. Why shouldn't Lia and David be happy?"

"They face so many problems, Emerson! They will be snubbed and insulted by ignorant Europeans who don't know any better, and if David is suspected of forging antiquities—"

A stifled exclamation from Ramses stopped me. "Oh, dear," I said. "I ought not to have said that."

"Why the devil not?" Emerson demanded. "You know perfectly well we had no intention of keeping this a secret from Ramses. We have been waiting for a suitable opportunity, that's all. Stop glowering, my boy."

Ramses's eyebrows, which are as heavy and black as his father's, slipped back into place. "Is this a suitable opportunity, sir?"

"It would appear so," Emerson admitted. "David is the one who must be kept in the dark, at least for the present. Peabody, may I impose on you to fetch the—er—object from my desk while I tell Ramses about it?"

"Don't trouble yourself, Mother," said Ramses. "This is the object in question, I expect."

He took the scarab from the pocket the kitten had not occupied.

"Damnation," said Emerson. "There is no hope of privacy in this house! I suppose you happened to run across it while you were looking for an envelope or a stamp?"

"A pen," said Ramses, bland as butter. "The drawer was not locked, Father. Since you intended to consult me anyhow . . ."

While Emerson told the story, the kitten climbed up Ramses's trouser leg, leaving a trail of snagged threads. It perched on his knee and began washing its face energetically but ineptly.

"Have you spoken with the dealer?" Ramses asked.

"There hasn't been time." Emerson took out his pipe and tobacco pouch. "We've got to go about this carefully, my boy. If the scarab is known to be a forgery, David is the first person who will be suspected. Everyone knows his history. When we first encountered him he was an apprentice of Abd el Hamed, one of the finest forgers of antiquities Luxor has ever produced. Since then he has become a qualified Egyptologist, with a thorough knowledge of the language, and he has made something of a name for himself as a sculptor. That scarab is not your usual clumsy fake; it was produced by a man who knew the language and the ancient manufacturing techniques. What the devil, I would suspect David myself if I didn't know his character so well."

"Father," Ramses began.

"Thanks to your quick thinking, we can keep the matter quiet for a time," I mused. "You purchased Mr. Renfrew's silence with the scarab. Presumably the dealer who sold it to him does not doubt it is genuine, and Griffith has not seen it, only a copy of the inscription. I suppose it really is a forgery?"

"Are you questioning my expertise, Peabody?" Emerson grinned at me. "I would be the first to admit I am not an authority on the language, but I have developed a certain instinct. The damned thing just didn't feel right! Besides, you will never convince me that the Egyptians of that period had the ships or the seamanship for such a voyage."

"Sir," Ramses said, rather loudly.

"You have translated the inscription, of course?"

"Yes, sir."

"Well? Don't be so cursed formal."

"It is a compilation from several different sources, including the Punt inscriptions of Hatshepsut and a rather obscure Greek text of the second century B.C. There are certain anomalies—"

"Never mind the details," I said, starting from my chair and hastening to the window. There was no sign of the motorcar; the sound I had heard must have been made by a gust of wind. "The conclusion seems irrefutable. What are we going to do about this?"

"Someone must talk to the dealer," said Emerson. "Inquiries will have to be indirect, since we don't want to arouse his suspicions. We should also attempt to trace the other forgeries."

"Others?" I had a good many things on my mind or I would have arrived at this conclusion myself. "Good heavens, yes! We must assume there are others, mustn't we?

Emerson chewed thoughtfully on the stem of his pipe. "Forging antiquities is a profitable business, and a craftsman as skilled as this chap won't stop with a single example. But if the others are as good as the scarab they won't be easily detected."

"Then they won't be easy for us to identify either," I said.

"How on earth are we to go about locating them? We certainly don't want people to suspect that a new, extremely skilled forger is at work."

Ramses rose to his feet, removing the kitten from his knee to his shoulder. "May I say a word?" he inquired.

"You can try," said Emerson, with a critical look at me.

"Then, with all respect," said Ramses, "are we not taking too much on ourselves? I doubt David would thank you—us, I mean—for keeping this from him. He's not a child, and it is his reputation that is being threatened."

"Not only his reputation," said Emerson, fingering the cleft in his chin. "You remember the case of young Bouriant. He ended up in prison for selling faked antiquities. It would be even more serious for David. He is an Egyptian, and he will be judged as such."

It was a sobering thought, but I soon rallied. "The cases are not parallel, Emerson; David is innocent, and we will prove it! Of course he will have to be told sooner or later, but just now he's in a frightful state of nerves; he deserves to enjoy his wedding and—er—and so on, without additional distractions. Surely we can clear this little matter up in a few weeks."

"How?" Ramses demanded with unusual heat. "How can we locate other forgeries unless we admit that that's what we're looking for? Would you care to estimate how many Egyptian antiquities have appeared on the market recently? We don't even know how long this has been going on! If the other forgeries (and yes, we must assume there are others) are as good as this, they'd never be suspected."

"The scarab is a bit too much," Emerson remarked.

Ramses nodded. "It's a superb piece of work, but the text is so intrinsically preposterous, one can't help wondering if he meant it as a private joke or a kind of arrogant challenge. The others may not be so easily detectable."

He had been pacing up and down. Now he stopped by the fireplace and stood looking at an object over the mantelpiece, shielded from heat and smoke by a recessed frame. The little alabaster head of Nefret was one of the first sculptures David had produced after he joined our family. Crude though it was compared with the work he had done since, it was an unnerving reminder of David's unique talent.

The firelight warmed Ramses's thin, impassive brown face. It also illumined the bloodstains on his shirt, the rents left in trousers and coat by the kitten's claws, and the curling locks that fell untidily over his forehead. His hair always curled when it was wet, and the kitten had been busily trying to dry it.

"For pity's sake, go and change, Ramses," I said. "And put the cat back where you got it."

Emerson jumped up. "No time. Here they are. We'll talk about this later. Not a word to anyone at present, is that agreed?"

A beam of light crossed the window and a series of triumphant hoots signaled the safe arrival of the motorcar and its occupants. Emerson started toward the door. Ramses returned the kitten to his pocket.

"Give me the scarab," I said quickly. "I'll put it back in your father's desk."

As I hastened from the room I heard the front door open, the sound of laughter and cheerful voices and, rising over them all, Emerson's hearty shout of greeting: "Salaam aleikhum! Marhaba!"

**2**

The Oriental man is keen about the white woman. If he marries her, his standards are such that he soon degrades her; and of course we are not going to allow our wives and sisters and sweethearts to have anything to do with them.

"Thank goodness that is over!"

I did not utter the words aloud. The ceremony was not over, and a reverent silence filled the ancient chapel of Chalfont Castle. But the fateful challenge had passed without a response, and they were husband and wife in the eyes of God.

I am not a sentimental person. My best lace-trimmed handkerchief was quite dry, but when the strains of the recessional burst out and David started down the aisle with his wife on his arm, the sight of their faces brought just a touch of moisture to my eyes. Lia carried a simple spray of ferns and white roses, and wore her grandmother's veil; the priceless old Brussels lace lay like snowflakes on her fair hair. They passed in a flutter of white and a sweet fragrance and David turned his head to smile directly at me.

They were followed by Ramses and Nefret, who were the only attendants. Nefret looked like the personification of spring, her white throat and coronet of golden-red hair rising out of the soft green fabric of her gown like a flower on a stem. I assumed it was she who had managed to keep Ramses from tugging at his cravat, mussing his hair, or smudging his linen; I had been too busy with other arrangements to watch him. With pardonable maternal pride, I concluded that he did both of us credit. In my opinion Ramses's appearance will never be as impressive as that of his father, but he carried his slender height well and his features were not unpleasing. Like David, he glanced at me as he passed. Ramses seldom smiled, but the solemnity of his countenance lightened a trifle as his eyes met mine.

Those glances acknowledged that without my support and intervention the match might never have taken place. In the beginning Lia's parents had been strongly opposed. As I pointed out to them, their opposition was based solely on the unconscious and unjust prejudices of their caste. My arguments prevailed, as they usually do. Was that why I had felt such strange uneasiness in recent days—why I had actually held my breath in suspense when the fatal question was asked? Had I really expected someone would rise up and "show cause" why those two should not be wed? Ridiculous! There was no legal or moral impediment to the marriage, and the views of narrow-minded bigots carried no weight with me. Yet if they were not happy together, or if tragedy ensued, the ultimate responsibility would be mine.

Emerson, who *is* very sentimental, though he does not admit it, had turned his head away and was fumbling in his pocket. I was not surprised when he failed to locate his handkerchief. He never can locate his handkerchiefs. I slipped mine into his hand. Face still averted, he blew his nose loudly.

"Thank goodness that's over," he declared.

I started. "Why do you say that?"

"Oh, it was very pretty, no doubt, but all that praying became tedious. Why don't young people just go off and—er—set up housekeeping, as the ancient Egyptians did?"

Chalfont Castle, Evelyn's ancestral home, is a gloomy old pile of a place and the Great Hall is the oldest and gloomiest part of it. The fabric dates from the fourteenth century, but early Victorian enthusiasm for the Gothic had resulted in some unfortunate additions and restorations, including several hideous carved oak chandeliers. Rain clouds darkened the stained-glass windows but a fire blazed on the hearth, lamps and candles twinkled everywhere, and flowers and greenery brightened the hoary stone walls. The floor was covered with Oriental rugs. The long refectory table had been spread with food; melodious sounds issued from the gallery at the north end, where the musicians were stationed.

Katherine Vandergelt joined me at the table and accepted a glass of champagne from the servant. "You do have the most unusual friends, Mrs. Emerson," she remarked with amiable irony. "Egyptians in native attire, servants mingling with their masters on equal social terms, and a former spiritualist medium who was only saved from prison by your kindly intervention."

She was referring to herself, though she was guilty of a certain degree of humorous exaggeration. Financial need and the desire to provide for her fatherless children had driven her to take up that questionable profession, which she had been happy to abandon. Her marriage to our wealthy American friend Cyrus had resulted from mutual attraction, with only a little help from me. I had no reservations about my part in that affair, for they had been exceedingly happy together. Like ourselves, the Vandergelts were on their way to Egypt where they spent the winters, sometimes with and sometimes without Katherine's children from her first unhappy marriage.

"Not to mention the aunt and uncle of the bride, whose encounters with ambulatory mummies and master criminals have only too often been featured in the sensationalist press," I replied, with an answering smile.

"I notice none of your kinsmen are here."

"Good Gad, Katherine, you have heard enough about my brothers to understand why they are the last persons I would want. My nephew Percy, whom you met when he was out a few years ago, is typical of the rest of them. I suppose you've read his wretched little book. He sent copies to everyone."

"It is extremely entertaining," said Katherine, with a smile that rounded her cheeks and narrowed her slanted eyes. I had thought when I first met her that she reminded me of a plump-faced tabby cat; her smile had the same touch of cynicism that marks the countenance of a feline—most of whom are cynics by nature as well as experience.

"So I have been informed. I have not the time to waste with such stuff. As for Emerson's family, it consists solely of Walter. There was an estrangement, I believe; when I suggested this might be a suitable occasion for mending relations, Emerson informed me it was a bit late, since both his parents had passed on. Naturally I never pursued a subject that was clearly painful to my dear husband."

"Naturally," said Katherine.

Evelyn and Walter did not mingle in local society, and they

knew quite well what their stuffy county neighbors thought of the match. That opinion was shared, alas, by most of our archaeological acquaintances, who regarded the Egyptians with whom they worked and lived as inferiors. Certain members of both groups would have come had they been invited, but only out of vulgar curiosity. We had decided, therefore, not to invite them. Only our closest friends and kin were there, and Katherine was certainly correct about the unconventional composition of the guest list.

Gargery was chatting with Kevin O'Connell and his wife. Kevin's quizzical blue eyes kept wandering from Daoud, almost seven feet tall in his towering turban, to Rose in a hat so loaded with fluttering silk flowers, it looked as if it were about to fly off her head. I did not doubt that he was mentally composing the story he would like to have written for his cursed newspaper. The gentleman and the journalist were always at war in Kevin, but I was certain that on this occasion the gentleman would keep his word, especially since Emerson had threatened to perpetrate various indignities upon his person if he published anything.

The children's laughing voices rose above the quieter tones of their elders. I still thought of them as children, but most of them were young men and women now; how quickly time passes, I thought with pleasurable melancholy. Raddie, the younger Emersons's eldest, had gone down from Oxford with high honors; a gentle, scholarly man like his father, he was chatting with Nefret, his head bent attentively and his mild blue eyes fixed on her face. The twins, Johnny and Willy, were in a corner with Ramses. Johnny, the comedian of the family, must have been telling some wild story, for I heard Ramses laugh out loud, which was a rare event. Margaret, Lia's younger sister, was romping with Bertie and Anna, Katherine's children. Evelyn was talking with Fatima, who had left off her veil and somber black in honor of the occasion. Emerson had taken Walter and Cyrus Vandergelt aside and was gesturing animatedly. I had no illusions as to the nature of their conversation.

Katherine laughed. "Isn't this typical—the men huddling together talking archaeology, and the women talking about . . . Stop me, Amelia; I feel an attack of matchmaking coming on."

"It is natural on such an occasion as this," I said. "Who will be next, do you suppose? Neither of yours; they are too young."

"Not too young to feel the first twinges. I am afraid Anna

gave Ramses rather a bad time last year. He handled it very gracefully, I thought."

"He has had a good deal of practice," I said dryly. "I cannot
imagine why they do it."

Katherine gave me a sharp poke in the ribs and I saw Ramses
at my elbow. "I beg your pardon," he said. "Have I interrupted
a private conversation?"

"Nothing private about it," Katherine declared, her eyes twinkling. "We were speculating about love affairs. What do you
think of Nefret and Raddie, Amelia? He appears rather smitten."

"He appears absolutely hypnotized," I said, for I too had observed Raddie's bemused look and sentimental smile. "She is flirting scandalously with him."

"She's just keeping her hand in," said Ramses tolerantly.
"Raddie's no match for her, though. I had better rescue the poor
chap."

The musicians who had been playing softly in the background
now struck up a waltz, and the bride and groom began the first
dance. They were soon joined by Walter and Evelyn. Ramses had
removed Nefret from her prey; her apple-green skirts flared as he
spun her in a wide circle. Johnny was dancing with a young lady
named Curtis or Curtin, who had been at Saint Hilda's with Lia.

I saw no more of the others at that time, for my husband
seized me in his masterful grip and led (or, to be more accurate,
lifted) me onto the floor. Waltzing with Emerson requires one's
full attention; it is the only step he knows, and he performs it
with the energy that marks all his activities. Fortunately my dear
Evelyn had instructed the musicians to play a great many waltzes.

Since there were fewer ladies than gentlemen present, we females were much in demand. During the course of the afternoon
I danced with most of the men, including Gargery and, to my
amused surprise, Selim, who was looking very pleased with himself and very handsome, despite the beard he had grown in order
to command more respect from his men. He explained he had
got Margaret to instruct him, and meant to get in all the practice
he could while in England, for he liked this new activity very
much and meant to teach his wives how to do it.

I cannot recall a happier day. Later, I wondered if some shadowy premonition had touched us all, inducing not the pain of
future loss but a greater joy in the present. Had we but known
this was the last time we would all be together.

It was late in the afternoon before the newly married couple retired in order to change into their traveling attire. We got them off at last, with much laughter and more tears and the usual ceremonies of farewell; and after the carriage had driven off through the foggy darkness to "an unknown destination," we returned to the Hall.

"Rather like a funeral, isn't it?" said Emerson. "As soon as the body or bodies of the participants have been sent away, everyone starts to have a good time."

The only person who heard this inappropriate remark was Cyrus Vandergelt, who had known Emerson too long to be surprised at anything he said. His lined, leathery face stretched into a broad smile. "I've already had a real good time. Never attended a wedding that was so much durned fun! I'll never forget Selim dancing Egyptian-style, with the bridegroom beating on a kettle and the best man blowing a toy whistle and the rest of us gathered in a circle clapping our hands."

"Neither will I," I said ruefully. "Perhaps we all had a little too much champagne."

"Have a little more, then," said Cyrus. "And let's finish up the occasion in style. Strike up the band! Whee!"

## From Manuscript H

Ramses had no difficulty persuading his parents they should not tell Nefret about the scarab until after the wedding. They left it to him to break the news; Selim and Daoud and Fatima had returned to Amarna House with them, and his mother and father were fully occupied with entertaining their guests and completing the preparations for departure. At least that was their excuse. They knew how Nefret would react to an accusation against her friend. So did Ramses. He decided it would be better to get her away from the house when he told her, in case she started shouting, so he suggested they take two of the horses out.

It was a gray, blustery day, and the wind whipped color into Nefret's cheeks. They turned an even brighter shade as she listened to what he had to say.

The explosion was less intemperate than he had expected, though she employed several expletives she had learned from Emerson and a few more Ramses hadn't realized she knew. Then her eyes narrowed in a look he had learned to dread even more than her fits of temper. "Have you spoken with the bloody damned dealer?"

"There hasn't been time. I thought I'd run up to London tomorrow."

"Not tomorrow. I promised to take Fatima to the shops."

"But—"

"You're not going to London without me, Ramses. We'll go the day after tomorrow."


It was late morning before they got off. Nefret didn't complain once about how slowly he was driving. That was a bad sign, and so were her furrowed brow and tightly clasped hands. She was off on one of her crusades, and when she got the bit in her teeth she could be as passionately illogical and unreasonable as his mother. They were in the city and across the bridge, heading for Bond Street, when Ramses felt obliged to remind her of something he knew she wouldn't like.

"You did promise you'd let me do most of the talking."

"I did." A flash of blue eyes. "But I wish to go on record as remarking that I do not agree with the method you have decided to follow."

"You've already gone on record," Ramses said. "Several times and at length. Look here, Nefret, I don't agree with it either. I tried to convince Mother and Father that we ought to tell David at once, and failing that, confront Esdaile with the truth. But you know how they are."

"Still trying to protect us and David." She sighed. "It is so dear of them, and so infuriating!"

"They aren't as bad as they once were."

"No. Once they wouldn't have told you about the scarab. All right, we'll try it their way, but I'm damned if I know how you are going to extract any useful information without admitting it wasn't David who sold him the thing."

"We'll see."

The shop was pretentious and the merchandise was overpriced, and the proprietor fawned on them like Uriah Heep at his most unctuous. Having members of the "distinguished family of Egyptologists" patronize his establishment was an honor he had never dared expect. It was well known that "the Professor" disapproved of dealers. Of course he was not like other dealers. The firm's reputation for integrity had never been questioned . . .

Extracting the information they wanted without giving away their real purpose was a delicate and prolonged business. While examining practically every object in the shop, Ramses managed to extract a description of the man from whom Esdaile had purchased the scarab. It was vague in the extreme, since Ramses didn't dare inquire about such details as height and hair color; as a close friend of Mr. Todros, he might reasonably be expected to know them already. Finally Esdaile offered them a sizable reduction on a string of amethyst and gold beads Nefret had admired—"as a token of goodwill, my dear young friends"—and Ramses felt it would be expedient to buy it.

"Have you found a customer for Mr. Todros's scarab?" he asked, counting out banknotes.

"And the other antiquities." Esdaile smirked and rubbed his hands. "They were unusually fine, as you know."

Nefret's mouth opened. Ramses jabbed his elbow into her ribs. "The others, yes," he murmured, realizing he ought to have anticipated this. "I hope they went to collectors who would appreciate them."

"Yes, indeed." Esdaile hesitated, but only for a moment. "Professional etiquette prevents me from mentioning names, of course. He is, however, an old acquaintance of your father's, and I don't doubt he has already—"

"Who?" Nefret barked, and then produced a particularly sickening smile as Esdaile stared at her in surprise.

"I shouldn't . . . But the ushebtis will soon be placed on exhibit."

Ramses said weakly, "In the British Museum?"

"There, I felt certain you knew already. Yes, it was Mr. Budge himself who bought them. He doesn't often buy from British dealers, you know, gets most of what he wants directly from the Egyptians, but I always let him know when I acquire something unusual, and when I told him the provenance of the ushebtis, he assured me he just could not resist."

Ramses stared at the dealer. He knew he must appear particularly feeble-witted. "Provenance," he repeated.

"Yes, from the collection of your friend's grandfather. The old man was your foreman, was he not? As Mr. Budge said, who would have better sources than the longtime reis of the distinguished Professor Emerson? Mr. Budge was so pleased, he was chuckling quite merrily when he left. He . . . Why, Miss Forth, what is wrong? Are you feeling faint? Here—a chair—"

Ramses wrapped his arm tightly round Nefret's rigid shoulders. "Fresh air," he said. "She gets these spells. That's all she needs, a breath of fresh air."

He snatched up the parcel Esdaile had made of the necklace, shoved it in his pocket, got a firmer, two-handed grip on his speechless "sister," and led her out. He had to drag her round the next corner and into the recessed entry of a building before he dared loosen his grasp.

"Did you think I was going to faint?" she demanded, eyes flashing.

"You? I thought you were going to fly at Esdaile shouting denials. The fat would have been in the fire then."

"I wouldn't have done anything so stupid. But to accuse a man who was the soul of honor—who is dead and can't defend himself against such a contemptible accusation—"

"Don't be so theatrical." He took her by the shoulders. She flinched, and he let go. "What is it?"

"I'll have bruises," Nefret said with grim satisfaction. "Did you have to be so rough?"

"Oh, God, Nefret, I'm sorry!"

"Maybe you did have to." With one of her bewitching, bewildering changes of mood, she moved closer, taking hold of his lapels and smiling up into his remorseful face. "You were a bit angry yourself. Admit it."

"Perhaps I was. But most people wouldn't think any the worse of Abdullah for collecting antiquities. Everyone does it— everyone except Father, that is. The Cairo Museum buys from dealers, most of whose stock is derived from illegal excavation, Budge buys from the tomb robbers themselves—"

"No wonder Budge was so pleased." Nefret ground her teeth.

"Yes. Father has criticized him privately and publicly for doing precisely what Budge assumes Abdullah must have done. Good Lord, half the tomb robbers in Luxor are relations of Abdullah's, and the other half were old acquaintances. And if Abdullah had done it behind his back, Father would be hurt and furious."

She bowed her head and did not reply. She's taking it badly, he thought, and reached for her hand. "Let's go home, dear. We've found out what we wanted to know."

"Mmmm." After a moment she looked up, slipped her arm through his, and said calmly, "We missed lunch. Let's stop somewhere for tea before we start back."

"All right."

"It's a good thing Aunt Amelia wasn't with us," Nefret said, as they walked to the motorcar. "You know how she feels about Abdullah. She will *explode* when she hears this!"

"I'm afraid you're right. She was devoted to the dear old fellow."

"She dreams about him, you know."

"I didn't know." He opened the door for her.

"Perhaps I shouldn't have told you. She hates being thought sentimental."

"I won't say anything. It's rather touching, really. Have you ever wondered . . ." He went round to the driver's side and got in. "Have you ever wondered what he whispered to her in those last moments before he died?"

Nefret burst into one of her delightful gurgling laughs. "Why, Ramses, I didn't know men were curious about such things! Of course I've wondered. She's never said, and I don't believe she ever will. We all miss him, but there was something very special between them."

"Yes. Well, where do you want to go for tea?"

Her choice of the Savoy surprised him—she usually preferred a less pretentious ambience—but he didn't become suspicious when she excused herself as soon as the waiter had seated them. She was back sooner than he had expected and even his uncritical masculine eye told him she had not been painting her face or smoothing her windblown hair.

"What are you up to now?" he inquired, helping her into her chair and resuming his own.

Nefret stripped off her gloves. "I happened to remember they were to be in town this week. You haven't met them."

"Who?"

"There they are." She stood up and waved.

There were two of them, male and female; young, well-dressed, obviously American. Both were strangers to him, but when Nefret introduced them he recognized the names. Jack Reynolds had been at Giza with Reisner the year before. He bore a certain amusing resemblance to his mentor, and an even stronger one to the former American President, Theodore Roosevelt, for he had the same stocky frame and bushy mustache and rather prominent teeth. Only the eyeglasses were missing, but he might come to that yet; he was still in his twenties.

The girl was his sister, dark-haired, pink-cheeked, pleasantly plump and breezily informal. She gave Ramses her hand and shook her head, dimpling, when he addressed her as Miss Reynolds.

"Say, now, we're already on first-name terms with Nefret, and she's talked about you so much I feel as if we're well acquainted. My name's Maude. Can I call you Ramses? I think it's just the cutest name."

"Shut up and sit down, Maude," her brother said, with an amiable grin. "You'll have to excuse her, folks, she's been badly brought up. But I sure hope you'll skip the formalities with us, Ramses. It's a real honor to meet you at last. I've read all your articles and your book on Egyptian grammar, and Mr. Reisner thinks you're just the smartest young fellow in the business."

"Oh, really?" A trifle overwhelmed by all this cordiality, Ramses realized his response had sounded stiff and pompous. Smiling, he went on, "The most complimentary thing he ever said to *me* was that if I kept at it another ten years I might be half as good an excavator as my father."

Maude stared at him, lips parted. Her brother burst out laughing. "That was a compliment, all right. I sure hope we'll see a lot of you folks this season. Where are you going to be working?"

"The Professor never tells us until the last minute," Nefret said, pouting prettily. "But say, now, Maudie, what have you been doing in London? I hope Jack hasn't made you spend all your time at that dusty old British Museum."

It was an outrageous parody of poor Maude's speech and mannerisms, but it passed unnoticed by the victim, who responded with matching vivacity. The girls discussed shops and gossiped about mutual friends while Jack talked archaeology and Ramses tried to listen to all three of them, wondering what the devil Nefret thought she was doing—aside from eating most of the sandwiches and ridiculing her friend. Finally she pushed her plate away and demanded a cigarette.

"We didn't mean to ignore you ladies," Jack said, with another of his hearty laughs. "I guess you get tired of all this Egyptology talk."

Nefret looked as if she were about to say something rude. Ramses hurriedly fished in his pocket and drew out his cigarette case and a parcel wrapped in tissue paper. He offered the case to Nefret and struck a match. In his haste he dropped the little parcel onto the table. The contents spilled out in a glowing tangle of purple and gold.

Maude sucked in her breath. "Say, that's pretty. Is it real?"

Nefret blew out a cloud of smoke, smiled at Maude, and said sweetly, "Genuine, do you mean? Ramses just now bought it for me, wasn't that cute of him? At Esdaile's. Do you know the place? This necklace is authentic, but be on your guard if you shop there; we—er—acquired something recently that was a very well-made fake."

"Why'd you buy it then?" Jack asked.

"We have our reasons," Nefret said mysteriously.

Ramses decided it was time to change the subject.

Darkness had fallen before they left the Savoy. One of the attendants brought the car round and lighted the lamps. Nefret slid into the driver's seat while Ramses was handing out tips.

"Well?" she demanded, inserting the vehicle into the stream of evening traffic along the Strand.

Ramses opened his eyes. She had never actually hit anything, but watching her perform the maneuver was a nerve-racking experience.

"Well what? Nefret, that omnibus—"

"He sees me."

"Now what are you doing?"

"Putting on my driving helmet. My hair's blowing all around."

"I noticed that. Why don't you change places with me? Assuming that regalia of yours takes both hands, and so does steering."

She made a face at him, but did as he asked, coming to a dead stop in the middle of the roadway. She drove like an Egyptian—and David, who was Egyptian, drove like a cautious little old lady. So much for stereotypes, Ramses thought, hurrying round the car as frustrated drivers of various vehicles hooted and yelled at them.

"What did you think of the Reynoldses?" she asked, tucking her hair under her cap.

"Surely you don't suspect *him* of being our forger?"

"I suspect everyone. Let me sum up what we know about the wretch so far." She turned toward him and began counting on her fingers. "First, he's a trained Egyptologist; you said yourself no amateur could concoct that text. Two, he's a relative newcomer to the field—"

"Possible but not certain. Esdaile bought the objects this past April, but we don't know that others weren't sold earlier."

"It's a reasonable assumption," Nefret said firmly. "Three, he's young—no wrinkled old man could pass for David. Four, he speaks English like a native, to quote Mr. Esdaile—"

"That eliminates Jack," Ramses said.

She let out a melodious whoop of laughter. "Now who's a bigot?"

"I didn't mean it that way," Ramses protested. "I only meant the American accent is—er—distinctive."

"Not if it's heavily overlaid with a fake Egyptian accent," Nefret said triumphantly. "Five, he knows a lot about us—David's name and general appearance, and his relationship with the family, the same for Abdullah. That confirms the assumption that he is an Egyptologist, and very probably one with whom we are acquainted."

"He could have got that information from the newspapers. Mother and Father have been prominently featured, especially by their friend O'Connell."

"Curse it, Ramses, we have to start somewhere! If you are going to disagree with every damned point I make—"

"All right, all right. You may well be correct on all those points. I can't take Reynolds seriously, though. For one thing, there's the little matter of motive. The Reynoldses must have private means. Archaeologists living on their salaries don't stop at the Savoy."

"We don't know the motive," Nefret argued. "It could be something strange and perverse. Don't laugh! People do have irrational motives."

"Indubitably."

"What did you think of Maude?"

"I thought you were extremely rude to her."

"I was, wasn't I?" Nefret chuckled. "If you want to know, *she* was rather rude to David last year. She didn't *exactly* treat him like a servant, but she came close. We haven't a lot in common, Maudie and I; Jack was the one who kept thrusting us at one another. He has the devil of a time believing women are interested in anything except clothes and flirting."

"You do hold grudges, don't you?"

"Where my friends are concerned, yes. Did you notice how she jumped when I mentioned Esdaile's?"

"She did not jump. That was me. I thought we'd agreed not to mention the forgeries."

"In connection with David. I didn't mention *him*. Anyhow, if the Reynoldses are innocent, as you believe, what I said won't mean a cursed thing to them."

The children were late returning. I hoped for a private chat with them about their discoveries, but I was forced to wait, for dinner had already been announced, and a few whispered words from Ramses indicated they had a great deal to tell us. Fortunately our guests retired early, as they were accustomed to do. It was some minutes before eleven P.M. when Emerson and I crept out of our room and made our way to that of Ramses.

Though she had attained the dignified status of housekeeper, Rose still insisted on cleaning Ramses's room with her own hands. It was a hopeless task; ten minutes after she had left, all the flat surfaces were again strewn with cast-off articles of clothing, books and papers, and the various objects featured in Ramses's current research. I will give him credit; he had made some attempt to tidy up, and a cheery fire burned under the Adam mantelpiece.

Nefret was sitting cross-legged on the hearthrug, with Horus sprawled across her lap. Horus was the largest and least affable of our current crop of cats, and Nefret's fondness for him was unaccountable to me. He did seem to return it, in his surly fashion, but she was the only one whose caresses he accepted. He tolerated Emerson and me, disliked David, and detested Ramses, who returned the compliment.

"I feel like a cursed spy," Emerson grumbled, flinging himself into an armchair. "I am still of the opinion that we ought to take Selim, at least, into our confidence. He is a sharp young chap, and has had a long acquaintance with forgers."

"Hmmm," I said. "Nefret, that is a very pretty necklace. A new purchase, I presume?"

"Ramses bought it for me."

My son was also sitting on the floor, his back against a bookcase, and the kitten on his lap. It had taken to following him about like a puppy. I suspected its devotion was not entirely altruistic, for several of Ramses's coats had developed suspicious greasy stains inside the pockets, and all our cats are extremely fond of chicken. I raised no objection, for I was pleased to see Ramses develop an attachment to one of the cats; he had been devoted to our dear departed Bastet, the progenitrix of the tribe, and had steadfastly refused to replace her with another. Bastet had traveled back and forth with us to Egypt, as Horus did now; but Ramses had concluded that the kitten was still too young to go out this year.

Glancing at me and then at his father, he said, "The beads are genuine, but they have been restrung—probably not in the original order. I felt it advisable to purchase something, Father, in order to conceal—"

"Yes, yes," Emerson grunted. "Well?"

Ramses repeated the description he had winkled (his word) out of the dealer. Emerson groaned. "Curse it! I had hoped the resemblance wouldn't be so close."

"It was really quite vague, Father. Fine-looking young chap; not as dark-skinned as most Egyptians (I wonder how many Egyptians he's encountered?); about my height and build."

"The turban was a mistake," Nefret said. "David never wears one."

"People expect Egyptians to wear a turban or a fez," Ramses said, stroking the kitten. "It's part of the costume. And a turban can be used to conceal one's actual height."

"There is more, isn't there?" I asked. "Out with it, Ramses."

As the tale unfolded, I found it difficult to restrain my outrage. When Abdullah and I first met, he had viewed me with deep suspicion and a certain amount of resentment. Not only had I, a mere woman, dared to express my opinions aloud but I had come between him and the man he admired above all others. Our strange friendship had developed and deepened over the years, and even before his heroic death he had earned my sincere regard. Abdullah's professional standards had been as high as those of any European archaeologist—aye, and a good deal higher than most!

"He would never have done such a thing," I said. "Never. He would have considered it a betrayal of our friendship."

Sympathy for my wrath enabled Emerson to control his own. Taking my hand, he patted it and spoke in the soft purring voice evil doers fear more than his shouts.

"Our unknown opponent is a clever bastard, isn't he? Abdullah knew every dealer and every tomb robber in Egypt. If he had formed his own collection of antiquities, it would have been of superb quality. The mention of his name gave the spurious antiquities a believable provenance and undoubtedly raised the price. The swine couldn't have known we would be the ones to discover the fraud, but by Gad, I could almost believe he anticipated even that possibility! You see the position he has put us in, don't you? In order to protect David, all we need do is maintain the fiction. No one would question his right to dispose of his grandfather's collection, but if the objects are found to be counterfeit—"

"Someone will find out," I said. "Sooner or later."

"There's a good chance it will be later rather than sooner," Emerson said. "If at all. It isn't that easy to identify a well-made fake, you know; there are several presently on display in various museums, including our precious British Museum! Budge couldn't spot a forgery unless it had 'Made in Birmingham' stamped on the base."

None of us replied to this (slightly) exaggerated assessment. Emerson's detestation of the Keeper of Egyptian Antiquities was familiar to us all. In fairness to my husband I should add that it was an opinion shared by many Egyptologists, if not quite to the same degree. Even if Budge realized the ushebtis were fakes, he was not likely to admit he had been taken in by them; but it would have been dishonorable to support the fraud by our silence, no matter how great the peril to David.

For a time only the crackling of the flames and the sleepy squeaks of the kitten broke the silence.

"At least we now know what to look for," said Ramses, in his cool, unemotional voice. "Any object that purports to have been sold by David or to have belonged to Abdullah. The more of them we can locate, the better our chance of establishing a pattern that may give us a clue as to this individual's identity."

"Quite right," said Nefret. "But how do you propose to go about it? We can't ask the dealers straight out whether they have recently purchased antiquities from David; they will wonder why he hadn't told us himself."

"Good Gad, that is true," I exclaimed. "We dare not arouse the slightest suspicion that the transaction was not legitimate. Then how . . ."

I did not complete the sentence. There was no need; we all knew the answer. My heart sank when I saw Emerson's face. His tight lips had relaxed, his eyes shone.

"By concealing our true identities," he said happily. "That is how. Disguised as a wealthy collector, I will say I have heard rumors about an outstanding group of antiquities that has recently come on the market—"

"No, Emerson," I said. "No, my dear. Not you."

"Why the devil not? I trust," said Emerson, glowering, "that you are not implying I cannot carry off a masquerade of that sort as competently as—as anyone."

He transferred the glare to Ramses.

Ramses's expertise at the dubious art of disguise was a source of irritation as well as pride to his father; not only had it been inspired by an individual for whom Emerson had a particular detestation, but it was a skill at which Emerson himself secretly yearned to excel. He has a fondness for theatrics and a positive passion for beards, possibly because I had deprived him of his, not once but twice! Unhappily it is a skill at which Emerson cannot succeed. His magnificent physique defies concealment, and his outrageous temper explodes under the slightest provocation.

Ramses remained prudently silent. I said, "I am not implying, Emerson, I am telling you straight out. There is no way of disguising the color of those sapphirine orbs or the strength of your chin and jaw, or your imposing height and impressive musculature."

The adjectives had a softening effect, but he was too set on the scheme to give in without an argument. "A beard," he began.

"No, Emerson. I know how much you like beards, but they are inadequate to the purpose."

"A beard *and* a Russian accent," Emerson suggested. "Nyet, tovarich!"

Ramses winced. Nefret's lips trembled. She was trying not to laugh.

"Oh, very well," I said. "I will go with you, also in disguise. Your wife? No, your mistress. French. A Titian wig and a great deal of paint and powder; champagne satin cut low over the—er—and copious quantities of jewelry. Topazes or perhaps citrines."

Emerson stared at me. I could tell from his expression that he was picturing me in the ensemble I had described. "Hmmm," he said.

"Father," Ramses exclaimed. "You can't mean to allow Mother to appear in public as a—a—"

Emerson burst out laughing. "Good Gad," he said, between chuckles, "what a prude you are, my boy. She didn't mean it, you

know. At least I don't think . . . Very well, Peabody, I give in.
We'll leave it to Ramses, eh?"

"Thank you, Father."

"The French mistress is an excellent idea, though," Nefret
said thoughtfully. "I won't even need the wig. A little henna will
do the job."

## From Letter Collection B

*Dearest Lia,*

*I ought to add "and David," since I know perfectly well
that in the first rapturous flush of matrimonial affection you
will want to share everything with him. But I hope, dearest,
that you won't share all my confidences with David. Do you
know (but you must) that you are the first and only woman
friend I have ever had? Aunt Amelia and I have become very
close, but there are some things she wouldn't understand. So
prepare yourself, dear Lia, for a spate of letters. Some may never
reach you, traveling as you are, but the act of writing will serve
as a substitute, however feeble, for those long talks we have
when we are together.*

*You'll never guess whom Ramses and I ran into in London
last week—Maude Reynolds and her brother Jack—you remember them—the Americans who were with Reisner last year. After the usual exchanges of "What a surprise!" and "How is it
you are in London?" I introduced everyone properly.*

*Ramses immediately began to slouch, the way he does when
he is trying to look inconspicuous and/or harmless. Absolutely
futile, of course, at least with females. Maude began babbling
and dimpling at him. He seemed to like it, for he actually smiled
at her. Perhaps it's because he's usually so solemn that his smile
has such an impact. If Maude hadn't been sitting down, she'd
have staggered.*

*Jack is a nice-enough chap in his obtuse fashion. If only he
wouldn't treat all women the way he does his bird-brained sister, with a mixture of affection and condescension! He explained
that he and Maude had been "doing" a European tour before
returning to Cairo for the winter season.*

*We took tea with them at the Savoy, where they were stay-
ing. Maude was as adorable as only she can be, black curls
bouncing, brown eyes wide, chubby cheeks pink. "Meow!" I can*

*hear you say. Very well, I admit it—I've always envied girls
who have that vivid autumnal coloring and ripe, rounded
shape—it's not just Maude's cheeks that are plump! I'm too
thin and I haven't any bosom, and I don't know how to be
adorable.*

*They asked after you and David, of course.*

**E**sdaile's revelations added a new complication to our search for
the forger. Ramses continued to urge that we make the matter
public, but even he was forced to admit that it would be cruel to
allow David to hear of it from strangers—an eventuality that well
might ensue once the word began to spread. Nefret, who had
been of his opinion, was won over to ours by this argument,
though it went against her nature.

Some preliminary inquiries were necessary; we could not personally call on every dealer and private collector in Europe. Emerson and I were still discussing how to go about these when
Ramses suddenly disappeared from the house. When questioned,
Nefret admitted she knew where he had gone, assured us he was
not up to anything illegal or dangerous, and politely refused to
answer any further questions.

He reappeared two days later, as suddenly as he had departed, and replied to our agitated queries by handing over a
sheaf of telegrams. A glance at one of them explained all. It had
been sent to a Mr. Hiram Applegarth at the Savoy, and read, TWO
FINE HEART SCARABS RECENTLY ACQUIRED FROM UNIMPEACHABLE
SOURCE STOP LOOK FORWARD TO YOUR VISIT.

Emerson, thumbing through the messages, let out a string of
swear words, ending with an emphatic "Damnation! Did you
telegraph every dealer in Europe? This must have cost a fortune.
And was it absolutely necessary to put up at the Savoy?"

"It was necessary to establish an impression of wealth,"
Ramses explained. "I had to give them a return address, and I
could hardly use ours."

"Since you did not ask your father or me for money, I presume you used Nefret's," I said.

"It is not *mine*," Nefret snapped, before Ramses could answer.
"It is *ours*. His, yours, David's, Lia's. We're a family, aren't we?
I've told you before—"

"Yes, my dear, you have." I studied my son, who looked back at me with a particularly enigmatic expression. When Nefret said, "What is mine is yours," she really meant it; but for some individuals it is easier to give than to receive, and for Ramses to accept assistance of any kind was truly remarkable. It was not only an acknowledgment of her equality, but a subjugation of that towering pride of his. I gave him an approving smile. "Well, we will say no more about it, since the procedure appears to have been effective."

"It gives us several possible leads, at any rate," said Ramses. "I—Nefret and I—had to act without delay. We are due to leave in a week."

It was true, and we were all anxious to be off. The dreary days of autumn were upon us; only a few yellowed leaves clung to the barren branches, and the last roses had perished in an early frost. The hours of darkness were lengthening, the wind blew chill and wet.

In short, the weather was ideal for criminal endeavors. That night the lodgekeeper and his family were snugly shut up in their house, curtains drawn against the rainy darkness. Our pampered and lazy dogs were not inclined to leave their warm kennel on such a night. We had spent the day sightseeing, and at my suggestion we all retired early.

At least I *thought* we had all retired early. I should have known Ramses would ignore my motherly advice. I never got round to asking why he was not asleep at that hour in the morning (two A.M., to be precise). His room is over the library, and his window was open (I am a firm believer in the benefits of fresh air), but I doubt anyone else would have heard the sound of breaking glass, muffled as it was by wind and rain. As the Egyptians say, Ramses can hear a whisper across the Nile.

It would not have occurred to Ramses that he might want assistance. He went down alone to investigate.

The sounds that followed his discovery of the burglars would have wakened the dead. Even Emerson, who is a heavy sleeper, and who had good reason to be weary that night, shot out of bed. He immediately fell over a chair, so I got to the door before him, but I heard his breathless curses close behind me as I ran along the hall. There was no time to lose, no time even to assume a dressing gown; the sound that had waked me was the explosion of a firearm.

I might not have known precisely where the action was taking place had I not seen a white form ahead of me. Ghostly and palely glimmering, it fled along the dimly lighted hall until it reached the top of the stairs, and then . . . For one extremely disconcerting moment I thought it had taken flight. A solid thump and a loud "Damn!" assured me the form was human—Nefret's form, to be precise—and that she had slid down the banister in order to save a few precious seconds. Picking herself up at once, she dashed along the corridor that led to the library.

My descent was of necessity less precipitous. Emerson, who can cover the ground quite rapidly once he is fully awake, ran smack into me at the bottom of the steps. Catching me to him as I tottered, he looked wildly around and bellowed, "Where the devil . . . ?"

There could be no doubt of the answer; sounds of struggle and the destruction of furniture issued from the direction of the library, and the lights in that chamber shone out into the corridor. Emerson said a very bad word and went on, pulling me with him.

A scene of disaster met our eyes. Rain blew in through the shattered windows, and broken glass littered the floor. Chairs had been overturned and books toppled from the shelves. A motionless body lay facedown by the desk; several drawers stood open, and their contents had been strewn across the carpet. Also on the carpet were two men, rolling back and forth as they struggled. One of them was a heavyset individual wearing rough, dark clothing; his right hand gripped a pistol, and his right wrist was gripped by his adversary, who was, as the Reader must have anticipated, my son, attired only in the loose cotton trousers he preferred to a nightshirt. Light as a windblown leaf, Nefret danced round them, her knife raised, waiting for an opportunity to strike. She jumped aside, swearing, as the burglar flung Ramses over onto his back—and onto the broken glass. His hand did not lose its grip, but the expletive that burst from his lips proved him a worthy son of his father.

"Stand out of the way, Nefret," said Emerson. Seizing the burglar by the collar of his coat, he lifted him up into the air and removed the pistol from his nerveless grasp. Ramses got slowly to his feet, streaming blood and gasping for breath. When he got it back, his first words were directed at Nefret.

"Damnation! Why didn't you go after him?"

Emerson looked from the motionless body on the floor to the

squirming body he held at arm's length. "Was there another one?" he inquired.

"Yes," Nefret said, through her pretty white teeth. "I didn't go after him because I thought possibly Ramses might need assistance with the other two. Silly little me! Do forgive me!"

"But he got the scarab, damn it!"

"Are you certain?" I asked, as Emerson shook the burglar in an absentminded sort of way and Nefret glared at her brother.

"Yes," Ramses said. "When I switched on the lights, that fellow actually had it in his hand. I went for him, and he tossed it to the third man, who rather lost his head, I think, because he went straight out the French doors without stopping to open them."

"What was that one doing?" Emerson inquired interestedly, indicating the fallen burglar.

"Trying to interfere," said his son.

"He had a pistol, too, I see," said Emerson. "You may as well pick it up, Peabody, my dear; I doubt if he is in any condition to use it, but it is always wise to take precautions. Ramses, apologize to your sister."

"I apologize," Ramses muttered.

"Now that I come to think about it, I'm rather flattered," Nefret said, with one of those abrupt changes of mood some people found so charming (and some other people found so exasperating). She started toward Ramses and let out a little scream; she had trod on some of the broken glass.

Emerson picked her up in the arm that was not holding the burglar and transferred her to a chair. "Be careful where you step, Ramses, you aren't wearing shoes either. It's too late to go after the one that got away. I'll wager this gentleman will be glad to tell us everything we want to know."

He smiled affably at the burglar, a burly fellow whom he continued to hold with one hand, as easily as if he had been a child. The entire household had been aroused, and a good number of them had joined us, shouting questions and brandishing various deadly instruments. The burglar glared wildly at Emerson, bare to the waist and bulging with muscle—at Gargery and his cudgel—at Selim, fingering a knife even longer than Nefret's—at assorted footmen armed with pokers, spits, and cleavers—and at the giant form of Daoud advancing purposefully toward him. "It's a bleedin' army!" he gurgled. "The lyin' barstard said you was some kind of professor!"

By the time we got things sorted out, the gray dawn was breaking. It had taken me a good twenty minutes to get all the broken glass out of Ramses's back and Nefret's feet, and I doubted I would ever get the bloodstains out of the carpet. The burglars had been removed by our local constabulary. The one on the floor had regained consciousness but insisted, between groans, that he could not walk and must be carried on a litter. He did appear to be rather crippled.

The other burglar had been anxious to cooperate but he could offer no means of tracing the man who had hired him and his associates, as he had approached them in one of the foul grog shops in London where such petty criminals (I am informed) are to be found. Disguised as before in turban and brown skin, the villain had paid a small amount down, with the promise of a larger sum upon delivery. He had described the object he wanted in precise detail, and showed them a picture postcard of a scarab in order to make identification easier. He had even given them a rough plan of the house, indicating Emerson's study as the most likely place where the object would be hidden.

After digging in his pockets, Bert (the burglar) produced this paper, and I was not surprised to see that there was no writing at all on it, only an emphatic X marking the room in question. The scoundrel had taken no chances of any kind. Instead of arranging a rendezvous in London, he had indicated he would be waiting outside the gates of the park, where he would hand over the rest of the money in exchange for the scarab.

The futility of pursuit was obvious. The villain must have heard the shot and seen lights go on all over the house; he had known immediately that the plan had gone awry. Had he dared wait long enough to receive the scarab from the third burglar? We might never know. No trace of burglar, scarab or villain was found, though as soon as it was light enough we conducted a thorough search of the grounds. The rain had washed away footprints and the tracks of motorcar, cart, carriage, or cycle.

I made all the searchers change into dry clothes and then we gathered in the small dining room for a belated and hearty breakfast. Gargery was still annoyed because he had not arrived on the scene in time to hit someone with his cudgel.

"You ought to have told me and Bob and Jerry you had got yourselves into mischief," he said reproachfully. "We'd have stood guard."

"There was nothing to tell, Gargery," I assured him. "We had no reason to anticipate any such thing. I still can't account for it. Why would he—whoever he is—go to such lengths to get the thing back?"

"Obviously," said Ramses, "because there was something about the confounded thing that might betray his identity. But what?"

"You observed nothing?" I asked.

"No," said Ramses, visibly chagrined.

"Even more to the point," said Nefret, "is how the fellow knew we had it."

"Hmph." Emerson rubbed his now bristly chin, with a sound like a file rasping on metal.

"We can discuss the ramifications of that question later," I said. Selim and Daoud were listening with amiable interest. They were quite accustomed to our little criminal encounters, but sooner or later one of them, probably Selim, was going to ask for additional details. Under ordinary circumstances they would have been among the first to be taken into our confidence. Under these circumstances I preferred to delay the revelation.

"It will all be gone into at the proper time," I continued. "Get a little more sleep if you can, or at least rest awhile longer."

"England is a dangerous country," Selim remarked. "We should go back to Egypt where you will be safe."

### From Letter Collection B

*Dearest Lia and David,*

*I understand Aunt Evelyn has already written you about our little burglary, so I make haste to reassure you. Aunt Amelia telephoned poor Mr. O'Connell and scolded him dreadfully for reporting the story, but his wasn't the only newspaper to print it. I fear every journalist in England is familiar with the name of Emerson! The accounts were exaggerated, as they always are; the only fatality was the Professor's favorite bust of Socrates, which was smashed to smithereens by a bullet. No one was hurt, except one of the burglars.*

*In case Aunt Evelyn didn't mention it, we will soon be following in your footsteps, at least as far as Italy. Poor Daoud has sheepishly admitted that he suffered horribly from seasickness on the voyage over, so we will go by train to Brindisi and board the steamer there instead of sailing direct from London.*

*The Professor has graciously consented to stop along the way in order to show our friends various places of interest. Knowing the Professor, you will not be surprised to hear that the itinerary includes only cities with museums and shops containing Egyptian antiquities . . .*

By the time we reached Brindisi I was not the only member of the party who was glad to leave Europe for sunny Egypt. It had rained in Paris and snowed in Berlin, and on our arrival in Turin we had been greeted by a horrid mixture of sleet and snow. Daoud had been struck all in a heap by the phenomenon of snow; he had stood openmouthed and staring on the Wilhelmstrasse till his face turned blue and his feet turned to ice. He was now suffering from a heavy cold, and was as miserable a man as I have ever seen. (Except for Emerson, who is almost never ill and who behaves like a fiend when he is.)

As soon as we boarded the ship I put Daoud to bed, rubbed him with wintergreen, bundled him up in flannel, and stuffed him full of sleeping medication. The weather was blustery and the sea was rough; Fatima took to her berth, and Selim, who shared Daoud's cabin, declared he did not intend to leave it until we reached Alexandria. They were not the only sufferers; a mere handful of passengers appeared at dinner that night. Even dampened tablecloths did not prevent the plates from sliding and the glasses from toppling. Thanks to the soothing effect of whiskey and soda (a panacea for numerous ailments, including mal de mer), the rest of us were unaffected, and the indisposition of our poor friends providing us with an opportunity for a council of war, we gathered in Emerson's and my stateroom after an excellent, if somewhat lively, meal.

It was really quite cozy, with water lashing across the porthole and the oil lamp swinging wildly, casting fascinatingly distorted shadows across the small room. The solid and surly bulk of Horus helped anchor Nefret to one of the bunks. Emerson's strong arm held me on the other, and Ramses elected to sit on the floor with his feet braced against the wall.

"So how many have we identified?" I inquired.

Ramses extracted a dog-eared list from his pocket. "Seven, including the original scarab. Unfortunately we were only able to purchase three of the remaining six—two scarabs with royal car-touches and a small statue of the god Ptah. The others had al-ready been sold. I've gone over all three and there is no obvious flaw in any of them. When we get to Cairo I will try a few chem-ical tests."

"If we still have them when we get to Cairo," muttered Em-erson, who was inclined to take burglaries of his home personally.

"Nonsense, Emerson," I said. "There is no way the forger can trace these objects to us. No one could possibly have recognized Mr. Applegarth, or his—er—friend."

*I* certainly would not have recognized Ramses in his role of a middle-aged, wealthy American collector; even his accent was a devastatingly accurate imitation of our friend Cyrus's voice. Nefret accompanied him, not in champagne satin and citrines, though the crimson ensemble she selected was almost as con-spicuous. The only thing that could be said for it was that it con-cealed her identity quite successfully. It had been obvious to my eye at least that she had stuffed several handkerchiefs into her bodice, and there had been enough paint on her face to disguise three women.

"We still don't know how he traced the first scarab to us," Ramses said.

"We can hazard a guess, can't we?" Nefret demanded. "I dropped an extremely broad hint to Jack Reynolds that day at the Savoy."

"Yes, but that doesn't narrow the possibilities enough," said her brother irritably. "Jack may have passed the remark on to someone else. Mr. Renfrew may have broken his vow of silence. The culprit may have returned to Esdaile's and learned we were there asking about 'Mr. Todros.' Someone else may have been indiscreet."

"It wasn't me," Nefret said indignantly. "You always blame me for talking out of turn. It isn't fair."

Ramses gave his sister a sour look, but nodded. "We are be-ginning to get a picture of the fellow, though, aren't we? If he is not actually an Egyptologist, he has had extensive training; if he is not an artist himself, he has connections with someone who is. He is annoyingly well-acquainted with our habits, our habitat, and our circle of acquaintances. None of the dealers he ap-proached knew David personally, but *he* knows David well enough to ape certain of his characteristics, including David's preference for English over other languages, though he also speaks German and French and some Arabic."

"He is an expert at disguise," Nefret contributed.

"Not really," Ramses said. "It doesn't take much expertise to darken one's complexion and assume a false beard and a turban."

A particularly violent lurch of the vessel set the oil lamp swinging. The play of light and shadow across Emerson's scowling face turned it into a diabolical mask. I knew what—or rather of whom—he was thinking. Only the Master Criminal could rouse Emerson to such ire.

We had never known his real name or his true appearance. He *was* an expert at disguise and the cleverest criminal we had ever encountered. For years he had ruled the iniquitous underworld of antiquities-smuggling and -fraud like the genius of crime he was. He had all the qualities Ramses had mentioned, and others as damning—a sardonic sense of humor and, as he had once admitted to me, some of the world's most expert forgers in his employ.

"Out with it, Emerson," I urged. "It is Sethos you suspect, is it not?"

"No," said Emerson.

"You always suspect him. Admit it. Do not suppress your feelings; they will only fester and—"

"I do not suspect him. Do you?"

"Not in this case. He swore that he would never harm me or those I love—"

"Don't be maudlin," Emerson snarled. "You may be fool enough to believe the bastard's protestations of noble, disinterested passion, but I know better. Curse it, Peabody, why did you have to bring him up? He can't be behind this business."

"I agree, sir," Ramses said.

"Oh, you do, do you? May I ask why? And," Emerson added, "I beg you will not repeat your mother's fatuous and inaccurate assessment of that swine's character."

"No, sir. A man who can imitate an elderly American lady and a foppish young English nobleman would never have assumed such a clumsy disguise as this one. He would have appeared as Howard Carter or Wallis Budge—or you."

**Drawing my sword, I ran the fellow through the arm. He ran off squealing and dripping blood. The girl knelt at my feet. "Allah bless you, Effendi," she whispered, pressing her lips to my dusty boots. Gently I raised her . . .**

We arrived at Alexandria before sunrise, but owing to the inevitable procrastination that prevails in the East, it was after luncheon before passengers and baggage were disembarked. The quay was aswarm with local merchants, all of them pushing and shoving and shouting at the top of their lungs. Even the most importunate gave way before Emerson, who strode along like a pharaoh. I will not be accused of boasting, I believe, if I say that by now we were known to most Egyptians, and those who did not know us were soon apprised of our identities by the hails of greeting: Marhaba, Sitt Hakim! Salaam aleikhum, O Father of Curses! It is Nur Misur, the Light of Egypt, who has returned! Welcome, Brother of Demons . . .

That, I regret to say, is my son's Egyptian soubriquet. He was greeted thus familiarly by beggars, cutpurses, and procurers, and he appeared to know all of them by *their* names.

I had raised my parasol, since the sun's rays were strong, so I did not observe an approaching individual until a soft expletive from Ramses made me look up. Though the individual was only of medium height, the resplendent uniform of an officer of the Egyptian Army (which has been compared by unkind persons to that of a Viennese bandmaster) and his arrogant stride made him seem taller. His features, which I had once thought bore a certain resemblance to my own, were partially obscured by a particularly oversized example of a military mustache. Mustache, hair and eyebrows had been bleached to a sickly brown, and his face was red with sunburn.

He was almost upon us before Emerson saw him. Astonishment stifled my husband's speech for a strategic moment.

"Why, Percy," I said. "What the devil are you doing here?"

My least favorite nephew whipped off his fez and bowed. With an engaging smile he indicated the gold braid, the epaulets, the sword, the sash, and the rows of gilded buttons. "As you see, my dear Aunt Amelia, I have joined the Egyptian Army. I hoped you would not have heard of it; I wanted to surprise you."

The express train from Alexandria to Cairo takes over three hours, but Emerson was still swearing when it pulled into the Central Station. Percy had not detained us long; he had explained that he had been seconded to "Alex" on a special mission of great importance and that he had been unable to resist the temptation to be among the first to welcome us. He was obviously aching to be asked about the nature of his mission, so he could look mysterious and important. None of us obliged him.

"I wonder if he's been temporarily assigned to the Alexandria police or the CID," Ramses mused. "Russell has been ordered to stop the import of hashish and cannabis, and he will need additional personnel if he's to have any hope of success."

"Damn and blast!" said Emerson. Ramses's suggestion succeeded in catching his attention, however, and he gave over general swearing for specific comment. "Hmmm. Additional manpower won't do Russell any good, there are too many miles of coastline to cover. What he needs is an informant who is working for one of the big men like Abd el-Quadir el-Gailani, and who can give him advance warning of a delivery."

"Obviously," said Ramses.

His father shot him a critical look. "I strictly forbid it, Ramses. I need you on the dig."

"I hadn't intended—" Ramses began.

"I should hope not!" Nefret exclaimed. "Our primary aim is to find that damned forger. Let Percy play spy and make a fool of himself. I wonder if he swaggers when he's asleep?"

"Enough about Percy," I said firmly. "I do not intend to associate with him and I am heartily sick of discussing him. We have arrived; Emerson, kindly assume your coat and your cravat and your hat. You too, Ramses. Nefret, put Horus on his lead."

Since it was necessary for Nefret to sit between Ramses and the cat, like a mama separating quarrelsome children, Ramses had the corner seat, with Nefret next to him and Horus sprawled insolently across the remaining space. Horus put up a fuss about the lead; he was as spoiled as a fat pasha and had no intention of walking if he could bully someone into carrying him. No one offered, however, not even Emerson.

Waiting to greet us were a number of our loyal men, members of Abdullah's extended family, who had worked for us for many years. Some resided in Luxor, some in the village of Atiyah, south of Cairo. Their cries of welcome were directed at us all, but the returning wanderers were the center of attention this time. I could see that Selim and Daoud were anxious to get home, where the whole village would be waiting to hear the tales of their adventures, so we bade them a temporary farewell and got ourselves and our baggage into cabs.

Traffic worsened every year; now motorcars disputed the right of way with carts and horse-drawn cabs and camels and donkeys, not to mention the pedestrians who had to risk life and limb crossing the major thoroughfares. It took almost half an hour to drive from the railroad station to the dock, but not even my impatient spouse complained of the delay. It was so good to be back—to breathe the hot dry air, to see roses and bougainvillea blooming in December, to hear again the familiar din of Cairo—the mournful chorus of "La lahu illa-Allah" that heralded a funeral procession, the shouts of sellers of licorice water and lemonade. And to see, when the brief journey ended, the familiar shape of my beloved dahabeeyah on which I had spent so many blissful hours.

Emerson had purchased the boat and named it after me. I could not bear to give it up, though it had become inconveniently small for our extended family and our ever increasing library (not to mention Nefret's ever increasing wardrobe).

Now back on her native heath, properly veiled and attired and ready to resume her duties as housekeeper, Fatima had worked herself into a state of anxious self-reproach. She should not have gone to England. She should have stayed in Cairo to make certain the dahabeeyah was in readiness for our arrival. No one knew how to do it but she. Her niece Karima had no sense. Her nephew, Karima's husband, was lazy and worthless and—worst of all—a man. The floors would be dirty, the beds unmade, the food inedible . . .

In my opinion Karima had performed a good deal better than dear old Abdullah had done when he was in charge of the housekeeping arrangements, but as we passed from room to room, Fatima subjected her to a running commentary of criticism. Announcing that she would have to do it all over again, Fatima fluttered off to her room to change from her good clothing and I dismissed Karima with thanks and compliments. She was very glad to go.

We become spoiled and jaded as we mature, I suppose. The bathing arrangements, which had so impressed me on my first inspection of the *Philae* (as she was called then), now seemed infuriatingly inadequate. I was the last to avail myself of them, and thus the last to join the others in the saloon. Located in the bow of the ship, this large chamber had long windows, with a wide divan under them. Ramses and Emerson had begun unpacking the boxes of books we had brought with us, but had stopped midway as men always do, leaving books on the floor, on the chairs, and on the tables. Nefret reclined on the divan with Horus across her feet; he was growling and rending papers that appeared to be the remains of letters and envelopes. Sitting cross-legged on the floor, Ramses was perusing a ponderous tome in German and Emerson was rummaging in the cupboards under the cushioned divan.

"Don't start scolding, Peabody," he remarked, observing my expression. "We cannot put the books away, the shelves are already full. We need more space, curse it."

"On that we are agreed, Emerson. I suppose you expect me to find a house and get it ready—repairs, furnishings, servants—"

"Who said anything about a house?" Emerson demanded. "All we need do is clear out a few tables and chairs—"

"And beds? We could sleep on the floor as well as sit on it, I suppose. Emerson, we have had this conversation a dozen times. You know we promised Lia and David we would let them have the *Amelia* when they join us; young married persons will want their privacy. You are only objecting because you resent giving up a few hours of your precious excavation time in order to assist me in a project which can only be of benefit to us all. And furthermore—"

"Sit down and have your whiskey, Mother," said Ramses.

"Sit down where? No, thank you, Nefret, I prefer not to hob-nob with Horus, he appears to be in a particularly evil mood this evening."

Horus bared his fangs at me. Ramses cleared the most comfortable overstuffed chair, removing the books to the floor. "Here you are, Mother. I'll get you your whiskey and your messages."

The genial beverage had its usual soothing effect. Accepting the pile of envelopes he handed me, I said, "All for me? I presume you have perused yours. Was there anything interesting in them?"

Ramses said, "No."

Since that was the answer I had expected, I turned to my own messages. A nice plump letter from Evelyn I put aside, to be enjoyed at my leisure. The others were notes of welcome. What a pleasure it was to see the familiar names, to anticipate meeting soon again with such dear friends as Katherine and Cyrus, Howard Carter, Mr. and Mrs. Quibell, and all the rest. One message was from an unexpected source; perusing it, I let out a little exclamation of surprise.

"Well, fancy that! Here is an invitation to luncheon from Miss Reynolds. You remember her and her brother, Emerson; we met them last year."

"I remember them, but I see no reason why we should improve our acquaintance with them," said Emerson. "We have too many cursed friends as it is. They interfere with one's work."

"Not our professional colleagues, Emerson. Mr. Reisner speaks very highly of young Mr. Reynolds, and his sister is quite pleasant for an American. She says she has heard we are looking for a suitable house—"

"And where did she hear that?" Emerson demanded.

"Not from me, Emerson, I assure you."

Nefret cleared her throat. "I told you Ramses and I met them in London. I may have mentioned, in the course of conversation, that we were thinking of taking a house."

"Ah, I see. That explains it. Are you and she such good friends, Nefret?"

"No," said Nefret. After a moment, she went on, "Maude's kindly gesture was not prompted by her interest in *me*."

"What? Oh! Ramses, did you—"

"Yes, Mother," said my son, in the exaggerated drawl he adopted when he was trying to annoy me. "I held her hand, looked deep into her eyes, and murmured passionate phrases into her ear while her brother wasn't listening. She was putty in my hands. Later I lured her away and demanded she find us a house."

"Ramses!" I exclaimed.

Nefret shook her head. "Really, Ramses, it's no fun teasing you anymore."

"Was that what you were doing?" my son inquired.

"Enough," I said severely. "You are too old to be poking fun at the poor young lady. I shall accept her invitation, and I expect both of you to behave yourselves."

"What the devil, Amelia," my husband exclaimed. "I did not come to Egypt to lunch with young ladies. I came here to excavate, and that is what I intend to do, first thing tomorrow morning. Naturally I expect you and the children to accompany me."

"Accompany you where? You have not condescended to tell us where we will be excavating this year. Really, Emerson, you have carried your habit of reticence to an extreme no person of character could possibly accept. Do you expect us to trail meekly at your heels through the sandy wastes of all the Memphite cemeteries? I will not stir one step until you tell me where we are going."

Emerson gave me a particularly maddening grin and reached for his pipe. "Guess," he said.

We had spent a fairly peripatetic life the past years, since Emerson had got into a quarrel with M. Maspero, and a falling-out with Mr. Theodore Davis, who had the concession for the Valley of the Kings at Thebes, where we were working at the time. Maspero had offered Emerson any other site in Thebes except the Valley of the Kings; Emerson, cursing royally, had declared he would have the Valley of the Kings or nothing.

Nothing was what he got, and in a typical fit of temper he determined to—as he put it in his extravagant fashion—shake the dust of Thebes from his feet forever. Four hundred miles to the north, across the river from the modern city of Cairo, lie the ruins of the ancient capital of Memphis and the cemeteries that had served it for thousands of years, and it was this region to which Emerson proposed we should transfer our activities.

I was a trifle put out, since we had built a comfortable house in Luxor and I had finally got it arranged just the way I liked. However, there were compensations. I refer, of course, to pyramids. To claim that I have a passion for pyramids is one of Emerson's little jokes, but I would be the first to admit that they are my favorite monuments.

"Which one would you like, Peabody?" Emerson had inquired, when we first discussed the matter. "The Great Pyramid, or one of the others at Giza?"

I had endeavored, more or less successfully, to conceal my exasperation. "Don't offer me any pyramid I would like in that offhand manner. You know perfectly well that the concession for Giza has been divided between the Americans, the Germans, and the Italians. M. Maspero is not likely to remove any of them as a favor to you."

"Hmph," said Emerson. "Very well, Peabody, if you are going to take that attitude—"

"What attitude? All I said was—"

It would serve no useful purpose to report the remainder of that conversation. I was, of course, correct; we had not been allowed to work at Giza, nor did I have any reason to suppose that we would be able to do so this season.

"Guess?" I repeated. "What nonsense! I refuse to engage in these childish, irresponsible—"

"I will, then," Nefret said quickly. "Is it Abusir, Professor?"

Emerson shook his head. "Abu Roash?" Ramses suggested.

"Even better," said Emerson smugly.

I am by nature an optimistic individual. Hope rose from the ashes of resentment. "Dahshur, Emerson?" I cried eagerly. "Don't tell me you have got Dahshur?"

Emerson's superior smile faded, and his eyes fell. Rather than admit he was ashamed and regretful, he began to swear. "Hell and damnation, Peabody! I know how much you want to go back to Dahshur; do you suppose I do not? Those pyramids are far more interesting than the ones at Giza and the cemeteries around them have never been properly investigated. I would give ten years of my life—"

"Don't talk like a fool, Emerson," I said.

Emerson's face darkened. "She means," said Nefret, "that we wouldn't exchange ten years of your company for all the pyramids in Egypt. Isn't that right, Aunt Amelia?"

"Certainly. What did you suppose I meant?"

"Hmph," said Emerson. "Well. Maspero is holding on to Dahshur for himself, curse him."

"Everyone wants Dahshur," Ramses said. "Petrie and Reisner

have also applied for it, without success. So, if not Dahshur, where? Lisht?"

Emerson shook his head. "I suppose I may as well tell you. It is really excellent news. I know you will be as pleased as I. Zawaiet el 'Aryan is the place. Pyramids. Two of them."

"Damnation!" I exclaimed.

"I am shocked to hear you use such language, Peabody. You told me once you were aching to excavate at Zawaiet el 'Aryan."

"Didn't Signor Barsanti investigate those pyramids in 1905?" Ramses asked, as I struggled to regain my composure and Emerson, avoiding my eyes, began to speak very loudly and very quickly.

"Barsanti is an architect and restorer, not an excavator, and the reports he published were shamefully inadequate. The pyramids at Zawaiet el 'Aryan may not look like much—"

"Ha!" I said.

"—but they have a number of interesting features. Remember the sealed, empty sarcophagus, and the—"

I cut Emerson short. "Have you got permission from M. Maspero?" I asked.

Emerson turned a cold blue eye on me. "I am deeply hurt that you should ask, Peabody. Have you ever known me to make a claim that was not true?"

I decided not to mention the examples that came to mind. "I was not questioning your word, only your—er—interpretation of what M. Maspero may have said. He *is* French, you know."

"But Reisner is not," said Emerson triumphantly and undeniably. "A blunt, straightforward chap, like all Americans. He was at Zawaiet el 'Aryan for a time last year, but he's got too much on his plate already, what with his concession in the Sudan and his work at Samaria, not to mention Giza. It was he who persuaded Maspero to let us have Zawaiet el 'Aryan."

"Kind of him," I murmured. Mr. Reisner was a friend and an admirable scholar, but if he had been present I might have lost my temper with him. His plate was indeed filled, with several of the most delectable sites in the Middle East. He was handing us the crumbs.

Well aware of my feelings, Emerson said, "The site is only a few miles south of Giza, you know, so a house there would be convenient."

"I am so glad you agree," I said sweetly. "After we have lunched with Miss Reynolds and her brother, we will have a look at the place she mentioned. I will tell Fatima to press your good tweed suit, and you can wear that pretty sapphire-blue necktie I gave you last Christmas. The one you keep misplacing."

The dimple (or cleft, as he prefers to call it) in Emerson's prominent chin quivered. "I neglected to pack that particular object of apparel, Peabody."

"I thought you might, so I packed it for you."

For a moment Emerson's temper hung in the balance. Then a twinkle replaced the glare. "Very well, Peabody. A compromise, eh? I will not appear in public in that damned tie, but I will go to luncheon and I will have a quick look at the damned house— on the Wednesday. Tomorrow we will visit the site."

"Tomorrow we have an engagement with Miss Reynolds, Emerson."

After a while Nefret said she was going to retire and fled from the room, carrying Horus. Finding he could not get a word in, Ramses soon followed suit, leaving me and Emerson to thrash it out. It ended as I had known it would, with Emerson apologizing for calling me an unreasonable bully of a woman, and demonstrating that in one area at least he was master in his own house. His attentions are particularly irresistible when he is in that irritated frame of mind.

Before we retired Emerson set fire to the sapphire-blue necktie and threw the blazing remains overboard.


At one time it had taken over an hour to reach the pyramids from the center of Cairo. Slow and dusty the trip may have been; but I have fond memories of jogging along in an open victoria, crossing the bridge over a river as yet uncontaminated by Mr. Cook's tourist steamers, and following the road that led past shady palms and green fields to the pyramid plateau. Now motorcars and cycles mingled perilously with donkeys and camels and carriages, and an electric tram carried passengers from the end of the Great Nile Bridge to the Mena House Hotel, near the pyramids. The suburb of Giza—not to be confused with the village of the same name—had become fashionable in recent years and was growing rapidly. As Emerson is frequently heard to remark, not all modern conveniences are improvements on the old ways.

The house the Reynoldses had taken was one of the new villas, with a view of the river and the Zoological Gardens. We were not the only guests; Miss Maude had invited several of what I must call the younger generation of Egyptologists. I felt certain this was meant as a delicate attention to Emerson, whose boredom with ordinary social engagements was well known. From what I had heard, Miss Maude's usual "set" consisted of the sort of people we took pains not to know—frivolous young women and supercilious young officials.

We were acquainted with most of the other guests—Jack Reynolds, of course, and another of Reisner's assistants, Geoffrey Godwin; Rex Engelbach and Ernst Wallenstein, a shy new member of the German Giza expedition, who was so paralyzed at finding himself in the presence of Emerson he never spoke a word the entire time. There was also a young classical scholar named Lawrence, who had done a bit of excavating in Syria and was spending a month with Petrie at Kafr Ammar. The only women present were Nefret and myself, Miss Maude, and a vague little old lady, an aunt or cousin who acted as nominal chaperone to the brother and sister. The Reynoldses treated her rather like a large fragile parcel, taking her out of one place and putting her down in another, where she remained, smiling dimly, until she was moved to another location. I could not imagine that she would prevent Miss Maude from doing exactly as she pleased.

At first the young men were frightfully deferential to Emerson, which depressed him a great deal. It was Mr. Lawrence who broke the ice—or rather, who jumped into the crashing hole Emerson had broken by criticizing Mr. Petrie.

"I consider it an honor to be working with Professor Petrie this season," he said stiffly. "He speaks of *you*, sir, with respectful admiration."

"The devil he does," said Emerson, with the greatest good humor imaginable. "We have been friendly enemies for years, and I know precisely what he thinks of me. He can teach you a thing or two about excavation, if you don't die of ptomaine poisoning first. Why he has not long since expired is a mystery to me; he leaves half-eaten tins of food standing about until they turn green, and expects his people to finish the vile stuff. Peabody, do you remember the time Quibell staggered into our camp at Mazghuna asking for ipecacuanha?"

I stopped him before he could elaborate—descriptions of digestive disorders are not suitable for the luncheon table—but his jovial manner had put the young men at ease, and an animated archaeological discussion ensued, dominated, of course, by Emerson. When he announced where we would be working, Jack Reynolds, on my right, exclaimed in surprise.

"Zawaiet el 'Aryan? I knew Mr. Reisner didn't intend to put in another season there, but I cannot conceive why you should be interested in the place. We found very little of interest. Isn't that right, Geoff?"

There could not have been a greater contrast between two men—Jack, hearty and red-cheeked and sturdily built, Geoffrey as fair as a washed-out watercolor and as shy as Jack was outspoken. A delicate flush of embarrassment touched his pale cheeks at finding himself the focus of Emerson's fixed regard, which has a devastating effect on persons of a sensitive nature. "I must agree," he murmured. "The site is not worthy of your talents, Professor."

"Bah," said Emerson vigorously. "You have not the proper attitude toward archaeology, Mr. Godwin." And he proceeded to tell Geoffrey what his attitude ought to be. Nefret, seated next to the young man, took pity on him and distracted Emerson with a teasing question.

Realizing we had heard almost nothing from Ramses—an unusual circumstance indeed—I found him engulfed by Miss Maude, who had placed him next to her. The manners of young American ladies are very free and easy, but it did not take me long to realize that Nefret's hints about Miss Maude's interest in my son were unfortunately correct. She had turned her back on Mr. Lawrence, who was on her other side, and was chattering nonstop, without giving Ramses a chance to speak. This, as I could have told her, was not the way to win his regard.

After luncheon the ladies retired to the sitting room and the gentlemen went into Jack Reynolds's study. I never permitted this absurd variety of segregation in my own home, but I put up with it on this occasion because I was anxious to become better acquainted with Miss Maude. A closer examination of her person confirmed my earlier impression; she was dressed expensively and uncomfortably in the latest fashion, her dress having been made with a hobble skirt so narrow, she had to shuffle like a Chinese lady with bound feet. She appeared to be anxious to ingratiate herself with me and Nefret, whose neat but simple frock she studied interestedly. Her conversation was boring in the extreme, however; it consisted primarily of gossip about her friends and questions about Ramses. Nefret, as bored as I, let her sense of humor get the better of her. The stories about her brother

with which she regaled Miss Maude became more and more outrageous, and I was finally forced to put a stop to them.

"If we are to look at the house this afternoon, we must be
getting on," I announced. "What are the men doing in there?"

Drinking brandy and smoking was what they were doing. I
was pleased to observe that Ramses's glass was untouched, and
that Emerson had none. My husband was fidgeting, since the conversation had turned from Egyptology to a subject that interests
him very little—firearms. Jack was showing off his gun collection,
which was contained in a locked cabinet against one wall.

"What do you need all of those for?" I asked, contemplating
with pursed lips the row of deadly weapons.

Jack was obviously not accustomed to having females invade
his sacred male domain, much less ask absurd questions. "Why,
for hunting, Mrs. Emerson. And protection, of course. Snakes, you
know."

"My husband uses a teakettle," I said. "Emerson, are you
ready to go?"

Grinning, Emerson came to join me. Cold-eyed and unsmil-
ing, Ramses did the same. He disapproved of hunting for sport.

Everyone insisted on accompanying us to inspect the house
Miss Maude had located. It was a pleasant walk of less than a
mile, along a road shaded by lebbakh trees, with the rippling
waters of the river on the left, but I do not think Miss Maude
enjoyed it very much. Her narrow skirt and ankle-strap shoes
made it necessary for her to cling to someone's arm, but she had
to settle for that of her brother, since Nefret had taken possession
of Ramses. It was pure malice that motivated Nefret, I believe,
for she did not require assistance; her ankle-length skirt and low-
heeled slippers made locomotion for her as easy as for a lad.

We were shown round by the custodian, a mournful-looking
individual in a dusty galabeeyah. The house was ideal, in size
and in location. It was a little north of the village and a trifle
south of the new suburb, set apart in its own ample grounds. It
had been built by a former minister of state whose career had
taken a sudden turn for the worse. A man of foresight, he had
got out of the country with his head still on his shoulders and a
fortune in jewels sewn into his clothes. The villa, as it should be
called, testified to his good taste if not to his prudence. It must
have cost a pretty penny, for the construction was solid and the
design an attractive combination of antique charm and modern
comfort. Three wings of two stories each surrounded a large

courtyard with a tiled fountain in the center. The entrance from the street led to the courtyard through a large and handsomely decorated takhtabosh, a reception hall open on one side to the court. Beautiful mashrabiya screens masked the windows of what had once been the harem, and there were several bath chambers in the European style. Another advantage was that the place was not far from the main road and the electric tramway that led from Cairo to the Pyramids.

After I had looked at each and every chamber I joined the others (who had tired of poking into cupboards and inspecting plumbing) in the courtyard, and announced my decision. "The place suits admirably. We will be settled in before Christmas, on which day I hope you will all join us for a fitting celebration."

Miss Maude's large brown eyes widened. "So soon? My dear Mrs. Emerson, it took me three weeks just to get the spiders removed from our house!"

"I have some experience in these matters," I said. "I will just go round to the office of the agent this evening and settle the business. We will have our people from Atiyah here tomorrow morning; Selim will be in charge, he can find—"

"Selim?" Emerson had been talking with Jack Reynolds. He whirled round. "I cannot spare Selim, Peabody. I want him at the site tomorrow."

"You cannot begin excavating tomorrow, Emerson."

"Why the devil not? That is why I am here," said Emerson, teeth bared and brows lowering. "To excavate. Not to sweep floors or help you select curtains and pots and pans and furniture."

The sight of Emerson in one of his little tempers, his shoulders thrown back, his blue eyes blazing and the cleft in his chin vibrating, never fails to thrill me. I replied, "I don't expect you to do anything of the sort, my dear. You may prowl the site to your heart's content, but you will have to do it without Selim. I need him." Turning to Geoffrey, who, like the others, had followed our exchange with considerable interest, I explained, "Selim is our reis, you see. The members of his family have worked for us for many years. Many of them reside in Atiyah, a village just south of here."

"Oh, yes," Geoffrey said, nodding. "Professor Emerson's trained men are the envy of all other excavators. David Todros, whom I met last year, is one of them, I believe."

"Not exactly," Ramses said. "David is a fully qualified archaeologist. He is now a member of our family as well, having recently married my cousin."

"So that is settled," I announced.

"No, it isn't," Emerson announced. "I'll tell you what, Peabody; we will compromise, eh? Compromise," he explained to the young people, "is essential to domestic as well as international peace. Mrs. Emerson and I are almost always of one mind, but compromise smooths over those little differences that occasionally occur. We will have a look at the site tomorrow and after that you can clean and scrub to your heart's content! How's that, my dear?"

It is impossible to resist Emerson when he thinks he is being clever, and anyhow, domestic discussions are best not conducted in public. "Very well," I said. "We had better be going. I am indebted to you, Miss Reynolds, for your help in this matter, and for a delightful luncheon."

We parted on the most amiable terms, and as we boarded the tram I said, "It will be nice to have such agreeable young persons as neighbors."

"Just so you don't expect me to spend all my time drinking tea and gossiping with Maude," Nefret said. "Goodness, how boring she is! She was quite rude to Mr. Lawrence, I thought. You weren't very polite either, Ramses; don't you like him?"

"I find him frightfully public-school, but I don't know him well enough to like or dislike him. I ran into him when I was in Palestine with Reisner. He had been working at Carchemish."

"He's not an Egyptologist?" Nefret asked.

"No."

"He can't be a suspect, then."

"The least likely suspect, I should say," Ramses replied with a faint smile.

"What are you talking about?" Emerson demanded.

"The forger, of course," said Nefret. "Surely you hadn't forgot about that little matter, Professor. If we are to track him down—"

"We won't do it by suspecting every Egyptologist we happen to run into," Emerson said in exasperation. "Order and method—"

"Don't seem to be getting us anywhere," Nefret declared. "Are we going to the suk this evening, Aunt Amelia?"

"Yes. We must begin shopping for"—I glanced at Emerson—"curtains and pots and pans and furniture."

Emerson's well-cut lips curved in an expression that was only distantly related to a smile. "Don't think you can put me off that way, Peabody, I am too familiar with your underhanded methods. Shopping for pots and pans is not your main purpose. You plan to question the antiquities dealers—to interrogate them, badger them and bully them. Not without me, my dear. You have a bad habit of annoying the wrong people."

"A nose for crime, rather," said Nefret, smiling. "You were planning to let me go with you, weren't you, Aunt Amelia?"

"Certainly. I need your advice about the curtains."

We enjoyed a hearty chuckle over this little joke. At least Nefret and I did.

When we reached the dahabeeyah I told Fatima about the new house and left her happily collecting buckets and scrub cloths, brooms and cleaning materials. Then we went to the office of the agent and signed the papers. It did not take long. Egyptians do not waste time haggling with Emerson.

There are now modern establishments in Cairo that sell a wide variety of European goods, and certain stretches of certain streets are almost indistinguishable in appearance from those in any city; but the Khan el Khalil still retains its air of Oriental mystery, especially after dark. The narrow lanes are roofed with matting and the merchants squatting on the mastaba benches before the small shops resemble figures out of the *Arabian Nights*.

We went first to the sellers of fabric, where rainbow-colored silks and damasks woven with gold and silver threads shimmer in the glow of copper lamps. Since I knew precisely what I wanted (I always do) and what its cost should be, it did not take me long to select stuff for curtains and draperies. Emerson rolled his eyes and muttered, however, so I decided not to try his patience by looking at furniture. We would have to make do with the beds and chests and tables from the dahabeeyah until replacements could be received.

A queer sinking sensation overcame me when we neared the establishment of the dealer we had determined to visit first. Not premonitions of the unknown future but memories of the past prompted the feeling; for here, at the witching hour of midnight, Emerson and I had discovered the body of the former owner hanging from the ceiling of his shop. Hardened as I am to crime, the sight of that gross body and hideous, swollen face had left a very nasty impression. The shop was now owned by the son of Abd el Atti, who was a lesser man than his father had been in every way. Aziz Aslimi had once had a shop on the Muski, in

the European quarter, but he had proved to be such a poor busi-
nessman that he had to give it up and return to the Khan el Khalil.
The memories that haunted me probably did not disturb Aziz in
the least. He was not a sensitive man. Nor, I thought, was he a
criminal, except in the broad sense that applies to almost every
antiquities dealer in Cairo. None of them can afford to be overly
scrupulous about the origins of the merchandise they handle.

The place was small and the doorway narrow; we had to step
aside to allow a customer to emerge—a stooped gray-haired man
wearing a frock coat of old-fashioned cut, and a limp white neck
handkerchief. He squinted nearsightedly at us, touched his hat,
muttered, "Verzeihen Sie mir, guten Abend," and limped away.

"We're treading a bit too close on his heels," whispered Emerson, taking my arm. "Hang on a minute, Peabody."

I could not see that it mattered, since his own mother would
not have recognized Ramses unless she had—as had I—beheld
the transformation, but we waited for a bit before going in. Mr.
Aslimi pretended to be delighted to see us and insisted we drink
coffee with him.

The same prolonged courtesies occurred at the other establishments we visited, so it was late before we returned to the
*Amelia* to find Ramses, in his own persona, waiting for us in the
saloon.

"What luck?" he inquired.

"None," I replied. "I ought not have allowed your father to
accompany me. He has not the patience or the temperament for
such delicate inquiries. One cannot gain information by shouting
at people and threatening them—"

"I never raised my voice," Emerson exclaimed indignantly.
"As for threatening people, it was you who told Aslimi—"

"Now, Professor darling, don't get excited." Nefret perched
on the arm of his chair and put an affectionate hand on his shoulder. "I doubt there was any information to be gained. You were
no more successful, Ramses, were you?"

Ramses shook his head. "I anticipated as much. Remember
that the fellow has been careful to avoid purchasers who knew
David by sight, or who would know he is not an Egyptian."

"Unless he *is* an Egyptian," I said.

"Bah," said Emerson. "Don't start muddying the water, Peabody. We can now be reasonably certain the swine hasn't approached any of the Cairo dealers."

"And that substantiates our earlier deductions," Ramses said.

"The fellow is English or European. Or," he added, glancing at Nefret, "American. Why should he take the risk of peddling his fakes here when he can get better prices, more safely, from European dealers? We know he was in Europe and England this past summer; that's when all the objects were sold, and none of them came on the market before April. That suggests this is a recent operation."

"Not much help," Nefret grumbled. Then she brightened. "Let's make a list of suspects."

"Premature," Ramses said, looking down his nose at her.

"I don't agree," I said. "We have deduced all that is possible from the scanty information at our disposal. Why not speculate—theorize, rather—a bit? It can do no harm and might lead to something."

"You've made one of your outrageous lists, I suppose," Emerson said resignedly.

"I have made a list, yes. As for outrageous—"

"So have I," Nefret said quickly. "Who is first on yours, Aunt Amelia?"

"I believe I could hazard a guess," Ramses murmured.

"Pray do," I said, with a suspicious look at him.

"Howard Carter."

Nefret gasped, Emerson swore, and I said severely, "Have you been snooping in my papers again, Ramses?"

"No, Mother. I know how your mind works. Carter has three things against him. He is an artist and an Egyptologist, and he has no income of his own. He passed three years without a position, scraping a living as best he could, and he is still dependent on the caprices of patrons like the Earl of Carnarvon. The temptation to build up a little nest egg would be understandable."

"You are assuming that the motive behind this is greed," I said.

"A logical assumption, isn't it? There may be strange, perverse motives that elude me—" He looked at Nefret, and his rare smile warmed his austere features. "But the only such motive that comes to mind is resentment of David or of our family in general, and that is surely far-fetched. There are simpler, more direct ways of getting back at us."

"Quite," Emerson grunted. "I refuse to discuss strange perversions. The most obvious motive is the need or desire for money. That might well apply to Carter, but your sweeping de-

scription of him as an artist is balderdash. The fellow we're looking for is a sculptor, not a painter."

"The two categories are not necessarily exclusive," Ramses
said, before I could offer my opinion. "And the forger and the
scholar need not be the same person."

"That might be considered another point against Carter," Emerson admitted. "He's been working in Luxor for years, as Inspector for the Antiquities Department, as a dealer, and as an
excavator. He is probably on first-name terms with every forger
in Gurneh."

"He would not need a forger, since he is an artist himself," I
pointed out. "The same is true of the other individuals on my
list."

"Come, come, Peabody. How many such individuals can
there be?" Emerson demanded.

"You would be surprised, Emerson. What about Signor Barsanti?"

"Ridiculous, Peabody. He's fifty years of age if he's a day,
with no stain on his character. I thought we agreed our suspect
is one of the younger lot."

"An assumption only, Emerson. Altered circumstances may
drive a formerly honest man to crime. Signor Barsanti was originally hired as a conservator and restorer. A man who has learned
how to restore a work of art has learned how to imitate it. Then
there are Mr. Quibell and his wife. Annie was copying reliefs at
Sakkara when we first met her, if you recall; I'll wager she knows
enough about the language to produce the fakes single-handedly.
Mr. and Mrs. de Garis Davies have produced copies of Theban
tomb paintings that are almost the equal of our dear Evelyn's,
and—"

"Why in heaven's name would they—any of them—do such
a thing?" Emerson exploded. He caught my eye. "All right, Peabody, all right. We'll leave motive aside for the moment. Who
else?"

"Karl von Bork. Though ordinarily I would dispute the assumption that husband and wife should be regarded as a single
entity, I fear that Karl and Mary fall into that category. She was
an artist, and a good one, when he, and we, first met her. It should
be added," I added, "that they are solely dependent on Karl's
earnings and that they have several young children. Children are
a considerable expense, what with one thing and another, and a

man who would not stoop to crime on his own account might do so in order to provide for those he loves."

"As von Bork did once before," said Emerson, looking grave. "Curse it, Peabody, I must confess you have made a serious case."

"But he's a friend of ours!" Nefret exclaimed.

"So is Mr. Carter," said Ramses. "Hadn't you realized that if the culprit is an Egyptologist he is bound to be a friend, or at least an acquaintance?"

"No, but see here," Emerson exclaimed. "We cannot dismiss the possibility that there are two people involved, and that the artist at least is Egyptian. The late and unlamented Abd el Hamed was the only one I've known who had that degree of talent, but this person may be unknown to us—a forger of unusual ability, discovered and trained by our hypothetical . . . Oh, good Gad! There is no solid ground here; we are fencing with shadows."

"True," I said. "It is time we went on the offensive! If we threw out a few hints to some of the likely suspects—"

Emerson jumped to his feet with a roar. "I knew it! I knew you'd come to that! I absolutely forbid you to run randomly around Cairo accusing people of criminal activities! One would have supposed that by this time you might have learned not to put your head under the blade of a guillotine in order to get a good look at the executioner. Concentrate on the damned house. There's enough to be done there to keep you out of mischief."

"There certainly is a great deal to be done," I replied pleasantly. "And it will be accomplished more quickly and easily if I can count on your wholehearted cooperation. I refer to all three of you. To leave me with the tedious tasks of cleaning and moving while you are enjoying yourselves with our pyramids would be unfair. You agree, of course."

"Of course," Nefret exclaimed.

"No reasonable individual could deny your premise," said Ramses.

"Bah," said Emerson.

"So that is settled," I said, with more optimism than confidence. "We had better retire now if we are to go to the site tomorrow."

"Would you mind very much if I didn't come with you tomorrow?" Nefret asked. "There is a visit I must make. They will be expecting me."

I glanced at Emerson. I could see by his grave look and compressed lips that he did not like the idea any better than I did, and that he knew as well as I that it would be futile to object.

"You must do as you think best, Nefret," I said.

"She will anyhow," said Ramses. "Do you mind if I come with you, Nefret?"

Her blue eyes flashed. "As a chaperon, Ramses, or a body-guard?"

"As a friend."

"You do know how to get round a girl, don't you?" She smiled and offered him her hand. When he would have taken it, Horus bit his finger.

### From Manuscript H

"How much farther?" Ramses asked.

"We're almost there." Nefret took a firmer grip on his arm and hopped neatly over a steaming pile of camel dung. She did not look at him. Keeping one's eyes fixed on the ground was expedient in the alleys of el Was'a, where one had to walk a sort of hopscotch pattern around piles and puddles of noxious substances.

The narrow twisting lanes were crowded, but not as crowded as they would be later in the day, when the shutters covering the ground-floor windows would be raised and the women would take their places behind the iron grilles, gesturing and calling out to the men who paused to inspect them as if they had been animals in a zoo. The area between the Ezbekieh and the Central Train Station was so notorious it was featured on certain tours, though not those of the respectable Mr. Cook.

Just now they were the only foreigners in sight, and Nefret was approximately as inconspicuous as a tigress in her boots and trousers, her golden head bare. People stared and whispered, but made way for them. The camels and donkeys did not. Ramses pulled Nefret to one side to let a cart rumble past. Mud splashed his boots. He hoped it was mud.

"Couldn't you have selected a more salubrious location?" he asked.

"You know better than that. They wouldn't have come to me. I had to go to them."

The house was one of the tall narrow blank-fronted houses of medieval Cairo. There was no sign or nameplate, and after Nefret had rung the bell they were subjected to an intense scrutiny through a narrow slit in the door before chains rattled and bolts squeaked. These sounds were accompanied by a high-pitched ululating cry which most Europeans would have taken for a distress signal. Ramses knew what it was; he was not surprised when the door flew open and Nefret was surrounded by a group of women, all shrieking with joy and all trying to hug her at once.

One of them, a middle-aged woman wearing a physician's white coat over her long tob, advanced toward Ramses with a firm stride and an outstretched hand. Her abundant black hair was heavily streaked with gray and she spoke Arabic with a strong Syrian accent.

"Marhaba, Emerson Effendi. You honor our house."

"Just call him Brother of Demons," said Nefret, laughing. "Ramses, this is Dr. Sophia."

He had not met her, but he had heard Nefret and his mother speak of her with admiration and respect. She deserved both; Syrian Christians were slightly more liberal in their views than most Middle Easterners, but Sophia Hanem's medical degree from Zurich had been acquired after long years of struggle with her family and her government. Nefret had been fortunate to find her to take charge of the clinic.

Ramses was left to cool his heels in the office while Nefret went with the doctor on her rounds. It was a bright, sunny room, lit by wide windows opening onto an interior courtyard, its scrubbed tile floor and whitewashed walls a striking contrast to the filth of the exterior. A girl who could not have been more than thirteen brought him tea; he could not help wondering whether she was one of the pathetic children the clinic had succeeded in freeing from degradation and virtual slavery. Some of the girls were even younger. It was quite some time before Nefret returned, and she did not linger over her farewells. The doctor was not offended at her brusque manner; she smiled rather sadly at Ramses and shook her head. He nodded, to show he understood.

His mother had warned him. "She is always in a wretched mood after she has visited the place. Don't be put out if she snaps at you. She isn't angry at you, but at—"

"At the miserable sights she has seen and at her inability to put them right. Never mind, Mother, I'm quite accustomed to being snapped at by Nefret."

The door closed behind them. Nefret let him take her hand

and draw her arm through his. He didn't know what to say to her. In her present mood an expression of his admiration and sympathy might be taken amiss. He had just about decided to risk it, when she stiffened and stared—not at him, but at two men wearing European clothing and matching tarbooshes. Both were smoking cigars. Catching Nefret's eye, the taller of the two came to a sudden stop, spoke briefly to his companion, and strode toward them. The crowd parted like the Red Sea before Moses. An officer, even in mufti, had that effect on the citizens of el Was'a.

"Good heavens, Miss Nefret, what are you doing here?" Percy tossed his cigar away and removed his fez. "Let me escort you to safety."

"I am perfectly safe," Nefret said. "And I know precisely what I am doing. May I ask, Lieutenant, for what purpose *you* have come here? The brothels in the Wagh-el-Birka are more to English tastes."

No lady was supposed to know that word, much less be familiar with the relative amenities of the Cairene establishments. Percy turned beet-red and glared at Ramses, who was choking with horrified amusement.

"I say! See here, Ramses, this is your fault. Bringing her here—teaching her about—about—"

"I really wouldn't take that approach if I were you," Ramses said earnestly.

It was too late. Nefret was almost as red in the face as Percy. "Ramses hasn't taught me a damned thing about brothels," she shouted. "Do you suppose I would ever speak to him again, or let him touch my hand, if I believed he would go to such places? A man who would take advantage of those poor women is the lowest form of life on earth. What about you, *Lieutenant* Peabody? You haven't yet told me why *you* are here."

Ramses no longer found the situation amusing. She was so angry she was shaking, and Percy had gone a very ugly color, and people were edging closer, staring. A nasty public scene wouldn't serve any useful purpose.

"On duty, are you, old chap?" he suggested helpfully and with only a slight touch of sarcasm.

"Yes." A hint was all Percy needed. Ramses almost admired him for being so quick to recover. "Sometimes the men come here. We do all we can to discourage them, of course."

Ramses nodded encouragingly. "Well done. Shall we leave

him to it, Nefret? Father and Mother will be waiting for us at Shepheard's."

"Yes, of course. I'm sorry, Percy, if I misjudged you." She smiled at him.

That was the trouble with Nefret—one of the troubles with Nefret, Ramses amended. She was as changeable as a spring day in England, blowing a gale one moment, sunny and bright the next. Some people made the mistake of assuming that because her emotions were so volatile they were not sincere and whole-hearted. He knew better. Nefret was perfectly capable of knocking a fellow flat on his back one minute and bandaging his broken head the next.

"You misjudged Ramses too," she went on. "It was my own idea to come here. I thought you knew I had opened a clinic for the prostitutes. They have no other medical services available, and they are in great need of them."

"Oh. Oh, yes. I had heard, but—but I never supposed you would come here yourself!" The storm clouds gathered again on Nefret's brow, and Percy said earnestly, "I cannot begin to express my admiration for your courage and compassion. But my dear Miss Nefret, I find it hard to forgive you for believing I would be capable of such contemptible behavior. You can only make it up to me by allowing me to escort you safely to the hotel."

"I think I can manage," Ramses said meekly. "We don't want to interfere with you in the pursuit of your duty."

Leaving Percy smirking and fondling his mustache, they headed back along the lane. "Stand up straight," Nefret muttered. "Why are you slouching?"

"Am I?"

"You sounded like a perfect fool."

"Did I?"

Nefret laughed and gave his arm a squeeze.

They were within easy walking distance of Shepheard's. One of the ironies visitors often commented upon was the proximity of the "Red Blind" district to the most elegant hotels in the city.

"It is good to have you back," Nefret said shyly.

Shyly? Nefret? Ramses glanced down at her in surprise. "I haven't really been away," he pointed out.

"Not this past summer, but you haven't spent the entire season with us for several years."

He recognized the implicit reproach and tried to think of a

way of responding to it without admitting it. "The truth is I was finding Mother's dear dahabeeyah, as she will call it, rather too confining."

Nefret laughed. "I know what you mean. It wasn't so much the cramped quarters as the feeling that Aunt Amelia knew every move one made and overheard every word one said."

"The new house will be a great improvement. Mother has actually proposed giving us an entire wing to ourselves. I suspect that was Father's idea."

"They really are sweet," Nefret said with fond condescension. "She still blushes like a prim Victorian maiden when he looks at her in a certain way, and he keeps inventing feeble excuses to get us out of the way when he wants to be alone with her. Do they really believe we don't know how they feel about one another?"

"They enjoy the game, perhaps. I wonder if we could persuade Mother to let us have keys to our own rooms."

"I shall insist upon it," Nefret said firmly. "Confess, Ramses; she anticipated I would want to visit the clinic and ordered you to go with me."

"No. Honestly." It had been his father who gave the order. Not that he had needed it.

In fact, there was probably no part of Cairo where Nefret could not walk unscathed and unmolested. A sentimentalist would claim that her efforts on behalf of the lowest and most degraded members of the population had made her an object of veneration. Ramses, who was not a sentimentalist, suspected that the reverse was true. Most Egyptian males despised women in general and prostitutes in particular. They hadn't objected when she decided to open a free clinic for the fallen women of el Was'a, but they certainly had not admired her for it. No; Nefret's immunity was due in part to her nationality and in even larger part to the blunt hints he and David had dropped in certain quarters—and perhaps in largest part to the fact that she was under the protection of the famous and feared Father of Curses.

They passed the Coptic Church—another of the juxtapositions moralists appreciated—and walked toward the Ezbekieh and the Sharia el Kamal. Ramses took out his watch.

"We're late. They'll be waiting."

But they weren't. As the minutes passed, Nefret began to fidget. "Something is wrong," she declared.

"They can't have got into trouble already," Ramses argued,

trying to convince himself as much as her. He knew his mother. "Selim is with them—"

"Aunt Amelia can get into trouble anywhere, anytime." Her eyes narrowed as a new idea struck her. "You don't suppose she lied to us, do you? Maybe they didn't go to Zawaiet el 'Aryan. Maybe they went hunting for the forger!" She pushed her chair back. "We'd better look for them."

"Where? Be sensible, Nefret. It's more than likely that Father came across something interesting and lost track of the time. You know how he is when he's working, and Mother is almost as bad. He won't let her get into mischief."

An Englishman in the East who shows a yellow streak lets the whole side down and endangers every other Englishman. Our innate moral superiority is our only defense against a a mob of howling savages.

**K**nowing that Ramses would be with her lessened my anxiety about Nefret's venture into one of the most noxious regions of the city, though in fact she was probably safer in any part of Cairo than she would have been in London or Paris. There was not a miscreant in Egypt who did not dread the wrath of the Father of Curses, not a villain who did not know Emerson's wife and daughter were sacrosanct. As Emerson had once put it in his poetic fashion, "Should a hair on her head be ruffled or a fold of her garment disarranged, I will tear out your liver."

So that was all right. With my mind at ease about Nefret, I rose before dawn so that we could leave for Zawaiet el 'Aryan as soon as the sun was up. The old thrill of archaeological fever ran through me as I assumed my working attire of boots and trousers and multi-pocketed jacket, and buckled on my belt with its fringe of useful accoutrements—brandy in a small flask, water in another, matches and candles, scissors, twine, to mention only a few. Emerson still complained about the—as he expressed it—superfluity of them and the noise they made banging against one another, but I knew he was only teasing. How often had one or another of those useful devices saved us from a terrible fate!

I tucked my little pistol into one pocket, a nice clean white handkerchief into another, and took up my parasol. I was ready!

Emerson had already gone up to breakfast. Ramses was with him, his coffee cup in one hand and a book in the other.

"What is that?" I asked, for I thought I recognized the volume.

"*Annales des Service*," said Ramses, without looking up.

"Signor Barsanti's report on Zawaiet el 'Aryan?"

"One of them."

"Well?"

"Well what? Oh. There are some points of interest."

"What points?"

"Finish your breakfast, Peabody," said Emerson.

"I haven't begun yet."

"Then begin. I want to get off. You should read the report for yourself."

"I would have done had I been given sufficient warning of your intentions."

Emerson pretended he had not heard. "Where is Nefret?"

Ramses closed the journal and put it aside. "Getting dressed, I suppose. There is no hurry; we needn't leave for a while."

"Then she has not changed her mind about visiting her clinic?"

"No, sir, I believe not. It will be all right, Father."

"Hmph," said Emerson, stroking his chin. "Yes. We will see you at Shepheard's for luncheon, then. Don't be late."

One of our men took us across the river, to where Selim was waiting with the horses we left in his care each summer. The original pair of thoroughbred Arabians had been gifts to David and Ramses from our friend Sheikh Mohammed; over the years they had produced several equally beautiful offspring. Selim had brought Risha and Asfur for us, and was mounted on Nefret's mare Moonlight. I thought our youthful reis appeared a trifle hollow-eyed and said as much to my husband.

"It really was inconsiderate of you, Emerson, to get Selim out so early. He has probably been up till all hours these past nights, celebrating and being welcomed home by his friends—"

"And his wives," said Emerson. "I wonder if he taught them to waltz?"

I deemed it advisable to drop the subject.

The inundation had begun to recede, but sheets of water still covered some of the fields, reflecting the sky in a shimmer of light. Herds of buffalo grazed among the reeds and white herons floated in the pools. In the distance the pale limestone of the desert plateau was crowned by the majestic shapes of the pyramids of Giza.

There were two routes we might have followed. As I believe I have pointed out (and as every informed Reader ought to know anyhow), a strip of fertile soil borders the river on either side. Since cultivable land was precious (and, at some seasons, actually under water), the ancients built their tombs in the desert. We could follow the coastal road south and then turn inland to reach Zawaiet el 'Aryan, or we could climb the slopes of the plateau at Giza and then ride south across the desert. As I pointed out to Emerson, it would not be much out of our way to pay a little visit to *the* pyramids. Emerson replied that this was quite true, so long as we had a little look and not a prolonged stop.

We were, in fact, past the Great Pyramid and proceeding around that of Khafre, when an exclamation from Emerson drew my attention toward an approaching form which hastened to intercept us, waving and calling out as he came.

"Why, Karl," I exclaimed as he came panting up. "How nice to see you. I didn't know you were coming out this year."

Karl von Bork whipped off his pith helmet, mopped his perspiring face, and made each of us a formal, Germanic bow. He was a bit stouter than he had been when we first met him, but his smile was as broad, his mustaches as luxuriant and his speech as effusive.

"Guten Morgen, Frau Professor, Herr Professor! A pleasure and an honor it is to see you again! Aber ja, I am with the so distinguished Professor Junker, assisting him work on the archives of the German Institute in Cairo and in supervising the excavating of the Western Cemetery, which, as you know—"

"Yes, we do know," said Emerson. "Hallo, von Bork. Read your article in the *Zeitschrift*. Bloody nonsense, you know, what you said about the early dynastic royal tombs being at Sakkara."

"Ach, so? Aber, Herr Professor, the Abydos monuments—"

I interrupted Emerson in the middle of an emphatic rebuttal. "Karl, you should not stand bareheaded in the sun; replace your hat at once. How is Mary? And the children? You have three, I believe? Or is it four?"

I ought to have known better than to ask; Karl whipped a thick sheaf of snapshots from his breast pocket. It took quite a while to examine them, since each image was accompanied by a detailed commentary on the beauty, intelligence, and medical history of the individual depicted. I was pleased to hear that Mary had fully recovered from the illness that had affected her a few years earlier. I had always had a fondness for her; she had worked for us as an artist during the Baskerville case and her marriage to Karl was one of the few pleasant results of that unhappy business.

For a time Emerson politely endeavored to conceal his boredom—like most men, he is profoundly disinterested in all children except his own—but eventually he interrupted with a question about the season's work. Karl asked where we were working, expressed surprise that we had not selected a more interesting site, and offered to show us his new mastaba.

"Not today," I said firmly. "No, Emerson, I mean it. We must go on at once if we are to be back in time to meet Nefret and Ramses."

"Ach, ja, entschuldigen Sie, ich habe to ask forgotten. Sind sie gesund, das schöne Mädchen und der kleine Ramses?"

"He is not so kleine now," I said, laughing. "Thank you for asking, Karl, they are quite well. We will make arrangements to meet soon again. Come, Emerson. At once, Emerson!"

The pyramids are visible for miles around, and as we rode southward my wistful gaze followed them until Emerson, who was well aware of my sentiments, bade me rather sharply to stop looking over my shoulder and pay attention to where I was going.

"We are almost there," he cried, pointing.

I wondered what the devil he was pointing *at*.

At that time Zawaiet el 'Aryan was one of the most obscure archaeological sites in Egypt. For obscure, read "boring." The two words are often synonymous in this context, since interesting sites are the ones visited by tourists. No tourists ever came to Zawaiet el 'Aryan.

I could not help but suspect this was one of the reasons why Emerson favored the site. My esteemed spouse is admirably indiscriminate in his antipathies, but, with the possible exception of certain of his fellow archaeologists, there is no group he despises more than tourists. It was fruitless to point out, as I often had, that many of them were moved by a genuine if uninformed interest in the antiquities, and that ignorance should be pitied, not condemned. Emerson's reply was simple and to the point. "They get in my way, curse them."

They would certainly not be in his way at Zawaiet el 'Aryan.

"There it is," he announced in sonorous tones. "The Layer Pyramid."

I believe I may say without fear of contradiction that no woman alive has a greater attachment to her husband than I to mine. Personally and professionally, Emerson is supreme. Just then, as my eyes fell upon the shapeless pile of rubble ahead, I had to bite my lip to keep from shouting at him. In some places a few layers of dressed stone were visible. The rest of the cursed thing was only a low rounded hill, about forty feet at its highest point.

"Is there a substructure?" I inquired hopefully.

"Hmmm? Oh, yes. A shaft, several passages, a presumed burial chamber. Empty. Hmmm. I wonder . . ."

The last word floated back to me. Emerson was riding away.

"Where are you going?" I shouted.

"I want to have a look at the other pyramid. It's off to the northwest."

I am by nature an optimistic individual; I look on the bright side and hope for the best and find a silver lining in the darkest cloud. For some reason my rational good spirits failed me that day, and my mood passed from bitterness to extreme aggravation when I saw what Emerson was pleased to call "the other pyramid." Not even a pile of rubble marked its location. There had never been a superstructure of any kind, only a huge trench leading far down into bedrock. Drifting sand had almost filled it.

Emerson dismounted. Accompanied by Selim, he began prowling round the elongated hollow that marked the trench, and I heard him remark, "We'll want fifty men and the same number of basket carriers at the start. As soon as the survey is finished . . . Peabody! Don't you want to have a look?"

He hastened to me and pulled me from the saddle with such impetuous enthusiasm that my foot caught in the stirrup and I toppled into his arms. "A little stiff, this first day out?" he asked.

Pressed against his broad chest, enclosed in his strong arms, I looked up at him and felt my wrath evaporate like raindrops in the sunlight of his smile, the warmth of his blue eyes. He was so happy with his wretched ruins of pyramids, so unquenchably (if inappropriately) romantic!

"Trim but nicely rounded," he murmured, embracing the region in question and tucking a lock of loosened hair under my hat. "You never change, my dearest Peabody. Your figure is as shapely and those jetty locks are as untouched by silver as when

I first saw you in the Museum of Boulaq. Have you sold your soul to the devil in exchange for eternal youth?"

I saw absolutely no reason to mention the little bottle of hair coloring I kept in a drawer of my dressing table. A husband's illusions should not be shattered, and anyhow I didn't use it often enough to matter.

"I might ask you the same question, my dear Emerson," I replied. "But perhaps this is not the proper time—"

"Anytime is the proper time. Curse it," he added, as the bridge of his nose came into contact with the brim of my pith helmet.

"Selim—"

"The devil with Selim," said Emerson, removing my hat and tossing it aside.

The interlude was brief but refreshing, and it left Emerson in a conciliatory frame of mind. He went so far as to ask my opinion as to which "pyramid" we should tackle, and my own mood was so forbearing I did not comment sarcastically on the word. I cast my vote in favor of the Layer Pyramid. Emerson grinned.

"You want to crawl into the cursed substructure. Really, Peabody, your penchant for dark, hot, dirty tunnels makes me wonder about you."

"Ah," I said, my interest reviving. "There are dark, hot, dirty tunnels in the substructure?"

Emerson chuckled. "Very dark and very dirty. Shall we have another look?"

Selim, who had tactfully disappeared behind a ridge, now returned, and I said, "We should start back, Emerson, we promised we would meet the children at two."

"Plenty of time," said Emerson, as I had expected.

So we headed back toward the other structure (the word "pyramid" stuck in my throat), which was farther south but closer to the cultivation. It is possible to see for quite a distance in that clear dry air (after the morning mist has dispersed, and providing there is no wind to raise clouds of sand). I was unable to resist glancing back toward Giza from time to time; the pure perfection of those triangular silhouettes drew my eye like a magnet. We had not proceeded far when I beheld other shapes advancing in our direction. I called out to Emerson to stop.

"There are three individuals on horseback advancing in our direction, Emerson. I think—yes, it is Miss Maude and her brother and Mr. Godwin. I expect they are looking for us."

"Why?" Emerson inquired.

"We did mention yesterday that we were planning to visit the site. It is a delicate attention."

"You and your delicate attentions," Emerson grumbled. "Idle curiosity would be nearer the mark. Haven't they anything better to do than bother me?"

"Probably not. Mr. Reisner is still in the Sudan, and their season does not begin till January. No doubt they wish to give you the benefit of their experience at the site."

The young people were soon with us. Miss Maude looked very businesslike in a divided skirt and matching coat and a pair of well-cut tasseled boots. I had not supposed she meant to offer the benefit of *her* experience, since she had none; my supposition as to her reason for coming was soon confirmed, for her ingenuous countenance fell when she realized Ramses was not one of the party.

Geoffrey remained modestly silent, allowing Jack Reynolds to do most of the talking. He had spent several weeks excavating in the cemeteries adjoining the pyramid (as he called it) and offered to show us round.

Emerson was graciously pleased to accept and we went on together, with Miss Maude trailing disconsolately in the rear. Listening to Jack's comments, I was increasingly impressed with his competence, though, as he was the first to admit, they had not spent enough time at the site to enable him to answer many of Emerson's pointed questions.

According to Jack, the monument had in fact been completed. It had been a step pyramid like the magnificent tomb of Zoser at Sakkara, with fourteen steps or layers. The original height was impossible to calculate, since the upper layers had disintegrated into a mass of formless rubble. Mr. Reisner had cleared the base along the east side and part of the north; the rest still lay hidden under heaps of debris. On the north side a great breach gaped, exposing stone steps that descended at a steep angle before disappearing into the darkness below. Even in the short space of time that had elapsed since Mr. Reisner cleared it, sand had half-filled the opening.

"The entrance to the substructure?" I inquired, leaning over to peer in.

"Yes, ma'am. Do be careful, Mrs. Emerson, if you lost your balance you would roll quite a long way." Geoffrey took me gently but firmly by the arm.

"Ten meters to the bottom of the stairs," said Emerson. "Then a long gallery which makes a right-angle turn to another stair, with several corridors opening off from it; one leads to an empty burial chamber. The plan indicates a perpendicular shaft going straight up to the surface from the end of the first gallery. Its upper entrance must be . . ." He shaded his eyes with his hand and went trotting off.

We followed Emerson to the west, where a largish dimple, or concavity, suggested a hollow beneath. "Here's where the shaft reaches the surface," Emerson said dogmatically. "What's in it?"

"In it?" Jack repeated, looking puzzled.

"There must be something in it," said Emerson slowly and patiently, "or we would be able to see the bottom. It was not left open by the men who constructed it in the first place; that would have constituted an invitation to tomb robbers. Are you with me so far?"

"Yes, sir, that is obvious," said Jack.

"Ah. I am glad you agree with me. So the builders of the shaft must have filled it with something, eh? Barsanti indicates the existence of masonry in the upper portion. Reisner's report makes no mention of it. What I am endeavoring to discover, in my clumsy fashion," said Emerson, "is whether the original filling is still there—and what it consists of—and how far it extends—and whether the shaft contains anything else, such as offerings or funerary deposits or subsidiary burials."

Jack had, I believe, begun to sense something odd in Emerson's manner, but having very little sense of humor he could not quite put his finger on what it was. A line in Geoffrey's thin cheek deepened into a dimple, but he tactfully repressed his amusement. "So far as I know, Professor, no one has excavated the shaft," he said. "Our team certainly did not."

"Good gracious," Emerson exclaimed. "How I admire your courage! If the material, whatever it may be, that fills that shaft, had fallen down into the passageway, you might have been buried alive."

"We spent most of our time on the subsidiary graves and the exterior of the pyramid," said Jack. Emerson's sarcasm had become too exaggerated to ignore; the young man was biting his mustache and glowering.

"Oh, bah," said Emerson, tiring of the game. "The published reports are shamefully inadequate. Where are Reisner's field notes?"

Jack was visibly taken aback. "I couldn't say, sir. I'm sure he would be delighted to show them to you, but without his permission I couldn't possibly—er—even if I knew how to locate them."

"Never mind," Emerson muttered. "I'll have to do it all over again anyhow."

"Emerson," I said. "It is getting late."

"Yes, yes. Just hang on a minute, Peabody."

And without further ado he began to climb the crumbling slope, scrambling agilely upward above a miniature avalanche of pebbles and broken stone.

"Goodness to gracious, look at him go!" Jack exclaimed, staring. "I wouldn't have believed a fellow his size could move so fast."

"He surpasses his own legend," said Geoffrey Godwin with an odd little smile. "Do you know, Mrs. Emerson, that before I met the Professor I doubted most of the stories I had heard about him?"

"The only apocryphal stories are the ones about his magical powers," I said with a laugh. "Though he performs a superb exorcism when called on to do so. As for the other tales, it is impossible to exaggerate where Emerson is concerned."

"The same is true of the rest of you," Geoffrey said gallantly. "You too have become a legend in Egypt, Mrs. Emerson, and Ramses is fast becoming one."

"I have no idea where you got that impression," I replied. I did, though. Maude must have repeated some of the absurd stories Nefret had told her.

Poised on the summit, one hand shielding his eyes, Emerson scanned the surrounding terrain. His splendid physique was outlined against the sky, and his black hair gleamed like a raven's wing. I wondered what the devil he had done with his hat.

"What's he doing?" Maude asked.

Her brother chuckled indulgently. "There's not room in that little head of yours for archaeology, is there? If you'd paid more attention to my brotherly lectures, you wouldn't have to ask. He's looking for buried tombs. Sometimes shadows define a sunken area or a stretch of wall. He won't see much this time of day, though. Sun's too high."

Evidently Emerson came to the same conclusion, for he started back down. "Be careful!" I shouted, as a stone rolled under his foot and thumped to the ground. Geoffrey said something to Jack in a low voice, and Jack called, "It's easier going on the other side, Professor."

I had been about to point this out myself. The descent was more dangerous than the ascent, since a misstep would send the climber tumbling head over heels, with little hope of stopping himself until the rocky ground did it for him. On the east side much of the stone had been exposed, offering a rough sort of staircase. Emerson followed Jack's suggestion, moving horizontally along the slope for a space before continuing his descent. He was within twenty feet of the bottom, moving with the same grace and agility he had displayed while ascending, when he suddenly stopped, stooped, and lost his footing. Staggering and swaying, he flailed his arms wildly as he strove to regain his balance. At one point his body was almost perpendicular to the side and I felt sure he was gone, but with a mighty effort he gathered his forces and threw himself back against the facing with a thud that roused the direst of forebodings as to the condition of his ribs.

I was, of course, already running toward the spot where I had fully expected him to land with an even louder thud. I began climbing, and I was not surprised to see Selim, who had remained aloof from the group, climbing beside me.

Emerson was flattened against the slanting surface, his back to me, one scraped, bleeding hand clamped over the edge of a stone. He turned his head and looked down.

"Confound it, what are you doing up here? Get out of my way, Selim, and drag her with you."

"Drag who?" I cried. The side of his head must have banged against the rock. Blood matted the hair at his temple and trickled down his cheek.

"Whom," Emerson corrected, with an infuriating but reassuring grin. "To be precise—you, Peabody. A mild crack on the cranium does not necessarily induce amnesia. Damnation," he added, "the whole bloody lot of them is on the way up."

It was a slight exaggeration; Maude had remained below, wringing her hands and bleating like a sheep. Emerson's profane adjurations stopped the young men before they had got very far; they retreated, Selim followed, and Emerson swung himself down beside me, assisting my descent with helpful gestures and suggestions. "That stone is loose, try the next one over . . . what the devil did you think you were doing? . . . almost there . . . if I had fallen I would have swept you down with me. Your heart may be pure, though I have my doubts, but your strength is not the strength of two, much less ten. How dare you take such chances, you adorable idiot?"

The last words were mumbled, since we had reached the ground, where we were surrounded by our anxious companions. Maude cried out and covered her eyes when she saw Emerson's face. It did present a rather horrific spectacle, smeared with blood and dust and perspiration. Geoffrey put a steadying arm round the girl.

"I tried to warn you, sir," he exclaimed. "I almost took a tumble on that stretch myself last year; it is very unstable."

"So I observed," said Emerson. "I got it, though."

And from his pocket he took a large potsherd of pale buff ware. On it, in black paint, was a row of hieroglyphic signs.


We refused Miss Maude's kindly suggestion that we stop at her house for sartorial and medical repairs, since we were already shockingly late. The water in my canteen and my small medical kit sufficed to restore Emerson to relative respectability. The cuts and abrasions were numerous but shallow; wounds on the head and face always bleed quite a lot. We went straight to the tram station at Mena House, where we left the horses with Selim and bade farewell to our youthful acquaintances. Jack Reynolds assured us in parting that they would be delighted to lend us a hand if we wanted assistance at the dig, since they would not be starting work officially for several weeks.

Once arrived in Cairo, we took a cab to the hotel. During the drive I made Emerson put on the cravat I had brought, smoothed his hair with my folding comb, and shook the sand off his coat. He submitted to these attentions with sullen resignation, remarking only, "Aren't you going to wash my face and brush my teeth?"

I shook my head. "I have done the best I could, Emerson, but I am afraid the children are going to get something of a shock. You look dreadful."

The children were not the only ones who reacted to Emerson's appearance with consternation. Every head of every diner turned to stare as my imposing and unkempt husband entered the dining salon. Nefret had been watching the door; she jumped up and hurried to meet us.

"Professor darling, what happened? Come back to the daha-beeyah at once and let me examine you."

"What, now?" Emerson drew her hand through his arm and led her back to the table. "I need food, not fussing, my dear; we have had a busy morning."

"So it would seem," said Ramses, who had risen and was holding a chair for me. "You are not seriously injured, Father?"

"No, no, just a bump on the head. I'll tell you all about it as soon as we have ordered. I'm ravenous. Where is the cursed waiter?"

Emerson is well-known to the staff at Shepheard's. He is, I expect, part of the training given new waiters: how to fold a ser-viette, how to pour wine, how to deal with Professor Emerson. (Ignore his eccentricities of dress and speech, and obey his orders instantly.) The response to his summons *was* virtually instanta-neous, and after I had ordered my modest repast I turned to the children.

"How was your morning, my dears? Nothing out of the or-dinary occurred, I presume?"

"If you are referring to murderous attacks or inexplicable happenings, the answer is no," said Ramses.

Nefret, who had opened her mouth, closed it again. Emerson handed the menus to the waiter, unfolded his serviette, and began describing the interesting features of the Layer Pyramid. Ramses asked a number of questions. Emerson began drawing on the tablecloth.

"Don't do that," I said. "Where is your notebook?"

Emerson reached into his pocket. Instead of the notebook he withdrew the potsherd he had found that morning.

"What is that?" Ramses asked, reaching for it.

"The cause of your father's little misadventure," I replied, as Emerson investigated his other pockets.

I proceeded to give a well-organized account of the events of the morning. Nefret's expressive countenance indicated some amusement as I described our encounter with the Reynoldses and Geoffrey.

"Poor Maude," she murmured. "All that way for nothing."

Ramses, intent upon the potsherd, ostentatiously ignored this comment.

"The young fellows seem very keen," said Emerson oblivi-ously. "We may take advantage of their offer to give us a hand for a few weeks. Both of them know the site."

"They might have warned you about the loosened stones," said Ramses.

"Good Gad, there was no need to warn me; I could see for myself that the cursed structure is falling apart. I was a bit careless, that's all." Emerson finished his soup and beckoned the waiter. "It seemed a strange place to find a potsherd of that size lying out on the surface. Our first artifact, eh? I couldn't make anything of the inscription, though."

"Just random hieroglyphs," said Ramses. "Hieratic, rather—Middle Kingdom type. Perhaps some apprentice scribe was practicing."

"Get the dirty thing off the table and eat your pilaf," I ordered.

"Yes, Mother."

"What are we doing this evening?" Nefret asked.

"Shopping."

Emerson groaned.

"Not you, Emerson. All you do is complain and look at your watch. Nefret and I will attend to the purchase of necessary furnishings. You and Ramses can begin packing books."

"There is no hurry," Emerson began.

"Considering the rate at which you pack books, there is. I intend to be moved in before Christmas. I instructed Selim to meet us at the house tomorrow with a full crew—carpenters, masons, painters, and cleaning persons."

Emerson's brows drew together. "I told Selim—"

"I countermanded your order."

### From Letter Collection B

*Dearest Lia,*

*It is most inconsiderate of you to be elsewhere when I yearn desperately to talk with you. A honeymoon is no excuse. Something happened this afternoon that has left me feeling wretched and uncomfortable, and I must confide in someone. You will see, as I proceed, why I cannot confide in Aunt Amelia or the Professor or Ramses. Especially Ramses!*

*I told you in my last that Percy had turned up. I wish you could have been there when he greeted us; I suppose he had no idea how absurd he looked in that ostentatious uniform, with his pink sunburned face and his huge mustache. His reception*

*would have discouraged a less confident man. Aunt Amelia
went absolutely rigid and her gray eyes took on a steely glitter;
the Professor let out one of his ripest oaths and would have
elaborated on it if I had not pretended to lose my footing and
stamped heavily on his foot. Ramses? Well, my dear, what
would you expect? He's become even more the stone pharaoh.
I used to be able to break through his shell by teasing him, but
these days he doesn't turn a hair, no matter what I say or do.
If I walked into his room stark-naked he would just blink and
ask if I weren't afraid of catching cold.*

*I seem to be losing the thread of the narrative, as Aunt
Amelia would say. To resume: I didn't suppose we would see
much of Percy, even after we heard that he had returned from
Alexandria; the young officers spend most of their time at the
Turf Club or the socially acceptable hotels or at various private
parties. I underestimated his persistence. He didn't call on us—
I think it has dawned on him that the Professor wouldn't be
pleased to see him—but he invited me to several parties and
dances. I refused, by return messenger, explaining I had no time
for social activities.*

*This wasn't strictly true, since we have seen more than I
would like of Maude Reynolds and her set. She and her brother
are such close neighbors, it's impossible to refuse all their invitations. I don't mind Geoffrey and Jack; they have been very
helpful on the dig and I've become rather fond of them, especially Geoff. He turned up at the house one morning with a
cartload of flowers—roses, poinsettias, lemon and orange trees
and various climbing vines, which he proceeded to plant with
his own hands all round the courtyard. He couldn't have done
anything to please Aunt Amelia more; the two of them were at
it all morning, digging and fertilizing and watering and discussing horticulture.*

*Ramses and I have had the devil of a time trying to satisfy
both the Professor and Aunt Amelia; he wants us on the dig
every day, and she wants us at the house. It's like walking a
tightrope! We will be making the move in a few days—inshal-
lah!*

*I'm losing the thread again. You can guess why. I will gird
up my loins (figuratively speaking! as Aunt Amelia would say)
and get it over.*

*Most men take the hint after one has consistently refused
their invitations. The young officers here in Cairo are often more*

persistent; their gaudy uniforms and swashbuckling ways make quite an impression on girls fresh out from England, and some of them find it difficult to believe any woman can resist them. It couldn't have been a coincidence that Percy turned up, in person, when I was alone on the dahabeeyah. Aunt Amelia had dragged Ramses and the Professor (protesting loudly) to help her at the house, and had ordered me to finish packing—I admit I'd kept putting it off. Now don't tell me I oughtn't have seen him, Lia; when Mahmud brought me his card he was already on the boat and in the saloon. I thought I could get rid of him before the others came back.

A less conceited man might have realized he was not welcome. I was wearing the same clothes I wear on the dig—boots and trousers and shirt. I defy you to define a less seductive costume! I settled myself in a straight chair instead of sitting on the divan, so he wouldn't have an excuse to sit next to me. I told him I was busy and asked flat-out what he wanted. He didn't waste time, I'll say that for him. Before I knew what was happening, he was leaning over me, so close I could see the separate hairs in his mustache.

The trouble with straight chairs is that they fall over very easily. For every action there is, we are told, an equal reaction; I was afraid that if I let fly with hand or foot, I would end up on my back entangled in the chair legs—an ignominious and, under those circumstances, vulnerable position. I looked him in the eye and said, "Sir! How dare you?"

It sounded so silly I could hardly keep a straight face. However, I had used it effectively on certain earlier occasions. Percy backed off, looking foolish. I slipped out of the chair and stood behind it.

"You claim to be an officer and a gentleman," I said. "If you cannot behave like one you had better go."

"Forgive me," he mumbled. "I couldn't help myself. You are so lovely, so desirable—"

"So it was my fault that you behaved like a cad?" (Another of those words that seems to be effective, though I'll be cursed if I know exactly what it means!)

"You don't understand. I want to marry you."

I laughed—not a genteel, ladylike giggle, but a hearty guffaw. It was completely spontaneous, but I suppose I couldn't have done anything more offensive if I had tried. He flushed darkly, and I got myself under control—for the moment.

*"No," I said. "Not under any circumstances. Not if you were the last man on earth. Not if the sole alternative were a slow painful death by torture."*

*"You don't mean it," Percy said.*

*I managed to hold on to my temper. I was quite proud of myself, for really, can you imagine a more infuriating statement? I said quietly, "The others will be back before long. If you are still here when the Professor comes—or Ramses—"*

*"Ah," said Percy, sneering like a stage villain. "Are you really going to let Aunt Amelia marry you off to cousin Ramses? I thought you had more spunk. He's not man enough for you, Nefret."*

*That was when I lost my temper. You remember our discussion of that interesting episode in Percy's book? David wasn't supposed to tell you what Ramses had admitted to him, and you weren't supposed to tell me; but we tell each other everything, don't we? You swore me to secrecy, as David had sworn you. Lia, I broke my word! I couldn't help it. That he should dare sneer at Ramses! I informed Master Percy that he wasn't fit to blacken Ramses's boots, and called him a sneak and a liar and a coward—among other things. I wasn't too coherent, but by the time I ran out of breath the whole story had come out.*

*I didn't fully comprehend what I had done until I saw Percy's face. It had gone all patchy red and white, as sunburned skin does after a bad shock.*

*"I didn't know," he muttered.*

*"Obviously you didn't, or you would not have written such rubbish, knowing we could challenge it."*

*"It's true?" He caught himself. "I mean to say—you would take his word instead of mine?"*

*"Really, Percy, you are too ridiculous!" I didn't feel like laughing, though; I had begun to realize what a mess I'd made of the business. "Ramses didn't tell me anything. He didn't want anyone to know."*

*"Then how did you find out? I mean to say, what makes you think—"*

*"He confirmed it, but only after some of us reasoned it out for ourselves."*

*"Some of us," Percy repeated.*

*"Not Aunt Amelia and the Professor, at least I don't believe*

so. We swore we would keep it to ourselves. Please . . ." The word came hard, but I got it out. "Please don't say anything."

Percy threw his shoulders back and stuck out his chin. "I would obey your slightest wish, Nefret, but this puts me in an impossible position. Ramses deliberately deceived me—for the best of motives, I am sure—but now that I know the truth I must give him the credit he deserves. An officer and a gentleman could not act otherwise."

I cringe when I remember the hackneyed clichés in which I begged him not to act like an officer and a gentleman. Yes, I had to beg. Whether he would actually have humiliated himself I don't know; that sort of thing is not his style; but I didn't dare take the chance. I knew Ramses would be furious if he found out I had given him away. Finally Percy reluctantly agreed—as a favor to me.

After he had gone I was trembling so hard I had to sit down. You know my frightful temper, Lia; I lose it too quickly, and when I've got my wits back, I feel guilty and ashamed. Not of embarrassing Percy—he deserved it, though I admit he behaved surprisingly well. I would have expected him to storm and shout and deny everything. But I can't forgive myself for betraying Ramses. The promise was unspoken, but it should have bound me. You won't say anything, will you? Not even to David.

**From Manuscript H**

It was almost midnight when Ramses left the dahabeeyah, wearing only a pair of cotton drawers. After he had lowered himself into the water he waited for a moment; hearing no challenge from the guard on the opposite side of the boat, next to the dock, he struck out toward the spot several hundred yards downstream where he had left his clothes. The abandoned hut, hardly more than a pile of tumbled mud-brick, was one he and David had used for a similar purpose when they prowled the suks and coffee shops in various disguises. Ramses still regretted having to abandon his persona as Ali the Rat; it had served him well for several years, until one of their more unpleasant adversaries had discovered Ali's true identity.

That night he would be himself. A disguise would negate the

purpose for which he was going through this tedious performance. Since he had known he would have to swim ashore, he
had left a change of clothing at the ruin. It was a confounded
nuisance but he couldn't risk the possibility that the night watchman, who was one of Selim's innumerable cousins, might tell his
father he had gone ashore when he was supposed to be sound
asleep in bed. Achmed would as soon cut his own throat as lie
to the Father of Curses.

Pulling the bundle of clothing from a crevice in the wall, he
rubbed himself dry and dressed, wondering wearily why he had
the misfortune to belong to a family of such boundless energy
and amiable inquisitiveness. It was almost impossible for him to
get away from them without interminable explanations. If he
didn't show up at the dig his father would demand to know
where the devil he had been; if he didn't turn up for meals his
mother would subject him to one of her endless inquisitions; if
he wasn't available whenever she wanted him, Nefret would assume he had gone off on some mysterious, possibly dangerous,
mission without telling her. That would have been a violation of
their First Law, which David had invented and insisted upon; it
was a sensible precaution, considering the situations they often
got into, and Ramses took pains to conform to it because if he
didn't, Nefret wouldn't. She probably would not consider the
note he had left for her a legitimate substitute for verbal notifi-
cation, but there was some consolation in the knowledge that if
he didn't get back in time to retrieve it before she found it, he
would probably be dead.

In the note he had told her where he was going, but not why.
He hated admitting his reasons even to himself; they were un-
founded, disloyal and unfair, but they made an unpleasantly convincing syllogism. David was dedicated to the nationalist cause.
Causes need money. David had indicated that he wouldn't touch
the money Lia's parents had settled on her. Would he have fewer
scruples about dealing in forged antiquities in order to lend financial support to the cause in which he ardently believed? He
wouldn't have been the first man to be corrupted by a noble ideal.

An hour after he had left the boat, Ramses was in the same
coffee shop he had visited twice before, asking the same question
and getting the same answer. Nobody had seen the man he
wanted. Nobody knew where he was.

Ramses paid the waiter and stared gloomily at the small cup
of coffee. Damned if he'd drink the stuff; he'd been swilling coffee

for three nights in a row, and caffeine jangled along his nerves. He rose to his feet, deliberately conspicuous in his European clothing. He hadn't hoped anyone would lead him to his quarry, but Wardani certainly knew by now that he was being asked after, and by whom. It would be Wardani's decision as to whether to make contact.

He chose the darker streets on his way back to the river, waving away the cabdrivers who accosted him hoping for a fare. Once he had left the boulevard he encountered only a few people, their faces muffled against the cool night air. He could have shouted with relief when one of them veered toward him and a hand closed over his arm.

"Do not move or cry out," said a quiet voice. "Do you feel the point of the knife?"

"Yes." It was scarcely more than a pinprick, below his left shoulder blade.

Another shadowy form closed in on his right, and he was blindfolded, quickly and efficiently.

"Children's games." He spoke Arabic, as they had done, and one of them let out a muffled laugh.

"Come, then, Brother of Demons, and we will play the game you have chosen."

He moved with them, letting his other senses compensate for the loss of sight. When they stopped he could have retraced the route without hesitation, and identified the establishment they entered. The smell was unmistakable. The British authorities were trying to stop the import of hashish, but so far all they had accomplished was to make it scarcer and more expensive. Ramses waited until the door had closed behind him and his escorts before he acted.

"So then," he said to his guide, whom he now held against the wall with the fellow's own knife at his throat. "Shall we find a more comfortable place in which to talk?"

As he had suspected, the guide was Wardani himself. He had grown a beard, which blurred the shape of that arrogant chin and strong jaw. Unperturbed and smiling, he glanced at the man who lay groaning on the floor. "More childish games, my friend. That was unnecessary and unkind. You knew you were in no danger with us."

"I dislike being dictated to in such matters."

"You were showing off," Wardani corrected. "Avec quel panache, mon brave! If you will be good enough to return my knife, I will escort you to my humble quarters."

He led the way up a flight of broken steps at the end of the corridor. The other man got painfully to his feet and followed, so close on Ramses's heels that his harsh, uneven breathing was audible even over the groaning of the loose boards. He sounded annoyed, but Ramses did not look back or move more quickly. To show uneasiness would have been a false move in the stupid little game they were playing.

The room Wardani entered was small and shabby, lit only by a smoking oil lamp. Wardani sat down on the divan and motioned Ramses to take a seat beside him.

"Coffee? Mint tea?"

"No, nor hashish, thank you." The smell was fainter here, but still perceptible. Ramses wrinkled his nose. "This isn't the hideout I would have chosen. Raiding hashish dens has become a popular sport for the young bloods in the police force, and that beard does not alter your appearance very effectively."

"An acquaintance of mine lent me the room for this occasion only," Wardani said calmly. "I move frequently."

"Then you haven't taken up the drug trade in order to raise money?"

A spark of anger flared in the dark eyes. "Do you mean to insult me? Drugs are the curse of my people. I am as anxious to stop the trade as are your police, but they go about it the wrong way. Education . . ."

Ramses let him lecture. He had a deep-rooted distaste for men who spoke of "my people" in that proprietary tone, but he didn't question Wardani's sincerity. The fellow was a born demagogue, with a resonant, flexible voice, a fine command of resounding clichés, and a superb sense of theater. Wardani was not his real name; he had adopted it as a gesture of respect for one of the "martyrs" of the cause—a young student who had assassinated the moderate prime minister, Boutros Ghali Pasha, the previous year. Another of those futile, flamboyant gestures that did more harm than good for the cause it claimed to serve, Ramses thought in weary disgust. The youthful assassin had been executed, and the murder had brought on harsher treatment of the nationalists.

The other man had left the room. He came back with a tray holding two small cups of Turkish coffee. The very sight of the black liquid made Ramses's nerves twitch, but it would have been a grave error to refuse Wardani's gesture of hospitality. Finally he interrupted the speech. "I've heard all this before."

"Yes, of course you have. How is the bridegroom?" Wardani crossed his legs and smiled.

"Well and happy."

"As he should be, having plucked such a blossom." His smile broadened. "Now, my friend, don't glower at me, you know I meant no offense. I respect and revere all women. They are the future of Egypt, the mothers of the new race."

"Balderdash," Ramses said rudely. They had been switching languages, from French to German to Arabic, as if Wardani were testing Ramses's knowledge or displaying his own. Ramses continued in English. "I know the rhetoric. I sympathize with your aims but I deplore your methods. Leave David out of it, Wardani."

"Ah, now we come to it. I wondered why you had gone to such pains to seek me out."

"When they catch up with you—and they will, now that Kitchener is in the saddle—you'll be sent to prison or to the oases—and David with you. He can work for the cause in other ways."

"What ways?" Wardani asked softly.

The air was thick with smoke from the lamp and from the cigarettes Wardani had smoked incessantly, lighting one from the stub of another. Ramses shrugged and accepted a cigarette from the tin the other man offered.

"Writing articles and giving speeches," he suggested. "Continuing the work that has earned him respect in a profession few Egyptians have been allowed to enter. His success and the success of others like him will force the British to acknowledge your demands for equality."

"In another hundred years, perhaps," Wardani said. "But perhaps . . ."

For God's sake, get to the point, Ramses thought. He had a fierce headache but he wanted the other man to introduce the subject.

"Madame Todros is, I believe, the daughter of wealthy parents," Wardani murmured.

Finally, there it was. Ramses lit another cigarette and began talking.

By the time he left the place his headache had assumed mountainous proportions, but he had accomplished his purpose. If

Wardani had not abandoned hope of acquiring Lia's money for "the cause," he was less perceptive than Ramses believed him to be. That subject had led more or less directly to the one that really concerned Ramses, and there, too, he hoped he had made his point.

He decided he could forgo the healthful exercise of swimming, so he took a cab directly to the dock. There was no keeping this business a secret any longer. He'd have to confess next day, not only to Nefret, but to his parents.

The night watchman roused instantly at Ramses's soft hail, and shoved a plank across the gap between dock and deck, displaying neither surprise nor curiosity. The men were accustomed to the peculiar habits of the Emerson family.

Ramses plodded along the corridor leading to his room. He was dead-tired, and his automatic defenses had dropped as soon as he was safely on board; when he opened his door and saw the slight form lying on his bed, the shock was so great he almost cried out.

She'd left a lamp burning. Apparently she remembered the incident some years ago when she had come on him without warning and he had half-throttled her before he saw who it was. Recovering himself, he moved silently to the side of the bed and stood looking down at her.

The shutters were closed and the room was warm. She lay on her side, facing the door, one hand under her cheek. The lamplight burnished the damp curls on her temple to copper, and brushed her quiet lashes with gold. As a concession to his mother's notions of propriety she had put on a dressing gown, if that term applied—it looked more like a bridal dress, translucent white silk and lace ruffles and bits of ribbon.

A sharp pain in his chest reminded him he hadn't breathed for a while. He let the air slowly out of his lungs, remembering a particularly asinine statement he had heard from one of the asinine young officers at the Turf Club. "One doesn't behave like a cad with a lady." The permutations had entertained him off and on for days. Was it permissible to behave like a cad with a woman who wasn't a lady? What was the precise definition of "lady," and, for that matter, "caddish" behavior? To behave like a cad with a sleeping lady must be even more reprehensible. However, considering he was in for an extremely unladylike tongue-lashing when she woke up, some small degree of caddishness might be allowable. He bent over her and laid his palm lightly on the curve of her cheek, brushing the coppery curls with gentle fingers.

Her eyes popped open.

"Caught in the act," she said.

"Dead to rights," Ramses admitted.

He removed his hand and watched her pull herself to a sitting position.

"I had to come here to find your message," she said accusingly. "The conventional method would have been to slip it under my door."

No use asking why she had gone to his room. She did that sort of thing all the time, whenever an inspiration or an idea or a worry struck her.

"This wasn't your first expedition, was it?" she demanded.

"No."

"Did you find him?"

"Yes."

"Thank goodness. You look exhausted. Lie down, why don't you?"

She moved over, in a flurry of filmy white, to make room for him.

"No," Ramses said. "Kind of you, but . . . What are you doing, softening me for the slaughter? Get it over, Nefret, so I can lick my wounds and go to bed."

"I'm not going to scold you. I understand why you couldn't take me with you."

"You do?"

"Don't sound so surprised. I have sensible moments, you know. You can save the detailed report until morning; just tell me whether Wardani admitted . . . said it was David who . . ."

Her wide, imploring blue eyes met his as if she expected him to know how the sentence should end. Physical fatigue and other distractions muddled his thinking. It took him a few seconds to comprehend.

"You wondered? Then I wasn't the only one who . . ."

"What fools we sound," Nefret said ruefully. "My poor dear, I knew you'd feel guilty, you always do, and you mustn't. I love David, too, and I had my doubts as well. It didn't really dawn on me until the other evening, when Aunt Amelia was coolly discussing her suspects, and you pointed out that they were all friends, people we would ordinarily trust and admire, and then I realized that David was the most obvious suspect of all, and that although he would never be dishonest on his own account, he might consider his cause more important than his principles, and ... I hated myself, but I couldn't get the idea out of my head."

"Neither could I. I think we can now, though."

"Really? Truly?"

He laughed a little at the childish questions. "I said I think. But Wardani insisted he knew nothing about the forgeries, and if he was lying he did a damned convincing job of it."

"You asked him point-blank?"

"I had to be fairly direct, there was no other way. He seemed to be completely thunderstruck. I only hope I didn't put ideas into his head. However, he was quick to agree when I pointed out that if David were accused of dealing in forgeries it would damage not only David's reputation but that of all Egyptians, and of the movement and its leader. He's frightfully self-conscious about honor and that sort of thing. So I decided I might as well tell him everything. He said, in that grandiloquent style of his, that in this at least we were allies, and that he would see what he could find out. I believed him. Naive of me, no doubt."

"No, you did the right thing. Are you going to tell the Professor and Aunt Amelia?"

"I expect I had better, don't you? Mother may have had doubts as well. She can be awfully cold-blooded at times."

"She's cold-blooded about some things and hopelessly sentimental about others. I think David is one of the others—along with you and me and the Professor."

"Me?" Ramses repeated, in surprise. "Good Lord, over the years she's suspected me of every crime in the calendar. With good and sufficient reason, I admit."

She moved with her habitual decisiveness, swinging her feet onto the floor and rising.

"Get some sleep," she ordered. "And, Ramses ..."

"Yes?"

She put both hands on his shoulders and looked up at him. "I know how much you miss David. You can't confide in me as you do in him—men have their little secrets, just as women do!— but I wish you'd share some of your worries with me."

"I shared this one."

"After I caught you red-handed." But her smile was very sweet and her face was very gentle. "I can always tell when you're bothered about something, you know. Don't be so hard on yourself. Admit you feel better now that you've told me."

"Yes, I do." He smiled at her. "Thank you, my girl."

A rather odd look passed over her face.

"You're tired, too," Ramses said. "We'll break the news at breakfast, then. After Father has had his coffee."

When she had gone, he undressed, swearing when he saw the small hole and spot of blood on the back of his shirt. Perhaps Fatima could mend it before his mother noticed. That was unlikely, though, she noticed everything, and she would have something to say about ruining another shirt.

Tired as he was, he lay awake for a while thinking, not about David's difficulties, but about Nefret. He wanted her as he had never wanted another woman, but he had resisted the temptation to demonstrate his feelings because he didn't want to risk losing what she had given him that night—sympathy and affection and an understanding so complete it was like communicating with part of himself. Anyhow, there was no way of forcing that kind of love, especially with someone like Nefret. It came or it didn't, sudden as a bolt of lightning, unpredictable as English weather.

Eventually he fell asleep.

**Surrounded by a circle of swords, I fought on. Had it not been for the girl . . .**

**M**y decision to find larger quarters had been taken none too soon. Tempers were becoming strained. Various persons were getting on other persons' nerves. Horus always got on everyone else's nerves, and confinement—for Nefret would not allow him to roam the noisome streets of Cairo—got on *his* nerves. Emerson grumbled and procrastinated when I asked him to pack his books and complained bitterly when I got Mahmud to do it; Ramses went about looking like a ghost, with dark circles under his eyes; Nefret brooded. When I asked if she was worried about something, she said she missed Lia and David.

We had all been disappointed to learn they did not mean to join us until after Christmas. David had been offered a wonderful opportunity to assist in restoring the frescoes of the palace of Knossos in Crete. He had always been interested in the Minoan influences on Egyptian art, and this invitation from Sir Arthur Evans, one of the most distinguished names in archaeology, was a tribute to David's growing reputation as a skilled copyist. Lia, it was clear, did not care where she was so long as she was with him.

In my opinion, this news was not enough to account for Nefret's uncharacteristic behavior. Hers was not a temperament given to gloomy introspection. With a young unmarried lady one particular explanation for mental perturbation comes to mind, so I set myself to determine whether a particular young man was responsible. Jack Reynolds and Geoffrey Godwin were the most likely suspects, I thought. Both were nice-looking, young, gentlemanly, well-educated, and professionally engaged in Egyptology. A fond parent or, as in my case, an individual in loco parentis, could hardly ask for more.

However, careful observation convinced me that Nefret did ask for more, and that she had not found what she wanted in either man. Her manner with Geoffrey was gentler than her teasing exchanges with the lively young American, but there is a certain look . . . I did not see it—and I am seldom mistaken about such things.

One mystery was solved when Ramses told us about his meeting with the leader of the Young Egypt party.

We were having breakfast on the upper deck, as was our habit, and Emerson was swearing, as was his habit, about the smoke and the stench and the increased river traffic. Ramses was late in joining us. The dark circles under his eyes were particularly prominent that morning, so, though I make it a point to allow the young people a proper degree of privacy, I felt obliged to ask him what he had been up to.

It would be inaccurate and unfair to say that Ramses often lied. He seldom had to; even at a tender age he had been a master of equivocation and his skills had become honed with time. On this occasion he replied that he had intended to inform us of the matter that very morning and would do so at once if I liked. Taking this with the usual shakerful of salt, I invited him to proceed.

Though the narrative raised innumerable questions, we let him talk without interruption—I because I knew the futility of trying to interrupt Ramses, Emerson because he had only had one cup of coffee and was not fully awake, Nefret because (my infallible instincts informed me) she knew already.

"You think he was telling the truth, then?" said Emerson, when Ramses stopped talking. "I am relieved to hear it. I had wondered . . ."

"You, too, Professor?" Nefret exclaimed.

"The suspicion was painful but unavoidable," Emerson said. "I gather we all shared it, and were reluctant to say so."

"Not I," I said, helping Ramses to eggs and bacon. "I won't scold you for wearing yourself out unnecessarily, Ramses; if your mind is now at ease, the effort was worthwhile. But I could have told you not to bother."

"Your intuition, I suppose?" Emerson inquired, taking out his pipe.

"It is based, in my case at least, on long experience and a profound understanding of human nature."

"Bah," said Emerson mildly. "I'll wager you didn't think of the nationalist cause as a possible motive for David's wanting money. I confess I did not. That's the devil of a complication, I must say. Kitchener is determined to crush the radical nationalists, and Wardani is his principal quarry. Is David deeply involved with the movement?"

"Not so deeply that he is under official suspicion," Ramses said. "At least I believe not. I hoped I could persuade Wardani to keep David at a distance. I may or may not have succeeded."

"Can't you talk some sense into David?" Emerson demanded. "You are his closest friend."

"I tried." Ramses had not touched his food. It was always difficult to know what he was thinking—as opposed to what he was saying—but there was an unusual degree of emotion in his voice when he went on. "It was a serious error on my part."

"Why?" Nefret demanded.

"Because I was smug and condescending. I didn't mean to be, but that's how it must have sounded—a kindly lecture, for his own good. It is precisely that attitude that Egyptians like David and Wardani resent in us. And when he talked about Denshawai . . . He's become obsessed with it, and who the devil am I to tell him he ought not care?"

The word is probably meaningless to most of my readers. Though the incident had occurred only a few years before the time of which I write, and had stirred up considerable furor even in the British press, it had soon been forgotten. We have very short memories where injustice to others is concerned, especially when we are the ones responsible for it. The incident had been one of the darkest blots on the British administration and a source of shame to all decent Englishmen.

The mud-brick towers of dovecotes are familiar features in the Egyptian scene, for the peasants raise pigeons for food. When a party of British officers went pigeon hunting at the village of Denshawai, the villagers were understandably enraged; as a distinguished British writer pointed out, it was as if a party of Chinese sportsmen had begun shooting the ducks and geese swimming in the pond of a Devonshire farmer.

A temporary truce was reached, but a year later the sportsmen returned to Denshawai. They were only a few hundred yards from the village when they began firing, and the infuriated villagers attacked them—not with guns, for they had none, but with rocks and wooden staves. In the ensuing struggle four Egyptians were shot, and an officer who had been beaten died while hastening to bring help to the others. Medically speaking, his demise was due to sunstroke and overexertion, but the authorities decided to make an example of the case. Twenty-one villagers were sentenced, four of them to death, some to penal servitude, and the rest to fifty lashes. The sentences of hanging and flogging were carried out at the place where the incident had occurred, and the villagers, including the relatives of the condemned, were made to watch.

Emerson had been one of those who protested the dreadful business, in impassioned letters to the English newspapers and in personal interviews with Lord Cromer. Even now his face flushed darkly with indignation when he remembered.

"Cursed if it doesn't make me want to join Wardani myself," he muttered.

Ramses had regained his customary composure. "Quite. Mother would say two wrongs don't make a right, and the end does not justify the means, and so on; more to the point, retaliation in kind only makes matters worse. The Denshawai affair provoked the assassination of Boutros Ghali, which led in turn to harsher treatment of the nationalists. To all intents and purposes the movement is dead. So may Wardani be if they track him down and he resists arrest."

"Hmmm, yes." Emerson tapped the ashes from his pipe. "Perhaps I might have a word with David."

"It would be better coming from you than from me," Ramses admitted.

"We'll keep him too busy to get into mischief," Nefret said. "I'm sure Lia will cooperate."

By concentrating all my considerable efforts and forcing my assistants to do the same, I got the house ready in record time. Fatima whirled through the rooms like a small black tornado directing the activities of the workers Selim had delivered. They were all friends and relations of his and Fatima's, and they worked diligently and intelligently. Selim did not want to be there; aided and abetted by Emerson, who did not want to be there either, he kept inventing excuses to absent himself. I got a little help from Nefret, none at all from Ramses, a great deal from Daoud and his wife Kadija, and a considerable amount of interference from Maude Reynolds, who turned up every morning offering her assistance. As soon as she found out Ramses was not there (he usually was not), she disappeared and I saw her no more.

One wing of the villa was soon ready for occupancy. The tiled floors gleamed, the walls shone with whitewash, the insect and rodent populations had been persuaded to find other lodgings, and Fatima was busily hemming curtains. We moved our possessions on the Thursday, and on the Friday, which was the day of rest for our Moslem friends, I decided I was entitled to a little holiday of my own. The others had been at Zawaiet el 'Aryan almost every day, for at least part of the day (whenever they could get away from me, to be precise); almost every evening I had to listen to Emerson's enthusiastic description of his activities.

I went to Emerson's new study to tell him I would join him that day, anticipating the pleasure the news would give him. I had left him shelving books. The books were still in the boxes, the shelves were empty, and Emerson was nowhere to be seen.

After searching the house and discovering that the rest of them had got away from me too, I went to the stable. Part of the building was already occupied by what Ramses called Nefret's menagerie. She collected abandoned and injured animals the way some young girls collect jewelry. In less than a week, she had acquired a large, homely yellow dog, an orphaned gazelle, and a hawk with a broken wing. The latter would be returned to the wild as soon as the wing healed, unless it became so attached to her it refused to leave. A good many of the creatures did. The dog—one of the least attractive specimens of the canine species I had ever encountered—had to be shut in the shed when she left the house to keep it from following her. What we were going to do with the gazelle I could not imagine.

The previous day Selim had brought the horses from Atiyah. The Arabians were gone from the stable, as I had expected. Only one of the hired animals, a skittish bay mare, remained in her stall. She rolled a critical eye in my direction when I instructed Mohammed to saddle her.

Mohammed also looked dubious. "The Father of Curses told me not to—"

"Never mind what he told you. They have gone to Zawaiet el 'Aryan, I suppose? Well, I am going there too. Please do as I say."

"But, Sitt Hakim, the Father of Curses said I should not let you go alone."

"Nonsense. You don't suppose I would lose my way, do you? I, who know every inch of the terrain from Abu Roash to Giza, from Sakkara to Abusir?"

I tend to exaggerate just a bit when I speak Arabic—it is a habit I got from Emerson—but the general sense of my claim was accurate.

Mohammed shook his head mournfully. He knew he was in for a lecture from Emerson if he did not accompany me, and a scolding from me if he insisted on doing so. The lecture was not imminent; the scolding was. His decision was not surprising.

"At least you will take your parasol, Sitt."

He gave the word the English pronunciation, and very odd it sounded. My parasol had come to be regarded as a weapon of extreme magical potency. In addition to its psychological effect, it is the most useful all-round implement imaginable, serving as walking stick, sunshade and—since my parasols are made with stout steel shafts and rather pointed tips—weapon. I assured Mohammed I would go fully armed.

Then I heard a low growl and saw in the shadows two green-glowing orbs. No wonder the poor horse was nervous. Horus must have been there the whole time, staring her out of countenance and imitating a lion.

"I will have something to say to *you* later," I informed the cat, and led my steed out of the stable before mounting.

It was a beautiful morning, clear and still—a perfect day for pyramids. Annoyance has an unfortunate effect on one's literary style; phrases like "work my fingers to the bone" and "sacrifice my own inclinations to the needs of others" dominated my musings. However, I am not the sort of person who allows resentment to spoil her pleasure. When I found my errant family I would express myself in a few well-chosen words; until then, I would enjoy the passing moment and the moments to come.

If I had been the sort of person who broods on her injuries, I would have found an additional cause of resentment in what had been going on at the site during my enforced (by duty) absence. After our first visit I had gone looking for the reports of Signor Barsanti, which I had last seen in the hands of Ramses. They were not in the bookshelves in the saloon; they were not on the upper deck; they were not on Ramses's desk in his room. I finally ran them to ground under a chair in the saloon and sat down to read them at once before someone else carried them off and misplaced them.

Honesty compels me to confess that the pyramid was a good deal more interesting than I had believed. As Emerson had said, in his quaint fashion, it is the interiors of pyramids that fascinate me, perhaps because they recall childhood fantasies about caves and underground passages, crypts and buried treasure. He can speculate about construction methods and fossiliferous limestone and angles of inclination and headers and stretchers all he likes; for my part, I will take a long, dark, complicated substructure any day. This one appeared to be quite nice, and I did not believe for a moment that Signor Barsanti had explored it properly.

Before I had gone a mile, whom should I chance to meet but Geoffrey Godwin, strolling along with his hands in his pockets.

"Why, Mrs. Emerson," he exclaimed, removing his pith helmet. "What an unexpected pleasure!"

"Is it really?"

A shy smile crossed his face. "A pleasure, certainly; unexpected—well, not entirely. I happened to run into the others a little while ago. They said they were on their way to Zawaiet el 'Aryan and that you would probably follow as soon as you—er—"

"Discovered they had eluded me," I finished. "That was Emerson, I suppose. He was quite correct. I am on my way there now, Mr. Godwin."

"Alone?"

"Yes, why not?"

"No reason at all," he said quickly. "Only your horse appears a trifle nervous."

"I can handle her," I assured him, gathering the reins more firmly into my hands as the wretched beast tried to kick a passing donkey.

"Of course. Look here, Mrs. Emerson, I am staying with Jack and Maude for a few days; he is working on an article, and Maude is in Cairo, so I can borrow one of the horses and be with you in a few minutes."

"Kind but unnecessary," I assured him. "I am not a lady tourist."

He stepped back with a smile and a shrug. "You are going by way of the pyramids, I suppose."

"I may just stop for a word with Karl von Bork. He is there today, I believe?"

"Yes, ma'am. Herr Junker's season begins earlier than ours. If you are certain—"

My leave-taking was perhaps somewhat abrupt; he seemed willing to go on talking interminably, and I was in a hurry.

Karl was indeed at work on one of the mastabas in the Great Western Cemetery, one section of which had been assigned to the Germans—though, to be strictly accurate, I should say "the Austrians." Herr Steindorff, the original excavator, had been replaced by Herr Junker of the University of Vienna. He was not present that day; it was Karl who popped up out of the ground with a beaming smile and an offer to show me the tomb. Tempted though I was (for it looked to be a most interesting tomb), I declined, explaining that I was on my way to our site and that I had only stopped by to proffer an invitation to supper that night. Karl accepted, of course. Then he offered to accompany me, urging his case with such vigor that I was forced to leave him as abruptly as I had left Geoffrey.

Really, these men, I thought. One would suppose I was incapable of taking care of myself.

My spirits rose as I went on, following the dimly defined path that led across the plateau. Sun and solitude, blowing sand and silence! The empty blue sky above, the light-bleached barren ground below! Remembering the concern of my two young friends, I laughed aloud. This was my spiritual home, this the life I loved. There was not the slightest possibility of losing my way.

The mare had settled down and I had no difficulty controlling her until someone began shooting at us.

The first shot made her start and shiver; the second, which struck the ground just ahead of us, made her rear. I did not fall off. I dismounted. I admit I did it rather hastily. It is the better part of wisdom to take cover when someone is shooting at you.

Lying flat behind a low ridge, I watched the cloud of dust that marked the flight of my faithless steed and considered my next move. What to do, what to do? I had covered more than half the distance, and was, I calculated, less than a mile from my destination—an easy walk for a woman in fit condition, which I always am, but an upright figure would be a tempting target, and I was not keen on crawling all the way. To remain in my present position was probably the safest course. However, there was no way of knowing how long I might have to remain there before someone happened along or my unseen adversary abandoned the hunt. A few hours under the burning rays of the solar orb, and I would be baked like a sun-dried brick. Once he got to digging, Emerson was likely to go on until darkness fell, and he might return to the house by way of the road along the river, instead of following the desert path.

There seemed to be no point in hanging about. I was fully armed. My parasol and my knife were of no use unless I could come to grips with the fellow, but I had my little pistol. Raising my head, I took stock of my position.

Behind me the silhouettes of the Giza pyramids showed against the sky. The river, I knew, was below and on my left, though owing to my lack of elevation I could not see it. There was nothing else to be seen but the typical landscape of the plateau—pebble-strewn sand and piles of barren rock. Behind one such heap of stone my opponent must be concealed. The sun was high. It was later than I had thought. Time to be up and doing!

I extracted my pistol from my pocket and removed my pith helmet. Placing the latter article on the tip of my useful parasol, I raised it slowly. The result was most gratifying. Another shot rang out. Rising instantly to a sitting position, I fired in the direction from which (in my opinion) the bullet had come. I was about to fling myself flat again, in anticipation of an answering shot, when I beheld a horse and rider galloping toward me from the direction of Giza. What audacity the fellow displayed! He made a perfect target, or would have done had he not been moving so rapidly. For this reason I missed him with the first shot, and fortunately, before I could fire a second time, he had got close enough for me to recognize who it was. Catching sight of me, he reined up, leaped from the saddle, and flung himself upon me, bearing me to the ground. He was stronger than his slight frame had led me to expect; limbs and body weighed heavily on mine.

"Really, Mr. Godwin," I remarked breathlessly. "I am taken aback by your impetuosity."

"I beg your pardon, ma'am." He blushed and shifted his weight into a position that was slightly less intimate but just as effective in preventing me from moving. "Was I mistaken? I assumed those shots were aimed at you."

"I believe they were, yes. I appreciate your courageous attempt to shield my body with your own, Mr. Godwin, but there are several dozen sharp stones pressing into my back. The fellow has gone, I expect."

A rapid fusillade of explosions interrupted me. They were distorted and muted and it was obvious to me that they came from a considerable distance, but Mr. Godwin's chivalrous impulses overcame his common sense. With an exclamation of alarm he mashed me flat again.

"Curse it!" I gasped. "The villain is in rapid retreat, I tell you; I hear hoofbeats . . . Oh, dear. Oh, dear! Do get up, Mr. Godwin, before something really dreadful happens."

Alas, the warning came too late. The hoofbeats were approaching, not retreating; they stopped; and over Mr. Godwin's shoulder appeared a face set in a hideous grimace, teeth bared, cheeks dark with choler, eyes blazing. Mr. Godwin rose precipitately from the horizontal to the perpendicular.

"No, Emerson!" I shrieked. "No, don't strike him! You are laboring under a serious misapprehension."

"Indeed?" Holding the unfortunate young man by the collar, Emerson checked the blow he had been about to deliver. He did not, however, unclench his fist.

"Mr. Godwin was protecting, not attacking me." I scrambled to my feet. Other riders were approaching. Emerson, on Risha, had outstripped the rest.

"Ah," said Emerson. "My apologies, Godwin."

"Put him down, Emerson," I suggested.

Emerson did so. The young man tugged at his collar and smiled bravely. "Quite all right, sir. I don't blame you for having the wrong impression. Someone was shooting at Mrs. Emerson, and I—"

"Yes, yes. We heard the shots too, and came to investigate. I thought they might have been aimed at my wife. People frequently shoot at her."

The others had come up to us—Nefret on Moonlight, and Ramses riding David's mare Asfur. Nefret slid from the saddle and hurried to me. The sight of her reminded Mr. Godwin of his manners. With a murmured apology, he removed his pith helmet.

"Don't fuss, Nefret, I am unscathed," I assured her, as she ran anxious hands over my frame. "But Mr. Godwin appears to have suffered some injury. Is that blood on your brow?"

"Is it?" He put his hand to his head. "Oh. Yes, I remember

now; I wasn't wearing my hat at the time, I came away in something of a hurry. I suppose you didn't observe the fellow, Mrs. Emerson—a shifty-looking native with a black beard? He was on horseback; I noticed him when you stopped to chat, for I thought it somewhat odd that he would wait all that time and then follow when you went on. I didn't like his looks or the way he watched you . . ."

Emerson reached for him as he staggered, but it was Nefret's arms into which he sank. His weight bore her slowly but inexorably to the ground, where she took his head onto her lap.

Ramses had not dismounted. Lounging in the saddle, he looked down on the tableau with a slight curl of his lip. "Very prettily done," he remarked.

"Go to the devil, Ramses," said Nefret.

Geoffrey's faint lasted only a few seconds. Blushing, he quickly removed himself from Nefret's arms and assured her he was quite unharmed. Such appeared to be the case; the abrasion that had scored his scalp was only skin-deep. However, I insisted he return with us to the house so I could clean it properly. My horse had apparently vanished into the Ewigkeit where, so far as I was concerned, the confounded beast could remain; so Emerson took me up with him on Risha and we let the young people draw ahead.

"What have you been up to now?" my husband inquired.

"I don't know what you mean, Emerson."

"Yes, you do. What did you say, and to whom, that might have provoked this performance?"

"Nothing, I assure you."

"No veiled hints? No random threats?"

"No, Emerson, truly. At least I don't think so."

"Instigating an attack is one way of identifying an enemy, I suppose," Emerson mused. "It is not one of which I approve, Peabody."

"Honestly, Emerson, I do not understand it. Our investigations have been singularly—embarrassingly, one might say—unsuccessful. The only encouraging aspect of this attack—"

"I felt certain you would find one."

"Well, but it must mean that the forger is here—in Egypt, in Cairo, perhaps in Giza! The disguise he assumed this morning was the same he used in Europe."

"Including the shifty look and the sinister appearance?"

"Don't be sarcastic, Emerson. Geoffrey may have exaggerated

a trifle after the event—he is a sensitive, imaginative young fellow. It was the man's behavior that aroused Geoffrey's suspicions."

"Hmph," said Emerson. "I wonder."

### From Manuscript H

The old fakir ambled aimlessly along the narrow lanes of the suk. Nefret gave him only a passing glance; he was obviously a member of one of the orders of dervishes, a little taller and a great deal dirtier than most. Daoud, who had been proud to be asked to escort her that evening, drew her out of the path of a vendor balancing a huge tray of bread and indicated the open doorway of one of the shops. Racks of slippers of all types and sizes were on display outside; Nefret did not pause to inspect them but entered the small room, in whose doorway the merchant stood bowing and smiling.

When she came out of the shop sometime later, the old fakir was surrounded by a group of young hooligans who were jeering and laughing at him. With a shocked exclamation Daoud started toward them. The fakir was not in need of his assistance, however; he began laying about him with his tall staff and cursing fluently. The young villains dispersed and the fakir sat down in the middle of the path, mumbling and dribbling. He wore no turban; long straggling strands of graying hair fell over his face.

"They are bad boys," Daoud said disapprovingly. "He is a very holy man."

"But perhaps a little lacking in his wits?" Nefret suggested delicately.

"His mind is in heaven and only his body remains on earth."

"God be kind to him," Nefret murmured. Something about the weird figure seemed to interest her. She edged closer. "Rather an attractive arrangement of rags. A thing of shreds and patches, or would one call it a coat of many colors?"

"It is called a dilk," said the literal-minded Daoud.

"Hmmm. Oh, I almost forgot—go back, please, and tell Mr. el-Asmar I want another pair of slippers just like the ones I ordered, but in black, and this much shorter." She measured the distance with thumb and finger. "They are for Lia. Her feet are smaller than mine."

Daoud's face broadened in a smile. "Ah! It is a good thought.

We will have a grand fantasia when they come, with gifts and music and much to eat."

"We will." She squeezed his arm affectionately. "I'll wait for you here."

After he had edged his large frame through the doorway, Nefret reached into her bag and took out a few coins. Jingling them in her hand, she went to the fakir, who had subsided into a shapeless lump, his hair over his face.

"If that is the odor of sanctity, I'd prefer damnation," she said in a low voice. "Why are your disguises so repulsive?"

"Filth keeps fastidious persons at a distance" was the barely audible reply. "Obviously you aren't one of them. Ruhi min hina, ya bint Shaitan. (Get away from here, daughter of Satan.)"

He dared not look up, but he heard her soft chuckle and her louder response. "How rude!" She dropped the coins at his feet and moved away.

Peering through the matted tangle of hair, Ramses saw Daoud emerge from the shop. Neither of them looked in his direction, but he waited until they had gone a little way before scrambling to his feet and following.

"**H**mph," I said, when Nefret had finished describing Ramses's costume. "Very picturesque, upon my word. Why were you following Daoud and Nefret? He is large enough and faithful enough to protect her."

Slouching upon the divan, with his feet on the rim of the fountain, my son replied, "He would gladly lay down his life for her, but by the time that regrettable event occurred it might be too late for Nefret. After what happened to you this morning we cannot take too many precautions."

"I don't need to be protected," Nefret said predictably. "I had my knife."

For the first time we were enjoying the amenities of the courtyard of our new abode. Consciousness of a task well done filled me with satisfaction as I contemplated it. Wicker settees and chairs, small tables and hassocks had been arranged around the fountain, where a jet of water tinkled musically. The plants Geoffrey had brought were the finishing touch; selected with the taste of an artist and planted with loving care, they had turned a bare courtyard into a garden. The pots containing orange and lemon trees, hibiscus and roses, were local products; their simple lines and softly burnished surfaces suited the ambience and were reminiscent of their ancient counterparts. Certain styles of pottery have not changed in general appearance for thousands of years.

"My adventure today has one positive aspect," I remarked. "If any of you entertained lingering doubts about David's guilt, they have surely been dispelled."

"You are assuming that the attack on you is related to the other business," Emerson said. The lamp on a nearby table illumined his scowling countenance.

"Surely it would be too much of a coincidence if they were unrelated," said Ramses.

"Not at all. Your mother is always getting into unpleasant situations. She goes looking for them. She attracts them. She revels in them."

"What nonsense!" I exclaimed.

"All the same," said Ramses, while Nefret hid her amusement behind her hand, "there are only two possibilities. Either Mother's recent—er—misadventure is not related to the inquiries we have been making, or it is. The second alternative seems most likely. Mother doesn't have *that* many old enemies lurking about. At least . . . Do you, Mother?"

"Hmmm," I said. "Let me think. No, not really. Alberto passed on a few years ago, quite peacefully, I was told by his cellmate, and it seems most unlikely that Matilda—"

"Don't go down the list, it would take too long," said Emerson. "We will accept the second alternative as a working theory. Do you have more to say, Ramses?"

It was a foolish question. Ramses always has more to say.

"Yes, Father. We may derive from that alternative certain other likely possibilities. First, the man we are after is somewhere in the Cairo area. Second, he has decided we—or Mother—constitute a danger to him. Third, it is a more complex business than we had supposed, with more at stake than a modest profit. We've known a few forgers in our time, and more than a few peddlers of stolen antiquities. How many of them would have committed murder to prevent exposure?"

"Several," said Emerson grumpily. "Especially . . . Close your mouth, Peabody, and don't swear. I told you, I do not suspect Sethos this time. I was thinking of that villain Riccetti."

"He has been in prison since the hippopotamus affair," I

pointed out. "I believe we would have heard had he been released."

"The prize that time was an unrobbed royal tomb, with all its contents," Ramses said. "That sort of thing does inspire exaggerated activity on the part of criminals."

Nefret's eyes sparkled. "You don't suppose . . ."

"We can't count on having that sort of luck twice in a lifetime," said Emerson. He sighed. "This is only a simple, vulgar case of fraud, I fear."

"The word 'vulgar' is not entirely apropos, Father," Ramses said.

"No," Emerson agreed. "The forgeries aren't the usual sort of thing at all. I cannot spare much sympathy for the buyers; it serves them right if they have been swindled. They have no business buying antiquities anyhow. I'd be tempted to let the fellow get away with this if it were not necessary to clear David."

Leaning forward, his hands clasped, Ramses said with unusual heat, "Then it's time we stopped being so tender of David's feelings and reputation. Even if we could afford that luxury, which I don't believe we can, it is bloody damned stupid."

"Don't—" I began.

"Swear," said Ramses between his teeth. "I beg your pardon, Mother. Don't you realize David is bound to hear about this sooner or later? The word will spread, it always does. Collectors communicate with one another, dealers approach valued customers. God knows how many other fakes there are in various antiquities shops; we were only able to locate a small percentage of them. I'm surprised one of our acquaintances hasn't mentioned Abdullah's 'collection' before this. Believe me, David won't thank us for keeping him unaware. It's a damned—excuse me, Mother—insult."

The silence that followed his statement was tantamount to tacit agreement. It was obvious that he was not the only one to arrive at this depressing conclusion. It had certainly occurred to me.

"You write to David, don't you?" I asked.

"Now and then. Not as often as Nefret writes Lia."

"Men are wretched correspondents," said Nefret with a sniff. "I've said nothing to Lia. You aren't suggesting that we break the news to David in a letter, are you, Aunt Amelia? I don't like that idea one bit."

"I wasn't suggesting it. I only wondered whether David had

said anything that might indicate he had got wind of the business."

"I've heard nothing from him to make me believe that," Ramses said. "Nefret?"

"Lia would have told me," Nefret said positively.

"Then what do you suggest we do?" Emerson demanded. "Confound it, Ramses, it's all very well to say we must change our strategy, but unless you can come up with a useful idea—"

"I suggest we stop tiptoeing around the bush, if I may be permitted to mix a metaphor," said Ramses. "We must take Daoud and Selim into our confidence. If we have not settled this business by the time David and Lia arrive, he will have to be told. We might also ask Mr. Vandergelt's advice. He is in closer touch with the world of collectors and legitimate dealers than we, and surely not even Moth—— surely no one could suspect him of dealing in forgeries."

"That is quite all right, Ramses," I said. "An imputation of realistic skepticism is not one I find offensive. It is, in my opinion, a useful idea. Katherine and Cyrus are above suspicion and we can count on their discretion. They are spending the Christmas season with us and will arrive shortly; we will tell Selim and Daoud at the same time, and have a council of war!"

Fatima came trotting in to announce dinner and we all rose from our chairs except for Nefret, who had to detach Horus claw by claw before she could move.

"It is agreed, then," said Emerson. "Just try and keep out of trouble till then, eh, Peabody?"

"I cannot imagine why you are directing your warnings at me, Emerson. We must all take care."

"Hmph," said Emerson. "No more visits to the suk, is that understood?"

"Why the suk?" I demanded. "It was not in the suk that I was attacked. You only want to keep me from shopping. I haven't purchased all my Christmas presents yet, and there is—"

"Enough!" Emerson exclaimed, clutching at his hair. "If you must go I will go with you, and Ramses, in some loathsome ensemble or other, and Daoud and the entire crew. Stop arguing and come to dinner."

"Our guest has not yet arrived, Emerson."

"Guest? What guest? Devil take it, Peabody—"

"Karl," I said, cutting into Emerson's complaint with the skill of long practice. "I asked him this morning. He should be along soon."

"Since we are confiding in all and sundry, do you propose to tell von Bork about the forgeries too?" Emerson inquired.

"I thought I might mention the subject of forgeries in general," I admitted. "Just to observe his reaction."

"Oh, well, that should settle the matter," said Emerson. "The moment you pronounce the word he will drop his fork, turn pale, and confess."

It would not have surprised me greatly if Karl had done just that—supposing he was guilty, I mean. In my estimation he was too timid and too much in awe of me to be a good criminal. Either he was innocent or he had become more hardened than I supposed, because my introduction of the subject failed to induce any of the reactions Emerson had described. Karl was interested, however, and treated us to a long lecture on some of the forgers he had known and some of the methods they employed.

After he had bade us good night we gathered round the fountain for a final cup of coffee, and Emerson remarked sarcastically, "So much for your latest scheme, Peabody. It didn't work, did it?"

"Oh, Emerson, don't be silly. I did not suppose Karl would break down and confess. He does know quite a lot about faking antiquities, though, doesn't he?"

With the arrival of guests imminent and the social activities attendant upon the season unavoidable, Emerson was all the more determined to get as much work out of us as he could. I had only been teasing Emerson a little when I said I had not finished my shopping. Most of it was done, and archaeological fever was rising in my bosom. It was with beating heart and spirits aflame with anticipation that I stood one morning by the newly exposed stairs and prepared to descend into the substructure of my pyramid.

Emerson refused to allow it.

"Confound it, Peabody," was how he began. He went on for a considerable time.

We had quite a large audience. Nefret and Ramses were there, of course, and our men. We were still discussing the matter when we were joined by Maude and Jack Reynolds.

I was not surprised to see Jack, since he had been assiduous in his attentions to us, turning up almost every day and prov-ing—as even Emerson grudgingly admitted—to be of consider-able assistance. I was not surprised to see Maude, either. She was becoming something of a nuisance—to me, at any rate. Whether Ramses felt the same I was not prepared to say. He had not ap-peared to encourage her, but it was always difficult to know what Ramses was thinking, much less doing.

Dimpling, Maude joined him and Nefret, who had removed themselves to a discreet distance while Emerson and I chatted. Selim had done the same. He was humming under his breath and shuffling his feet. I thought I observed a familiar rhythm: one two three, one two three . . .

Jack was not so tactful as Selim. "You folks arguing again?" he inquired with a broad toothy smile.

"We are not arguing," I explained.

"Yes, we are," said Emerson. "I ought to know better. She always gets her way. Very well, Peabody, you can come with me this time. Only control your exuberance, if you please, and don't push me into the shaft or trample me underfoot trying to get ahead."

"You will have your little joke, Emerson," I said.

Jack gaped at me, showing an even greater number of teeth. "But Mrs. Emerson, why do you want to go down there? The place is absolutely empty and it's very dark and dirty and close."

I did not reply to this inane remark but followed Emerson, who had already started down the stairs.

That word most probably gives my Reader an inaccurate im-pression, for the steps were so worn and broken they more re-sembled a ramp than a staircase, and the angle of descent was steep enough to render progress somewhat hazardous. After a time the passage entered the rock and the slope became gentler. It was not such a long passage—a bit over a hundred feet—but the darkness that soon enveloped us made it seem longer. I won-dered what Emerson was going to do about light. The candles we carried were adequate for the limited space of the passage, but whether we could keep them lighted in the bad air of the lower regions was another matter.

Not that there was much to see. The walls were squared off but not smoothed or plastered, the ceiling had a number of cracks running across its surface. This was not a good sign; the rock appeared to be of rather poor quality, and there is always the danger of a collapse. None appeared imminent at the moment, however, or so I told myself.

Finally Emerson stopped and put out his arm. "Slowly," he called, his deep voice booming in hollow echoes. "Very slowly, if you please, my dear."

His warning to me had been quite unnecessary. To proceed precipitately through the passages of a pyramid is something I never do. Even if I had not known there was a deep shaft in this particular pyramid, I would have been on the lookout for some such thing; the builders of these monuments constructed pitfalls and other dangers in the hope of foiling tomb robbers.

Emerson's muscular arm formed a barrier as effective as a steel railing. He had come to a halt several feet from the shaft. Above, a square opening stretched up into darkness. The lower extension of the shaft had been partially bridged over by several stout planks. On the left-hand wall of the shaft I saw another dark opening.

"The passage goes on through there," Emerson said, indicating this side opening. "I've had a quick look round—"

"Well, Emerson, really! You knew how desperately I have anticipated exploring the substructure! You might have waited for me."

Emerson chuckled. It was an eerie sound in those dark depths. "You have no more sense than a child," he said fondly. "Look up, Peabody."

He caught me round the waist and helped me out onto the plank that crossed the shaft.

There was not much to see in the emptiness overhead even when Emerson held his candle up at arm's length. Then I made out a rough ladder leaning against the wall. "Have you been up there?" I demanded.

"Selim held the ladder for me," replied Emerson calmly. "I don't recommend the ascent, however. There is an entrance to another passage approximately ten feet above; it appears never to have been finished. What concerns me—"

He broke off with a grunt of disgust. Looking back up the passage, I beheld the twinkle of several candles. Others had followed us.

I muttered a subdued "Curse it!" for in my opinion exploring a new pyramid should not be regarded as a social event. Emerson emitted a much louder expletive. "Ramses!" he bellowed. "Keep everyone back, I don't want people jostling one another on the edge of a deep drop."

He then handed me his candle and helped me back onto the rock floor of the passage.

"I want to go over there, Emerson," I said, indicating the opening to the left.

"I'm sure you do, Peabody. Just hang on a minute."

"And down there into the shaft."

"You cannot and may not." Emerson rubbed his chin. "As I was saying . . . Confound it, Reynolds, get hold of your sister and keep hold of her. Ramses, why did you let her come down here?"

"It was not his fault," Nefret said.

"Yes, it was. He is in charge when I am not on the spot. If I failed to make that clear to you, Reynolds, I am doing so now."

"It wasn't Ramses's fault," Maude insisted. "Or Jack's. He spoils me terribly. Brothers do, don't they, Nefret? Good gracious, Professor, it isn't the first time I have done this sort of thing, you know. I wouldn't have missed it for the world."

Her attempt at bravado did not quite come off. There had been a decided quaver in the voice that pronounced those brave words. Of all the faces whose relative pallor shone in the shadows, hers was the palest.

Hands on hips, lightly balanced on the edge of the abyss from which he had warned the rest of us, Emerson studied the girl. "Indeed? Come and have a look, then."

Taking her by the arm, he pulled her forward till she stood beside him. One look into that seemingly bottomless chasm put an end to her bravado. She let out a breathless little squeak and clutched at Emerson. His one-handed, seemingly casual grip could have held a much heavier weight than hers; steady as a rock, he passed her back to her brother, who had sprung forward with a cry of alarm as she swayed.

"That is just the sort of thing I mean," said Emerson in tones of mild vexation. "Too many people milling about in a confined space. A stumble or slip, a dizzy spell, and over you'd go, taking, as it well might be, others with you. The bridge isn't fixed, a careless step could easily dislodge it. Escort your sister back to the surface, Mr. Reynolds. She is not fit for this sort of thing."

"Indeed I am!" Now secure in her brother's grasp, Maude had recovered. "It has never happened before. Truly!"

Emerson had held on to his temper longer than I would have expected. He now lost it. His roar of "Damnation!" was sufficient to express his feelings; the Reynoldses beat a hasty retreat, and Ramses—who had, astonishingly, not spoken a word—joined his father on the edge of the shaft.

"Poor girl," I said to Nefret. "One can only admire her courage. She was trying to overcome a fear of deep dark places, one must suppose."

"She was trying to impress a certain person," said Nefret. "Or perhaps she planned to swoon gracefully into his arms."

"How uncharitable, my dear."

"I have spent more time with Miss Maude than you," said Nefret grimly. "More time than I would have liked. I assure you, Aunt Amelia, she has not the least interest in archaeology or in pyramids."

Emerson and I passed the remainder of the morning inside the pyramid. It was quite delightful. A detailed description would be out of place here, but readers of superior intellectual capacity will no doubt wish to refer to Emerson's and my book published by the Oxford University Press. The substructure was fairly extensive and in a delightful state of dilapidation, for the ceiling had given way in several places, so that we had to crawl through narrow spaces that scored our bodies—particularly that of Emerson, whose frame is considerably larger than mine. The horizontal gallery into which the opening in the side of the shaft led continued for some distance and descended another shorter flight of stairs before emerging into a small room which might have been the burial chamber. The candles we carried had only a limited beam. One walked in a small bubble of light enclosed by blackness. The constriction of vision constricts the mind as well; one sees not the whole but a series of small separate segments. The air was hot and stifling. The brain does not function well under those conditions.

According to the plan Signor Barsanti had published, a second passageway led to a long corridor paralleling the north side of the pyramid. He had indicated there were niches cut into the wall of this passage. The very regularity of his plan aroused suspicion; had he really measured each niche so accurately? Were they really so regular in size? What was their function?

To determine the answers to those questions was one of our missions that morning. Selim preceded me, holding the light, and Emerson followed, paying out a steel measuring tape. Notebook in hand, I jotted down the numbers Emerson called out to me. We followed the intersecting corridor to its end and then retraced our steps and followed it to its other end, making notes all the while.

"The niches are surely storage spaces," I said, my enthusiasm not one whit dimmed by the fact that I could hardly draw a deep breath. "Look there. Isn't that—"

Emerson caught hold of my belt and pulled me back. "Come out of it, Peabody, we've been down here over two hours. You are wheezing."

Selim, who had accompanied us, was the first to step onto the plank, and although I could have managed quite well unassisted, he and Emerson insisted on holding my hands as I crossed. Hot and sticky though he was, Emerson paused for a moment to look down into the lower part of the shaft.

"Clumsy arrangement," he remarked disapprovingly, indicating a rope that had been tied round the plank. "That's how we've been removing the rubble, hauling up filled baskets from below. We'll have to rig up something more solid if we are to go on with this."

"It was good of you to oblige me, Emerson," I said. "It is a very nice pyramid after all. I apologize for my disparaging remarks about it."

Nefret was waiting for us when we emerged. "Goodness, how hot and sticky you both are! Come into the shade and have a drink. You were gone such a long time I had begun to be worried."

"Obviously Ramses was not," I said, as he came sauntering toward us, hands in his pockets and hat on the back of his head.

"Did you enjoy yourself, Mother?" he inquired.

"Very much. I am surprised you didn't join us."

"When oxygen is limited, the fewer people who breathe it the better. I assume there is nothing down there for me?"

"No inscriptions, if that is what you mean," his father said hoarsely. "There is plenty to do, however."

"The most exciting thing," I said, wiping mud from my face, "is that the shaft is deeper than Barsanti indicated. He did not finish clearing it! The floor is not cut stone but rubble and sand!"

Emerson gave me a companionable grin, his teeth gleaming in the muddy mask of his face. "I suppose you want me to dig the rest of the cursed stuff out."

"How can you doubt it?" I took the cup of tea Nefret handed me, and went on with mounting enthusiasm. "There may be other passages opening off it farther down, leading to the *real* burial chamber. Even you must find that prospect exciting, Ramses."

"Enormously," said Ramses.

"Don't let archaeological fever get the better of you, Peabody," my husband warned. "It is deuced unlikely there is anything down there except rubble. I don't mind sparing two or three of our fellows to finish clearing it, but there are more important projects."

"Such as the surrounding cemeteries," said Ramses. "I had a look from the top of the pyramid while you were down below. The area to the north looks promising. I believe there is at least one large mastaba Mr. Reisner didn't find."

"Oh?" Emerson jumped up. "Show me."

I caught hold of his sleeve. It was soaking wet, like the rest of his shirt, partly from perspiration and partly from the water he had poured over his hot face. "Emerson, sit down and rest a bit first."

"Later, my dear, later."

Smiling, I watched him stride off, in animated conversation with Ramses. At least Emerson was animated. Ramses seldom was. I did hope he could find something to interest him. Over the past years he had been something of a scholarly vagabond, studying in one city and working in another, never spending more than a few months a year with us. Emerson missed him a great deal. He had never told Ramses so, for fear it might sound like a reproach and a demand. He must go his own way and follow his own path, said Emerson nobly.

Ramses was a skilled excavator—no man trained by Emerson could be anything else—but his primary interest lay in the various forms of the Egyptian language, and it was most unlikely we would find inscriptions here; none of the earliest pyramids had them, and this was clearly a very early pyramid.

"A nice mastaba," I murmured. "Full of potsherds with graffiti all over them."

### From Manuscript H

"I did knock," Nefret said virtuously.

Ramses looked up from his book. "I didn't say 'Come in.' "

"When you *really* don't want me to come in you lock the door." She was looking extremely pleased with herself, eyes spar-

kling, lips parted, cheeks flushed. Her hair had come loose from
its knot and her face was streaked with dust. "I have a surprise
for you. Come and see!"

He put his book aside and rose. "You haven't adopted another animal, have you? Mother has barely become resigned to
that mangy dog. A camel or a family of orphaned mice would be
the last straw."

"Narmer is going to be a perfectly splendid watchdog," Nefret insisted. "As soon as I teach him to stop barking at scorpions
and spiders. Stop trying to be sarcastic, Ramses, and come."

She led him into the opposite wing and flung open a door.

"What's this?" he asked. The room was sparsely furnished in
true Egyptian style. Along one wall ran a wide, low divan covered with printed cotton; the wall above it was filled with shelves
containing books and prints. A few European-style chairs had
been provided for those who preferred them. Oriental rugs in
glowing shades of crimson and burgundy covered the floors.

"Our sitting room. I told you I was going to ask Aunt Amelia
if we couldn't have our own quarters. My room is on one side,
and yours is on the other. There are connecting doors."

He hoped his face didn't betray his feelings. It was bad
enough having her in the same house. Connecting doors . . . I can
always lock myself in and throw the key out the window, he
thought wryly.

This part of the house had been the harem. Exquisitely carved
wooden screens covered the windows, admitting light and air
through pierced holes that formed part of the decoration. Ramses
inserted several fingers into the holes and shook the screen. It
was firmly fixed on both sides. "This won't do," he said.

"Curse it, I hadn't thought of that. You're right; we may want
to get out the window."

"Ibrahim can probably fit the screens with hinges and han-
dles. It would be a pity to remove them altogether; they're quite
handsome." He moved away from the window. "Very nice, my
girl. How did you manage it?"

"I nobly offered to move us over here and give our nice clean
furnished rooms to the Vandergelts. Then I enlisted Kadija and
her daughters to do a whirlwind overnight cleaning. I washed
the floor myself. On hands and knees!"

"It's very clean."

"What an effusive compliment!"

"What more can one say about a floor? Did you also paint the walls?"

"I thought I'd got all the paint off my hands." She inspected them critically.

"Under your nails. It doesn't show very much."

"But you saw it, Sherlock." She gave him an amused smile. "I didn't do it all. Geoff helped me."

"Geoff."

"Yes, he's been sweet. Now come and see your room." She opened the next door. "Doesn't it look nice? I helped paint your walls too. I hope you like the color. I bought new furniture for both of us—your old mattress is as lumpy as a sack of coal, you ought to have asked for a replacement years ago—so all you need do is move your books and clothes and things."

The walls were pale blue. The curtains and the matching coverlet were printed with improbable flowers ranging in color from magenta to pink.

"Cheerful," said Ramses.

Her face fell. "You hate it."

"No, dear, really. The flowers are—er—cheerful."

"Men have such dull tastes," said Nefret. "If you really can't stand the pattern I'll get something else. Plain or stripes. Come on, I'll help you move your things."

"Now?"

"The sooner the better. You haven't unpacked your books anyhow."

She would have carried the heavy boxes herself, or dragged them, if he had let her. When she got behind the bureau and tried to push it, her forehead wrinkled with effort and the tip of her tongue protruding, he began to laugh helplessly. It was that or give her a brotherly hug, and he hadn't dared do that for years. "Leave off, Nefret. I'll take the drawers out and empty them into the elegant new bureau you supplied."

"That would make better sense, wouldn't it?" She pushed the damp curls back from her forehead and grinned at him. "I'm so excited I'm not thinking straight. I insist on helping, though; you'd just turn the drawers upside down and dump the contents."

"Let me carry them." He caught hold of the drawer in time to keep her from dropping it.

"What on earth have you got in there?" she demanded.

"Rocks? Oh. I might have known! Potsherds! Really, Ramses. They're crumbling all over your cravats. What's this?"

The loose tissue-paper wrapping fell away as she lifted the object out of the drawer.

Similar statuettes depicting Egyptian gods and goddesses with human bodies and animal heads were sold in the better souvenir shops on the Muski and in the hotels. This example was approximately a foot high, with a falcon's head atop a male body wearing the typical knee-length kilt and wide jeweled collar. The baked clay had been painted in colors bright enough to make one's eyes water, the kilt in stripes of red and white, the collar in turquoise and orange with touches of gold. The beak of the bird, the tall plumes crowning its head, and the sandals on the human feet were also gilded.

"Good heavens," said Nefret, inspecting it with a mixture of amusement and disgust. "I hope this isn't your Christmas gift for me."

"It's for me. From Maude." Carrying the drawer, he started to leave the room.

"Really?" Nefret drawled. "Stop a minute. It's meant to be Horus, I suppose. The young Horus, defender of his father, opponent of Set, falcon of gold, and so on. Very appropriate."

"Hardly. Father isn't Osiris or about to be, and it's generally he who rescues me, instead of the other way round. I would greatly enjoy coming to grips with our friend Sethos, but father has always taken care of that as well. What an unbridled imagination you have."

The criticism did not deflect her from her purpose. "When did she give it to you?"

"Last night."

"Oh. You saw her last night?"

"She asked me to stop by." He could feel her eyes boring into the back of his neck. Might as well have it out, he thought, and turned to face her.

"Any further questions?" he inquired.

Nefret looked from him to the statue and back again. "There is a certain resemblance."

"Especially the head."

Nefret chuckled. "Your nose is a bit large, but it does not in the least resemble a beak. I meant from the neck down. Especially the chest and shoulders. You really shouldn't go about on the dig without your shirt, it's not fair to the poor girl. She couldn't take her eyes off you the other day."

Ramses clenched his teeth to keep from swearing. It was at times like this that he was tempted to shake his beloved till her teeth rattled. Her blue eyes were bright and merciless and her smile full of mockery.

He hadn't been able to think of a reasonable excuse for refusing Maude's invitation, especially when she gave him that pleading look and explained she had a gift for him. The little statue had left him at something of a loss for words—he couldn't imagine why she should have supposed he would want such a travesty—but he managed to thank her properly. She had then gone on to apologize for her "dizzy spell" in the pyramid that morning, while he drank the coffee she had pressed upon him and tried to think of a graceful exit line. It was not a private tête-à-tête—the aunt-in-residence (he could never remember the poor little old lady's name) sat knitting in the corner the whole time—but after he had said good night, Maude had followed him, out into the starlit garden.

Nefret had told him more than once he didn't know a thing about women. She had been right this time. He had taken Maude for a spoiled little creature who was accustomed to getting what she wanted. She was; but no woman would have said the things she had said to him unless she was past caring about her pride. It had been horribly embarrassing and rather pathetic, and when she started to cry . . .

Nefret had always had an uncanny ability to read his thoughts. "Did she cry?" she asked sweetly. "And then you kissed her? You shouldn't have done that. I'm sure you meant well, but kissing someone out of pity is always a mistake."

"Have you quite finished amusing yourself?" Ramses asked, in the icy voice he knew she particularly disliked.

After a moment her eyes fell and her face reddened. "You do know how to make a person feel like a worm. All right, I apologize. She's in love with you. That isn't funny, for her or for you. Have you—"

"No!"

"How did you know what I was going to say?"

"The answer is no, whatever you were going to say. From what I've heard, she is always fancying herself in love with someone, and my chief attraction is the fact that I'm new on the scene. She's already run through most of the officers and all the Egyptologists of a suitable age. She'll find a new hero next year, if not next month."

Nefret folded the tissue around Horus, defender of his father, and replaced him in the drawer. "Have you got a gift for her?"

"Do I have to? Confound it, I suppose I do. I've no idea what."

"It is a bit tricky," Nefret mused. "You want to be polite but not encouraging. Leave it to me, I'll find something appropriate. I'll get something for Jack too—from the family. That will make it more impersonal."

"See here, Nefret—"

"Don't you trust me?"

"No."

"You can this time. I promise."

Experience has shown that the native official has not reached the stage of intellectual development which would enable him to make the proper decisions or the degree of moral courage to face the consequences of those decisions.

## From Letter Collection B

*It is good of you to write so often, Lia dear, for I suspect there are other things you would rather be doing. I love to read your letters; your happiness shines in every word and every phrase and every repetition of David's name. (You do mention him rather frequently, you know!)*

*But your happiness misleads you, darling, when you claim to detect—how did you put it?—the blossoming of new interests and affections in me. Lovers always want everyone else to be in love! Sometimes I wish I could feel that way about someone—head over heels, insanely, madly, passionately! There have been times in the past when I thought I was beginning to succumb—you remember Sir Edward and Alain K., and one or two others—but it died in the bud, to continue your horticultural metaphor. You say it is unpredictable and uncontrollable, so I suppose there's nothing I can do to avoid or encourage it. I only hope to goodness I don't fall uncontrollably in love with someone like M. Maspero or Mahmud the cook. He has two wives already. (Mahmud, not M. Maspero.)*

*As for my current admirers, as you call them, let me set the record straight. Jack Reynolds has indicated, not too subtly—subtlety is not one of Jack's characteristics—that he would propose if I gave him any encouragement. He reminds me of a very large clumsy dog who wants to make friends with a cat, but who has no idea what the cat wants. Will it scratch or purr when he pats it with a large clumsy paw? At least I know Jack is no fortune hunter. He and his sister are quite well-to-do. Their grandfather manufactured some esoteric but essential component of what Americans term "overalls." I think I've made a few dents in his assumption of male superiority, at any rate. He told me the other day I was a swell little kid (!).*

*He and Geoff Godwin are unlikely friends, as different in character as they are in appearance. No, Geoff is not at all effeminate! You knew him last year, though not well, I believe. Surely you were not misled by his delicate features and slight build and the fact that he's fond of animals and flowers? He has developed a rather nasty cough lately, but he insists there is nothing serious wrong and works all the harder after I've expressed my concern. The other day a wall collapsed on the dig and he was the first one on the spot, throwing stones aside and digging with his hands to free one of the men who was temporarily buried under the debris.*

*Let me hasten to add that the victim wasn't hurt except for bumps and bruises. That sort of thing happens all the time, you know. I only mentioned it to prove you were mistaken about Geoff. I am not at all in love, but I am fond of him and I feel rather sorry for him. Not that he complains. It was Jack who told me that Geoff's family has been exceedingly unkind to him. They're all huntin', fishin' squires and he is a swan in a family of ugly ducks—the only one who cares about reading and poetry and art.*

*Maude is still a nuisance. Ramses is usually able to deal with this sort of thing himself—I'd be afraid to ask how—or rather, when I do ask, he tells me to mind my own business! With some of the others it has been mostly his appearance, I think, and that indefinable aura of . . . what can one call it? Desirability? He's quite nice to look at, if one admires the lean, dark type—and you obviously do, since it is also David's type.*

*With Maude it's gone beyond that. When he's in the room her eyes follow him the way a dog watches his master—and that's how he treats her, kindly and gently and with only the*

*slightest touch of irritation when she gets in his way. I don't
think Ramses is ever going to fall head over heels either. Perhaps
some people just don't have the capacity for it.*

*I ought not have worried you about that business with
Percy. It is like you to take part of the blame on yourself, but
there wouldn't have been any harm in your telling me the true
story if I hadn't blurted it out to the one person in the universe
Ramses didn't want to know of it! I am thoroughly ashamed of
myself, but I don't suppose any real damage has been done, has
it? After all, what can Percy do to injure Ramses?*

I spoke seriously to Emerson about finding Ramses a mastaba.
He replied that it was not a question of finding one, the cursed
things were all over the cursed place. When I would have pursued the subject he informed me that Ramses could excavate mastabas to his heart's content as soon as we had finished a proper
plan of the site. "First things first, Peabody!" The trouble with
most excavators . . .

Royal pyramids are, as a rule, surrounded by the tombs of
private persons who (one must suppose) believed that proximity
to the king's remains would assist their survival in the next world.

The mastaba tombs consisted of two parts: a superstructure
of mud-brick shaped like the mastaba bench that gave them their
names, rectangular in shape with sloping sides; and a substructure sunk deep into the underlying rock, where the actual burial
rested. Some of the larger mastabas around the Giza pyramids
are beautifully decorated and inscribed. Mr. Reisner had of course
kept these for himself. I do not blame him; I simply state the fact.

There were cemeteries of private tombs around our pyramid.
Mr. Reisner had excavated a few of these the previous year, finding that they ranged widely in date, from the crude grave pits of
the earliest dynasty to equally poor burials of a period two thousand years later. He had therefore left them to us. He was, of
course, perfectly within his rights to do so.

Reisner had not published these tombs, so the results of his
(somewhat cursory) excavations had to be extracted (by detailed
and ruthless interrogation) from Jack and Geoffrey.

The two young men put up with Emerson's bullying for two
reasons. Firstly, because no one dares disagree with Emerson.

Physically, professionally and vocally, he dominates any group. Secondly, because I endeavored to make the encounters as pleasant as possible in other ways, interrupting Emerson's lectures with my little jokes and encouraging others to speak.

The last of these encounters took place one evening in our charming courtyard. I had issued invitations as if it were to be an ordinary social occasion, but Jack and Geoffrey must have known what they would be in for. They came anyhow. The presence of Nefret, smiling and silently sympathetic, was no doubt a factor. Ramses was present. He was neither silent nor sympathetic. I had also invited Maude, since I supposed she would come whether I did or not.

The only other guest was Karl von Bork. He had taken to hanging about rather like one of the stray dogs Nefret insisted on feeding. I could hardly turn him away; he was an old friend and I knew he was lonely for Mary and the children. He was always bringing me little gifts from the bazaar in Giza village—a gracefully curved pot or a silver bracelet or a scrap of bright embroidery.

His customary loquacity seemed to have deserted him that evening. To be sure, it would have been difficult for him to get a word in, since Emerson immediately began quizzing Jack and Geoffrey.

Geoffrey was more helpful than Jack, who spent part of the time trying to fend off Emerson's criticisms of Reisner and the rest of it gazing sentimentally at Nefret.

"I did regret we were unable to do more in the area west of the pyramid," Geoffrey said in his quiet, well-bred voice. "The tombs were all early dynastic and some had not been plundered. One, which contained some rather pleasant bits of ivory and carnelian jewelry, was that of a woman. Beside her lay the tiny bones of a newborn child. It is that sort of thing, isn't it, that brings the past to life."

"Hmph," said Emerson, waving away this touch of sentimentality. "So you suggest proceeding with that cemetery on the west?"

"It is entirely up to you, sir, of course."

"No, it is up to Ramses," said Emerson. "Mrs. Emerson has been nagging me about the interior of the pyramid and I will probably have to spend some time on that project since—"

"Really, Emerson," I exclaimed. "How dare you accuse me of nagging? I never nag. I simply pointed out that it behooves us to excavate all the way down to the bottom of the shaft in order to ascertain whether there is an entrance to a lower passageway."

"I hardly think so," said Jack Reynolds with a superior smile. "The shaft can't be much deeper."

"So far," said Emerson mildly, "we have gone down another five meters, without reaching bedrock."

"What? Oh. Well, now. Er—have you found anything?"

"Bits and pieces," said Emerson. "Bits and pieces."

That was all we had found, in fact—bits and pieces of the ubiquitous pottery, fragments of basketry and scraps of wood— but Emerson's portentous tone and mysterious looks suggested something much more interesting. Having aroused the curiosity of our visitors, he proceeded to change the subject.

"I am leaving the cemeteries to Ramses for the moment. I believe he plans to begin in the area to the north. And now it is getting late." Emerson rose and tapped the ashes from his pipe. "Time for everyone to go home."

The two young men sprang to their feet like soldiers who have been given an order. Maude followed suit, pouting. Nefret exchanged glances with Ramses, cleared her throat and squared her shoulders.

"There's no need to leave so soon. We'll just retire—er—go up to our sitting room where we won't disturb you, Professor."

"What? Where? Oh." Emerson exchanged glances with *me*, coughed, and shuffled his feet. "Oh. Yes."

Karl was the only one to decline the invitation. He was some years older than the others, and I think he felt his age that night, for even his mustaches drooped as he bowed over my hand and Nefret's in his formal German fashion. We said good night and I led Emerson away.

"When did that happen?" he inquired.

"The sitting room? Now, Emerson, you know we agreed that Ramses and Nefret are entitled to more independence."

"Yes, but—"

"Nefret asked some time ago if they might not have a place of their own where they can entertain their friends. She furnished it herself and very attractive it is."

"Certainly. But—"

"This is the twentieth century, Emerson. Old-fashioned notions about chaperonage are passing away, and a good thing, too. Surely you trust Nefret to behave like a lady at all times."

"Of course! But—"

"We have no hold on her except that of affection, my dear. Or on Ramses, come to that. It is sometimes necessary to slacken the reins a trifle if one wishes to keep a high-spirited young creature under control."

Emerson's furrowed brow smoothed out. "Peabody, you do talk the most infernal nonsense at times."

"Your decision to give Ramses a nice mastaba of his own is the same sort of thing, Emerson. We want to keep him happy and contented so he won't go wandering off again, to Saint Petersburg or Capetown or Lhasa."

"Why would he want to go . . . Oh. I happen to want the cemetery excavated anyhow, Peabody, but you're right; we do want the lad to be happy with us. I have a feeling, however, that it may take more than a nice mastaba to content him."

The children began work on our north cemetery next day. Daoud and several of our other trained men were with them, and Emerson had taken on thirty unskilled workmen and the like number of basket carriers. According to Jack, their group had excavated a large mastaba in this area the previous February. There was no trace of it now; drifting sand had filled the hollow again. If I hadn't seen the same thing so often before, I would not have believed how quickly the feeble efforts of man can be expunged by the hand of nature. I was a little surprised that Mr. Reisner had not continued excavating in this area, since his mastaba had produced fragments of handsome hard-stone vessels inscribed with the name of a hitherto unknown king. However, this was paltry stuff compared to the elegantly decorated tombs he was finding at Giza. One would not expect him to give something of *that* sort to another excavator.

I went first to the little shelter I had caused to be set up nearby. I always make it a point to arrange a rug and a few chairs and a table and other modest comforts in a shady place so that we can retire to it for refreshment and occasional rest periods. Unnecessary discomfort is inefficient as well as foolish. Usually I was able to find an empty tomb or cave, but here the terrain was so flat I had to content myself with an awning of canvas. Removing my coat and discarding my parasol, I rolled my sleeves to the elbow and loosened my collar. It is always warm inside pyramids.

Going in search of Emerson I found him with Ramses and Nefret, their heads bent over one of the plans. "Here, then," Emerson was saying, as he jabbed at the paper with the stem of his pipe. "Make sure you—"

"Emerson!" I said rather loudly.

Emerson jumped, dropped his pipe and said a bad word. "What do you want?" he demanded.

"You. You said I could go inside today. If you do not care to accompany me I will take Selim, but I thought it only fair to inform you that I am about—"

"Oh, damnation," said Emerson. "I am coming. I only wanted to—"

I turned on my heel and marched off. Selim, who had been watching with a grin, fell in step with me. We had not gone two yards before Emerson caught us up. He was wiping the dust off his pipe with his shirttail.

"Peabody," he began, in a voice like thunder.

"Leave Ramses alone, Emerson."

"I only wanted to—"

"Is he competent to do the job?"

"Curse it, I trained him myself!"

"Then let him do it."

We stamped along side by side in silence. Then Emerson said, "Have I mentioned recently that you are the light of my life and the joy of my existence?"

"And have I mentioned that you are the most remarkable man of my acquaintance?"

Emerson chuckled. "We will elaborate on those statements at a later time, my dear. At the present time I can best demonstrate my affection by taking you into your pyramid."

However, when we reached the shaft we met an unexpected and ominous check.

Our men had been pulling the filled baskets up by hand, an increasingly onerous task as the shaft deepened, until Selim had employed his engineering talents in constructing a more efficient apparatus. A framework of stout beams supported a series of pulleys and a roller onto which the rope could be wound by means of a handle. Attached to the end of the rope was a sort of box, open on top, which served as a container for filled baskets or for people. A foot lever pushed something or other that would stop the rope unwinding too suddenly. Selim would have explained it all to me—indeed, I had a hard time *stopping* him from explaining it all to me. I had assured him I had complete confidence in him and that I would take his word for it that the device was entirely safe.

It was no longer there. With an emphatic swearword Emerson knelt on the edge of the chasm and looked down. Then he looked up. He pronounced another even more emphatic swearword. "Damnation! Clear out, everyone. Get back."

"What has happened?" I demanded. I thought I knew, though, and Emerson's reply confirmed my suspicion.

"Rockfall," said Emerson, towing me along the inclined passage. "How the devil it could have happened I don't know; when I examined the upper part of the shaft the other day, the fill looked to be fairly stable. No one is going down there again until I have made certain there is no danger."

A shudder ran through me when I remembered that day. Emerson's head had been within a foot of the lowest level of stones. If one had fallen then . . .

We made our way back to the surface and retired to my shady shelter, where I dampened a cloth and removed the worst of the dust from my face and hands. Emerson's ablutions were quicker and more comprehensive: removing his shirt, he poured a jar of water over his head and shoulders and shook himself vigorously.

"That's better," he remarked. "Now then, Peabody, I will leave you to write up those notes while they are fresh in your mind."

"Where are you off to? Don't go out in the sun without your hat. And your shirt."

"It is too warm," said Emerson, retreating in haste.

My admonitions were purely formal. I knew he would pay no attention. Keeping a hat on Emerson's head is a task beyond even my powers, and I have never been able to break him of his habit of removing articles of clothing while he works. An ordinary man would have suffered from sunstroke, heat prostration and sunburn, but Emerson is not an ordinary man. After a week in Egypt he is tanned to an even, handsome shade of brown and he never seems in the least inconvenienced by the heat.

As for where he was going, I knew the answer, so after I had finished tidying myself I went after him.

Ramses was not wearing a hat or a shirt either. He and Emerson stood at the edge of a trench looking down. The cutting was approximately two feet wide and four feet deep, and Nefret was at the bottom of it. I could not see what else was there, since her crouching body hid the bottom of the trench. I took some comfort in the fact that she was wearing her pith helmet.

"What a nice neat deep trench," I said. "Er—should Nefret be down in it?"

"She thought she saw a skull," Ramses said. "You know how she is about bones. However, your point is well taken, Mother. Nefret, there isn't room to work down there. Come up and we'll widen the trench."

Nefret straightened. She held a brush in one hand, and I now made out a distinctive rounded shape half-buried in the earth at her feet. The trench was deeper than I had thought; the top of her head was an inch or so below the upper surface. She raised her hands. "Right you are."

Ramses leaned over and took hold of her arms just above the elbows, braced his feet, and swung her up onto solid ground.

Emerson squatted and squinted at the side of the trench. "Cut stone," he muttered. "How long—"

"A little over three meters. I will of course make precise measurements once we have cleared the entire enclosure. So far we have located three of the four corners and I decided to do a trial trench on this side in order to—"

"You need not explain," said Emerson, rising. "Just make sure you . . . Er, hmmm, yes, Peabody. Time for luncheon, eh?"

By the end of the day it was evident that Ramses had come across something rather interesting. The tomb was of considerable size, indicating that it had belonged to a person of some importance. The use of cut stone for the outer walls was another indication of the owner's status. However, the roofing stones had been supported by internal walls of mud-brick, and by wooden beams, which had collapsed, precipitating the ceiling onto the floor in a jumble of blocks. Mixed in with the fallen stones and drifted sand were a number of hard-stone vessels, some of which had been smashed. In short, the interior of the mastaba was a mess, and Ramses had set about clearing it in the approved style, dividing the area into sections and excavating each from top to bottom before proceeding to the next.

I allowed Emerson one look—since I was rather curious myself—before we started for home.

"I see you have braced that wall," he remarked with exaggerated unconcern.

"Yes, sir. You always tell me not to take the slightest risk."

Especially not where Nefret was concerned, I thought. The

wall was beside the scattered bones, which had now been exposed, along with a few rough pots and broken beads. The lower portions of bones and artifacts were still sunk in the matrix of hardened mud and Nefret was trying to get a final photograph of the unsavory ensemble. Selim, atop the wall, held a reflector of polished tin with which he directed the slanting rays of sunlight into the trench.

Emerson glanced uneasily at the bracing beams. They looked to be effective—one plank diagonally across the questionable section, a smaller but sturdy bit of wood propping it, the pointed end of the latter pushed deep into the ground.

"That will do, Nefret," he said. "Er—you agree, Ramses?"

"Yes, sir," said Ramses, quite without expression.

I had asked Karl to have supper with us that evening. Emerson made the usual objections; he always objected to company as a matter of principle, though in fact he quite enjoys professional discussions and does not allow the presence of guests to discommode him in the slightest. He was kindness itself to Karl, pressing him to take a whiskey and soda and remarking in his blunt fashion, "You appear rather seedy, von Bork. Something on your conscience, perhaps?"

"Really, Emerson!" I said.

Karl's mustaches twitched. He might have been trying to smile. "I know the Professor well, Frau Emerson. He is right, in fact; my conscience troubles me that I must leave my Mary und die lieben Kinder so much alone. A letter from her today tells me that meine kleine Maria has been ill—"

"Nothing more than a childish cold, I expect," I said cheerfully.

"So Mary said in the letter. She would not wish me to worry." Karl sighed. "How I wish I could have them here with me, where there is no snow or cold rains. But the University does not provide quarters for us and my room in the village would not be suitable. Those who work for Herr Reisner are fortunate to have such a comfortable house."

Mr. Reisner's permanent expedition quarters, named Harvard Camp, after one of the institutions that supported his work, was a model of its kind, but I doubted very much that "Herr Reisner" would have welcomed a subordinate's wife and four small children.

The courtyard had become our favorite place and we retired there after supper for coffee. Before long an explosion of barks burst out. "Visitors," said Nefret in a pleased voice. "You see how useful Narmer has become."

"He has given over barking at scorpions and spiders," Ramses admitted. "But he still howls at other dogs, cats, birds—"

"Who is it?" Emerson demanded. "Peabody, did you invite someone? Curse it, we have work to do."

"It is probably Geoff," Nefret said coolly. "He offered to help me develop photographs this evening. Nothing to do with you, Professor darling."

"Hmph," said Emerson.

It was Geoffrey, and Jack, and Maude. She was dressed "to the teeth," as Nefret vulgarly put it, in a very low-cut frock with a skirt so tight she could scarcely walk, and a hair fillet from the center of which a white egret plume rose straight up into the air like a signal flag. Their habit of popping in was becoming something of a nuisance; I really did not blame Emerson for glowering and growling. Maude explained that they had no intention of disturbing us (as if they had not already done so), but had stopped by only to deliver Geoff and ask if Ramses would care to go into Cairo with them, to an evening party and dance at the Semiramis Hotel.

Ramses actually hesitated for a few moments before shaking his head. "Another time, perhaps. As you see, I am not properly dressed and I would not like to detain you."

He had of course changed clothing after we returned from the dig, but since his father refuses to dress for dinner I cannot insist on Ramses's doing so. His collarless shirt and unpressed flannels were certainly not appropriate for a stylish hotel.

"You have work to do," said Emerson firmly.

"All work and no play make Ramses a dull boy," Jack said with a jolly chuckle.

"Would that it would," I murmured—a seemingly enigmatic statement that produced a puzzled look from Jack and a faint smile from the individual referred to.

The Reynoldses finally left, without Ramses. Nefret and Geoffrey went off to the darkroom—with Ramses—and Emerson and Karl settled down with their pipes to discuss Fourth Dynasty mastabas. Why Emerson should have selected this subject I did not know; our mastaba was obviously much earlier and far less interesting than the fine tombs the Germans and Americans had found at Giza. I left them to it, for I was strangely restless that evening. As I paced up and down along the arched colonnades that lined the courtyard I heard Emerson invite Karl to come round next day and have a look at our mastaba, for all the world as if he had found something worth looking at. Karl accepted, of course. Poor lonely chap, he would have accepted an invitation to a hanging if he could be with us.

As I passed the door of the darkroom I stumbled over something that turned out to be Horus. He had been lying or crouching on the threshold, sulking, one presumed, because he had not been allowed in.

When I went down to breakfast next morning Nefret told me Geoffrey had asked if *he* might come by to see our mastaba.

"That makes two," I said. "Emerson has also invited Karl. Will Mr. and Miss Reynolds also be dropping by? I will tell Fatima to pack extra food and perhaps a bottle of wine."

Emerson looked up from his plate. "Dear me, Peabody, I believe you are being sarcastic. What's wrong with you this morning?"

"I did not sleep well."

"Oh?" Emerson reached for the marmalade.

"I lay awake for hours. I am so glad you were not disturbed."

Emerson pushed the marmalade jar away, mumbled something and left the room rather precipitately. It was probably the wisest thing he could have done, but it left me without an object for my (admittedly unreasonable) annoyance. I looked at Ramses. He jumped up, mumbled something and left the room so precipitately that he stumbled over Horus. They swore at one another, and Horus came, limping, to Nefret for sympathy.

"He isn't injured," I said. "I think he deliberately puts himself in people's way so he can complain."

Nefret supported her chin on her hands and looked gravely at me. "I am sorry you did not sleep well. Did you have one of your famous premonitions?"

"No," I admitted. "Nor a bad dream, like the ones you used to have."

I had dreamed of Abdullah, as I did from time to time. The setting of those visions was always the same. We were standing at sunrise atop the cliffs at Deir el Bahri, on our way to the Valley of the Kings. Over the years Abdullah and I had got in the habit of stopping there after we had climbed the steep path, to catch our breaths and enjoy the view, which he loved, I think, as much as I. Re-Harakhte, the falcon of the morning, lifted over the eastern cliffs and spread the light of his wings across river and fields and sandy waste, and over the features of the man who stood at my side.

When we first met, Abdullah's beard had been grizzled. In the dreams hair and beard were black without a trace of gray; his face was unlined, his tall frame erect and vigorous. Dreams carry their own internal logic; I was never surprised to see him looking as I had never seen him in life, I was only glad to be with him once more.

"The wedding was very lovely," I said, as one reports the news to a friend one has not seen for a time. "We were sorry you could not be there."

"How do you know I was not?" Abdullah's black eyes twinkled as they did when he was teasing me. Then he grew sober. "It is well for them, Sitt; but there are stormy waters ahead."

"What do you know of stormy waters, Abdullah, who never sailed the ocean?"

"Does not your faith teach you that those who have passed the Portal know all? I know of storms, at any rate, and I have seen the sky darken over your path."

"I wish you wouldn't be so cursed literary, Abdullah. If you mean to warn me of danger, you might be more specific." He smiled and shook his head, and I went on, "At least you can tell me whether we will pass safely through the peril that threatens us."

"Have you ever met a storm you could not weather, Sitt? But you will need all your courage to face this one."

Then I woke with his words of farewell echoing through the darkness. "Maas salama—Allah yibarek f'iki."

I had no intention of repeating that conversation to Nefret. She would have thought me hopelessly fanciful and superstitious. It had disturbed me enough to trouble my slumber for the remainder of the night, and it had reminded me of the duty I owed my dear old friend.

"I would be in a happier frame of mind if we were making some progress with our investigation of the forgeries," I admitted. "We don't seem to be getting anywhere."

"Perhaps something will result from our council of war. When do the Vandergelts arrive?"

"Tomorrow."

"Unless the cursed boat runs aground," said a voice from the next room. "Why can't Vandergelt take the train like a sensible man instead of clinging to his confounded dahabeeyah?"

"Because he chooses."

"Hmph," said the voice.

I did not really want another boiled egg, but I cracked one and began to peel it. "Has Ramses heard anything from Mr. Wardani?"

"No." Meeting my skeptical eye, Nefret added firmly, "He would have told me—us."

"He hasn't been creeping out at night, I hope. I don't like that, it is too dangerous."

"I don't like it either. He promised me he would not. Aunt Amelia, are you ready to leave now? You have surely tormented the Professor long enough."

I could hear Emerson stamping and swearing outside. "It doesn't do to allow a man to become too confident of his authority," I explained.

"I see," said Nefret, dimpling.

When we arrived at the site we found Geoffrey already there, talking with Selim and Daoud. "Practicing my Arabic," he explained, shaking hands all round. "Daoud has been telling me about some of your exploits, Professor. You have certainly led an interesting life!"

Emerson looked suspiciously at Daoud, who looked away. "Don't believe a word he says. Daoud, stop telling lies about me and get to work. Where is Karl? Where are the workmen? Confound it, this traveling back and forth wastes too much time. Tents. That is what we need, a few tents. Selim—"

"Emerson, do keep quiet for a minute," I exclaimed.

"Herr von Bork went to have a look at the mastaba," Geoffrey said.

Ramses turned on his heel and went off, almost running. Nefret laughed. "He's afraid someone will touch his precious rubbish without his permission. Are you coming, Geoff?"

He took her arm. It was quite unnecessary, but she permitted it and even, I thought, leaned toward him as they walked along.

"Hmmm," I said. "I wonder . . ."

"So do I," said Emerson. "I thought I had it here. I could have sworn it was in this notebook."

He had dumped the contents of his knapsack out onto the table and was rummaging through the papers in his usual haphazard fashion. I asked what he was after, found it stuck between the pages of his notebook, and was about to deliver a little lecture on order and method when I heard a woman's scream and a rumbling crash. Both came from the north side of the pyramid.

Emerson was ten feet away, running at full speed, before the echoes of the crash died. I followed as fast as I could, my limbs shaking with apprehension. Nefret was not much given to screaming.

When I arrived on the scene, the cause of the disaster was easy to ascertain. The wooden props had slipped or broken or given way, and the wall had collapsed in a tumble of stones and dirt onto a form that lay facedown and unmoving on the floor of the trench. The form, as I immediately realized, was that of Ramses. Geoffrey knelt at his side, digging the dirt away with his hands. Nefret was squirming in the grasp of Daoud, who let out a gusty sigh of relief when he saw Emerson.

"The effendi ordered me not to let her go down there," he explained.

"Quite right," Emerson said. "There is not enough space for more than one person. Hang on to her, Daoud. Clear out of there, Godwin."

He emphasized the order by catching hold of Geoffrey's coat and dragging him bodily out of the trench. Dropping neatly down into the excavation, he began to dig Ramses out with the strength and skill only he could have demonstrated. The greater part of the debris was confined to Ramses's legs and lower back. For once he had been wearing his pith helmet, and I observed that his head was resting on his folded arms, so that it was entirely possible that his nose and mouth were not full of sand. He appeared to be unconscious, however. Emerson ran anxious hands over his arms and legs before turning him carefully onto his back.

Ramses's pith helmet immediately fell off. He had not buckled the strap. There was only a little blood on his face, which was not nearly as pale as that of his father, and I could see that he was breathing nicely, but Emerson lost his head just a bit; he slipped his arms under Ramses's knees and shoulders, and I do not doubt that his well-nigh supernatural strength, intensified by parental anxiety, would have been sufficient to raise the lad bodily out of the excavation, if a duet of cries from Nefret and me had not stopped him.

"Don't move him yet!" was the gist of our remarks.

Ramses's eyes opened. He looked at his father and then turned his head to examine his surroundings. "Damn it, Father!"

he gasped. "You've smashed that pot! It was a perfect specimen of blue and buff Eighteenth Dynasty ware!"

"Impossible," said Emerson. "What would such a thing be doing here?"

"The burial is intrusive. I would tentatively date it to—"

"Stop it!" Nefret's face was crimson. "Ramses, you bloody fool, is anything broken? Professor, don't let him sit up! Aunt Amelia—"

"Calm yourself, my dear," I said, watching Ramses, assisted by his father, rise stiffly but steadily to his feet. "And don't swear. There appears to be no serious damage."

Nor was there. After we had retired to the shelter he submitted with ill grace to Nefret's attentions. The shirt would have been ruined even if she had not insisted on cutting it off him. Nefret was almost as destructive with a pair of scissors as she was with a knife. She finally admitted—grudgingly, I thought—that scrapes, scratches and bruises were the extent of his injuries. Ramses denied this was due to luck or the grace of God; he insisted he had seen the prop give way and had immediately assumed a position that offered the greatest protection to the most vulnerable areas of the body. He sounded so smug I could hardly blame Nefret for accidentally spilling half a bottle of alcohol down his front.

Ramses was determined to go back to his mastaba and I could think of no way of preventing him. He condescended to accept a sip of brandy from the flask I always carry and stalked off, bare to the waist and trying not to limp. A nod from Emerson sent Daoud and Selim trotting after him. I hoped they would be able to prevent him from doing something foolish.

"I'll give him a hand, shall I?" Geoffrey, who had been sitting on the rug, got to his feet.

"I am glad to see you were wearing gloves," I said. "I can never get Ramses and Emerson to do so, and they are always mashing their fingers and scraping their knuckles." Gloves did offer some protection, but in Geoffrey's case I suspected a harmless touch of vanity. He had slender, aristocratic hands, and his nails were always carefully manicured. "We are indebted to you, Geoffrey, for your quick thinking and prompt action."

"I fear I was of little use."

"And I was of no use at all," said Karl heavily. He had flung himself down on the rug, his head in his hands. "Ach, Gott, it was a frightful thing to see. I felt certain he would be crushed from head to feet. I could do nothing. It happened so quickly . . ."

Emerson had taken out his pipe and was smoking. He claimed this dirty habit calmed his nerves, and it may have been so. Only I could have detected the effort it cost him to remain seated and speak quietly.

"Did you see what happened?" he asked.

Karl threw out his hands. "It happened so quickly! He had gone down to look at the pottery, and then Miss Nefret cried out . . . I did not see."

"Hmph," said Emerson. "Well, my dear Peabody, with your permission I believe we will leave the pyramid for another day. I think I will just—er—see if I can help Ramses."

"Of course, my dear," I said sympathetically. "Whatever you say."

Karl excused himself; he said he was too shaken to work any more that day, and went trotting off on the little donkey he had hired. The rest of us worked until after midday and then started for home. Geoffrey and Nefret were riding ahead, and when Ramses would have joined them Emerson called him back.

We went on at a walk, side by side. With my usual tact I remained silent, wondering which of them would speak first.

They spoke simultaneously.

"Father, I—"

"Ramses, you—"

They broke off, avoiding one another's eyes, and I said, "Really! You first, Emerson."

"It wasn't your fault," Emerson said gruffly.

"I was about to say the same thing, sir."

"Oh, indeed?"

"I am not trying to deny that the ultimate responsibility is mine. That has always been your attitude, sir, and I share it. However . . ." His voice rose. "I will be damned if I know what I did wrong!"

"Then what did go wrong?" Emerson asked.

"Any number of things might have happened. A slight earth tremor, a sudden subsidence of the area directly under the prop, a careless movement on the part of one of the men . . . I saw nothing out of the way. I only went down because Nefret was determined to get at those beastly bones of hers, and I wanted to make absolutely certain . . ."

"I understand," Emerson said. "Well done. Hmph."

"I'm not trying to excuse myself," Ramses insisted. "But we must consider the possibility that it was not an accident."

"Especially," said Emerson, stroking his chin, "since it would be the second accident in a single day."

"The rock fall in the shaft, you mean?" Ramses considered this. "That would rather strengthen the theory that a minor earth tremor was responsible. They do occur."

"Yes," Emerson said. "But it's a bit odd, isn't it, that this one occurred only here?"


The Vandergelts arrived on schedule. A telegram sent from Meydum, where they had tied up the night before, warned us of their arrival that morning, so we were all on hand to greet them. Emerson, of course, gave Cyrus barely time to eat luncheon before informing him that they must visit the site, and Katherine goodnaturedly agreed to go along, claiming she would not mind a bit of exercise after lazing about the boat for ten days.

"Whom else are you expecting?" Katherine asked, as we rode off across the plateau.

"Howard Carter is the only one who is staying at the house. He has been in the Delta looking for a new site for Lord Carnarvon. We have invited quite a large number for Christmas Day. I expect you know most of them."

"No doubt. Cyrus is so hospitable, he likes to keep open house for any archaeologists visiting Luxor. Will the Petries be coming? We heard he had been in hospital. I hope it was nothing serious."

"A surgical operation was necessary, but he is recuperating nicely. However, Mrs. Petrie felt he was not fit for a large party and of course she could not consider enjoying herself when he was ill. What is the news from Luxor?"

We were having quite a comfortable little gossip about mutual friends when Ramses, belatedly remembering his manners, or possibly directed by his father, turned back to accompany us. I informed him we did not require an escort, but he would not go away, and so we were forced to change the subject. A wink from Katherine assured me she would finish the story about Mr. Davis and the duchess at a later time.

When we caught the others up, Emerson was arguing with Cyrus about the age of the pyramid.

"Reisner mentioned it last year when he was in Luxor on his way south," Cyrus insisted. "Said it was Second Dynasty."

"Bah," said Emerson. "Far too early. You're familiar with the plan of the Step Pyramid? Beginning of the Third Dynasty, correct? This is clearly later. Admittedly it's falling apart, but the shoddy construction was due to the fact that this king, whoever he was, did not reign as long as Zoser. Come along inside and I'll show you—"

"No, Emerson!" I said firmly. "Cyrus is not dressed for such an expedition."

Impeccably attired in one of the white linen suits he had specially tailored for him, Cyrus stroked his goatee and smiled.

"Thank you, Amelia. I believe I will postpone that little treat. You know I'm not as crazy about the insides of pyramids as some people. How about the private tombs? Sometimes you find interesting objects in the private tombs."

"Will you never get over this dilettante's obsession with interesting objects?" Emerson inquired good-humoredly (good-humoredly for Emerson, that is). "The only objects I care about are those that would enable me to identify the builder of this pyramid. If it's private tombs you want, come have a look at the West Cemetery. So far the graves are small and poor, but I am determined to make a complete clearance of the area, unlike some other excavators, who . . ."

They went off arm in arm, with Emerson continuing to lecture and Nefret trotting alongside. After inquiring whether we wanted him to stay with us—to which we replied with a decided negative—Ramses followed the others.

Watching the tall erect figure of my son I let out a little sigh.

"Something is worrying you," Katherine said, with the intuitive sympathy of a friend. "Something to do with Ramses?"

"I am not worried. Not at all. But I do wish he would settle down. He can't seem to make up his mind what he wants to do."

"My dear Amelia! For a young man his age he has already accomplished a great deal. The beginning Egyptian grammar, those volumes on the Theban temples—"

"That's just the trouble, Katherine. He has been working too hard and not taking proper care of himself."

"Aren't you contradicting yourself?" Katherine asked with a smile. "You just want him to stay home so you can fuss over him."

"I have never been one of those doting mamas, Katherine,

THE FALCON AT THE PORTAL

you know that. The truth is Emerson has missed him a great deal."

"Emerson?"

"And Nefret, of course."

"Of course."

"Well, never mind. Allah will decree, as dear Abdullah would have said. Would you care to go inside the pyramid?"

"Not today or any other day." Her amused and affectionate smile faded into sobriety. "Nor will Cyrus, if I can prevent him. Since you left he has been increasingly bored and restless. Luxor is just not the same without you. I believe Cyrus would even abandon his beloved castle and ask for permission to excavate in the Cairo area in order to be near you. It would please me, too, but I don't want Cyrus climbing around inside pyramids. Can't you find him a nice safe group of tombs?"

I took the hand she offered and gave it a little squeeze, for I was greatly moved at this declaration of affection, but I could not help smiling a little at her naïveté. She had learned a great deal about Egyptology since she married Cyrus, but her chief interest in the subject was how it would affect her husband.

"My dear Katherine, nothing would delight me more than having you and Cyrus as neighbors again. Would that it were in my power to do as you ask, but we have absolutely no influence with M. Maspero these days; as you see, my dear Emerson has been forced to settle for insignificant cemeteries and unfinished pyramids. However, Cyrus is on better terms with M. Maspero than we. Perhaps with a little judicious flattery . . . What sort of tombs did you have in mind?"

"It is a matter of complete indifference to me, Amelia dear, so long as the tombs in question don't have deep shafts and collapsing tunnels." She leaned closer and lowered her voice. "Cyrus would rather die than admit it, but he is not as young as he once was."

"None of us is," I said. "Not even Ramses and Nefret."

"It is a silly cliché, isn't it? But you know what I mean. Your enthusiasm for deep, pitch-dark passageways filled with bat guano and moldering mummies is one I cannot share."

"Ah, well, tastes differ," I said cheerfully. "And a good thing, too, Katherine, or we would all be fighting like Kilkenny cats over the same things."

Dinner that evening was a merry meal. Cyrus had brought several bottles of champagne and insisted on toasting everyone and everything. His final toast was in the nature of an announcement.

"Here's to you, folks, our best friends and near family. We've missed you so durned much, we've decided to give up the house in Luxor and move to Cairo—isn't that right, Katherine? I'm gonna see M. Maspero after Christmas and ask him about a firman for next season."

Our expressions of pleasure and surprise made Cyrus beam. He then began to question Emerson about possible sites.

My contributions to the conversation were spasmodic, for I was preoccupied with our forthcoming council of war. We had determined to hold it that evening; Howard was due to arrive next day, and the following day was Christmas. In my opinion it is a good idea to get unpleasant business over with as quickly as possible. Parts of it at least would certainly be unpleasant. We had asked Daoud and Selim to join us after dinner, and I was trying to think how best to manage the business as I led the way into the lantern-lit courtyard.

The main thing was to keep the discussion under firm control and not let it wander off into unproductive displays of emotion. I felt reasonably certain Emerson could not manage this. He believes he is rational and unsentimental, but he is mistaken.

There was one individual whom I could count on to refrain from emotional displays, so I drew him aside while the others were settling into their chairs. "Ramses, I believe the best way of going about this is to tell our friends how we found out about the fakes and what we have done to pursue the matter. Narrate it as you would a story, or perhaps a statement to the police—"

"You want *me* to do it?" Ramses asked, his emphatic black eyebrows drawing together.

I took this as an expression of surprise rather than refusal. "Yes, why not? You have more or less conquered your youthful tendency toward verbosity. Be succinct and factual. Include all the pertinent details but none that are superfluous. Avoid expressions of opinion. Assure our friends that never for a moment did we doubt David's integrity, but do not dwell at excessive length on the warmth of our feelings and the strength of our commitment to—" I broke off in mid-sentence and looked closely at him. It was rather dark in that corner of the courtyard. I stood on tiptoe in order to see his face more distinctly. "Are you by any chance grinding your teeth, Ramses?"

"No, Mother."

"Your lips are compressed to a degree that often expresses exasperation."

"I am not exasperated, Mother. Rather the reverse, in fact. But," he said, glancing over my head, "here are Daoud and Selim. Tell me when you want me to begin."

"I will give you your cue," I promised.

Daoud, the Beau Brummel of the family, had dressed for the occasion in silken robes and an astonishing turban. Selim looked very handsome in less extravagant but elegant garments. Fatima served coffee and Emerson offered brandy. I was among those who accepted the latter beverage and Cyrus gave me a questioning look.

"All right, folks," he said in his amiable American drawl. "Something's up, I reckon. Here we are sitting around in a circle for all the world like a board meeting, and Amelia's drinking brandy instead of whiskey and soda, and Emerson's chewed halfway through his pipe stem, and Miss Nefret's as fidgety as a bird when a cat's near its nest. Do Selim and Daoud know what this is all about, or are they in the dark too?"

"They won't be for long," I said. "Nor will you. You are right, Cyrus. We have something to tell you—all of you. I beg that you—including Selim and Daoud—will contain your expressions of surprise, distress or indignation until you have heard the entire story, for it would be an unnecessary waste of time to comment—"

Ramses cleared his throat. "Yes," I said. "Proceed, Ramses."

He told it quite well, beginning with the visit of Mr. Renfrew with the scarab, and his accusation of David. The only reaction from Selim was a sharp intake of breath. Daoud's honest brow furrowed, and Nefret went to perch on a hassock beside his chair, her hand on his.

No one spoke until Ramses had concluded the narrative with a statement of the negative results of our visits to the Cairo dealers. "We will find the man, though," he said, meeting Selim's dark gaze.

"Quite right," I said briskly.

Cyrus brought his big hand down on his knee. "Well now, that's a thunderbolt, and no mistake! I was wondering how to bring up the subject."

"Damnation," said Emerson mildly. "You bought one of the fakes, Vandergelt? Why didn't you mention it?"

"I didn't know it was a forgery," Cyrus protested. "Consarn it, Emerson, I still don't think it is. What had me in a stew was the provenance—the alleged provenance, I guess I should say. It seemed real strange that David would be selling Abdullah's collection to dealers instead of offering it direct to friends like—well, like me. He'd have got a better price, and done me a favor."

"That did not arouse your suspicions?" Emerson demanded. "Really, Vandergelt, an old hand like you ought to have known better."

"Well, maybe so." Cyrus took out one of his favorite cheroots. He made rather a long business about lighting it, and after waiting in vain for him to elaborate, Emerson bared his teeth in a humorless smile.

"You see what we are up against," he remarked to the room at large. "Vandergelt knows us well; he knew and respected Abdullah. Yet even he was willing to believe in this apocryphal collection."

"I wouldn't think the less of Abdullah if he had done such a thing," Cyrus said defensively. "Doggone it, Emerson, I admire your principles but they are sure unrealistic. And I could understand why David might decide to dispose of the objects without telling you. You'd have raised Cain."

Selim spoke for the first time, in a voice as flat and sharp as a knife blade. "My honored father had no collection of antiquities."

"You're sure?" Cyrus asked. The young man's eyes flashed, and Cyrus held up a conciliatory hand. "I don't doubt your word, Selim, I'm just trying to get things straight."

"Abdullah was a man of honor and my friend," said Emerson. "I would not have blamed him for doing what most men, Egyptian and English, have done. I do not believe he would have done it behind my back."

"He would not," Selim said. "But this story makes no sense, Father of Curses. You say the objects are fakes. If that is so, and you are never wrong about such things, then it is not my father but David whose honor is in question. Collecting antiquities is not a crime. Selling forgeries is. Would David go to prison if he were proved guilty?"

Daoud let out a bellow of alarm. The complexities which had been clear to Selim's quick intelligence had confused our simple friend, but he understood the last sentence.

Nefret squeezed his hand. "He is not guilty, Daoud, and we will prove it. This is where we need your help. The forgeries are perfect, even better than the ones made by David's former master, Abd el Hamed. Have you heard of anyone like that?"

Daoud shook his head. Simple is not the same as stupid; there was nothing wrong with Daoud's brain, it just moved a little slower than some. "I cannot think of such a man. Can you, Selim?"

"Not in Gurneh." Selim sounded positive, as well he might. Like his father, he had a wide acquaintance with the antiquities dealers of his hometown. "But Egypt is long. Aswan, Beni Hassan—any village could produce such a genius. Better than Abd el Hamed, you say? That is hard to believe."

"You can have a look for yourself," Ramses said. "As I said, we were able to buy several of them. I'll get them, shall I, Father?"

Emerson nodded. "I don't suppose you brought your purchase, Vandergelt? What was it?"

"I did bring it. Had to; bought it in Berlin, didn't trust the international mails to get it home safe."

He and Ramses went off. The atmosphere had changed; it was rather like the feeling of relief that follows a violent family argument (a condition with which I am only too familiar). How well they had all taken the news! A refreshing sense of renewed optimism filled me. With these resolute allies and dear friends to assist us, the case was as good as solved!

Nefret, who prided herself on her ability to brew the thick dark Turkish coffee, started another pot; Selim leaned back and lighted a cigarette; Daoud gave me a questioning look.

Ramses was soon back, carrying the box in which we had stored the artifacts. Emerson pulled up a small table and drew one of the lamps closer. He unwrapped the objects and passed them one by one to Selim, who examined them carefully before handing them to Daoud.

"You are right, Father of Curses," Selim admitted. "They are as good as any fakes I have seen. There is no mistake in the writing?"

"No," said Ramses. "But—" He broke off as Cyrus came back to the table.

"Took me a while to find it," he explained. "Can I see those?"

He inspected them as closely as Selim had done. "All right, I give up," he said at last. "What's wrong with 'em?"

"Nothing," Ramses said. He lined them up on the table: two scarabs and a small statue of a male figure wearing a strange tight-fitting garment and an odd little skullcap. "We got the leftovers," he said. "The best pieces were snapped up as soon as they appeared on the market, which was, as nearly as we can determine, in late spring of last year. The scarabs, like the one that was stolen from us, are made of faience. Molded, in other words, from a substance that isn't difficult to manufacture. It would not require a great deal of artistic talent to take a mold from a known piece and change certain details that would add to its historic value."

"What is your point, Ramses?" I asked.

"Only that that sort of artifact could be produced by a person who knew the history and the hieroglyphs but who would not have to have unusual artistic talent. So could the figurine. It is carved of alabaster, a relatively soft stone, and the simplicity of the forms of the garment and cap make Ptah perhaps the easiest of all the gods to sculpt. The face and hands are conveniently scratched and worn, you observe, and the scepter he carries has been broken off."

"Hmmm," I said. "Cyrus, you look like the cat who has swallowed a canary. What is it?"

"I admire your reasoning, young fellow, and I sure hate to knock it down," Cyrus said. "But maybe you'd better have a look at this."

Carefully he unwrapped the cotton wool enclosing the object. At first glance there was nothing particularly impressive about it—a small, rather lumpy seated figure carved of a brownish substance. Before I could get a closer look, Emerson rudely snatched it from Cyrus's hand.

"Hell and damnation," he remarked and handed it, not to me, as I might reasonably have expected, but to Ramses.

"Let me see!" Nefret, less conscious of her dignity than I, came up behind Ramses and leaned against him so she could look over his shoulder. "I don't understand," she said, after a puzzled look. "What is so remarkable about it?"

"Would you care to see it, Mother?" Ramses asked. Very gently he lifted the little hand that rested on his shoulder and leaned forward.

"The dealer said this was from Abdullah's collection?" Emerson asked.

"Yep." Cyrus grinned.

"It is ivory," Ramses said. "The image is that of a king wearing the White Crown and the close-fitting mantel assumed during certain ceremonies."

"How old is it?" I asked, intrigued. "Or rather, how old is it supposed to be?"

"No doubt about that," Ramses said. "There is a line of hieroglyphs on the base. No cartouche—they didn't use them at that date—only a royal title and a name. The Horus Netcherkhet."

"Zoser," said Cyrus. "Third Dynasty, builder of the Step Pyramid. There's only one other statue of him known. Well, Emerson, my friend?"

Emerson reached for his pipe. "Vandergelt, I apologize. This would have taken me in too. The details of costume and technique, even the hieroglyphs, are entirely accurate for the period. How he aged the ivory I don't know; put it through a camel, perhaps. How much did you give for it?"

"Less than it was worth if it's genuine, far too much if it isn't." Cyrus's grin faded. "I don't want to call anybody a liar, but let me just ask one question. Has anybody talked to David about this business?"

"No." Ramses took it upon himself to answer. "We ought to have done so, perhaps, but with the wedding less than a week away..."

"It may have been an error, but it was kindly meant," Katherine murmured.

I decided to intervene, since we were getting off the track. "You still harbor doubts, Cyrus. Look at it this way. The man who sold these objects was not David, and that means he selected David as a scapegoat, and that means he is a forger and a criminal. The logic is inescapable."

"Ah," said Cyrus.

"And that," said Emerson dogmatically, "means your ivory king is a forgery. The digestive tract of a camel—"

"Yes, sure," Cyrus said. "All the same, my friends, I believe I will take very good care of this little object until you've had that delayed chat with David."

**7**

They have not the *flair* for self-governance, but they are
fine fighting men, when led by white officers.

**From Manuscript H**

The message came the day before Christmas. It was only a
note from one of the antiquities dealers in Cairo saying he had
the gift he had been asked to find, and Ramses would have
thought nothing of it if it had been directed to his mother. However, the messenger had insisted on delivering it personally into
his hands, and said he had been instructed to wait for a reply.

Ramses scribbled a few words on the back of the note and
went looking for Nefret.

How she and his mother had persuaded, bullied or bribed
Emerson to close down the dig for a few days he didn't know;
he suspected Nefret had painted a pathetic picture of a suffering,
tight-lipped Ramses concealing two broken legs and several
cracked ribs. What they really wanted was time to prepare for a
sentimental English Christmas. Mysterious parcels filled every
cupboard and drawer, the smell of spices wafted from the
kitchen, and the two of them had hung lanterns and ribbons and
palm branches and other tasteless objects all over the house. He

found Nefret in the courtyard, perched precariously on top of a long ladder tying a bit of greenery to one of the arches.

"Where the devil did you get that?" he asked in surprise. Mistletoe was not indigenous to Egypt.

He steadied the ladder as she scrambled down. "In Germany. The berries kept falling off, so I put pins through them. It should be inaugurated, don't you think?" Standing on tiptoe, she pulled his head down and kissed him on the mouth.

As a rule he managed to avoid those generous, agonizing, sisterly kisses. This time she was so quick he hadn't time to move, or even turn his head. Knowing it meant nothing to her, he did his best not to respond, but when she stepped back her eyes were puzzled and her cheeks a little pinker than usual.

"Aesthetically and horticulturally it lacks a certain something," he said, glancing up at the withered leaves and blackened berries. "But I suppose it's the thought that counts. If you have quite finished playing the little woman, come over here where Mother can't hear. I've something to tell you."

She was quick to reach the same conclusion he had reached. The flush in her cheeks deepened and her eyes sparkled with excitement. "I take it you did not ask Aslimi to find a rare and beautiful and very expensive antiquity as a Christmas gift for me or Aunt Amelia?"

"I ought to have done, oughtn't I?" A wrinkled globule bounced off his head and onto the floor.

"Don't be silly. It's an assignation! When?"

"I sent back to say I'd come at once."

"Not alone."

"There's not the least risk."

"Then there's no reason why I can't go with you. Come to the Professor." She took his hand and pulled him toward the stairs.

Emerson was in his study working on his notes. When Nefret burst in, without knocking, he looked up with a frown. It deepened into a formidable scowl when she explained.

By that time Ramses knew he wasn't going to get away without Nefret. The problem now was to keep his father from accompanying them. If what he suspected was true, Nefret's presence would be excellent camouflage and it wouldn't frighten their correspondent away, but Emerson was another matter. He stood out in the suk like a lion in a herd of deer, and Wardani had no reason to trust him.

"What makes you think the message is from Wardani?" Emerson demanded. "Aslimi was one of the dealers we questioned about the forger."

"Why would Aslimi be so roundabout? Wardani promised to let me know if he found out anything; he would have to do it indirectly, and this is unlikely to rouse suspicion: a harmless visit to the suk, in broad daylight."

"And it's even less likely to arouse suspicion if I am with Ramses," Nefret added.

Emerson gave in, but he insisted they take two of the men with them. Ramses didn't object to that; the Egyptians weren't as conspicuous as his father and he could order them to stay at a distance.

"Try to be back before your mother notices your absence," Emerson said with a sigh. "If she should ask I will tell her where you have gone—as I may have mentioned before, absolute candor between husband and wife is the only possible basis for a successful marriage, but—"

"We understand." Nefret kissed him on the cheek and danced away—to get her hat, as she claimed.

"Look after her," Emerson muttered.

"Yes, sir."

Nefret looked particularly demure in a flower-trimmed hat and long linen coat, spotless white gloves, and a pair of frivolous bow-trimmed slippers. As they walked along the dusty tree-lined road toward the station, she slipped her hand through his arm and moved closer. He shortened his steps to match hers.

"Thank you, my boy."

"What for?"

"For letting me come along. Without so much as an argument!"

"Just don't use that knife unless you must."

"Knife? What knife?"

He turned his head and looked down at her. Nefret grinned. "Yes, sir. How would you define 'must'?"

Ramses pretended to ponder the question. "When I'm bleeding to death at your feet and someone has both hands round your neck."

"Oh, all right. I can manage that."

He kept a wary eye out and a hard grip on her arm as they

made their way through the crowded streets of the suk. Hassan and Sayid had been told to stay well behind and not enter the shop. Aslimi was engaged with a customer, to whom he was trying to sell a flagrantly fraudulent amulet. He started violently and turned pale when he saw them. That wasn't evidence of anything in particular except that Aslimi was a miserable little coward and a rotten conspirator.

The poor devil was so petrified, Ramses had to carry on both sides of the conversation. "That object you found . . . Ah, in your office? We'll just go back and wait till you've finished with this gentleman. Take all the time you like. We're in no hurry."

Wardani was sitting at Aslimi's desk with his feet on a chair. Rising, he bowed to Nefret and nodded at Ramses. "Bolt the door, please. Welcome, Miss Forth. I had not expected you, but it is a pleasure to meet you at last."

"You were listening at the door," Ramses said, drawing the bolt.

"Looking through the keyhole," Wardani corrected, with a flash of white teeth. He was wearing European clothing and steel-rimmed eyeglasses; beard and hair were a dusty gray. He examined Nefret with an interest that verged on insolence, but did not quite go over the line, and waved her to a chair. "Please sit down, Miss Forth. It was clever of you to bring her, my friend; I should have suggested it myself. No gentleman would allow a lady to accompany him if he anticipated violence."

Nefret settled herself in the chair with a thump. "I can be just as violent as Ramses, Mr. Wardani, and it was I who insisted on accompanying *him*. You have news for us?"

"The best of news, which is that there is none," Wardani said. He took out a heavy silver cigarette case and offered it to Ramses, who had taken up a position behind Nefret's chair. It would not have occurred to him to offer it to a woman. Ramses watched, with considerable amusement, as Nefret plucked a cigarette from the case. "Thank you," she said.

"Not at all," said Wardani, recovering with admirable aplomb. "You will forgive me if I do not offer you coffee. I would rather not linger; Aslimi is supposed to be one of us, but he is such a coward he may betray me out of pure hysteria."

"It was good of you to take the risk of coming here," Ramses said.

Wardani grinned and daintily removed a bit of tobacco from his lower lip. "Could I allow you to surpass me in daring? You took the risk last time. You knew, I think, how great a risk it was. Listen, then. I have connections in every corner of this city and in every trade. There have always been forgers of antiquities; I know their names and their work, and so do you. None of them can be the man you want. No dealer in this city or in Luxor has handled objects that belonged to your reis. Most of them know David by sight; all of them know him by name. None have bought antiquities from him. I would not say this if it were not true."

"I believe you," Ramses said.

Wardani wasn't as much at ease as he wanted them to believe. He kept shooting glances at the door. "So. I have given you your Christmas gift, yes? Your forger is not David. He is not an Egyptian. He is one of you—a sahib." His upper lip curled back when he spoke the word. It gave his face quite a different aspect; one saw the ruthlessness behind the charm. "So that is it, yes? If I learn more I will find a way of informing you."

It was a dismissal. Nefret rose and offered him her hand. "Thank you. If there is anything I can do in return . . ."

He took her hand; folding back the cuff of her glove, he pressed his lips to her wrist. The intimate gesture was another test; like a naughty child he was trying to see how far he could go without provoking an angry response.

Not much further, Ramses thought.

Nefret's response was perfect—a soft laugh and a measurable pause before she withdrew her hand from his grasp. Wardani grinned appreciatively.

"One more thing. It has nothing to do with your business, but it may be of interest. I offer it as another gift to a charming lady. There is a rumor that one of yours has invested heavily in that other trade of which we spoke. He is an Inglizi, but no one knows his name."

"I see."

"I am sure you do. I go that way, through the back. You will wait two minutes and then unbolt the door. And I think"—another flashing white smile—"it would be kind to purchase something from poor Aslimi, yes?"

"We'll have to buy something," Nefret said, after the curtain at the back of the room had fallen into place, "in case Aunt Amelia asks why we went to Cairo."

"I thought you had learned the futility of trying to keep things from Mother. However, so long as we're here, I may as well see if Aslimi has something rare and beautiful and very expensive."

Aslimi started and squealed when they came out of the back room. Ramses noticed his nails were bitten to the quick. The prospect of a sale revived him, and by the time they left with their purchases—none of which met Nefret's criteria—he was a much happier man.

"You did believe him, didn't you?" Nefret asked. "You weren't just being polite?"

"I do believe him, actually. What a mountebank the fellow is!"

"I rather like him."

"So do I. You understood the point of that so very casual final comment, I suppose."

"It was the drug trade he meant?"

"Yes."

"So it was his oblique way of telling you you owe him a favor in return. Payment, in other words."

"You're getting the hang of it."

"I've always had the hang of it." Nefret took his arm and gave a little skip, reminding Ramses he was setting too rapid a pace. He was anxious to get out of the suk. Crowds made him nervous, especially when Nefret was with him.

"A simple business transaction," she went on cheerfully. "Information in exchange for information."

"He wants rather more than information," Ramses said thoughtfully. "He can't lay an accusation against an Englishman; coming from him, it would be ignored or dismissed. He knows I would do it, though, and I'd be hard to ignore if Father backed me up. Which he would."

"I hate to think an Englishman would become involved with such a dirty trade."

"My dear girl, morality has nothing to do with business. The opium trade made a number of honest British merchants rich. We even fought a war to force the foul stuff on the Chinese."

"I know. Wouldn't it be wonderful if Percy were the villain?"

"Too good to be true, I'm afraid." He laughed, and so did she; but there had been a note in her voice that made him ask, "Has he been annoying you?"

"You needn't get all brotherly and protective. If he annoyed me I'd deal with him."

Had that been an answer? He thought not.

Nefret glanced over her shoulder and beckoned. Their two escorts, who had remained prudently behind, hurried to join them. They were a handsome family; Daoud's son Hassan had the same gentle brown eyes and large smile as his father. Taking Nefret's parcels, he said, "Did you find a good present for the Sitt Hakim?"

"I think she will like it," Nefret said.

Emerson claimed he had never agreed to attend the ball at Shepheard's that evening. He had not—not in so many words—but I had informed him of the affair several days earlier and he had not said he would *not* attend. Emerson appealed to Cyrus, but he got no help from that quarter. Cyrus was sociably inclined and had been looking forward to squiring his wife to the affair.

The ball did not begin until midnight, but we planned to dine at the hotel beforehand. Evening dress was de rigeur. Emerson had accepted this, though he did not like it and never would. On this occasion he got himself into his stiff shirt and so on with a minimum of grumbles and with the usual assistance from me. He then obligingly assisted me to button my frock and my gloves. Neither of us employs a personal attendant, though I must say Emerson could use one—if only for the purpose of locating the articles of clothing he misplaces or kicks under the bed, and sewing on the buttons that pop off his shirt because of his impetuous method of removing that garment, and pressing the clothes he leaves lying on the floor, and mending the holes made by sparks from his pipe, and removing the spots of blood that only too frequently stain his clothing, und so weiter, ad infinitum, so to speak.

As I was saying, before understandable wifely vexation distracted me, neither Emerson nor I enjoy being waited upon except by one another. To have Emerson kneel at my feet in order to lace my boots, to feel his fingers moving lightly down my back as he unfastens the buttons of my frock . . . But perhaps I had better say no more. Any woman of sensibility will understand why I would never exchange Emerson's attentions for the more efficient but far less interesting assistance of a lady's maid. Fatima and her staff—most of them related to her by blood or marriage— did most of the mending, cleaning and washing for the entire family and would have done more had we allowed it.

When I was ready I went to see if Nefret needed my help,

but found she was already dressed. Fatima was fussing over her hair and one of Fatima's stepdaughters, the child of her late husband's second wife, stood by watching attentively. Elia was a pretty girl, barely fourteen, and she aspired to the post of lady's maid to Nefret, whom she admired enormously. Nefret was no more keen on that kind of attention than I, but she did not want to discourage the girl, who was intelligent and ambitious and who was attending school under our auspices.

"I don't want to hurry you, my dear, but the others are waiting," I said, smiling at the bright face reflected in the mirror.

"I am ready." Nefret jumped up from the dressing table. "Except for my wrap . . . Oh, thank you, Elia. Don't tell me Ramses is waiting, Aunt Amelia, he is never on time."

However, he emerged from his room as we left Nefret's. I straightened his cravat and brushed a few cat hairs off his sleeve, which he permitted with his usual absence of expression. We then proceeded in splendor to our carriages and to the hotel.

I had been told that Shepheard's was no longer considered the most fashionable hotel in the city. Younger members of the smart set preferred the Semiramis or the Savoy. So far as I was concerned, this was all to the good, since we were not as likely to encounter any of the silly creatures when we went there. My own sense of humor has been highly commended, and I have no objection to pleasant little jokes, but some of the tricks these "upper-class" officials and officers played would have disgraced a schoolboy. Carrying off the handsome statues of Nubian maidens that stood at the foot of the great staircase, and putting them in people's beds, was among the most harmless of their "stunts." They were fond of making fun of other people, especially those whose accents, education, nationality and social status differed from theirs.

Shepheard's was greatly changed since my first visit—in point of fact, it had been entirely rebuilt—but it was part of the history of Cairo, rich in memories of the great and the infamous, with many of whom, both great and infamous, I had been personally acquainted. Every part of the splendid structure held delightful memories: the suite of rooms on the third floor, on the carpet of whose sitting room the mysterious Mr. Shelmadine had writhed in convulsions after telling us of the hidden tomb of Queen Tetisheri; the magnificent entrance hall, with its lotus columns painted in shades of apricot, russet and turquoise, where Emerson had snatched me from the arms of a masked abductor;

the shadowy alcoves and soft divans of the Moorish Hall, where Nefret had spent an unchaperoned quarter of an hour with the dashing and unprincipled Sir Edward Washington.

I do not greatly exaggerate when I say I knew everyone of importance in Cairo. I disliked a good many of them, but I knew them all. For the Europeans who lived there or returned every winter, Cairo had some of the characteristics of a narrow-minded, provincial village. The various social circles overlapped but did not coincide, and the social strata were as rigid as any caste system. Egyptian Army officers were of a lower stratum than officers of the British Army of Occupation, and both were inferior to the British Agency set. The jealousy, the vicious gossip, the cliques and struggles for promotion and prestige were all perfectly ridiculous to those of us who were outside the pale and happy to be there.

Outside all the circles—somewhere in outer darkness—were the Egyptians whose country this was.

We had an excellent dinner and a good deal of champagne, and then went to the ballroom. I am very fond of the terpsichorean arts; after I had danced with Cyrus and Emerson, Ramses dutifully propelled me about the floor, dutifully returned me to a chair, and vanished. No sooner had he done so than a gentleman approached and begged leave to introduce himself.

"I would have asked your husband to perform this office," he explained, "but I can't see him anywhere. My name is Russell, Mrs. Emerson. Thomas Russell."

I was extremely interested. Mr. Thomas Russell was then head of the Alexandria police and I had heard him described as an exemplary officer. I said as much, adding that my various encounters with the police officers of Cairo had not given me a high opinion of that group of individuals.

"I can understand why," Russell said politely. "I have long looked forward to making your acquaintance, Mrs. Emerson, since you and your family have a considerable reputation for catching criminals. I am being transferred to Cairo, as assistant commissioner, and I hope I may eventually merit your approval, as certain of my colleagues have not."

I congratulated him upon his promotion—for so, in fact, it was, Cairo being headquarters for the entire country—and, the music having begun, he asked me to dance.

"We will have to consider that we have been properly introduced," I said jestingly. "Looking for Emerson would be a waste of time; he is probably hiding in the shrubbery smoking his pipe and fahddling with the dragomen."

Russell laughed. "Yes, I know the Professor's habits. Is your son also smoking in the shrubbery? I don't see him either."

"Do you know Ramses?"

"I almost had the honor of arresting him a few years ago," Russell said. My look of surprised displeasure wiped the smile off his face. Quickly he added, "Only a little joke, Mrs. Emerson."

"Ah," I said distantly.

"Allow me to explain."

"Pray do."

"I didn't know who he was, you see," Russell said. "I walked into a café in Alexandria one afternoon and found a group of young fellows—Egyptians, as I believed them all to be—listening to an orator who was holding forth on the iniquities of the British occupation, as he called it—"

"Isn't it?" I inquired.

"Er—well. This was not long after the business at Denshawai, and we were all a bit on edge; I thought the discussion was getting somewhat heated and so I told them to go about their business. Your son refused—quite politely, and in impeccable Arabic, but quite decidedly. Like most of the others, he was wearing European clothes, but he wore them like an Egyptian, if you know what I mean."

"Yes, I do know."

"I wasn't accustomed to being talked back to by Egyptians, especially young firebrands like those. He appeared to be the leader—he was the one doing all the talking, anyhow—so I identified myself and told him to make himself scarce or I'd arrest him. He then gave me one of the most irritating smiles I have ever seen and identified *himself*, in English as impeccable as his Arabic had been! By that time the others had melted away except for one chap whom Ramses introduced as David Todros. The young devil—excuse me, ma'am—then invited me in the coolest manner to take drinks with them."

"That sounds like Ramses," I admitted. "He never mentioned the incident to me, Mr. Russell. Ramses is inclined to keep his own counsel."

"So I understand. I had heard of him—everyone in Egypt knows your family, Mrs. Emerson—and I was amused by his sangfroid, so I accepted the invitation. We had quite a long talk. I don't suppose he's ever considered taking up police work? I could certainly use a chap who looks like an Egyptian and speaks Arabic like a native."

Clearly Mr. Russell did not know of Ramses's escapades as Ali the Rat and other equally disgusting personalities. Devoutly I prayed he never would. I replied that my son was destined for a career in Egyptology and, the music ending, Mr. Russell gave me his arm in order to lead me off the floor.

"A word of warning, if I may," he said, in a low voice and in quite a different tone. "You may have wondered why I remembered the name of your son's friend. It is a name that appears in the files of the Cairo police, Mrs. Emerson. If young Todros is still a friend—"

"He is now related to me by marriage, Mr. Russell. He espoused my niece in November."

"What? Married?"

I gave him back stare for stare. After a moment he smiled wryly. "All the more reason to heed my warning, then. Try to keep the boy out of trouble. K won't stand for nationalist unrest."

"Thank you for the warning."

"Thank you for the dance, ma'am. If Ramses should ever change his mind about Egyptology, send him to me."

**From Manuscript H**

Ramses shared his father's dislike of formal dinners and balls. In a way these events were harder for him than for Emerson, who didn't give a damn about anything except Egyptology and refused to pretend that he did; who preferred the company of his Egyptian friends to that of officials, officers and "the best people," and made no bones about that either. Ramses had not attained that level of sublime rudeness; he doubted he ever would, not so long as his mother was anywhere around. He made a point of dropping by the Turf Club and the hotel bars from time to time, rather in the manner of an explorer investigating the bizarre customs of the Masai or the tribes of West Africa. He couldn't stand it for very long at a time. They set his teeth on edge, these arrogant outsiders, they were so convinced of their superiority to all other nations and races and persons of other social classes.

The ballroom filled rapidly. Ramses kept moving; he had become expert at eluding the determined matrons who bore down on unattached men, towing a recently arrived female. Many of the young women had failed to find a husband at home and were on their way to India where, presumably, men had fewer choices; since their aim was marriage and their requirements few, the damsels were perfectly willing to try their hands in Cairo first.

He danced with his mother and with Mrs. Vandergelt, observed Nefret looking extremely bored as she talked with the Finance Minister, and escaped to the Long Bar. Maude and her "set" had not turned up, but he had a horrible premonition they would. Nefret had mentioned that the family meant to attend, and he had seen Maude glance in his direction. Or was he becoming one of those egotistical asses who thought every woman he met was after him? Not in this case, he feared. She was an embarrassment, and he didn't know what to do about it. One couldn't tell a perfectly harmless girl point-blank that she was a bore and a bother, and demand she leave him alone. Women had it easier. They could be as rude as the occasion demanded if a fellow was a nuisance.

If they were ladies, that is. If they were not, they were fair game for worse than boredom. No, women didn't always have it easier.

He was brooding quietly over his whiskey when he heard a rustle of skirts and looked up to see Nefret.

"I thought you'd be here," she said. "Move over."

Before he could stand up she had squeezed in next to him on the curved banquette. He slid over and raised a hand to summon the waiter. That unfortunate individual looked wildly toward the bar, where Friedrich, the head steward, stood in lordly splendor. Friedrich shrugged and rolled his eyes. Women were not allowed in the Long Bar except on New Year's Eve, but Nefret went where she pleased and few people had the courage to try and stop her. Certainly not Friedrich. Or Ramses.

"What were you brooding about?" she asked, stripping off her gloves.

"Women."

"Any woman in particular or women in general?"

"What would you like to drink?"

"Champagne."

"You had quite a lot at supper."

"And I am going to have more now."

"All right, one glass. You aren't supposed to be here, you know; some stuffy sahib is sure to complain and then Friedrich will be in trouble." He waved the waiter away and looked closely at her. The alcove was dark, lighted only by a candle on the table, but he could read Nefret's feelings by the curve of her lower lip or the tap of a finger. "What's wrong, Nefret?"

"Nothing's wrong. What makes you suppose . . . Oh, curse it!"

The officer standing in the doorway was in mess kit—gold and crimson, sword and epaulets. He appeared to be looking for someone.

Ramses pushed the table away and stood up. "What are you doing?" Nefret hissed.

"What has Percy done, to make you so intent on avoiding him? It's not like you to cower in corners."

"I do not cower in corners!" Nefret got to her feet. She hadn't answered his question, but he thought she clung rather more tightly than usual to his arm as they made their way to the entrance of the bar.

Percy greeted them effusively. "I saw the Professor and Aunt Amelia in the ballroom, so I thought you must be somewhere about. Miss Reynolds is looking for you, Ramses, old chap. You'll give me a dance, won't you, Nefret?"

"I promised the next one to the Professor." She tugged at Ramses. "He'll be looking for me."

Percy followed them back to the ballroom. Emerson was nowhere in sight; he had probably gone out of the hotel looking for more congenial company among the vendors and beggars in the street. Ramses saw his mother dancing with Thomas Russell of the Alexandria police, and wondered if she was up to her old tricks, lecturing Russell about the inexplicable narrowmindedness of the police in refusing to hire women.

Then he caught sight of Maude, dancing with Geoffrey. They did not appear to be enjoying themselves; Maude's eyes wandered, and Geoff looked bored. He hadn't often accompanied the young Reynoldses on their social rounds, and Ramses wondered what had brought him out that night. He knew the answer, though. When Geoff saw Nefret his remote face brightened, and the moment the music ended he led his partner toward their group.

"I wasn't aware that you were acquainted," Ramses said, watching Percy click his heels and kiss Maude's hand. Geoff looked as if he wanted to kiss Nefret's, but didn't dare.

"Oh, yes," Maude said. "Imagine my surprise when Lieutenant Peabody introduced himself and told me he was your cousin. You don't see much of each other, do you?"

"Percy has his duties," Ramses said. "And we our work. He's not interested in Egyptology."

"Now, old chap, you know that's not true. I came to the conclusion that I could be of more use to my country in the military, but there were personal reasons why I had to abandon the study of Egyptology." Percy sighed. "My dear aunt and uncle don't care much for me."

"Really?" Maude exclaimed. "Well, I'm sorry if I spoke out of turn. I surely don't want to bring up a painful subject."

"It is painful to me," Percy said softly. "But you couldn't know that, Miss Reynolds. I fear Aunt Amelia has never forgiven me for certain boyish pranks. Mothers are like that. God bless their dear, prejudiced hearts!"

Nefret made a rude noise.

"It was a long time ago," Ramses said.

"I felt sure *you* didn't hold a grudge, old boy." Percy clapped him on the shoulder. "But they are playing a waltz, and I don't see Uncle Radcliffe anywhere about. Nefret?"

"This one is mine," Ramses said. "Excuse us."

They circled the floor in silence, to the saccharine strains of the waltz from *The Merry Widow*. Nefret was the first to speak.

"Uncle Radcliffe! He wouldn't dare call him that to his face."

"Are you sure there's nothing you want to tell me?"

"I don't know what you mean."

"He was suspiciously polite to me. And he's obviously gone out of his way to make Maude's acquaintance."

"They're part of the same 'set.' Idle, superficial snobs." She rested her head against his shoulder. "I'm tired. Will you take me home?"

"Of course."

When they went to his mother to announce their departure they found Emerson had already declared his intention of leaving: "And if you don't come along peacefully, Peabody, I shall pick you up and put you in a carriage. Carter is arriving at some ungodly hour in the morning, and we have two dozen people for dinner. And what is more . . . Oh. You are ready? Oh. Well, why the devil didn't you say so?"

Even the indefatigable Vandergelt was yawning, so they all left together. While they were waiting for the servants to bring their wraps and hats, Maude and her brother caught them up.

"Hey, you aren't leaving so early?" Jack exclaimed. "It's the shank of the evening, and you haven't given me a dance, Nefret."

Nefret made her excuses. Maude said nothing. She just stood there looking mournful. There was no sign of Percy.

Howard arrived in time for breakfast Christmas morning, and afterward we all sat down round the rather spindly tree in the sitting room to open our family gifts. Evelyn had sent a parcel and so had Lia and David, so we were quite some time about it. I had not expected Ramses would be enthusiastic over my Christmas gift to him—a dozen nice shirts, the buttons reinforced by my own hands—but any other offering would have paled by comparison with the one Howard brought him.

The contents of the wooden box would certainly not have roused many people to rapture—two battered, broken tablets of wood covered with a thin layer of plaster on which a hieratic text had been written—but Ramses flushed with pure excitement after he had removed the cotton wool and unwrapped the layers of paper.

"Are these the tablets Lord Carnarvon found a few years ago? Does he want me to . . . Will he allow . . ."

"He wants you to translate and publish them if you are interested." Howard burst out laughing. "I gather the answer is yes. Well, well, I feel like Father Christmas! I wish I could please all my friends as easily."

"I suppose he is calling them the Carnarvon Tablets," Emerson muttered. "Such vanity!"

"One must call them something," Howard said tolerantly. "It is a delicate attention to name a text after the person whose money financed the discovery—and it may inspire additional contributions!"

It was a very sensible attitude. I don't know why I should have remembered the night so many years ago when we had dined at Mena House with a very young, very idealistic scholar who said he was not interested in working for wealthy dilettantes.

"What is the text about?" I asked.

"It dates to the reign of Kamose and seems to describe the war against the Hyksos. Right up your alley, eh, Mrs. E.? The story of Sekenenre and the hippopotami which you so ably—er—

interpreted a few years ago precedes the events of this tale by
only a few years. Perhaps you can write a sequel."

"Not for a while. My next task will be a revision of the story
of Sinuhe. I was not entirely satisfied with my earlier—er—interpretation."

Howard laughed and accepted a honey cake from the plate
Fatima offered him. "Poor old Sinuhe! But what was wrong with
your earlier—er—interpretation, Mrs. E.?"

I had not meant to mention it, for that would have seemed
like boasting, but since he asked . . .

"An American publisher has just offered me a considerable
sum of money for my little fairy tales," I explained modestly.
"David and me, I should say, for it was his sketches that were
the attraction, I believe. He dashed off a set of them for 'The Tale
of the Two Brothers,' just for the sake of amusement, and the
reaction was so enthusiastic, we have gone into partnership! He
has recently sent me the drawings for Sinuhe, so I decided to take
advantage of the opportunity to correct some of my interpreta-
tions. I do not believe Sinuhe was guilty of—"

"You are mistaken, Peabody," said Emerson. "But," he added
quickly, "I refuse to discuss it now."

We sat down two dozen to dinner, for I had asked all of our
archaeological acquaintances who were separated from home and
loved ones. They came from as far away as the Delta and the
Fayum and included Petrie's lot, as Emerson called them; Mr.
Petrie was still in hospital, and in any case the Petries were not
noted for their lavish hospitality. Turkeys were easily obtainable
in Egypt, and Fatima had learned to make an excellent plum pud-
ding, so we had all the good old English fare, and Cyrus's champagne flowed freely. As I looked round at the smiling faces I was
humbly grateful that I had been able to perform an act of Christian kindness on such a day.

The fact that several of the guests were among my suspects
did not mar the gesture in the slightest. Nor did I have much of
an ulterior motive when I kept the wineglasses filled. The first
toast was offered by Howard—to me—and as I nodded a gracious acknowledgment I did sincerely hope he would prove to be
innocent.

After the usual healths had been drunk—to the ladies, to absent friends, to His Majesty, to President Taft—the young men
vied with one another in proposing amusing or touching toasts.
We drank to Mr. Petrie's stitches and the Carnarvon Tablets and

to Horus, who had been shut in Nefret's room and was howling like a banshee. We never followed the archaic custom of having the ladies withdraw and leave the gentlemen to their port and cigars, so when the meal was concluded I led the company to the courtyard. I had done my best to adorn it in festive fashion with masses of poinsettias in seried ranks, and colored lanterns hanging from the arches. There were still a few berries left on Nefret's mistletoe.

Most of the guests were known to one another and everyone seemed to be having a merry time, so I felt I could neglect my duties as hostess for a bit and indulge in a spot of detectival introspection. Withdrawing to a shadowy corner, I was somewhat taken aback to find it already occupied. I coughed loudly, and the two forms drew apart.

"Give Miss Maude a cup of tea, Ramses," I said. "Unless she would prefer coffee."

"Yes, Mother."

She shot me a distinctly unfriendly look as he led her toward the tea table, but I thought there had been a note of relief in his voice. At least I hoped there was. Not that I had anything against the girl, but she did not measure up to *my* standards as a daughter-in-law. Egypt did not seem to agree with her. I had observed at dinner that she was not looking her usual self, and she had only picked at her food. Perhaps she had not liked the gift Nefret had selected for her—a pretty scarf from Damascus, woven with silver and gold threads. Perhaps she had hoped for something more personal.

It was not the first time Ramses had got himself involved with a young woman, and it would certainly not be the last. I do not believe it was always *entirely* his fault. He had not given the girl any encouragement that I could see. Of course I had no way of knowing what he did behind my back.

I told myself, as I had done so often before, that the romantic affairs of the children were not my business, and turned my thoughts to more important issues.

The news the children had got from Mr. Wardani had not really changed the situation. I believed him, not because I had much faith in his truthfulness (for I have learned that noble causes have a deplorable effect on the morals of the persons who espouse them), but because his statement confirmed every other clue we had found.

It made the situation even more baffling. We had always believed that the culprit must be someone we knew—a colleague or an acquaintance, if not a friend. We were no nearer to discovering his identity, and yet he must think we were, or he would not have paid us so many interesting attentions. I did not believe the collapse of the mastaba wall was an accident. In light of that incident and the earlier attack on me, Emerson's seeming accident, our first day at the site, took on alarming significance. The interesting potsherd could have been put in position to divert his descent toward a particular section, and one of the stones insidiously undermined.

The burglary at Amarna House before we left England was of a different nature. No harm to any of us had been intended. The sole aim had been the retrieval of the spurious scarab. Two questions arose from that occurrence: how had the villain learned we had the thing in our possession, and why was he so bent on getting it back? The only possible answer to the last question was that we might have found on it some clue to the identity of the forger.

Perhaps, I mused, we had not given enough attention to that incident. Ramses was the one who had inspected the scarab most closely. In fact . . . Yes, he must have translated it, for he had been quite specific about the sources. If I knew Ramses, and I believe I may claim that I did—through the painful experience only a mother can acquire—he had written it down or at least made copious notes. We must have a look at that translation. I would never claim that my knowledge of the hieroglyphs is that of an expert, but one never knows when and to whom a sudden burst of inspiration may occur. They often occur to me.

Detectival fever had gripped me. New ideas burgeoned; new avenues of investigation were opening up. I had quite lost sight of my duties as a hostess when I was reminded of them by a shout from Emerson.

"Peabody! Where have you got to? What . . . Ah!" Questing round like a hunting dog, he had made out my form. Advancing, he demanded, "What are you doing lurking in the shadows? Are you alone?"

"Of course I am. What do you want?"

"Only your company, my dear." Emerson looked a little sheepish. His profound attachment makes him unreasonably suspicious—not of me, for he never doubts my fidelity, but of the hordes of male persons whom he suspects of having amorous designs on me. Taking my hand, he raised me to my feet and gave me a quick but hearty kiss by way of apology before leading me out of my quiet corner.

I was unable to concentrate on serious matters thereafter, for everyone was having a jolly time and I felt obliged to romp a bit with the young people. Champagne has a way of loosening people's reserve; it had a surprising effect on Clarence Fisher, Mr. Reisner's second-in-command, who had always seemed to me a particularly straitlaced, humorless individual. Eyeglasses askew and hair standing up in tufts, he joined in a game of musical chairs and bumped Nefret out of the last empty one with remarkable joie de vivre. Even Karl forgot his Teutonic solemnity and allowed himself to be blindfolded and spun about for blindman's bluff. I allowed him to catch me, since he would have fallen into the fountain if I had not got in his way, and then I caught Emerson—he had put himself deliberately in my path—and he caught Nefret, who pulled him under the mistletoe and kissed him soundly. I had to put a stop to the kissing after a while.

Nefret had brought David's drawings for Sinuhe down from my study. Howard was not the only one who expressed his admiration; several of the others crowded round as he looked through them, handling them with an artist's careful touch.

"Amusing," said little Mr. Lawrence, rising onto his toes in order to see. "What's the tale about, then? I don't know it."

I thought he sounded a bit patronizing, so I told him.

"Pharaoh was assassinated while his son, the Crown Prince Senusert, was fighting in Libya. There was a plot by some of the other royal sons to seize the throne from Senusert; but a spy got word to the prince and he set off for the palace as fast as he could go. 'The falcon flew, with his attendants,' as David has shown him here, quite beautifully, in my opinion—the stalwart young soldier-prince who was the embodiment of Horus, with the god in shadowy falcon form flying overhead. The next drawing shows our friend Sinuhe lurking near the tent where he overheard the conspirators talking of the plot. Sinuhe then hid in the bushes . . ."

I turned the page, and Howard burst out laughing.

"He's got the old boy's expression very nicely. Never saw a guiltier look."

"That is one of the questions scholars have debated," I explained, passing rather quickly over succeeding sketches, since Emerson was beginning to look surly. He does not like me to tell my little Egyptian stories. "Sinuhe was certainly guilty of something, for he fled from Egypt and almost died of thirst in the desert before he was rescued by a tribe of Asiatics, as he calls them. He became rich and successful in the service of the Asiatic prince. I am particularly fond of this drawing, which shows him with his wife, the prince's eldest daughter, and their innumerable children. Doesn't he look like a smug Victorian papa in fancy dress?"

Emerson cleared his throat. I went on quickly, "But as old age approached, he yearned for home. He sent a pitiful message to pharaoh, who told him all was forgiven and summoned him back from exile. He was clothed in fine linen and anointed with fine oil; a house and garden were given to him, and a tomb was built for him, and he lived happily until the day of his death."

"What happened to his Asiatic wife and children?" Katherine asked.

"He abandoned them," said Ramses. "He was a cad and a bounder and a dreadful snob."

"It wasn't very nice of him," Nefret agreed. She was looking at the last delicately tinted drawing, which showed the old man sitting in the shade of green trees beside a blue pool where lotus blossoms floated. In the distance one could just make out the shape of the king's pyramid, near which Sinuhe's tomb had been built. The wrinkled face had a look of peace that was very touching.

"But in a way one can understand how he felt," she went on. "No matter how much success and happiness he had attained, he was still an exile. He wanted to come home."

"He was a cad, all the same," Ramses said.

Nefret laughed, and Mr. Lawrence eyed Ramses askance. I believe he noticed the tone of irony in the words—in one word especially.

We finished the celebration with carol singing, as was our custom. Sentiment had succeeded merriment, and several of our guests choked a bit over the familiar and beloved songs. Karl broke down while attempting to render "Stille Nacht"; Jack Reynolds wrapped a sympathetic arm round his shoulders, proffered his own handkerchief, and took up the words in quite respectably accented German. I was pleased to see that the kindliness of the day had softened the American toward a man to whom he had scarcely spoken before; but I also made note of the fact that Jack could talk German. I hope I am as sentimental as the next person, but sentiment should not be allowed to interfere with the ratiocinative processes.

Emerson sang louder than anyone else but the rest of us managed to drown him out. He enjoyed himself a great deal.

The older guests began to drift away. Nefret remained at the piano, playing bits of melody and humming softly to herself. I went with Karl to the door and asked Mr. Fisher, who was leaving at the same time, if he would see Karl safely home. Karl kept assuring me of his profound admiration and trying to kiss my hand. "If at any time you wish me to die for you, Frau Emerson, you have only to say the word," he remarked. "You have been a friend to a lonely man and forgiven a sinner for a crime he will never forgive himself. Your magnanim———"

However, he got tangled up in the syllables and could not stop, so I pushed him gently into Mr. Fisher's grasp and said good night to both. They went off arm in arm, singing. Mr. Fisher was rendering "The Holly and the Ivy" and Karl "Vom Himmel Hoch." Both were off key.

When I returned to the sitting room, Nefret was trying to persuade Ramses to sing with her. He has rather a pleasant voice and they sound well together, but he hardly ever consented to perform in front of strangers. I supposed he considered it beneath his dignity. Geoffrey offered to take his place, so we had a nice little concert, with all the old favorites and some of the newest songs from the music halls and theaters. "When I was Twenty-One and You Were Sweet Sixteen" was popular that year; in the mellow lamplight, with the curls clustering round his brow, Geoffrey looked no more than sixteen himself, but he had a surprisingly robust baritone. I remember he rendered one of Harry Lauder's Scottish songs with surprising panache and an exaggerated accent that made us all chuckle. I had never seen him enjoy himself so much.

### From Letter Collection B

*Dear Lia,*

*I am peppering you with letters, aren't I? I had to respond at once to your last, for it seemed to hold a certain note of reproach. My darling Lia, no one will ever replace you as my confidante; certainly not Maude Reynolds! If I have mentioned her often, it is only because the confounded girl is always here! So it feels, at any rate. I've told you why. She and I could never*

*be friends; we have nothing in common; but I feel so sorry for
her I can't bring myself to keep her entirely at arm's length.
She's head over heels, Lia; it's one of the worst cases I've ever
seen. She has sense enough to know he prefers women with
intelligence and spunk, but her desperate efforts to impress him
are so pitifully inept! I told you about the time she followed us
down into the pyramid; it took a lot of courage, because she was
absolutely petrified with fear, and of course it backfired the way
such gestures often do. When she saw Ramses on Risha she
insisted on trying to ride, and made a perfect fool of herself
bouncing up and down in that stiff style. It's impossible to fall
off Risha unless he wants you off, but she came close.*

*Ramses is handling it well—he's had plenty of practice!—
but he's hating the whole business. You know, he's really very
sensitive under that stony exterior. It's that quality that really
attracts women, isn't it? Especially when the man in question
is also tall and strong and handsome.*

*But I meant to tell you about our Christmas. You were
sadly missed, my dears. Aunt Amelia and I did our best, but
our decorative skills couldn't begin to match David's. Your parcel arrived in good time, somewhat battered, but intact—you
shouldn't have taken the trouble, darling, but I loved the Greek
earrings . . . [Several paragraphs of miscellaneous gossip omit-
ted.]*

*The only other news of mild interest is that I have had two
proposals of marriage—that makes three this season, including
Percy's, which is of course the one I cherish most. Yes, Jack
Reynolds took the plunge, emboldened, I do not doubt, by Mr.
Vandergelt's champagne. I refused him cheerfully and amiably
and he informed me, cheerfully and amiably, that he would try
again. Why can't men take no for an answer? He was a perfect
gentleman, though, so I let him kiss me—on the cheek.*

*I'm not going to make fun of Geoffrey even to you. He
didn't so much propose as tell me he knew I wouldn't accept
him; nor should I, he wasn't nearly good enough for me, no one
was . . . You know the sort of thing. I've heard it before. There
was something oddly impressive about him, though—his quiet,
well-bred voice and pale, controlled face. "I only want you to
know," he said, "that if you ever need me, for any reason, at
any time, it would be the greatest honor and pleasure to serve*

*you." I was so moved I let him kiss me—not on the cheek. It was very sweet.*

☙

**W**e had a nice long gossip with Howard next day. He was very proud of the new house he had built near the entrance to the Valley of the Kings, and showed me innumerable pictures of it—a pleasant little domicile with a domed central hall. This indicated to me that he meant to go on working in the Theban area, and he admitted, when I inquired, that he and Carnarvon had not given up hope of getting the firman for the Valley of the Kings one day. Mr. Davis had lost some of his enthusiasm; he felt that the Valley was exhausted.

"Not true," said Emerson.

"Are you considering a return to Thebes?" Howard asked.

Emerson shook his head. "Not while Weigall is Inspector there. Can't stand the fellow."

"He hasn't been particularly cordial to me either," Howard said. "But what is one to do?"

Having no answer to this, Emerson relapsed into moody silence and allowed me to turn the conversation in the direction I desired.

"I understand that Mr. Weigall has been making a fuss about the sale of antiquities," I said cunningly.

Howard's long face lengthened even farther. "He accused *me* of negligence, if you can believe such a thing! The fellow sneers at everyone, even Maspero, who has been so kind to him."

"I find myself in sympathy with certain of his views, however," I continued. "It is a pity to see fine objects sold to private collectors."

This touched a tender spot, for Howard had become skilled at acquiring valuable antiquities for wealthy collectors—one of whom was his current employer. He looked a little chagrined, but defended himself spiritedly. "That's all very well, Mrs. E., and I agree in principle, but there's not the manpower for proper supervision, and Weigall knows it. As many priceless pieces have slipped through his hands as was the case when *I* was Inspector for Upper Egypt."

Howard mopped his perspiring brow, smiled apologetically

at me, and dropped his bombshell. "Speaking of antiquities, what's this I hear about Abdullah's collection?"

I spilled my tea, Emerson swore, and Ramses said, "What have you heard, Mr. Carter?"

"That it was being sold through various European dealers." His eyes moved from my face to that of Ramses, found nothing in that enigmatic countenance to assist him, and went on to that of Emerson, which expressed his emotions as clear as print. "I see I've spoken out of turn. Was it supposed to be a secret? Don't see how it can be, though."

Ramses did not say "I told you so," though he must have been sorely tempted. Glancing at his father, he said, "We have been meaning to take you into our confidence, Mr. Carter."

"Curse it, we may as well," Emerson grumbled. "It's going to come out anyhow. Abdullah had no collection, Carter. The objects purporting to have belonged to him are forgeries. The man who sold them gave David's name, but it was not David."

This statement was typical of Emerson—the bare facts, without elaboration or explanation. They had the same effect as a series of blows from a hammer. I therefore took it upon myself to add a few words, describing how we became involved with the business and what we had done to investigate it.

Emerson, of course, cut me off before I had half done.

"Enough, Amelia. Well, Carter, you may now express your skepticism and ask the usual idiotic questions. Are we sure the objects are fraudulent? How do we know the seller was not David? Have we—"

"No, sir," Howard said firmly. "If you say they are fakes, then I take your word. D'you know, I couldn't help wondering. I knew Abdullah pretty well—not as well as you, but I'd be likely to know if he had been involved in the antiquities game. I never had the slightest hint of such a thing. I should have known it wasn't true."

I got up from my chair and put my arms around Howard and gave him an affectionate hug. "Thank you."

Howard turned red with pleasure and pale with alarm—for he was only too well aware of my husband's jealous temperament. Emerson said only, "Hmph."

I had never *really* suspected Howard, and I was delighted to be able to enlist his aid. The theories he put forth were not especially useful, but they testified to his excellent heart.

Howard left us after dinner, with assurances of affection and support and a promise to stop for a longer visit at a later time. After a quiet evening with our dearest friends we parted for the night, with no forebodings of the tragedy drawing inexorably nearer.

Having "wasted" three days Emerson was wild to get back to the dig. He had us up at the crack of dawn. Cyrus and Katherine meant to spend the day in Cairo, so we let them sleep, though why Emerson's loud demands for haste did not rouse them I do not know. We were off soon after sunrise. Greatly as I had enjoyed the interval of amiable social intercourse and communion with friends, it was sheer delight to be abroad in the fresh morning air. We took the road along the cultivation (Emerson refused to allow me to get any closer to the Giza pyramids); the smooth ripples of the river were pink-tinged by reflected sunrise, and waterfowl splashed in the irrigation ditches. Nefret's high spirits demanded an outlet; she challenged Ramses to a race, and the two of them set off at a run. Our pace was slightly more sedate, but only slightly; I was mounted on David's lovely mare Asfur, and she moved like the bird after which she was named.

Increasing my pleasure was the prospect of another visit to the interior of our pyramid. Under Emerson's direction the men had braced the stones in the shaft above the passageway. In fact, I was fairly sure Emerson had carried out this hazardous task with his own hands, since he had come home one day with a mashed thumb which he vainly attempted to conceal from me. He was eager to try out his latest toy, a new and powerful electric torch which had been one of the Vandergelts's gifts to him. (Honesty compels me to admit that it was American-made.)

We were there so early that our men had not yet arrived, which of course made Emerson grumble and revert to his threat of camping on site. I assured him I would think seriously about it. (I had.) Nefret said she would like to have a look below, since Ramses had not found her any more bones, and then Ramses said he would go along too. He would have preceded the rest of us had I not demanded the support of his arm.

"Your father is quite capable of looking after Nefret in the event of an emergency," I said. "Have you any reason to expect something of the sort?"

"Only the fact that we have had several already. The site has

been left unguarded." He hesitated for a moment and then said,
"There were signs of the presence of a horse. Fresh signs."

"Surely not hoofprints in this sand."

"No."

"Oh. Well, I cannot imagine an enemy could arrange a trap
your father would not detect immediately."

The passage ahead looked like a lightning storm, as Emerson
flashed his splendid new light wildly from side to side. We
caught him and Nefret up and he turned a radiant face to me.
"Excellent. We must have a dozen more of them, eh? I wonder if
the beam will reach all the way down to the bottom of the shaft.
It's almost twenty feet now."

Selim had replaced the windlass that had been destroyed by
the rockfall, and the wooden cage hung empty from the supporting ropes. Emerson leaned over the edge and shone his torch
down into the depths.

Ramses's vision is as keen as his hearing. He breathed out a
single word. Before any of the rest of us could move, he kicked
the bar aside and leaped onto the cage. It went down like a plum-
met, and Ramses with it.

Reason told me he would not crash to the bottom, since the
length of the rope had been carefully measured. Reason did not
prevent me from letting out an involuntary cry. Emerson let out
a flood of bad language and jumped for the spinning handle of
the windlass. By sheer brute strength he managed to stop the rope
unwinding; but by that time most of it was already in the shaft,
and Ramses was at the bottom.

A light appeared below. It was the beam of the candle Ramses
carried in his pocket, and it illumined the chair frame and a huddled, featureless shape beside it.

There could be no doubt that the shape was that of a human
body, or the remains of one. If the individual had fallen clear from
the top, there was little chance he had survived, but I clung to
the hope that he had been partway down before he lost his hold.
I believed—how could I have assumed otherwise?—that some
poor deluded villager had penetrated the burial place of the pharaoh by night as his ancestors had done, in a search for treasure.

I do not know precisely when the truth began to dawn. Perhaps it was Ramses's rigid pose as he knelt beside the crumpled
form. He had placed his candle on the floor beside him. His body
was in shadow; the glow illumined only his motionless hands.
When he spoke he pitched his voice low. It came up the hollow

shaft like a series of groans, with long intervals between the words.

"Get something . . . to cover her. I'll . . . bring her up."

"Her," Emerson repeated. "Ramses. Who . . ."

He told us. "She's dead."

"Are you sure?" I asked.

"Yes. God, yes."

"Call out when you are ready," Emerson said. He gave me the torch and grasped the handle of the windlass.

Ramses removed his coat and bent over the body. Nefret was already running up the sloping passage that led to the surface.

The girl was—had been—small and slight, but only Emerson's phenomenal strength could have raised her weight and that of Ramses. When I moved to help him he grunted at me to get out of his way. Nefret came back, carrying one of the rugs from the shelter. She reached out to steady the cage and its burden, and Ramses swung himself onto level ground.

His coat concealed the head and the upper part of the body, but it was not long enough to cover the torn skirt or the small scarred boots. It was Ramses who lifted the half-shrouded form onto the rug and folded the sides over to cover it, but when he would have raised the pathetic bundle Emerson put a firm hand on his shoulder.

"I'll take her from here," he said gruffly. "Damnation, my boy, you are only human!"

Ramses turned his face toward the wall. I unhooked the flask of brandy and handed it to Nefret. We left them together, her arm round his bowed shoulders.

**I was an object of interest to the women of the tribes, who
seemed fascinated by my golden hair and fair skin . . .**

They did not remain below for long. Ramses was himself again,
his countenance no more expressive than that of the Sphinx; but
when he saw me kneeling by the roll of carpet he caught me by
the shoulders and pulled me away. "No, Mother. Don't. Not here,
and not now."

"And not you, Aunt Amelia," said Nefret.

Ramses turned to face her. "Nor you, Nefret. What are you
trying to prove—that *you* are more than human?"

"I have done my share of autopsies and dissections," Nefret
said steadily. "How did she die?"

"Take your choice. Fractured skull, shattered spinal cord, broken neck, pelvis, ribs . . ."

Emerson breathed out a string of curses. I said, "The face?"

"You would not care to see it."

"Then how can you be certain of her identity?"

After a long moment Ramses said, "Trust you to think of that,
Mother. I fear there can be little doubt. The hair was the same,
and the clothing."

"Especially the boots," Nefret said in a cold, dry voice. She
was looking down at the foot I had exposed. "They were specially

made for her in London. I doubt many women could get them on. I certainly could not. She was proud of her tiny feet."

We were no longer alone. Selim and Daoud, Ali and Hassan, had come; at a little distance, huddled together and watching in silence, were the local men we had hired.

"Enough of this," said Emerson, in the quiet voice no one ignored or disobeyed. "Selim, as you see, a sad accident has occurred."

Selim's wide dark eyes were fixed on the single small boot I had uncovered before Ramses pulled me away. "Is it the young American lady? God be merciful! How did it happen? What was she doing here?"

"It was an accident," Emerson repeated. "There was no negligence on your part or that of anyone else. Her brother must be sent for, and we must make arrangements to remove the—to remove her. Can you find a cart or wagon, Selim? It is not very dignified, but—"

"But it is better than some of the alternative methods of transport," said Ramses coolly. "As for Jack, it won't be necessary to send for him. He's come looking for us. Interesting. I wonder why? He cannot be aware of what has happened."

Nefret gasped, "Head him off, for heaven's sake! He mustn't see her."

She ran toward the approaching rider. I pulled the rug over the small boot and went after her. The news must be broken gently and the poor young man prevented from viewing the sad sight until he had had time to accept the truth.

We were all together, waiting, when Jack reined up, pulling the unfortunate horse back on its haunches. He flung himself from the saddle. Pushing past Nefret, he caught Ramses by the front of his shirt.

"Where is she? What have you done with her?"

He was several inches shorter than Ramses, but quite a bit bulkier, and he was very angry. Ramses did not move. Looking down his nose at Jack's red, distorted face, he said, "You had better explain what you mean."

"She's gone, that's what I mean! Last night! And you have the goddamned gall to stand there pretending you didn't . . . What the devil have you done? Where did you leave her?"

Ramses freed himself from the other man's grasp with a single sweep of his arm. "Control yourself," he said sharply. "I don't know where you got the idea that Maude and I were together last night; it's not true, but that is not important now. There is bad news, Reynolds. The worst kind of news."

"Worst kind? I don't understand." His eyes moved in bewilderment from Ramses to the tear-streaked face of Nefret. "Are you telling me . . . Are you telling me she's dead?"

"I am sorry," Ramses said.

Men are, I suppose, comprehensible only to other men. I certainly would not have expected a newly bereaved and affectionate brother to relieve his feelings with vulgar violence, but Ramses must have anticipated the movement; he twisted aside so that the blow Jack had aimed at his face only grazed his cheek. Emerson started forward with a loud expletive, but the fight, if it could be called that, was over almost as soon as it had begun. Jack's second wild blow gave Ramses the opportunity he wanted. His hands snapped into place with clinical precision, bending the other man's arm back and forcing him to his knees.

"Now, Mr. Reynolds, that is quite enough of that," I said sternly. "Tragic duties lie before you; face them like a man!"

My admonition had the desired effect; the firm but kindly tone struck chords of memory and of duty. Jack's burly shoulders sagged.

"Yes, ma'am," he muttered.

The frozen calm of acceptance had replaced the frenzy of disbelief. His time of greatest suffering lay ahead, but for the moment he moved and spoke like an automaton. He asked if he might see his sister and accepted my emphatic negative with no more than a dull stare. I was administering sips of brandy from my flask when I saw another person approaching, this time on donkeyback. It was Karl von Bork, come, as he explained, to see what we were doing and lend a hand if we needed one.

"Aber," he went on, his happy smile fading as he looked at Jack, mute, white-faced and swaying, and at our grave faces. "Aber, was ist's? What has happened?"

So I had to explain again. The story was beginning to sound like the wildest sort of fiction; I could hardly believe myself that it was true. Sentimental, tender-hearted Karl was so affected he did not think to ask uncomfortable questions, such as why the girl had come there and what had prompted her brother to follow her. Tears trickled from his soft brown eyes and dampened his mustache. I would have given *him* a sip of brandy, but when I took the flask I discovered Jack had emptied it.

"I can't stand much more of this," Emerson remarked in a

conversational tone. "Von Bork, stop blubbering and be a man. We need your assistance."

Karl wiped his eyes with the back of his hand and snapped to attention. I almost expected him to salute, but he did not.

"Ja, Herr Professor! Entschuldigen Sie, Frau Professor! I am your obedient servant, as always."

I was able to arrange matters in the most convenient and merciful fashion. Nefret and I arranged the crumpled body in a more seemly posture, for I had detected the first signs of rigor mortis. That meant that death had occurred at some hour in the early morning. It was not possible to be more exact, nor was the knowledge of much assistance. We did not linger over the unpleasant task, and it was not long before the donkey-drawn cart Selim had found set off for Giza with an escort of several of our men. Jack rode behind it; Karl trotted alongside Jack, looking a bit absurd on his little donkey, but full of sympathy and the desire to be of use. He assured me, in his high-flown Germanic fashion, that he would not leave "meinen Freund Jack" until someone relieved him.

Nefret had insisted on going with them. She was medically trained and she was a woman—in both capacities she could be of use, she claimed, and who was I to deny it? I promised I would come as soon as I could.

We returned to the shelter, and Emerson said, "Another day lost, curse it! We won't get any work out of those fellows today."

He referred to the local men we had hired; they had gathered in a group some distance away and were smoking and talking in low voices. The glances they kept shooting in our direction supported Emerson's pessimistic appraisal.

I knew, of course, that Emerson's offhand manner was only his way of hiding his real feelings, but I felt obliged to utter a gentle remonstrance. "How can you suppose that any of us are capable of going on with our work, Emerson? It would be callous in the extreme."

"Hmph," said Emerson. His brilliant blue eyes softened as he bent them upon his son. "Er—all right, are you, my boy?"

"Quite, sir. Thank you."

Ramses stood looking down at the bare ground, where the sand was disturbed and slightly indented. "There was very little blood," he said in a remote voice.

"Damnation," Emerson growled. "I was afraid of that." He

raised his voice in a reverberant shout. "Selim! Send the men home and come here, you and Daoud."

"Please," I said.

"Please, curse it!" Emerson roared.

Selim joined us, with Daoud close on his heels. Daoud's heart was as large as his body; Maude had never responded to his gestures of friendship, but Daoud loved all small young creatures of all species, and his honest face was a mask of distress. At Emerson's gesture they squatted on the rug beside us, in the position they found most comfortable, and Selim said soberly, "The men are worried, Father of Curses. They ask how could this have happened?"

"That is what we would like to know, Selim. It must have happened last night. Her brother is not the most conscientious of guardians, but he would surely have noticed her absence if she had not been at home last evening. What was she doing here alone in the dark?"

"Oh, Emerson, don't waste time discussing implausible, not to say impossible, theories," I exclaimed. "There is only one explanation that makes sense."

Emerson was filling his pipe. He put it down on the table (spilling tobacco all over the surface) and took my hand. "For once, my dear, I will not scold you for jumping to conclusions. I fear you are correct."

"All the same," said Ramses, "we had better examine the other possibilities, if only for the purpose of disposing of them. You may be certain they will be raised by others."

"An accident," Selim said, without much hope.

"It is possible, you know. The result of a wager or challenge." Ramses took a tin of cigarettes from his pocket. It was symptomatic of his state of mind that he neglected to ask my permission to smoke. He went on, "Maude and her set were playing a game of that sort one night a few weeks ago—daring one another to do various hazardous and pointless things. If Geoffrey and I had not restrained him, Jack, who had taken rather too much to drink, would have attempted to climb the Great Pyramid, in the dark and without assistance, in order to place the American flag on the summit. An investigative officer might be persuaded to believe Maude had come here to prove her 'pluck,' especially after . . ."

He paused to light his cigarette, and I said helpfully, "Especially after she had—what is the slang? I cannot keep up with it!—funked it that other time."

"In the middle of the night, alone?" Emerson demanded.

"I agree it is out of the question," Ramses said. "But accident is a more socially acceptable verdict than suicide."

"Suicide?" Emerson repeated in an incredulous voice. "Good Gad, what possible reason could she have for ending her life, a young, healthy, wealthy girl like that?"

"None," I said. "Morbid mental instability may lead an otherwise healthy individual to commit such an act, but she was not that sort. I will not entertain such a notion for a moment. It was murder. She was dead when she was thrown down the shaft. A fall of that sort would account for a fractured skull or broken neck, or any other kind of fatal injury. Ramses said there was very little blood."

"It is the only possible answer," Emerson said, fingering the dent in his chin. "And it explains why she was brought here."

"Not entirely," Ramses said. He started and dropped his cigarette. It had burned down to his fingers. "I appreciate your tactful efforts to leave me out of this, but we had better face the facts. She could have been dropped from a height anywhere along the plateau if the murderer's sole motive was to hide the nature of the injury that killed her. Bringing her to this out-of-the-way place inevitably involves us—me, to be precise. No matter what the verdict, my name will certainly come into it. If it was an accident, she may have been trying to overcome her fear of the place in order to make me think better of her. If it was suicide, some will believe she was driven to despair by rejection, or even by—" He had done his best to be cool and dispassionate, but he could not quite manage this. The dark eyes that were so often half-veiled by lowered lids and long lashes met mine in direct appeal. "It's not true, Mother," he said desperately. "You heard what Jack said—you know what he accused me of. I don't care what he thinks, so long as you believe me."

His appeal had been to *me*. It was *my* understanding he sought. Some mothers would have gone to him, embraced him, murmured affectionate—and useless!—words of comfort. In all candor I must admit that I was strongly moved to do just that. I knew Ramses would not like it, though.

"I believe you, my dear. Even if it were true—I know it is not, but even if it were—any woman who is fool enough to end her life on account of a man has only herself to blame."

"Oh, Mother!" His rare, unguarded smile illumined his face. "You have an aphorism for any occasion."

Emerson cleared his throat noisily and picked up his pipe. "Bloody waste of time, all this," he grumbled. "No one could possibly suspect—"

"Some of them will, though," Ramses said. "All the old cats in Cairo, of both sexes, are ready to believe the worst of a woman like Maude—young, pleasure-loving, undisciplined. Whether the verdict is murder, suicide or accident, the assumption will be that a man was responsible."

"Knowing the old cats of Cairo as I do, I fear you are right," I said with a sigh. "But let us not cross any more bridges until we come to them. We must get home; I told Nefret I would come as soon as I could. Selim, will you and Daoud come back with us? You may be of assistance."

"Aywa, Sitt Hakim, we will come and do what we can. It is a sad thing."

"Ramses," said his father, "how did you know she was down there? Oh, damnation, I didn't mean that the way it sounded. I only wondered what prompted you to jump for the rope. I couldn't see a thing."

Ramses reached into his pocket and pulled out a fragment of cloth. It was gold tissue, delicate as chiffon. "This was caught on a point of rock. It had been torn from the scarf we gave her."


As I had predicted, the investigation of Maude Reynolds's death was a travesty. Why put those concerned through the torment of a postmortem when the cause of death was obvious?

This was the question posed to me by Mr. Gordon, the American Consul, when I went to him to protest the proceedings, or the absence thereof. When I replied that it might be useful to discover whether she had been under the influence of drugs or alcohol at the time, or whether any of the bruises could have been made by human hands, or whether—

He cut me off with a shocked exclamation before I could go on, which was probably just as well, since my next suggestion would have shocked him even more. A complete medical examination would have cleared the poor girl's name. I did not believe Maude had been enceinte, but half of Cairo society did—the old cats, as Ramses had called them. It would have been useless to point out to them that the old-fashioned attitudes of their youth had changed—and thank God for it, in my opinion! A modern, wealthy young woman was not likely to take her life out of shame, or because there were no other ways out of that particular dilemma.

So Cairo gossiped and whispered—for a week. No scandal lasted much longer, there were always new sources of entertainment. Maude was laid to rest in the Protestant cemetery in Old Cairo. Walled all round, it was a pretty spot, filled with trees and imported shrubs, so that it resembled a village churchyard in England. The funeral was well attended and Jack was a picture of manly fortitude as he cast the first handful of dirt into the grave.

The verdict had been accidental death.

For the living, the pain had just begun. Whether Jack knew what was being said of his sister I could not tell. He would have been helpless to deny it, since not even the worst of the scandalmongers would have dared say it to his face. He had come out of his stupor of grief and was in a dangerous state of mind, sticking close to his house and, I was told, drinking heavily.

His friends, of whom I counted myself one, were relieved to know that Geoffrey had moved into the house and was staying with him. A few days after the burial the young Englishman sent a message to ask if he might see me. I responded at once, inviting him to tea that same afternoon, for I was anxious to be of help.

Upon my return from the dig I bustled about ordering special dainties and trying to make the ambience as pleasant as possible, for I had a feeling he might be in need of comfort. I was correct as usual. I would be the first to admit that the maternal instinct is not one of my most notable characteristics, but I daresay any woman would have been moved by the sight of the young fellow. His refined features were drawn and there was a hint of pallor under his tan. Sinking into a chair, he let his head fall back against the cushions.

"How good you are to have me, Mrs. Emerson. I feel better just being here. You have made the place a home."

"Its charm is due in large part to you, Geoffrey. I always say there is nothing like a garden to rest the soul. Your plants are flourishing, you see. It was a particularly thoughtful gesture for which I will always be grateful. What do you take in your tea?"

"Nothing, thank you." He leaned forward to receive the cup from my hand. His eyes moved round the enclosure; I suspected it was not the blooming plants and twining vines that drew his attention.

"Nefret will be here in a moment," I said.

His cheeks took on a warmer hue. "Not much escapes you, Mrs. Emerson. Though it was not my primary reason for asking to see you, perhaps I should take advantage of these moments alone to assure you that I have no intention of behaving in an underhanded manner with regard to Miss Forth."

Concealing my amusement at his formality, I assured *him* I would never harbor such suspicions.

"Not that I've had the opportunity," he said with a rueful smile. "I care for her very much, Mrs. Emerson. Her beauty would attract any man, but it was not until I had learned to know her and appreciate her unique qualities of mind and spirit, that my feelings developed as they have. If I believed she reciprocated them, I would ask the Professor's permission to pay my addresses."

"You think she does not?"

"She thinks of me as a friend, I believe. That is an honor I cherish for its own sake. She knows how I feel. I told her that I stood ready to be of service to her at any time and in any way, and that I would ask nothing of her except her good opinion. I hope for more, of course. I will never abandon hope, but rest assured I will not press my attentions upon her."

"In Nefret's case that would be a serious mistake," I said. "Your feelings and your behavior do you credit, Geoffrey."

Nefret soon joined us. Observing her warm but unselfconscious greeting, I concluded he (and I) had been correct in our assessment of her feelings for him.

As I had suspected, it was concern for Jack Reynolds that had prompted Geoffrey's visit.

"I don't know what to do," he confessed, brushing back a lock of fair hair that had fallen over his brow. "It is natural he should grieve for Maude—they were very close—but I had hoped he'd show signs of improvement by now. Instead he is sinking deeper into depression and despair. Mr. Fisher talks of starting work in earnest next week, and Mr. Reisner will be back before the end of the month, and he will expect us to have accomplished a great deal, and—and if Jack goes on at this rate, he won't be fit for work of any kind, much less the exacting schedule Mr. Reisner demands of his people."

"Mr. Reisner is not a monster," I said. "He will understand that Jack needs time to recover from his loss."

"How much time, though? Hard work is the best medicine for grief; I'm sure you are of that opinion, Mrs. Emerson, and I would have expected Jack to feel the same. This isn't like him. He's always been so strong. I can't help wondering . . ."

He broke off. "If there is something else tormenting him?" I prompted. "Some deeper, darker sentiment than simple grief?"

Geoffrey stared at me with respectful amazement. "How did you know?"

"Aunt Amelia knows everything," Nefret said. "You cannot shock or surprise her, so stop beating about the bush. You've been with Jack almost constantly. He must have dropped some hint."

"It is so unreasonable, so unfair—"

"He isn't satisfied that Maude's death was an accident," Nefret said. "That isn't unreasonable. We're not satisfied either. Does Jack have any particular suspicions?"

The young man's shoulders slumped. "Yes. That's really why I came. I felt I must warn Ramses—"

"What about?" The query came, not from one of us, but from Ramses himself, who had apparently materialized out of thin air, in that uncanny way of his. I deduced he had been in the work area washing pottery fragments, for his shirtsleeves were rolled above the elbows.

"I didn't know you were here, Godwin," he went on, taking a chair. "Haven't seen you since the funeral. Warn me about what?"

"Don't pretend you were not listening to the conversation," I said, pouring tea.

"I couldn't help overhearing some of it. What is Jack saying about me?" He took the cup from my hand and settled back, crossing one leg over the other.

"He's beside himself," Geoffrey muttered. "He's not responsible."

"You mean he's drunk most of the time," Ramses corrected. "In vino veritas—what he takes to be veritas, anyhow. Does he still believe I cold-bloodedly seduced his sister and . . . And then what?"

"And murdered her!" As soon as the words left his mouth Geoffrey looked as if he wanted to take them back. Ramses's affectation of callousness had angered him (as it may have been designed to do). Turning impulsively to me, he exclaimed, "Mrs.

Emerson, forgive me! I didn't intend to blurt it out that way. Jack is insane with grief and guilt. When he's in his right mind he knows better, but just now he's not in his right mind, and I'm afraid he may do something he would later regret."

"Something I would also regret?" Ramses inquired. "Has he threatened me?"

"More than threatened." Geoffrey passed a trembling hand over his face. "One night last week he took out that pair of pistols he's so proud of, and cleaned and loaded them."

"Revolvers," Ramses said absently. "The Colts."

"If you say so. I take no interest in such things. I hate firearms. It made me a little sick to watch him rub and polish them, as if he were caressing the confounded things. Finally he shoved both of them into his belt and started for the door. I asked where he was going, and he said . . . I can't repeat the words, not in the presence of ladies; the gist of it was that he was going after the villain who murdered his sister. He's a good deal stronger than I am, and he was beyond reason just then, but I got to the door ahead of him, turned the key, and removed it."

"How frightfully courageous," Ramses said. Nefret gave him a reproachful look.

Geoffrey shrugged. "Not especially. I knew he wouldn't use a weapon on me. If he'd been able to get close enough he'd have knocked me flat, but I made sure he didn't. It was rather pathetic and quite ridiculous—me skipping and ducking and Jack lumbering after me like a great clumsy bear. He wore himself out eventually, and I was able to get the weapons away from him. I did it for his sake as much as yours."

"Yes, of course. Well," Ramses drawled, "I'll have to do something about this, won't I? For Jack's sake."

"Stop talking like a fool, Ramses," I said sharply. "If you are thinking of marching over there and confronting Jack, you can dismiss the idea. The main thing is to stop him drinking. Leave it to me."

"Now?" Geoffrey exclaimed, his eyes widening as I put on my hat and removed my parasol from the hook near the door. "Alone?" he added, his eyes widening even more when neither of the others moved from their chairs.

"Certainly. I won't be long."

I always like to settle such matters as soon as they come to my attention, for procrastination is inefficient. In this case immediate action was advisable; it was still early and Jack had not had time to drink enough to render him beyond reason. Rather than risk a denial, I did not send in my card but proceeded directly to the sitting room, where the servant had told me I would find his master.

The sight of that once bright and cheerful chamber confirmed Geoffrey's pessimistic assessment. There was now no mistress in the house; the poor little old aunt (whose name I never did learn) had been so overcome by the tragedy that Jack had sent her home. Human nature being what it is, servants usually do no more than is demanded of them, and it was obvious that Jack demanded very little. Dusty sand covered every article of furniture, the floors had not been swept for days, and a strange unpleasant smell hung about the room. Jack had not changed from his working clothes. He sat slumped in a chair with his dusty boots on the table and a glass in his hand and a bottle on the table next to his boots. When he caught sight of me he moved so abruptly that he knocked the bottle over.

"That is a good start," I said, retrieving the bottle. Enough had spilled to make a reeking puddle, but there was quite a quantity left. Carrying it to the window, I poured the rest out onto the ground.

I will not bore the Reader with a detailed description of my subsequent actions. It did not take long to go through the house and confiscate several other bottles, with Jack following after me expostulating and protesting. I did not suppose I had found them all, and of course he could easily get more; it was the dramatic impact I counted upon. Having thus got his attention, I sat him down in the parlor and spoke to him gently but firmly, as his own mother might have done.

I moved him to tears; he bowed his head and hid his face in his hands. I administered an encouraging pat on the back and prepared to take my leave. Wondering if I dared attempt to confiscate his weapons as well as his whiskey, I took hold of the handle of the guncase and tugged. It was locked.

Jack looked up and I said calmly, "I am glad to find you keep dangerous weapons secure, Jack. You don't leave the key lying about, I hope."

"No. No, ma'am. I have been very careful about that, after one of them was stolen. It was one of the Colts, a forty-five caliber—"

"That is all right, then," I said, for I did not want to hear a lecture on weapons. What I had wanted to know was where he kept the key, but neither by gesture nor word had he indicated the answer to that.

"Good-bye, then, for now," I continued. "I trust in your promise of reformation, Jack. You are too fine a man to succumb to this weakness. If you are tempted, remember those angelic presences that even now watch over you; and come to me, at any time, if you are in need of earthly consolation."

Or words to that effect.

I was reasonably certain I had made Jack see the injustice of his suspicions of Ramses. Others were not so easily dealt with. Stories of Maude's involvement with various young men sprang up like noxious weeds, but there was no doubt that the name most often mentioned was that of my son. Apparently the poor wretched girl had made no secret of her infatuation. As young girls will, she had confided in her friends, and they had confided in their brothers and their fiancés and their mamas.

I heard none of this firsthand. My connections with British officials and their ladies were few, and the most venomous of the latter would not have dared mention the subject to *me*. It was Nefret who told me what was being said, and I had to force it out of her. I happened to be in the courtyard the afternoon she returned from a luncheon party, and one look at her stormy face was enough; I intercepted her when she would have started toward her room and made her come and sit with me.

She was one of those girls who really did look very pretty when she was angry; her eyes flashed and her cheeks took on a wild-rose blush. They matched the gown she was wearing that afternoon and the silk roses that adorned her elegant hat. The only discordant notes were her gloveless hands and the scraped knuckles on the right one. When she saw me staring at it she tried to hide it under her full skirts.

"Dear me," I said. "How did you do that?"

"I . . . uh . . . Would you believe me if I said I caught my hand in the carriage door?"

"No."

Nefret burst out laughing and gave me a quick hug. "I did, though. Did you think I was so unladylike as to punch another young lady on the jaw?"

"Yes."

"I was sorely tempted. Why do you suppose I went to that stupid woman's stupid little party? I wanted to know what they were saying about us. I knew some of them wouldn't be able to resist tormenting me—they think they're so *clever*, with their in-nuendoes and sly hints and pursed lips and sidelong looks! I was in complete control of myself until Alice Framington-French said she soooo admired Ramses for keeping a stiff upper lip after his *tragic loss*, and I said we all missed Maude, we had been very fond of her, and she said, well, but that was a bit *different*, wasn't it, and *really* couldn't I persuade Ramses it was time he settled down and stopped breaking hearts, that was a sister's role, wasn't it—oh, but of course he wasn't *really* my brother, was he, and then she and Sylvia Gorst exchanged one of *those* looks . . ."

She stopped to catch her breath. Nefret's way of talking in italics intensified as she became angrier. I was neither surprised nor angry—not very. No one has a nastier imagination than a well-bred lady. One must learn not to care what such people are thinking and saying or one will be in a perpetual state of agitation.

I said as much to Nefret, who nodded glumly. She took the pins out of her hat and began fanning herself vigorously with it. "I did *not* hit her. I just curled my lip and said yes, it was a pity *she* hadn't been able to catch Ramses year before last, she certainly pursued him hard enough, though not as hard as *Sylvia*, and then I thanked her for a *delightful* luncheon and stalked out and when I got in the carriage I slammed the door on my hand."

A noise like that of a cannon firing sounded without. I did not suppose I would ever become accustomed to the volume and spontaneity of Narmer's barking. He had a perfectly astounding voice for a dog his size; one was reminded of blasted heaths and spectral hounds.

"Someone is coming," Nefret said unnecessarily, while I dabbed at the tea I had spilled on my shoe. She was always trying to convince me of Narmer's usefulness as a watchdog.

"The Vandergelts are coming to dinner," I replied. "Go and tell that dog to behave itself, Nefret; you and Ramses are the only ones he will listen to. Last time the Vandergelts came he jumped all over Katherine and knocked her hat off."

Nefret hurried to obey, but my concern had been unnecessary; the barking cut off as if by a knife, and the door opened to admit the Vandergelts, and Ramses.

"We saw Ramses at the train station and brought him on with us," Katherine explained.

I turned my attention to my son, of whose absence from the

house I had not been aware until that moment. "You went to Cairo this evening?"

"Yes. I had an errand. Mrs. Vandergelt, won't you take this chair? It hasn't quite so many cat hairs as the others."

"Where is Horus?" Cyrus inquired. It could not be said that he got on any better with the cat than the rest of us, but he took an interest since Horus had fathered the kittens of the Vandergelts's cat Sekhmet. She had once belonged to us but had adapted quite happily to the pampered life she led at the Castle.

"In my room, I expect," Nefret said. "I'll go see, and change out of this frock."

"You might just look in at Emerson and tell him our guests are here," I called after her.

When Nefret reappeared she was wearing a blue shot-silk tea gown she had purchased in Paris at a price that had made me blink. She could well afford as many expensive gowns as she liked, and this one was particularly becoming; it deepened the blue of her eyes and had the lines only a top-flight designer can create. The effect that evening was marred by the bulky shape of Horus, who was hanging over her shoulder, his large hindquarters resting comfortably in the curve of her arm.

Emerson soon joined us and we settled down to catch up on the news. There was no one with whom we could be as comfortable as the Vandergelts. Before long Emerson was smoking his pipe and Cyrus his cheroot, and various masculine garments were strewn about the furniture. Ramses had removed his coat, tie and collar as soon as he entered the house, and Cyrus had been persuaded to follow his example. Emerson, as I hardly need say, had not had them on to begin with. Nefret had put Horus on the floor by the sofa, over his loud protests, so she could sit cross-legged as she preferred.

The Vandergelts had recently returned from a brief trip by dahabeeyah to Medum and Dahshur. They had decided to remain on board instead of returning to us, and I did not argue with them since I know one is more comfortable in one's own quarters. Emerson wanted to talk about Dahshur, but I put an end to that; there was still no hope we could get that site, and it was only rubbing salt in our wounds to discuss it. I knew Katherine was anxious to hear about the tragedy; they had left Cairo the day after our frightful discovery and had missed the funeral.

"I felt a little guilty about not attending," she said. "But we

scarcely knew the poor girl and we had already made our arrangements to sail."

"Why should you feel guilty?" Emerson demanded. "Funer-
als are a waste of time. You needn't bother attending mine. I
won't give a curse."

"How do you know you won't?" Cyrus asked.

Emerson does not at all mind being teased by Cyrus, for they
are the best of friends, but I did mind listening to my husband's
unorthodox opinions on the subject of religion—again. I had
heard them quite often. His eyes shone wickedly and his lips
parted . . .

"You were not missed," I said, cutting Emerson off with the
expertise of long practice. "There was a large attendance."

"All staring and nudging one another like tourists at a monument," Emerson growled. "Most of the people who attended
didn't even know the girl. Ghouls!"

Katherine looked from me to Nefret, who was staring fixedly
at the cat, to Ramses, perched on the edge of the fountain. "If
you would rather not discuss the subject, I understand," she said.
"But that is what friends are for, you know—to listen and perhaps offer useful advice."

"Doggone right!" Cyrus exclaimed. "We'd both feel real insulted if you didn't let us in on things like you've always done
before. That poor girl's death was no accident, don't tell me it
was, and you folks are in trouble because of it, don't tell me you
aren't. How can we help?"

Emerson heaved a sigh so deep, a button popped off his shirt;
Nefret looked up with a smile; and I said, "Ramses, if you will
be so good—pass round the whiskey!"

I brought our friends up-to-date on the circumstances surrounding Maude's death and the events that had followed. They
were not as indignant as I about the failure to conduct a postmortem. "It's more than likely they wouldn't have found anything to prove it was murder, anyhow," Cyrus said shrewdly.
"Even a bullet hole or a knife wound would be hard to see if the
injuries were that extensive."

"Death most probably resulted from the blow on the back of
her head," Ramses said. "It would have been difficult to prove it
was caused by the conventional blunt instrument rather than the
side of the shaft."

"You didn't tell us that," Nefret exclaimed. "How do you
know?"

"I can't be certain. But I've been thinking about it, trying to remember details. I told you there was very little blood on her clothing and on the rock surface. That suggests that she had been dead for some time when she was thrown into the shaft. The only area of extensive bleeding was on the back of her head. Her hair had been saturated."

"So she was struck from behind," I said. "At least it was mercifully quick and virtually painless. Can we deduce that if she turned her back on her killer he was someone she knew and trusted?" I answered my own question before Ramses or Emerson could beat me to it. "Not necessarily. He might have lurked in hiding and caught her unawares."

"But surely only someone she knew could have persuaded her to leave the house in the dead of night," Katherine said. "One must assume the attack did not take place in her room. Her brother would have noticed the—er—evidence."

"Well reasoned, Mrs. Vandergelt," said Ramses. "According to Jack, she had dined with him and retired at her usual hour. It was not until the following morning he realized she was gone and that her bed had not been slept in. There is no doubt but that she left the house of her own free will. One of the doors was unbolted and unlocked. Either someone roused her or she had arranged a meeting in advance—probably the latter, since she had changed her evening frock for riding clothes and had not gone to bed."

"So when Mr. Reynolds found her missing he came hunting for you," Katherine said. "Why? Don't look at me in that accusing fashion, Amelia, just think about it. The lady must have had a number of admirers; she was young, attractive and rich. This season her fancy seems to have fallen on Ramses. I don't mean to embarrass you, Ramses dear—"

"No," Ramses said. "That is—uh—I see what you are getting at, Mrs. Vandergelt, and I—uh—"

"You didn't suppose I had the sense to think of it?" She smiled affectionately. "I know you, you see; I feel certain your behavior in private and in public was exemplary. Why should her brother immediately suspect *you* of luring her away—for purposes of seduction, one must assume?"

Emerson swallowed noisily. "Good Gad, Katherine, what a cynic you are. You think someone put the idea into Reynolds's head?"

"It's a rather thick head, isn't it?" Katherine said calmly. "He hasn't much imagination or originality. And that scenario is so outrageously out of character for Ramses that no sensible person would entertain the notion for a moment."

"Thank you," Ramses said, very quietly.

"None of us entertained it," I assured him. "It is very kind of you to reassure Ramses, Katherine, but with all respect to your undoubted acumen, I cannot see this gets us any further. Unless you are suggesting that it was a former lover who killed her? And carried her body all that way in the hope of incriminating the man who had replaced him in Maude's affections... Hmmmm."

"Control your outrageous imagination, Amelia," Emerson exclaimed. "If the girl's death were an isolated incident, there might be another motive, but there have been—how many?—three, four other seeming accidents. Curse it, this must be connected with our search for the forger. She knew something—or he thought she did—"

"Accidents," Cyrus interrupted. "What accidents?"

"I suppose," I said musingly, "that the shots fired at me might have been aimed at someone else. Or something else. But there was no game in sight—"

"Shots," Cyrus gasped. He began tugging agitatedly at his goatee. "I ought to be used to you, Amelia, but consarn it, you make my blood run cold sometimes. What shots? When? How many amusing little incidents like that have there been?"

Emerson was disinclined to admit his near fall from the pyramid had been one of the incidents in question, but he was overruled by the rest of us; the ostentatious ostracon must have been placed where it was in order to lead him onto a treacherous stretch.

"The most maddening thing about them," I said, "is that we have no idea why the villain is after us. If we were hot on his trail he might wish to distract or destroy us, but we haven't discovered a single confounded clue as to his identity, and he must be aware of that. A sensible villain (if there can be such a thing) would avoid stirring us up."

Katherine and her husband looked at one another. Cyrus shook his head. Katherine shrugged.

"Are you thinking the same thing I am?" Cyrus demanded of his wife.

"I feel certain I am, Cyrus."

"What are you talking about?" I inquired.

"I don't understand how you could have missed it." Katherine turned back to me. "Could we be mistaken, Cyrus?"

"Durned if I see how, Katherine."

"Confound it!" Emerson shouted. "Vandergelt, are you trying to drive me to distraction with enigmatic hints and unanswered questions? You sound like my wife."

"All right, old buddy," Cyrus said with a grin. "You're off the track, and I'll tell you how. These accidents of yours don't have a blamed thing to do with the forgeries. They were designed for one purpose and one purpose only: Somebody's trying to drive you away from Zawaiet el 'Aryan!"

After an interval that seemed to last longer than it actually did, Emerson said, "Peabody, if you tell me you had already arrived at that theory, I will—I will never take you inside another pyramid!"

"Then I won't tell you, Emerson."

"But Mrs. Vandergelt, that is absolutely brilliant!" Nefret exclaimed. She clapped her hands and jumped to her feet—and trod heavily upon the tail of Horus, who had, I am convinced, spread himself out across as large a space as possible in the hope that someone would trip over him or give him an excuse to complain. He did complain, most vociferously, and attacked Nefret's trailing skirts with his claws. Nefret tried to raise both feet at once, got them tangled in her ruffles, and pitched forward into the arms of Ramses, who had sprung to her assistance. He swung her up out of the cat's reach. Seeing there was no sympathy to be got from Nefret, who was swearing over the rents in her skirts, Horus stormed out of the room, deliberately knocking over a small table and a footstool. Ramses was laughing; affronts to Horus generally cheered him up.

"Well, really, one can hardly blame the girls," Katherine whispered. "Goodness, Amelia, the lad is absolutely séduisant when he smiles!"

"Hmmm," I said. "He is not vain about his looks, I will say that for him. Kindly do not encourage him. Ramses, put her down."

"Yes, Mother."

He deposited Nefret on the sofa, and Emerson said sourly, "One can always count on a bit of comic relief in this house."

Nefret had been examining her ankles. "It might have been worse. You were quick as a cat, Ramses. Thank you."

"It isn't difficult to be quicker than that cat," said Ramses. "If

he gets any fatter we'll have to hire him his own donkey cart."
He caught his father's critical eye and sobered. "Mrs. Vandergelt,
you must think we are utter fools."

"I think," Katherine said, "that you have all been preoccupied
by your affection for David and Abdullah. You have been so intent on the business of the forgeries that you are unable to see
anything else."

"There was the burglary at Amarna House," I said.

Cyrus shook his head. "You can't connect that with the attacks on you here, Amelia. Its purpose was obviously to retrieve
the scarab. If Ramses hadn't interfered, they'd have left without
inflicting a scratch on anybody."

"Curse it!" I exclaimed. "Katherine, you have knocked the
bottom out of all my theories. I had eliminated several of our
suspects because they had alibis for one or another of the attacks.
Howard was in the Delta, Geoffrey was on top—er—that is, he
was with me when the unseen marksman fired his last shots.
They are cleared of wanting to drive us away from the site, but
not of being the forger. We must start all over again!"

Fatima appeared to announce that dinner was served. We
made our way to the dining room and Emerson said, "It's high
time we got David here. Curse it, he's been dawdling around
Crete too long."

"You know that if we had so much as hinted at danger to
any one of us they would have been on the next boat," I said.
"What did Lia say in her last letter, Nefret?"

"She accused me of hiding something from her," Nefret said
glumly. "Don't stare at me in that critical fashion, Aunt Amelia,
I haven't given anything away—and believe me, it's been
damned—excuse me!—very difficult, chattering cheerfully about
things that don't matter and trying to avoid mentioning anything
that might rouse her suspicions!"

"Speaking of the burglary at Amarna House," I began.

"We were not speaking of it," said Emerson. Fatima removed
his empty soup bowl and he said amiably, "Excellent soup, Fatima."

"We were speaking of it earlier," I said, determined not to let
him distract me. "I keep meaning to ask, and I keep forgetting—
so many other things have happened—the soup was excellent,
Fatima. Tell Mahmud."

"Yes, Sitt Hakim. Thank you."

"The burglary," Cyrus said. "I'm durned glad you brought

that up, Amelia, because I have also been curious about it. Why did the fellow take such a risk to get the scarab back? Obviously there was nothing about it that gave you a clue to his identity, or you wouldn't still be in the dark."

The rest of us looked expectantly at Ramses. He did not appreciate the attention. "I don't know the answer," he said shortly.

"It is a pity we didn't photograph the confounded thing," I mused. "But of course we did not anticipate losing it so soon. Do you have a copy of your translation here, Ramses?"

"I didn't write it down, Mother." Eyebrows drawn together, he took up his knife and began sawing at the portion of roast chicken with which he had been served. It was a trifle tough. Egyptian chickens often are.

"You just read it off the way you'd read English, I guess," said Cyrus, with a wry smile and a shake of his head.

"Yes, sir. However," said Ramses, after an appreciable pause, "I did make a copy of the hieroglyphic inscription. Would you care to see it?"

"Who, me?" Cyrus laughed. "No point in that, I can't read more than a few words."

"I would like to see it," I said. "Why didn't you mention you had a copy?"

"No one asked me," said Ramses.

Nefret threw a dinner roll at him.

"Let's have a look at it, then," said Emerson, as Ramses caught the roll and politely handed it back to Nefret.

"Now?" Ramses asked.

"When we have finished eating," I said. "If you and Nefret will stop playing childish games—and in the presence of guests, too!—we will be done all the sooner."

"I beg your pardon, Aunt Amelia," Nefret murmured. She gave Ramses a sidelong grin, however, and his thin lips turned up a bit in response.

While Fatima cleared the table Ramses went to find his copy of the text. We pulled our chairs closer as he spread the crumpled paper out. Unlike his normal handwriting, which rather resembles the amorphous shorthand squiggles of Egyptian demotic writing, Ramses's hieroglyphic hand is neat and easy to read— assuming, of course, that one can read ancient Egyptian. I would be the last to claim that my knowledge of the language is that of an expert, but the first few words were part of a familiar formula.

"Imy-re—er—hmmm," I read aloud. "The overseer of ships,

hereditary prince and count, sole companion. These are the titles of the high official who composed the text, Cyrus."

"Quite right, my dear," said Emerson, audibly amused. He put his hand over mine. "Supposing we let Ramses translate the entire text—without interrupting him."

"An excellent suggestion, Emerson," I replied graciously.

It was certainly an astonishing document. The Egyptians were excellent boatbuilders, and they knew something of astronomy. It was barely conceivable that by following the coastline and putting in to shore periodically to take on fresh supplies, a captain who enjoyed the favor of every god in the extremely extensive pantheon might have accomplished the feat. I didn't believe it, though; and as Ramses's interpolated comments made clear, almost every description in the text was plagiarized from much later sources. The man who had put it together was obviously familiar with those sources and with the Egyptian language.

"There are certain anomalies, however," said Ramses. "For one thing, this text begins with the titles and name of the man who ostensibly composed it. Proper protocol would demand that the date and the king's name and titles precede his. They are here, but they follow the titles of the official, and those titles are not in the order one would expect."

"I see what you mean," Emerson exclaimed. "The chap was a prince and count and sole companion and all the rest; why would he mention his post as overseer of ships before the other, higher titles? Is that significant?"

"If so, the significance eludes me," Ramses said rather snappishly. Vain about his person he was not, but he hated to admit his knowledge of Egyptian could fail, even in such a case as this.

"So the clue," I said, "that might have given us more information was not in the text itself."

Ramses said he had come to the same conclusion, but that the clue must have been minute in size, or concealed with such diabolical skill that he had not seen it. He added that since we no longer had the bloody—excuse me, Mother and Mrs. Vandergelt—the confounded thing, further speculation was a waste of time. With this I was forced to agree.

Since the following day was Friday, the day of rest for our men, Emerson had agreed to escort me to Cairo and spend the night at Shepheard's. He did not want to do this—he never does—and now he seized upon an excuse for calling it off.

"I don't like leaving the children alone, Peabody," he remarked sanctimoniously. "Vandergelt's idea, that someone is trying to prevent us from excavating at Zawaiet—"

"Has not changed the realities of the situation, Emerson," I explained. "They are in no more danger than they ever were, and I believe we can depend on them to take care."

"Quite," said the male "child" forcefully, while the female "child" pursed her lips and rolled her eyes.

"Hmph," said Emerson. "Very well. Er—Nefret, I have a large quantity of notes to be transcribed. It will probably take you most of the day."

"I had planned to go to Atiyah with Ramses," Nefret protested. "Kadija is expecting me."

"You can do that another time. We will be back early Saturday morning ready to get back to work." Observing her sulky expression, he changed his tactics. "I know you think me overly cautious, my dear, but as a favor to me, give me your word you will not stray far from the house tomorrow. Nothing can happen to you here."

Stripped to the waist, sabers in our hands, we faced one another. Ahmed was a hulking brute, his body seamed with the scars of many such encounters, his reach considerably longer than mine. My only hope was to wear him out with my greater agility and defensive skill. Weeping, the girl cried out to me . . .

## From Letter Collection B

*Dear Lia,*

*I don't know whether you will ever receive this—but I must tell someone, now, this instant—I must talk about him to someone—and there's no one here but Horus and he's not a very sympathetic listener, especially considering we put him out of the room last night, and the Professor and Aunt Amelia haven't come back and anyhow I promised I'd wait for him so we can tell them together. It's been less than an hour since he left me. It seems like days. How did you bear those endless weeks and months when you and David were apart? Especially that awful time when you feared you would never be together?*

*Do I sound completely insane? I am! Head over heels, madly, passionately! Perhaps writing it all down will clear my head. I hope you can read this. My hand is as unsteady as my heart.*

*It was all Percy's doing. Isn't that strange? You'd never have supposed a man I detested as much as I did Percy could be responsible for making me so blissfully happy!*

I was alone in our sitting room yesterday afternoon when Percy came calling. Aunt Amelia and the Professor were to spend the night in Cairo—she to indulge in "friendly social intercourse" at Shepheard's, and the Professor to consult someone at the German Institute—and Ramses had gone to Atiyah to talk to Selim about some supplies the Professor wanted. Percy didn't wait to be announced, he came straight up, with Fatima fluttering after him. A brisk knock was my only warning. When I saw him posing on the threshold, with poor Fatima behind him expostulating with him and apologizing to me, I was tempted to throw the inkpot at him.

Why didn't I? Because I was a coward and a fool. A coward because I dreaded what Ramses would say if he ever learned I had betrayed him—a fool because I believed Percy had some of the instincts of a gentleman. Whenever I had happened to run into him, there had been meaningful glances and little nods of understanding and a general air of mutual confidentiality— rather sickening and worrisome, but not threatening. I didn't believe Percy would really tell the truth and shame the devil (i.e., himself); that he would use the threat of self-exposure to blackmail me seemed too ludicrous to contemplate.

So I told Fatima she could go and offered Percy a chair. With a sweeping gesture he offered me a seat—on the divan. He was dressed with that extra smartness that is all wrong somehow—no single detail can be faulted, but all together they are a bit too much.

I remained standing. "I really am rather busy, Percy. What do you want?"

"A cozy little chat." He smirked at me, and then I realized he was drunk. Not drunk enough to stagger or slur his words, just enough to weaken his brain even more.

I dipped into my collection of clichés. "You are not in fit condition to be in the company of a lady."

"A little Dutch courage," Percy mumbled. "Don't be angry, Nefret. I've kept my part of the bargain, haven't I?"

"I don't recall striking a bargain. You had better go before Ramses comes back. I expect him any moment."

Another miscalculation on my part—but honestly, who would have supposed he'd be stupid enough to make the same mistake twice? He called Ramses several rude names, and lunged for me. He had me wrapped in a clumsy but temporarily

*effective bear's hug before I could skip aside. I said irritably,
"Let go of me."*

*"You don't mean that. All you high-spirited women are
alike; what you really want is a man who can master you."*

*I managed to avoid his clumsy attempts to kiss me while I
got one arm free and shifted my weight onto my left foot. I was
trying to decide what part of Percy to hit first, when the sitting
room door opened.*

*I'd lied to Percy; I had not expected Ramses back so soon.
The sight of him paralyzed me, and Percy managed to land a
kiss on my mouth. The next thing I knew there was a kind of
soundless explosion. It lifted Percy clean off his feet and sent
him flying, over a chair and against the wall; I stumbled back
and would have lost my balance if Ramses hadn't grabbed me
by the collar.*

*Then I got a good look at his face.*

*I threw myself against him and hung on with both hands.
For a second or two I was afraid he was too furious to care
about hurting* me. *Then the fingers that had gripped my ribs
relaxed and he said, "Get up and get out. I don't know how
much longer I can hang on here."*

*I didn't know how much longer I could hang on. That cool
voice hadn't deceived me. I got a tighter grip on his shirt and
leaned hard against him. I didn't dare raise even my head, which
was pressed against his shoulder; I had the feeling that if I
relaxed the slightest little bit he'd move me aside as imperson-
ally and efficiently as if I were a piece of furniture, and then
what he would do to Percy I didn't dare think. I could hear
Percy wheezing and groaning, but he wasn't much hurt; when
he finally moved it was at a trot. His footsteps faded into silence.*

*Ramses lifted me off my feet—and his—I was standing on
them. Holding me in one arm, he walked to the door and
slammed it.*

*"Unhand me," he said. "Don't bother pretending you're
about to faint, you've ripped my shirt and I think those sharp
points in my neck are your teeth."*

*"Put me down, then."*

*"Oh. Sorry." He lowered me to the floor.*

*"No, you aren't." I raised my head and examined his
throat. "No blood."*

*"Would you care to try again?"*

*"Stop it!" I put my hands on his shoulders and tried to*

shake him. "Can't you admit for once in your life that you're a human being, with human emotions? You wanted to kill him. You would have killed him. I had to prevent you, the best way I could."

"Why?"

The question took my breath away. I fumbled with my feelings like a clumsy-handed servant rummaging in a bureau drawer. When I understood, or thought I understood, I stepped back and swung at him. My wrist smacked into his raised hand.

"I suppose that can be taken as a reply." His eyes moved from my face to my throat. My shirt was open almost to the waist. I hadn't noticed. "Did Percy do that?" he asked.

"You did, I think. When you pulled us apart." It might have been true.

"Sorry."

"Please don't."

"Apologize?" He raised his eyebrows and curled the corners of his mouth. "Whatever you say. You appear a trifle agitated still. Sit down and I'll get you a glass of brandy."

"Not yet. I mean . . ." I couldn't stand to look at him. That travesty of a smile turned me cold. I pulled the edges of my shirt together. "I'm going to change. Will you stay here? Don't go away?"

"I'll be here." He crossed to the window and stood with his back to me.

You know how your eyes can deceive you at times—how a group of shapes and shadows can take on a certain form and then shift into another? It wasn't really like that; there was no physical change in him, he was exactly the same as he'd always been. I knew every line of his long body and every curl on his disheveled black head. I'd just never seen him before. You know what I'm trying to say, don't you? The change is in the heart.

I must have made some sound—a gasp, a wordless breath. He spun round, and there it was again. The features I knew better than I do my own were the same, but now I saw the tenderness those stubbornly set lips tried to hide, and the refined modeling of temples and cheekbones, and his eyes—wide open and unguarded for once, all his defenses down.

He stood quite still for a few seconds, watching me. Then he held out his hand. "Come here," he said.

I couldn't move. I felt as if I were standing on my head

*instead of my feet. The world had turned inside out and upside down.*

*"It's too late, you know," he said, in the same muted voice. "Too late for me, whatever you decide. Can you at least meet me halfway?"*

*I don't remember any interval between that rather heart-breaking question and the moment when his arms pressed me close and his lips settled onto mine.*

*Why hadn't I known? How could I have been so stupid? Why didn't someone tell me? He laughed at me when I said that. I love to see him laugh, Lia. His whole face changes, his eyes light up and his mouth softens and . . . I told you I was head over heels.*

*Not until Fatima scratched at the door and asked when we wanted dinner did I realize how much time had passed. We were sitting in the dark. He kissed me again and put me gently away.*

*"I'll tell her ten minutes. Will that be time enough?"*

*"Yes. No. Tell her . . . Tell her we don't want dinner. Tell her to go away."*

*I stopped writing because I heard Narmer bark and hoped . . . But it wasn't he. I can't stay here any longer; I'm going out to wait for him at the door. A few steps closer, a few seconds sooner . . . I'll pop this in an envelope and leave it on the table with the rest of the mail.*

*I hope you don't think I broke off at that interesting moment for literary effect, or because I was ashamed to admit what happened. I'm not ashamed. I didn't know it was possible to be so happy! Unless you are already on board ship, you will miss the wedding; I won't wait an extra day, even for you, my dearest friend. Not that I care about the conventions—but the Professor would be scandalized and Aunt Amelia would lecture—they don't understand, theirs was a different world—and my poor darling is so in awe of them he might lock himself in his room and refuse to open the door. Then I'd have to climb in the window! I would, too, to be with him. Thank goodness I had Ibrahim hinge the screens!*

*He couldn't help himself last night, it was all my doing . . . mostly my doing . . . When I remember, I feel as if my bones are melting. That's not the only reason I love him so much, Lia. He pretends to despise the gentleman's code of his class, but he is everything they claim to be and seldom are—gentle and strong and brave and honorable.*

**From Manuscript H**

Ramses didn't need to ask Ali who the visitor was. The horse was sweating and showing the whites of its eyes. Percy's horses always looked as if they had been ridden hard and handled clumsily. He delayed only long enough to tell the stableman to water it and rub it down. There was no one in the courtyard. He was almost running when he turned down the corridor toward their rooms. Even as a child there had been something about Percy that made his skin crawl with an emotion stronger than dislike and stranger than detestation. What he had learned about his cousin a few weeks ago made the very idea of his being alone with Nefret unendurable.

He didn't doubt she could take care of herself, but when he saw her in Percy's clumsy grasp, pure murderous rage drove every other thought and sensation out of his mind.

It felt wonderful.

The pressure of her body against his and the fingernails digging into his skin brought him back to his senses. Her face was ashen. Slowly and carefully he removed his hands from her waist. He hoped he hadn't hurt her. He hadn't meant to.

Percy had hit the wall with enough force to knock several photographs from a nearby shelf and was now on his knees clutching his midsection. A few carefully chosen words got him to his feet and out the door. He had better sense than to speak, but the look he gave Ramses was fairly eloquent. Well, they made quite a pretty picture, Ramses thought—the fainting girl clinging to her rescuer, her golden head against his breast, his manly arm supporting her. Percy was probably in no condition to notice that the arm round her waist was not embracing but lifting her. She was standing on his feet.

She had accomplished what she meant to do, anyhow. He hadn't broken Percy's neck. That was probably a good thing. She knew he was inclined to get himself worked up about killing people, and murdering a member of the family would have been unpleasant for everyone concerned.

It had been kind of her. Now if she would only go away and stop talking, and stop touching him, and give him a chance to get himself under control . . . She said she didn't want any brandy. She asked him to wait while she changed. Her hair was coming down and her lips were trembling and her dress was torn. Another wave of murderous fury darkened his vision and he went to the window, unable to look at her.

Then he heard an odd little sound, half squeak, half sob, and turned. When he saw her face his breath stopped. There was no mistaking that look, he had waited long enough to see it. He knew that if he went to her then, she would come unresisting into his arms, but he forced himself to hold back. One more step, the last, must be hers. Her choice, her desire as great as his.

When finally she moved, it was in a stumbling rush. They met halfway.

In the still darkness before sunrise, as she lay in his arms, he felt a drop of moisture on his shoulder and asked why she was crying.

"I feel like Sinuhe."

He laughed a little and drew her closer. "Not to me, you don't."

A breath of answering laughter warmed his skin. "You know what I mean."

"I think I do. But I'd like to hear you say it."

"Like an exile who has finally come home."

She slept then, but he lay awake, holding her, until the dawn light strengthened and she stirred and smiled.

When Emerson and I returned to the house that morning, they were waiting outside the door—an old man and a veiled woman holding a small, very dirty child. I took the woman for one of Nefret's pathetic charges; she was decently covered with a thread-bare dark blue tob (outer robe) without which no woman of any class would have dared appear in public; but the black eyes visible over the veil were heavily rimmed with kohl and the cheap ornaments dangling from face and head veils betrayed her profession. The man, whose dusty gray beard reeked with scented oil, wore a silk caftan, striped in gaudy colors and girdled with a colored shawl. Either they had not had the courage to ask for Nefret, or Ali had refused to let them in, for which one could hardly blame him.

I was about to speak to the woman when Emerson addressed the old man by name.

"How dare you dirty my doorstep, Ahmed Kalaan? You know where the clinic is; take her there."

The woman shrank back. The old man caught her by the arm. "No, Father of Curses, no. And do not send me to the kitchen as if I were a servant. I come as a friend, to spare you."

"Rrrrrr," said Emerson. "You vile, contemptible old . . ."

Words failed him. In fact I was sure they did not, for they seldom did, but the words he would like to have employed were too inflammatory for my ears, much less those of an innocent child. For all his bravado, Kalaan was not willing to risk the wrath of the Father of Curses. With a muttered oath he snatched at the child, whose face was hidden against the woman's shoulder. She clung desperately to her mother—for so I assumed the woman to be—but Kalaan's clawlike hands pulled her away and held her up so we could see her face. Her skin was brown, her curly hair black, her features rather delicate and, at the moment, almost witless with fear. She was a typical Egyptian child . . . except for one thing.

"See—see!" Kalaan gabbled.

"Good Lord," Emerson gasped. He looked at me. "Peabody—what—"

Though I was shaken to the core, I am accustomed to react quickly in a crisis. This was unquestionably a crisis. I said, "We cannot pursue this matter in the open street. Bring them in at once. Ali, open the door."

Kalaan's face split into a gargoyle grin. He thrust the child back into her mother's arms and strutted after me. Fatima, who was in the courtyard, let out a cry of protest at the sight of the trio. "Sitt Hakim—where are you taking them, Sitt? If it is Nur Misur they want, she is here, she wishes to see you and the Father of Curses—"

"Is Ramses here?" Emerson asked.

"Aywa. He came just before you and went with Nur Misur to his room. Do you wish—"

"Not now, Fatima," I said and closed the sitting room door almost in the poor woman's face.

Kalaan selected the most comfortable chair, lowered himself into it, and smiled insolently at me. He was in control now, and he knew it. He gestured brusquely at the woman, who came to him cringing like a dog who expects a beating. Her veil had been pulled away by the child's frantic grasp. She was younger than I had realized—even younger than she looked, perhaps, for the life she led ages a woman quickly.

"Sit down, my dear," said Emerson to me. He was holding himself in such rigid control, I trembled for his health. Before he could say more, the door of the sitting room opened.

Nefret did not bother to knock. She seldom did, and she had no reason now to believe we did not wish to be disturbed. She was holding Ramses by the hand, tugging at him as she did when she was excited about something she wanted us to share. They were both smiling.

The old man pulled the child roughly from her mother and stood her on her feet, holding her so that she faced Ramses. "Salaam aleikhum, Brother of Demons. See, I have brought your daughter. Do you accept her?"

Ramses shook his head. "No," he said hoarsely.

His face gave him the lie. The color had drained from it, leaving it white under his heavy tan.

The little girl slipped out of the old man's grasp and ran toward Ramses, holding out her arms and calling to him in a high, quavering voice. She was too small to talk plainly. I understood only one word. It was the Arabic word for Father.

His involuntary recoil stopped her as brutally as a blow might have done. She spread dimpled, dirty hands over her face and crouched down, like a threatened animal trying to make itself smaller. But before the child hid them, Nefret had seen what we had seen earlier—wide, dark gray eyes, of an unusual shade and shape—the exact shade and shape as mine.

Until that moment Nefret had not moved or spoken. The sound that came from her parted lips was wordless: a sharp cry like that of a wounded animal. Her blazing blue eyes shifted, first to the woman in her shabby garments, then back to the child. She did not let go of Ramses's hand; she flung it from her and ran stumbling from the room.

"Nefret, wait!" Ramses started to turn.

The child must have been watching him between her fingers. She let out a little whimper.

I am not a maternal woman, but I could bear it no longer. I

would have leaped to my feet if Emerson's hand had not held me back. His unblinking eyes were fixed on Ramses.

The old man cackled with laughter. "You see? You say no, but who will believe you if they see her face? For a price—a very small price—I will find a home for her among her own people, where she will be loved and desired, and hidden forever from the eyes of Inglizi."

Perhaps the child did not understand the unspeakable promise in the leering voice—I prayed she had not—but it was clear to the rest of us. I had thought Ramses could go no whiter, but I was wrong. He dropped to one knee and took the child's hands in his. His voice was steadier than mine would have been.

"Don't cry, little bird. There is nothing to be afraid of. I won't let him have you."

She threw her arms round his neck and buried her face against his shoulder. Holding her, he rose to his feet.

"I claim her," he said formally. "She is mine. Get out, Kalaan, while you are able."

Kalaan licked his lips. "What are you saying? Do you know what you are saying? You have dishonored this woman, who is my—uh—my poor daughter. Give me money and I will—"

"No," Emerson said gently. "I think if you start now, and move very quickly, you may make it out of the room before I lose my temper."

The old villain knew that purring voice. He scuttled toward the door, giving Ramses a wide berth. The woman crept after him. She did not look at Ramses, nor he at her. After they had gone, Ramses said, "Excuse me, Mother and Father. I will be back shortly."

He went out, carrying the child, who clung to him like a little monkey. Emerson sat down next to me, took my hand and patted it, but neither of us spoke until Ramses returned.

"I left her with Fatima, but I promised I would return in time to watch over her during the terrors of the bath," he explained. "What do you want to know?"

"She is not yours," Emerson said.

"No."

"Then who . . ." I did not finish the question. There was only one other man in Egypt through whom the child could have inherited my father's eyes. "Perhaps he does not know," I went on. "Should we not tell him?"

Ramses dropped into a chair and reached for a cigarette. "He has no legal responsibility. Do you suppose he would admit any other kind?"

"Hmph," Emerson said. "Peabody, my dear, let me get you a whiskey and soda."

"No, it is too early. But I might try one of those cigarettes. They are calming to the nerves, I have heard."

Ramses raised his eyebrows, but he provided the cigarette and lit it for me. It provided a distraction, at least. By the time I had got the hang of the business and had stopped coughing, I was ready to hear Ramses's explanation.

"She approached me one day in the suk, tugging at my coat and asking for baksheesh. When I looked down at her I saw ... You saw it too. Something of a shock, wasn't it? Once I had recovered I asked her to take me to her house. She thought I wanted ..." His even voice caught. Then he went on, "Her mother was under the same impression. After I had disabused her of the notion, we talked. She claimed not to know who the father was. She may have been telling the truth. Her clients don't often bother introducing themselves by name."

"Dear God," I whispered.

"God has nothing to do with it," said Ramses, offering me another cigarette. "The place was unspeakable—a single room, ankle-deep in refuse, swarming with flies and other vermin. I couldn't leave her there. I moved them to more salubrious surroundings and paid Rashida a sum of money each week on condition that she—er—retire. I got in the habit of dropping by from time to time in order to make certain she kept her promise. When Sennia began calling me Father I didn't have the heart to stop her. The other children with whom she played had fathers; she knew the word, and she was too young to understand, and ..."

"You became fond of her," I said.

"I am not entirely impervious to the softer emotions, Mother. After she had learned to trust me, there were times when she would gesture or laugh in a way that reminded me of—of someone else." He smiled at me, and his face was so young and vulnerable I wanted to cry.

"Why didn't you tell us?" I demanded.

"Should I come running to my mother with every difficulty? Oh, I would have told you eventually, but you had enough to worry about and this was no more your responsibility than it was mine."

It would have been strange if he had acted otherwise, I thought. He had never been in the habit of asking for help.

"I wonder how Kalaan comes into this," Emerson said thoughtfully.

"He is no more Sennia's grandfather than you are," Ramses said. "You know what he is. But he is a crafty old swine, and he set the stage well. Those rags she was wearing had been supplied in place of the clothes I had got for her, and I haven't seen her so filthy for weeks. As for what he hoped to gain by this—"

"Money, of course," I said. "No doubt he assumed we would want the business kept quiet. Though how anyone, even a—a vile creature like Kalaan—could suppose we would abandon that child—any child—to . . ."

"It's all right, my love," Emerson said, taking my hand.

Ramses put out his cigarette and stood up. "I must get back. She was trying not to cry, but I could tell she was frightened."

"I will come with you," I said. "The presence of a woman may reassure the poor little thing."

Ramses looked at his father, who said quickly, "Where has Nefret got to? She is wonderful with children, and she will want to apologize for misjudging you when she learns the truth."

"You didn't know the truth either," Ramses said. His face had hardened and there was a note in his voice that was new to me. "But you had enough faith in me to believe, even before I explained, that I was not a liar or a coward or a . . . Thank you for that. It means a great deal to me."

He strode out of the room without waiting for a reply.

"Oh, dear," I said. "Emerson, go to Nefret. She will be glad to learn she was mistaken, and anxious to make it up to him."

I hastened to the bath chamber, from which I could hear cries of distress. Fatima had given it up; she stood watching with a broad grin while Ramses tried in vain to persuade the child to let him put her into the bath. Water dripped from his chin and made dark patches on his clothing. "She has been bathed before," he explained defensively. "It must be the size of the tub that frightens her. Now, little bird, it is only water—see, I will just lower your feet . . . No? No." He wiped his face on his sleeve. "Mother, have you any ideas?"

"Now, what is this?" Emerson stood in the doorway, his hands on his hips, looking sternly at us. "What a roaring! Is there a lion here? Where is it? Where is it hiding?"

He began opening cupboard doors and throwing towels out

onto the floor, while the child watched him in wide-eyed fascination.

It is absolutely unaccountable to me why small children respond to men like Emerson. One would suppose a voice as deep as his and a form as large as his would frighten them into fits. Before long she was giggling as he tore the bathroom apart looking for the imaginary lion, but it was to Ramses she turned when the actual moment of immersion arrived. With my assistance Emerson pursued the lion out of the room and closed the door to prevent it from returning.

"My darling girl," he said, and took me in his arms.

"I am not going to cry, Emerson. You know I am not at all a sentimental person. It was just seeing how gentle he was with her, and how she clung to him. Oh, dear."

Emerson reached into his pocket and pulled out his handkerchief. He looked so surprised and pleased at actually finding it where it was supposed to be that we both started to laugh, a bit damply in my case.

"Well, well," said Emerson, "we'll find room for the little thing, won't we? She'll be no trouble."

I fancied she would be considerable trouble—all small children are—but I said, "Of course, Emerson. You know, don't you, that the old fiend's threats were right on the mark? No one will believe she is not Ramses's child, no matter how we deny it."

"Why the devil should we deny anything?" Emerson demanded. His chin jutted out. "We know the truth. They say— who says?—let them say!"

"That's all very well, Emerson, but this is not going to do Ramses's reputation any good. It has already suffered unfairly."

"Some men might take pride in that kind of reputation."

"That is unfortunately correct, but our son is not one of them. He won't show it, he never does, but this suspicion will hurt him deeply. And Nefret will . . . Where is she? Did you look for her?"

"Not yet. Shall we do so now?"

Nefret was gone. We were in her sitting room reading the message she had left when Ramses joined us.

"She says she has gone to stay with friends for a few days," I reported. "She must mean the Vandergelts. Ramses, don't be angry with her; if she had had time to think she would have known better, but it came as such a shock. Won't you go after her?"

Ramses stared at the note, which he was twisting in his fingers. "Go after her," he repeated. "Good God!"

"What is it?" Emerson demanded.

"I ought to have realized . . . Go after her. Yes, I must. I hope it's not already too late."

## From Manuscript H

The house to which he had moved Rashida and the child was in Maadi, some distance away from Rashida's old haunts and, he hoped, from a convenient supplier of hashish. It had been one of the way stations he and David had used when they were prowling the suks in various exotic disguises, for various illegal purposes. (They had been very young at the time; but that was probably no excuse for some of their activities.)

The old woman who owned the place—thanks in part to his subsidies—was elderly and half-blind, and she had been profoundly disinterested in their comings and goings. She was kind, though, in her vague way, and he had been paying her an additional small sum to make sure the child was properly looked after. Rashida's maternal instincts had been somewhat warped by her experiences; in her own way she was passionately attached to her daughter, but she couldn't always be depended on to do the things he wanted her to do. He had known that sooner or later he would have to introduce Sennia to his mother, and he had thought she'd be more likely to accept the child if the little creature could be got used to bathing, and wearing clothes, and certain modifications of her table manners.

Once again he had underestimated his mother. He ought to have known she'd come through—for the child, and for him.

The old woman was squatting on a bench outside the door of the house, blinking in the sunlight. She told him Rashida and the child had left early that morning and had not been back. Certainly he could look at their rooms. He was paying for them, wasn't he?

Rashida had not been much of a housekeeper, but one look at the room in which they slept told him that this disorder was significant. She had not meant to come back. The carved box in which she kept her few treasures was gone, and so were the pots of kohl and lip paint and henna. Lying across the bed was a crumpled bit of bright pink cloth—one of the little dresses he had bought the child. He picked it up and smoothed it between his hands. No doubt he had been a fool to believe Rashida's protestations of gratitude and reformation, but she had seemed so glad to be free of the life she led, even gladder that there was a way out for her daughter.

He finished searching the room. Half-buried in the ashes of the brazier were a few brown stubs of cigarettes with a faint, unmistakable smell.

He waited for an hour, pacing the floor in growing worry and impatience, even as he told himself there was no basis for his fears. Kalaan was one of the most notorious pimps in Cairo. He could have tracked the girl down and forced her to come back to him, with no ulterior motive except pour l'encourager les autres. She'd have admitted everything to him, she had been in his power too long to resist his demands or the drugs from which she had been cut off. The idea of blackmailing her protector would come readily to Kalaan's pragmatically filthy mind. She might even have agreed to go with him in the hope that the Inglizi would save her child. Ramses wanted to believe that.

If that were the case he would get her back, and put an end to Kalaan's activities by one means or another. It was his fault she had fallen back into Kalaan's hands; if he hadn't been so stubborn he would have told his parents the truth immediately, and this disaster would never have happened.

It was the most likely possibility. The only consolation—and a feeble one it was—was that if his worst suspicions were right, there was no way he could have anticipated this. No way of proving anything, either, unless he could find her before . . .

He could only think of one other place in which to look. By the time he reached Cairo it was early in the afternoon; the reeking alleys of el Was'a steamed in the heat, and most people were within. The hovel from which he had removed them was occupied by two other women. They took him for a customer at first; the terms in which he corrected that assumption made them cringe into a corner, and he had to waste more time reassuring them. They denied any knowledge of Rashida.

The sun was setting before he admitted to himself that the search was futile. He might not have abandoned it even then had it not belatedly occurred to him that he had another responsibility.

His first indication of the correctness of that assumption came from Ali the doorman. He was standing outside in the road looking anxiously up and down, and when he saw Ramses he came running toward him, white puffs of dust spurting up under his sandaled feet. "Allah be praised, you are here. Hurry, hurry."

He knew Ali well enough to know that the emergency was not dire, but he was not entirely prepared for what he found when he entered the courtyard, followed by the howls of Narmer. His mother, his father, and Fatima were there. His mother was clutching a glass of whiskey. On his father's knee was a small bundle wrapped in tweed. The face atop the bundle consisted of a mop of black hair, a fist, and a pair of enormous eyes, gray as storm clouds.

"Thank God!" his father exclaimed.

"Don't swear," his mother muttered.

"That was not swearing. That was a prayer, from the heart. See," Emerson went on in Arabic, "did I not tell you he would come back? I do not tell lies! He is here."

"She wouldn't go to bed," his mother said. He had never heard her sound so helpless. "We had to wrap her in your coat before she would stop crying. Ramses. Do something."

Ramses felt a sudden, insane desire to laugh. He was afraid, he was worried sick, he didn't dare think about quite a number of things; but he felt better, somehow. The bundle wriggled, and an arm appeared, reaching for him.

"I can't touch you until I wash," Ramses said, remembering where he had been that day.

She took her thumb out of her mouth and said something.

"What? Oh—wash? Yes. Of course. Right back," he added.

There wasn't time for a bath—the situation was obviously desperate—so he had to settle for washing hands and arms and face, and exchanging his European clothing for a galabeeyah. When he came back she squirmed out of the coat and off his father's knee, and ran to him. The little brown body was bare except for a cloth wrapped round her hips. Ramses picked her up, wondering what she made of that item of clothing; children of the poorer classes just squatted, wherever they happened to be. Her face and body were unmarked, except by the scratches and bumps a small child might normally acquire. He had made sure of that when Fatima bathed her.

He wrapped the coat round her and held her till she settled into the curve of his arm and put her thumb back in her mouth.

"It is time to sleep," he said. "You are safe now. Sometimes I must go away, but I will always come back, and when I am not here, they will watch over you. Do you know who they are? They are my mother and my father. We must obey them."

His mother coughed.

"And," Ramses said hurriedly, "they are mighty magicians! Now that they are your friends, no one can hurt you. Fatima is your friend too. Go with Fatima."

Fatima held out her arms and this time she went unprotesting, her eyes already half closed.

"I'm sorry," Ramses said, not quite sincerely. He was absurdly pleased that she had wanted him.

"Ha," said his father. "She seems to have inherited another family characteristic—stubbornness. What about a whiskey, my boy? You look as if you could use it. Where have you been all this time? Wasn't Nefret with the Vandergelts?"

"Nefret," Ramses repeated. The only positive feature of the afternoon's frantic search had been the fact that it kept him from thinking about Nefret. He didn't want to think about her. It hurt too much. "I wasn't looking for Nefret."

"Ah," said his father. He reached for his pipe. "Did you find . . . what is her name?"

"Rashida. No, I didn't find her."

His mother put her glass down on the table. She had drunk every drop, but her chin was firm and her shoulders were squared. "It has been," she said, "quite a day. I apologize for failing to realize that the welfare of that unfortunate girl ought to have concerned me. One cannot blame her for not contradicting the old villain's lies; a woman in her position cannot afford the luxury of morality."

"Well put, Peabody," said Emerson, his face softening. "We'll find her, Ramses, and I will personally dismember Kalaan and hang bits of his anatomy all round el Was'a. I wish I could do the same to every procurer in Cairo, but so long as there are men contemptible enough to use those women, there will be other men exploiting them. She is probably in hiding, you know. It may take a while to locate her. Where did you look?"

Fatima had come back down the stairs. She gave Ramses a smile and a reassuring nod, and then glided around the courtyard lighting the lamps. The crimson and orange of hibiscus blooms and the green of their leaves shone in the mellow light; the contrast between the quiet, murmurous beauty of this house and the places he had seen that afternoon was almost too much to bear. All at once he was so tired he could hardly keep his eyes open.

"The rooms I had taken for them are in Maadi," he mumbled. "She hadn't been there. I waited for over an hour—the old woman who owns the house promised she would send to me if Rashida came back. Then I went to the house where she'd lived before . . ."

"How long has it been since you have eaten?" his mother demanded. "You had no lunch, at least not here, and I do not suppose you had sense enough to think of it."

"I don't remember."

"Fatima, please tell cook to get dinner on the table."

"Yes, Sitt. It is ready."

His mother was right. (She always was.) The hot soup revived him, and by the time they reached the main course he was almost back to normal.

"What about Nefret's clinic?" his mother asked—they were still discussing ways of tracing Rashida. "Had she ever been there?"

"No," Ramses said. "She knew of it, but said Kalaan had forbidden his girls to go there. I am at somewhat of a loss as to where to look next."

"He will probably keep her hidden for a while," his father said. "Hell and damnation! I should have strangled the old buzzard this morning when I had the chance. Never mind; we'll track him down, and he will tell us what he's done with her."

"I hope so," Ramses said.

"What are you worrying about?" his mother asked. "One hates to think of her in the power of such a man, but she and many others have been in that position before. Do you believe he will harm her?"

It was a waste of time trying to spare his mother.

"I think she might be in danger," he admitted.

Fatima let out a hiss of distress. Since her trip to England she had become emancipated to the extent of not veiling herself in the presence of his father or himself—she was now part of the family, after all—and her plump, pleasant face was lined with worry. He patted the brown hand that was reaching for his plate.

"It'll be all right, Fatima."

"She is a bad woman," Fatima murmured. "But she is very young, Ra-meses."

It had taken him a long time to persuade her to use his name; she didn't do it often, and when she did, she pronounced it, not as the others did, but with an odd accent. When he was in a fanciful mood he wondered whether that was how the name had sounded in the thirteenth century B.C.

"She is not a bad woman, Fatima, only unlucky and unhappy and very young. She wouldn't have done this of her own accord," he went on. "She hadn't the guile or the malice even to think of such a thing. Someone made her do it—someone she feared more than she trusted me."

"Agreed." Emerson nodded. "When you went to her house that day, Kalaan found out about it—he would, of course. The seeds of the idea must have been planted then, and he saw the opportunity for a spot of blackmail. No good deed ever goes unpunished, my boy; never forget that. Good Gad, Kalaan may even have taught the little creature to call you Father."

"Someone may have done."

"You are worrying unnecessarily, I believe," his mother said. "Kalaan didn't get the money he expected from us, but he has no reason to be angry with her. She did as he asked. Why should he destroy a valuable piece of merchandise?"

Ramses pushed his half-filled plate away. His parents were watching him anxiously, their faces warm with concern. If he told them what he feared, they would think he had lost his mind. Maybe he had.

The following day brought one piece of good news—a telegram from David announcing their arrival on Wednesday next.

Emerson and I were at the breakfast table when Ali delivered the cable. Although I had applied myself with my usual efficiency to the innumerable alterations in our schedule necessitated by the events of the previous day, there were still a few matters to be settled. Ramses had not yet joined us. I knew where he was; immediately upon arising, I had gone to see how our small charge had spent the night, and had found her awake and demanding her abu.

"We will have to break her of that," I said to Fatima, who had taken the child to sleep with her. "What is she to call him, though?"

Fatima had no opinion on the subject. She had a number of opinions on other matters relating to the child, however, and we were discussing them when Ramses joined us. I left the three together and went down to breakfast. Emerson, already at table and drinking his coffee, was by then sufficiently aroused to be in a querulous mood.

"What are they all doing up there?" he demanded. "I thought you would bring her down with you. She will be hungry. Where is Ramses?"

Patiently I explained that no child of two, whatever its nationality, is a pleasant table companion, reminded him that Ramses had not been allowed to take meals with us until he was six, pointed out that the little girl had nothing to wear, and added that Fatima would make certain she had a suitable breakfast. The advent of Ali with the telegram distracted Emerson from the complaints he had undoubtedly been about to make.

"Finally," he exclaimed. "They have been long enough about it. Now we can get some work done. I want to leave for the site as soon as possible. Finish your breakfast, Peabody."

"I do not see how I can come with you today, Emerson," I said. "I must do a bit of shopping. The child hasn't a stitch to her name, or a proper child's cot, or a hairbrush, or anything she needs. We must fit up a room as a nursery and find a nursemaid; Fatima cannot look after her and carry out her other duties. Now I must also make certain the dahabeeyah is ready for Lia and David. I cannot take Fatima with me, since the child is getting comfortable with her, so—"

"Don't tell me about it, Peabody," Emerson growled. "Ah, here is Ramses. All right, are you, my boy?"

He looked as if he had not slept a wink. I handed him the telegram and had the pleasure of seeing his haggard face brighten.

"It will be good to see them," he said.

"It will be good to have them on the dig," said Emerson. "All these interruptions have wreaked havoc with my schedule. Yesterday was a total loss, and your mother is planning to waste the entire day in Cairo, and Nefret is off somewhere, and . . . I trust *you* have no other plans, Ramses?"

"No, sir."

Ramses said no more. Emerson's brow furrowed—not with annoyance, but with paternal anxiety. He knew better than to express it; instead he attempted a diversion.

"I have a new plan," he announced.

I said nothing. Ramses said, "Yes, sir," in the same polite, disinterested voice.

"If Vandergelt's idea is right, someone is trying to keep us away from the site. That means—it must mean—that there is something at Zawaiet el 'Aryan this chap doesn't want us to find. So," said Emerson triumphantly, "we will find it. Not by random digging or concocting baseless theories, but by methodical excavation that will sweep the site from side to side and top to bottom! Well? What do you say?"

"It will be a long job," Ramses said. He looked a little more alert, though.

"We'll hire as many men as we can use. With the four of us, and David and Lia and Selim and Douad, there will be ample supervision."

"Excellent, Emerson," I said, frowning at the list I had made out and adding another item.

Emerson looked over my shoulder and read the words aloud. "'Small enamel bath.' Hmmm. The trouble with your mother, Ramses, is that she has no maternal instincts to speak of."

I did not mind being the butt of Emerson's little joke, for it actually brought a smile to Ramses's face. Emerson popped a last bit of toast into his mouth and left the room, beckoning Ramses to follow. Ramses paused by my chair, bent his tall frame and gave me a quick, clumsy kiss on the cheek. In fact it landed on my ear, but it was meant for my cheek, I believe. When I turned toward him he stepped back, looking embarrassed.

"Watch over your father," I said in a low voice. "Unobtrusively, of course. He is superbly indifferent to his own safety, but the plan he has proposed is likely to be dangerous."

"I know. I will do my best, Mother."

"And look after yourself. Be careful. Don't take foolish chances."

"Yes, Mother. Thank you, Mother."

"Ramses?"

"Yes, Mother?"

"Don't worry about Nefret. I will stop by the Vandergelts and fetch her home."

"I am not worrying about her," Ramses said. "She is a free agent and will do as she likes."

I was a trifle put out with Nefret myself. We all sympathized with her feelings on the subject of men who consorted with the unfortunate women she was trying to help, but in my opinion her behavior had been somewhat theatrical. No doubt she had already had time to reconsider and feel ashamed of herself for jumping to conclusions about her brother. I had no objection to making her feel a bit more ashamed. By stopping to see the Vandergelts I could kill two birds with one stone, since I was anxious to apprise them of the situation.

Cyrus had caused the *Valley of the Kings* to be brought to the dock near Giza. It was only a short walk, but I accepted Ali's offer to get me a cab, since I meant to take Katherine and Nefret on to Cairo with me. We would have a pleasant morning shopping for the child and then return for luncheon at the house. Cyrus could meet us there or go to the site.

I got it all worked out during the five-minute drive to the dock. One of the ferries was just unloading, so I had to make my way through a throng of tourists to the southern section where the dahabeeyah was moored. One of the crewmen, lounging in the bow, saw me coming and of course recognized me immediately. He hastened to run out the gangplank and emitted a shout that brought Cyrus on deck.

"Why, say now, I didn't expect to see you so early," he exclaimed. "Figured you'd be on your way to Zawaiet."

"I hope I am not de trop, Cyrus."

"You could never be that, Amelia. Come and have coffee, we're just finishing breakfast."

Cyrus lived in princely style; the table was set with crystal and silver and every appointment was of the best. Golden damask draperies had been pulled back from the long windows of the salon, admitting a flood of sunlight that brought out the beautiful colors of the Persian rugs covering the floor. Katherine jumped up from her chair and embraced me.

"How lovely to see you, Amelia. We intended to come by this evening since we had not heard from you for several days."

"We have been somewhat preoccupied, Katherine. No doubt Nefret told you what happened yesterday. Where is she?"

"Why, Amelia, I have no idea." Katherine's smile faded. "Why did you think she was here? What happened?"

"Oh, dear," I said, feeling as if the breath had been knocked out of me. "You haven't seen her?"

"Now calm down, my dears," Cyrus said in his slow, soothing drawl. "Let's just figure out what the situation is and then we'll know what to do about it. First things first. Did Miss Nefret say she was coming to us, Amelia?"

"No. No, what she said—wrote, rather—was that she was going to spend a few days with friends. I assumed . . ."

"Sure you would. But we're not her only friends, and maybe a young thing like that would rather be with folks her own age. This was yesterday? Uh-huh. Well, we'll track her down, don't you worry. Now tell us what happened."

As Cyrus later confessed, he expected "the usual disasters you folks get into." He listened with friendly interest and occasional ejaculations of surprise, but when I had finished my tale he inquired, "Nobody dead, wounded or kidnapped? Well, that's a pleasant surprise! I'm relieved it's not serious."

Katherine, being a woman, came closer to understanding. "I am so sorry, dear Amelia. Sorry for Ramses, too. In wishing to spare you, he only made things worse, but he thought he was acting for the best."

"Spare me what? Do not suppose for one moment, Katherine, that I doubt his word. He is incapable of doing such a thing, and if he had, which he never would, he would shoulder the responsibility like a man! He nobly and generously came to the rescue of that innocent child! And now," I added bitterly, while Katherine made conciliatory noises and Cyrus patted my shoulder, "now he will suffer for it. If *you* suspect him—"

"My dear, I don't! You misunderstood. Ramses would no more do such a thing than—than Cyrus. You think that nephew of yours is the child's father?"

"He must be. Wait till you see her, Katherine. The resemblance is astonishing."

Katherine had poured coffee for me. I took a sip. "Excellent coffee," I said. "I am on my way to Cairo, Katherine, to get some things for the child. I thought you might like to join me. Cyrus, Emerson has gone with Ramses to Zawaiet. He has concluded your idea was correct, and he is determined to clear the site to bedrock."

"If that isn't just like Emerson," Cyrus exclaimed. "Tell him there's a rattlesnake in the bushes and he goes straight for it. I guess maybe I'd better get along over there and sit on a rock with a rifle. Cat, my dear, you going with Amelia?"

"I would love to. It will be delightful buying things for a child again. How old is she, Amelia?"

"We will discuss details on the way," I said, finishing my coffee. "We will lunch in Cairo, I think; it is later than I had

realized. You will both dine with us this evening? We have much
to talk about."

"We sure do," Cyrus muttered. "I'll just get my coat and be
on my way."

"And I will get my hat and handbag," said Katherine.
She fixed her steady, compassionate green eyes on my face.
"Amelia—"

"Later, Katherine. You and I have much to talk about too."

Men are very well in their way, and even more useful than
women in other ways; but they are simply incapable of compre-
hending certain things. The long ride into Cairo gave me a chance
to converse privately with a woman on whose intelligent advice
I relied. I had not realized how desperately I yearned to confide
in a friend. By the time we reached the Muski I was hoarse from
talking.

"I do apologize, Katherine," I remarked in some embarrassment. "I had not meant to say so much."

"You could pay me no higher compliment, Amelia. You are
my dearest friend; I owe my happiness to you. I only wish I could
do more to help. It is hard to see one's children in trouble and
be unable to relieve them."

"They are not children; they are young men and women, and
must solve their own problems. I deplore Ramses's unfortunate
habit of reticence; he has always been like that and probably always will be; but just between you and me, Katherine, I am very
proud of him. It is Nefret with whom I am vexed at the moment.
Really, life was much simpler when I had only murderers and
thieves to deal with."

Men may jeer, and they do, but shopping does have a salutary
effect. I had never bought clothing for a little girl; Nefret had been
thirteen when she came to us. It proved to be unexpectedly pleasurable. Katherine gently intervened once or twice, pointing out
the impracticality of the garment I was considering, and mentioning certain practical items that had not occurred to me. We
were loaded with parcels when we returned to the cab, and I had
ordered a number of articles to be sent on.

We took luncheon at Shepheard's. Katherine saw my eyes
wandering. "You are looking for Nefret, aren't you?"

"Foolish of me," I confessed. "It did occur to me, though, that
she might have come here. She hasn't many friends, you know.
She and Ramses and David have always been so self-sufficient—
too much so, perhaps. It will be a great relief to have Lia with us

again. I know Nefret talks to her more confidentially than she does to me."

"That is only natural," Katherine said.

"Yes."

"So you aren't going to call on her friends this afternoon?"

"It is too awkward, Katherine. How can I go round asking if they have seen her without admitting that she has run off and I don't know where the devil she is? Curse the girl, she has no business worrying us this way. Not that I am worried. Not at all. Gracious, look at the time. We still must stop by the *Amelia.*"

So we did, and found several of Fatima's nieces, including the much-maligned Karima, already hard at work. A brief discussion with Karima convinced me there was little for me to do. I knew Fatima would insist upon inspecting the premises herself and adding the final touches—including rosebuds in the washbasin and dried petals between the sheets. Not even Emerson had dared object to these procedures (in fact, I rather think he liked them though he would never have admitted it).

I dropped Katherine off at the *Valley of the Kings,* since she wanted to bathe and change before coming on to us. Ramses and Emerson had not yet returned, but the house was full of people, all women. One of them was Daoud's wife Kadija. The others, sitting meekly in a row in the kitchen, appeared to be prospective nannies.

It was as well the men were late, for they would undoubtedly have complained about the unnecessary fuss that ensued, as I inspected and approved the quarters Fatima had selected for the child and her attendant, unloaded and unwrapped my purchases, interviewed nannies, and greeted Kadija. Kadija was a very large, very dark-complected, very silent woman. At least she was usually silent with me; Nefret insisted she had a wicked sense of humor and could tell extremely amusing stories. On her mother's side Kadija was of Nubian blood; from the women of her mother's family she had learned the recipe for a certain magical ointment which she and Daoud smeared on everyone who required healing. Nefret had become a convert to its efficacy, so I had stopped objecting to it, though it turned the skin of the user a horrid shade of green.

I do not believe that child had set a foot on the ground since I left. Kadija was carrying her when I got there, and was only persuaded to put her down when I insisted she try on some of the garments I had purchased.

Sennia did not want to wear a dress. The little slippers were rejected even more forcibly. The enamel bath was well received, however, since splashing quantities of water about the room is a favorite occupation of the young, and so were several inconsequential objects I had just happened to acquire. We—Kadija, Fatima, and I and Basima, the proud winner of the contest for nursemaid—were sitting on the floor of the new nursery watching Sennia play when we heard voices down below. The child had been listening. She made a beeline for the door.

"Catch her, Kadija, she is unclothed!" I exclaimed.

Kadija's big gentle hands intercepted the fugitive and held her fast. "Now that you have come to live with the Inglizi you must wear clothing," she explained. "Put on a pretty robe. You want him to be proud of you, don't you?"

Ramses came straight up, as I had thought he would. Kadija's appeal had done the trick; we had barely time to get the anxious little creature into one of the new frocks before he appeared in the doorway. After he had admired the result she insisted on showing him her new possessions one by one. Every frock, every bit of underclothing, every ribbon and toy had to be examined and approved. Ramses was dusty and sweat-stained, but the lines of weariness in his face smoothed out as she trotted back and forth, and when she dragged the doll onto his lap he actually laughed.

"Mother, whatever possessed you? It is almost as big as she is."

"None of them had dark hair," I said disapprovingly. "It really is shameful. One would suppose flaxen curls and blue eyes are the only acceptable style of looks. Go and change, Ramses. Now that you have made your presence known, I presume she will allow you to absent yourself for a time."

After he had slipped out I had a few words with Fatima. She wanted to know how "that worthless Karima" was getting on with the cleaning of the dahabeeyah, and assured me she would herself supervise the final arrangements. Realizing that I could do with a bit of tidying myself, I betook myself to my room, where I found that Emerson had finished his ablutions and gone to the courtyard. When I joined him he immediately handed me a whiskey and soda and led me to a settee. We had a great deal to say to one another, but for some reason neither of us felt like talking. Emerson pulled up a hassock and lifted my slippered feet onto it. Then he sat down next to me and put his arm round me.

Whatever difficulties lay ahead—and there were sure to be many of them—we would face them hand in hand, side by side, and back to back.

I said as much to Emerson, who replied, "You are mixing your metaphors again, Peabody, but the sentiment is one with which I am in complete accord. Vandergelt told me Nefret was not with them; I take it you did not find her?"

"You may take it that I did not look for her. I didn't know where to start. Emerson—there is not the slightest possibility that she can be in danger, is there?"

"She certainly left of her own accord." Emerson took his pipe from his pocket. "Ali the doorman said she had a small valise with her. He asked if she wanted a cab but she said no. She set off on foot, in the direction of the tram station. If she doesn't come home tonight, we will begin tracing her tomorrow; but I cannot believe she is in danger. At least," he added glumly, "I wouldn't believe it if I could make any sense whatever of what is happening."

The howls of Narmer proclaimed the arrival of our friends. Katherine did not waste time. "Did the frocks fit? How did she like the doll? May I see her?"

"You women," Emerson growled. "Is that all you can think of, frocks and toys and babies? Er—suppose I just go and fetch her."

I persuaded him to serve beverages to our guests instead, and before long Ramses came down the stairs carrying the child. She was wearing one of the frocks I had bought—a nice little white garment with just a touch of broderie anglaise on the collar—and the red leather slippers. At the sight of so many people she burrowed into Ramses's shoulder.

I went to sit with Katherine and Cyrus, who had tactfully withdrawn some little distance, leaving Emerson to make a complete idiot of himself as he tried to persuade Sennia to talk to him. The deep rumble of his voice blended oddly with her brief, high-pitched replies. She really did sound like a little bird. At last she condescended to perch on Emerson's knee while he fed her bits of biscuit.

It was not until that moment that Katherine got a good look at her face. She sucked in her breath. "I begin to understand Nefret," she whispered. "The resemblance is uncanny, Amelia. She even has your chin."

"I fear she will one day, poor unfortunate child. Emerson, no more biscuits. They will spoil her appetite."

"What are you going to do with her?" Cyrus asked.

"There can hardly be any question of that, Cyrus. Even if Percy admitted his responsibility, he is no fit person to take charge of a child. He would hand her over to a randomly selected Egyptian family, pay them a small sum of money, and stroll away."

"She might be better off with an Egyptian family," Cyrus argued. "You could with complete confidence let Selim or Daoud or any one of them adopt her."

"They will be part of her family, Cyrus, as they are part of mine. Kadija would take her in a second. But she is half English, and I will not be a party to the sort of irresponsible callousness so many English persons of the male gender demonstrate toward the infantile victims of their brief encounters. It is a matter of principle."

Cyrus raised his glass in salute. His eyes were twinkling. "And a certain amount of bullheadedness? You're gonna outface the gossips and tell them to go to the devil? We're with you every step of the way, Amelia, but—well—isn't this going to be a little hard on Ramses?"

"I have given that full consideration, of course. Ramses is of my opinion, I know; he is even more bull—er—determined than I. There is no concealing her existence now, and you may be sure gossip will spread whatever we do. Cyrus, would you be good enough to get me another whiskey and soda? Thank you. Emerson, I said no more biscuits! I do not approve of bribing a child with sweets. It is time she went to bed. Growing children need a great deal of sleep. No, Ramses, do not take her up, she must learn to go with Basima."

A certain amount of protest followed this decision. It ended when Emerson slipped a biscuit to Basima and she held it in front of the child as she carried her off, as one leads a donkey with a carrot. I pretended not to see.

Katherine, chuckling, said, "She has quite a will of her own, hasn't she? Remarkable for an infant who has lived as she has. Amelia, what are you going to do about her mother?"

"That is a difficulty," I admitted. "The unfortunate creature seems to have disappeared; Ramses has been looking for her, without success thus far. If we can find her, we will of course protect and assist her, but . . . I dare not think what the child has seen and heard and experienced. Can we ever eradicate those memories?"

"Children that age learn quickly and forget easily, Amelia. I have a feeling she has been sheltered from the worst of it. A mother can do that—or try to do it."

Katherine's first husband had been a drunkard and a wife beater. I did not doubt she knew whereof she spoke.


During dinner an idea occurred to me that I was anxious to investigate. I saw no reason to explain it to Emerson, in case I was mistaken, so I simply informed him that I had not seen Jack Reynolds for several days and felt I ought not neglect that duty.

"He has been doing quite well, but men often relapse unless someone keeps after them," I explained. "Katherine will go with me, won't you, Katherine?"

We declined the offers of the gentlemen to accompany us, for I was afraid that if we did find Jack in a state of inebriation he might remember his old grudge and behave badly. Escorted by two of our men carrying lanterns, we set out on foot. It was a beautiful night and Katherine had said she would be the better for a bit of exercise.

We found Jack alone and in full possession of his senses. He was in his study, from which he emerged to greet us carrying the book he had been reading. I was glad to see the book was not a yellowback novel but the first volume of Emerson's *History*. The sitting room was neater than it had been on the occasion of my first visit, but it could have done with dusting and there was a faint whiff of that strange odor.

If Jack was not pleased to see us, he was faultlessly polite, offering us chairs and refreshments, the latter of which we declined.

"We were out for a stroll and decided to stop by for a moment," I explained.

Even a few days without the dire effects of alcohol had restored the young fellow to his former healthy looks and intelligence. "You stopped by to see if I had gone back to the bottle," he said bluntly. "The cure has begun and you need not fear I will give way again. As you yourself reminded me, I have obligations to carry out." His jaw protruded and his teeth were bared; I could almost see Mr. Roosevelt leading the charge on San Juan Hill.

"I am delighted to hear it," I said, hoping I spoke the truth. "We will not keep you longer, then. Is Geoffrey here?"

"I no longer need a nursemaid, Mrs. Emerson."

"You misunderstood my meaning, Mr. Reynolds. I asked after Geoffrey as I would ask after any friend."

"Well, then, he's not here. He went off yesterday—I don't know where. He left a message saying he'd be gone for a few days. I was away from home."

"I see. Good night, then."

He insisted on seeing us to the door, and when I gave him my hand in farewell, he held on to it. "If I was rude or abrupt, Mrs. Emerson, I hope you will forgive me. I will always be grateful to you for your help."

"What was that all about?" Katherine asked curiously, as we started back toward the villa. "I found his manner very odd, Amelia."

"Men are very odd, Katherine. I cannot say for certain what is on his mind. I thought I detected some resentment of Geoffrey, but I would not care to say whether Jack was angry because his friend had deserted him or because he had come to his assistance in the first place! The poor creatures do dislike admitting they are dependent on others for help. I must confess that concern for Jack was not my primary reason for calling on him this evening."

"You thought Nefret might have gone to him?"

"To Geoffrey, rather. She is better friends with some of the young men than with the young ladies of Cairo society, which is not surprising, considering that the latter are empty-headed ninnies. It is surely more than a coincidence that Geoffrey went off leaving such a vague message. If she was in some distress, as I believe her to have been, he would have offered himself as escort to—well, to wherever she wanted to go. Nor would he have betrayed her confidence to Jack. Yes, that must have been what happened. I confess I am relieved to know she is not alone."

"He is not the sort of man to take advantage, I suppose."

"Of Nefret?" I could not help laughing. "He is a perfect gentleman, and Nefret is not the sort of woman who is easily taken advantage of. Depend upon it, we will hear from her soon."

We did hear, the following evening. The letter was handwritten and delivered by messenger. "I hope you haven't been worried about me. We will be home in a few days, Geoffrey and I. We were married this morning."

**Ah, the wonder of those chill desert nights! How often have I laid [sic!] wrapped only in a blanket looking up at the canopy of stars and thinking of Him who made them. A man whose thoughts and acts are not ennobled by such experiences is beyond redemption.**

### From Manuscript H

The *Amelia's* gangplank was out and David was on deck, leaning on the rail and smoking his pipe. His thin brown face broadened in a smile when he saw Ramses, and he came with long strides to meet him.

"I hoped we'd see you this afternoon," he said. "You weren't at the train station this morning."

"I'm sorry, there was something else I had to do." He gripped David's outstretched hand. "I've missed you."

"I can't say that you have been foremost in my thoughts the entire time."

Ramses laughed. "Had that been the case I would question your sanity. So—"

"So stop behaving like an Englishman." David held out his arms. "Embrace me as a brother should."

The landing stage was used by the steamers that carried tourists from Cairo; only Emerson's prestige (and, Ramses suspected, a judicious application of baksheesh from Reis Hassan) had won the *Amelia* permission to use it. The location was within walking distance of the house, and the convenience of this outweighed the disadvantage of the crowds that filled the area several times daily. Some of them stared and whispered at the sight of two men in European dress embracing one another.

"The devil with them, as the Professor would say," said David, sketching an impertinent parody of a salaam at a staring woman. He was looking well, Ramses thought; his face was fuller and there was a new firmness in the set of his well-cut lips. Ramses had looked forward to this moment for weeks. Now there was so much to say he didn't know where to begin.

David saved him the worst of it. "Aunt Amelia told me about Nefret. Do you want to talk about it?"

"No. Why are we standing here? I haven't said hello to Lia."

"She can wait," said Lia's husband. "For God's sake, Ramses, don't pretend, not with me. What happened?"

"Mother told you about the child?"

"Yes. I won't ask why you didn't write me about her; you never tell me anything! It must have been a frightful shock having her turn up out of the blue with that filthy swine Kalaan. But there has to be more to it than that. Even Nefret wouldn't rush off and get married unless . . ."

"Unless she loved him."

"Do you believe that?"

"What I believe is immaterial. It's over and done with." The desire to pour out his anger and bewilderment to the one person who knew most of the truth was almost overpowering. He couldn't do that, though. Not even to David could he admit what had happened between Nefret and him. A man who had just had an arm or a leg amputated might feel the same, he supposed, the wound too raw to bear the slightest touch.

"It was clever of Kalaan to approach you instead of Percy," David said thoughtfully. "Trying to blackmail him would have been a waste of time. And of course everyone in Cairo knows you and your parents by sight and by reputation."

"That's the logical explanation," Ramses said. "If one were charitably inclined one would assume Kalaan didn't know the truth either."

"But the woman must know. Aunt Amelia said you've been searching for her."

"Not to force a public confession out of her, if that's what you suppose. No one would believe her anyhow. The damage is done." Indignation furrowed David's broad forehead, but Ramses

cut him off before he could protest. "It's done, I said. We have
several more pressing problems to deal with. I wish I could leave
you and Lia in peace for a while longer, but you know the family
too well to hope for that! What else did Mother tell you?"

"Quite a lot." David knew when to stop asking questions. He
put his hand on Ramses's shoulder and they started back toward
the boat. "What the deuce has been going on? Murder, assault—"

"The usual sort of thing," Ramses murmured.

"Yes, quite. Like the forgeries?"

"She told you about that too?"

David grinned reluctantly. "When she stopped for breath, the
Professor started in. I felt like a boxer reeling from a series of
hard hits to the jaw!"

"Well, you know Mother." He stopped to greet Reis Hassan,
and went on, "When she decides to confide in someone she lets
him have it all at once."

"I prefer it to her former habit of never telling us anything."

Ramses had not been on the *Amelia* since they moved. The
saloon looked strange without the clutter of books and papers
that had always filled it. David hadn't had time to scatter his
drawing materials and reference books about; the place was almost too neat for comfort.

Lia was sitting on the wide curving divan under the windows;
the setting sun framed her golden hair like a halo. One of the
servants must have delivered the messages and letters that had
come for them over the past weeks; a stack of envelopes was on
the divan beside her and her head was bent over the letter she
held in her hand. He noticed, because he had got in the habit of
noticing things, that it was several pages in length, and that it
absorbed her to such an extent that she failed to observe his presence until he was actually in the room. Thrusting the letter into
the pocket of her skirt, she ran to meet him. When she freed
herself from his hearty embrace, he saw there were tears in her
eyes.

"I'm glad to have you to ourselves for a bit," she said, taking
his hand and leading him to the divan. "We are dining with the
family this evening, and you know what that will be like—everyone talking at once!"

"I'm afraid you are in for several days of exhausting celebration," Ramses said lightly. "Selim has been organizing a fantasia
to which the entire village is invited, and Mother spoke of giving
a ball or dinner party in your honor."

"She can just forget that," Lia said emphatically. "I refuse—what's so funny?"

"You look exactly like Aunt Evelyn when she's in a temper. A nice little domestic cat pretending to be a tiger."

"She's not pretending," David said. The look he gave his wife made Ramses wish he were dead.

"I mean," Lia went on, "that we haven't time for balls and dinner parties, and no interest whatever in outfacing Cairo society. I find it hard to forgive you for not telling us, Ramses."

"About what?"

"Anything!" She gestured emphatically. "It was bad enough concealing the business of the forgeries from us, but you might have mentioned it when people started shooting at you."

"Mother," Ramses said meekly. "Not me, Mother."

"Oh, well, that's all right then!"

"I'm sorry."

She turned toward him and took his hand in hers. "No, I'm sorry. I shouldn't be scolding you; you've had enough to worry about. Do people really think you were responsible for that girl's death?"

Ramses blinked. Lia was always taking him by surprise. Like her mother, she looked fluffy and sweet and naive, but she had the same gift for going straight to the heart of the matter regardless of tact.

"I remember her from last year," Lia went on. "I didn't know her well and I didn't like her very much, but she didn't deserve to die that way, at the hands . . . Oh, Karima. Yes, thank you, we will have tea now."

It took a while to arrange the trays and dishes to Karima's satisfaction. When she had gone, Lia picked up exactly where she had left off. "At the hands of someone she knew and trusted."

"Did Mother tell you that?" Ramses asked. "We don't know for certain."

"It's obvious! She was a frivolous, overly confident woman, but she wasn't stupid enough to wander around alone at night. She was meeting someone, and that someone was not a lover."

"I'm afraid to ask how you arrived at that conclusion," Ramses murmured.

"She was in love with you," Lia said coolly. "And it wasn't you who was with her that night. Therefore—"

"Lia!" David exclaimed.

"It's true, isn't it? I don't know why men find these things so embarrassing! There are only two things that could have brought Maude out of the house that night: an invitation from a man she loved, or a threat from a man who had some hold over her."

"Good God," Ramses said helplessly. His face was burning. Perhaps it was his mother who had mentioned poor Maude's infatuation, but he feared Lia had got the information, along with a plethora of embarrassing commentary, from Nefret. "I—I don't know what to say."

"Something sensible, I hope," said his cousin. "You didn't do anything to encourage her, did you? I thought not. Then why do you feel guilty? Is my syllogism right or not?"

"Was that a syllogism?" He got a grip on himself. "All right, I see where you're going. You've overlooked something, though. What if she received a message purporting to be from me?"

"Unlikely in the extreme," Lia said, shaking her head so decidedly that her bright curls sparkled in the sunlight. "You saw a good deal of one another during the daytime and evening hours. If you wanted to arrange a rendezvous, you had only to whisper a word in her ear. She'd have to be pretty stupid to respond to a written message. Anyhow," she went on, before either of the men could object to this dubious generalization, "too many other unpleasant incidents have occurred for this to be unrelated. I think she knew something about those incidents and their perpetrator. Maybe she threatened to expose him. Maybe he realized her loyalty to him had been weakened by her love for another man—a man whom he had already attacked."

"Loyalty to whom?" David demanded. "You can't be referring to her brother!"

"Why not?" She turned to Ramses, her eyes narrowed. "You thought of it too, didn't you?"

He put his cup in the saucer and leaned back. "Allow me to commend you for having a mind almost as suspicious as mine. I suspect everybody, including Jack. He wouldn't even have to lure her out of the house. She might have been killed in her own room, or in the courtyard. No one looked for bloodstains. The servants don't sleep in the house and the aunt wouldn't notice a full-scale war. He had all night to dispose of the body and return home."

"That would mean Jack was the one who shot at Aunt Amelia and arranged the other accidents," David said thoughtfully. "Any idea why?"

"Mr. Vandergelt suggested one possible motive," Ramses said, "that the accidents were designed to drive us away from

Zawaiet el 'Aryan. It was pure luck that none of them resulted in a serious injury. Had one of us been killed or badly hurt, Father might have canceled the excavation."

"That suggests that there is something at the site this person doesn't want found. A tomb?"

"Zawaiet isn't the Valley of the Kings or even Giza, David. It's one of the most unpromising sites we've ever explored; there's nothing there but an empty collapsing pyramid and cemeteries of poor graves. Evidence of a crime, perhaps? Mother does have a gift for finding corpses. 'Every year, another dead body,' as Abdullah used to say."

Lia's face softened. "Dear Abdullah. Aunt Amelia is even more determined to clear his name than David's."

"We've rather lost sight of that issue recently," Ramses admitted. "I'm still not entirely convinced that the attacks on us are unrelated to the forgeries, but I'll be damned if I can see *how* they are related. We were getting absolutely nowhere with our investigation. The point about Zawaiet is that Jack worked there for several months last year. He is one of the most likely persons to have found something, or buried someone, or—or God knows what!"

"He wasn't the only one," David pointed out. "Mr. Reisner and his crew were there too."

"Mr. Reisner isn't here. Jack is. Only two other members of that crew are presently at Giza, Mr. Fisher and Geoffrey. Nefret's . . ." It was the first time he had said it. "Nefret's husband."

"I am indebted to you and Cyrus for rallying round this evening," I said to Katherine. "I am afraid it may be a bit sticky."

We were alone in the courtyard. Everything was ready; the dining table set, the flowers arranged. Cyrus had gone up to join Emerson in his study. I had no idea where Ramses had got off to. For the past few days he had spent all his spare hours in the filthy alleyways of Cairo, trying to find the miserable girl whose silence had supported the untruthful accusation against him. He had not even accompanied us to the railroad station to meet David and Lia; a rumor had reached him from one of his sources that Rashida had been seen the previous night and he had gone immediately to investigate. When he returned to the house later that day he said only that his informant had been mistaken. I hadn't seen him since.

"I feel certain you are worrying unnecessarily," Katherine said in her comfortable way. "You said you had seen Nefret this morning and told her about the child?"

"I had already written her. I knew she and Geoffrey were staying at Shepheard's; I ought to have called earlier, but I took the coward's way out by writing first."

"You were still angry with her."

"Yes," I admitted. "And not only on Ramses's account. I had always believed we were close, Katherine; why should she keep her engagement to Geoffrey a secret from me?"

"They were engaged?"

"They must have had an understanding, if not a formal engagement. A woman doesn't turn to a stranger when she is in distress."

"Not unless the foundations of her world have been utterly shattered," Katherine murmured.

"What do you mean?"

"I don't believe I know myself. It was only a passing fancy." She gave herself a little shake and returned to the subject at hand. "The understanding may have been quite recent. She didn't question your explanation, did she?"

"No; she said she ought to have known, and that she hoped he would forgive her, and . . . That was odd. She never mentioned his name—Ramses, I mean. She kept saying 'he' and 'him.' Geoffrey wasn't there. I don't know whether that was due to tact or his fear of facing me!"

"You don't dislike the young man, do you?"

"Quite the contrary. He is of good family—not that that sort of thing matters to me!—well-bred, cultured, and a first-rate archaeologist. That does matter, you know, especially to Emerson. No doubt it will work out for the best. But we have a number of things to decide. Geoffrey is committed to Mr. Reisner for the rest of this season, and you may be sure Emerson won't allow Nefret to shirk her duties on account of something as inconsequential as a honeymoon. And where are they to live? Harvard Camp is a bachelor establishment and I don't like the idea of them staying with Jack Reynolds. They had better come here to us."

"You might wait to see what they have to say on that subject," Katherine said with a smile.

A sharp but abortive yip from Narmer informed me of the

identity of an arriving individual. Only Ramses and Nefret could get the confounded dog to hush and it usually took her longer than it did him.

My deductions were correct as usual. Seeing Katherine, Ramses raised his hand to his head, discovered he was not wearing a hat, and lowered it again.

"David and Lia will be along in a few minutes," he announced. "She couldn't decide which hat to wear. They all looked much the same to me."

"Oh, is that where you were? Did you have tea with them?"

"Yes. Are you ready for your usual, Mother, or will you wait for Father and the others?"

"I will wait, thank you."

"Mrs. Vandergelt?"

"Thank you, Ramses, I will finish my tea."

I watched him walk to the sideboard. Except for his wind-blown hair he looked quite neat and tidy, in a nice tweed suit and a tie. It was not like him to begin drinking so early, though.

"You had better go up and see Sennia," I said. "Otherwise she will come looking for you."

"Of course." He put his empty glass down and mounted the stairs.

Another outburst from the dog, this one of longer duration, brought Emerson and Cyrus out of the former's study.

"Damned dog," said Emerson. He went out of the house, and I heard him and Narmer barking at one another. The dog appeared to regard Emerson's shouts as an attempt at friendly conversation. The barks faded into frustrated yelps when Emerson issued Lia and David in and closed the door.

Lia was laughing as she brushed at the dusty pawmarks on her frock. "It's good to be home," she declared, and hugged everyone in turn.

I rather expected Emerson would try to carry them off to his study to show them the plans of the site and explain at tedious length what he meant to do; but he seemed not quite himself. He had not gone with me to the hotel that morning, so this would be his first meeting since her precipitate marriage with the girl he loved like a daughter. I wondered if he had been hurt—no, I *knew* he had been hurt by her failure to share her feelings with him. Not that Emerson would ever have said so. I only hoped he would behave himself and not take it out on Geoffrey.

He and Nefret were so close on the heels of Lia and David, I wondered whether they had lingered until after we were all assembled. Both of them had reason to expect remonstrances or expressions of resentment, and there is safety in numbers. Nefret flew into Lia's arms, leaving the rest of us to converge on the unfortunate youth she had espoused. He carried it off quite well, I must say; mine was the first hand he clasped, but it was Emerson he addressed first, with a manful acknowledgment of error.

"I hope you can find it in your heart to forgive me, sir. I ought to have spoken to you and Mrs. Emerson; I ought to have waited a decent interval. I have no excuse except that I love her so very much."

"Well, hmph," said Emerson.

It was a more gracious response than I had dared expect.

Everyone was trying hard to behave normally. Geoffrey continued to command my regard; his congratulations and best wishes to the other pair of newly married persons were nicely expressed, and his manner toward me was that of an affectionate son. I could have wished he had not been quite so considerate of my advanced age and female frailty, settling me tenderly in a chair and supplying unnecessary footstools and cushions, but it would take a while, I supposed, before he was entirely at ease with me.

We settled down around the fountain and the entire household staff appeared with food and drink. They were all related to David in some degree or other, and they had been waiting eagerly to greet him and his bride. It was amusing to see Geoffrey stare as David took the tray of little sandwiches from Fatima so that she and Lia could hug one another. David went round the whole grinning circle, kissing cousins on both cheeks and shaking hands with more distant kin, and then Fatima bustled them out, with a last fond look at David.

"The fantasia is the day after tomorrow," I said. "I forgot to tell you, Nefret. You—and Geoffrey—will come, of course."

One day, I thought, I might be able to add his name to hers without having to stop and think about it.

"Of course," she said, and smiled at me.

I had never seen her look lovelier. She was wearing a new frock and her cheeks were brilliant.

Ramses had not made an appearance, and I began to wonder whether he was sulking or had climbed out a back window. I ought to have known better. Avoiding awkwardness was not his habit; he had, rather, waited until he was sure of being the focus of all eyes. He was carrying the child when he came slowly down the stairs.

The only word that occurs to me is "bedecked." Her frilliest frock, her largest hair bow, her most lavishly gilded slippers, and several strings of sparkling beads (which I had not purchased) adorned her small person. She looked like a full-blown pink rose.

Four new faces were too much for even a child of her astonishing self-possession. She buried her face in Ramses's shoulder and clutched him round the neck, but not before the others had seen her features clearly.

"Good Lord!" Geoffrey breathed. He was sitting next to me on the settee; I was the only one who heard him. Ramses emitted noises suggestive of strangulation, which made Sennia giggle and loosen her grip.

"She's a bit shy with strangers," he said easily. "Just ignore her till she gets used to you. Here is the lion, little bird," he went on in Arabic. "He wants to speak to you."

Whereupon Professor Radcliffe Emerson, the Father of Curses, holder of innumerable honorary degrees, scourge of the underworld and the greatest Egyptologist of this or any other age, growled and tickled her on the back of her neck.

It was impossible to ignore *him*, but we did our best. Lia's eyes were bright with tears of emotion. Nefret got slowly to her feet. I will never know what she meant to do, for at that moment, with the awful inevitability of an omen sent by some inimical deity, the massive, brindled form of Horus emerged from behind a potted plant, tail lashing and teeth bared.

We had not seen him for three days. He had disappeared the same morning Nefret left the house, and I would be the first to confess that I had not spent a great many minutes wondering what had happened to him. He was heading purposefully toward Nefret when the child's high-pitched chirps attracted his attention. Emerson had persuaded her to come to him, and she was investigating his pockets, for it had not taken her long to learn there was usually something in them for her. She and the cat caught sight of one another at the same moment.

If a cat's jaw could drop, Horus's did. He stopped dead in his tracks, staring.

Everyone in the room was familiar with the cat's vile temper, including Geoffrey, who still bore the scars of a recent attempt to make friends with Horus. Several of us moved at once. Ramses jumped up, I reached for a pitcher of water, Emerson wrapped his muscular arms protectively about the child and Nefret lunged for Horus. A scene of utter pandemonium ensued as our frantic efforts to intercept the beast countermanded one another; Horus slipped through Nefret's hands, bit Ramses's thumb, shook the water off his back (most of it had splashed onto the floor) and sat down with a thump at Emerson's feet, still staring. The child compounded the confusion by squirming and demanding to be put down so she could talk to the little lion.

"Be calm," I implored. "Everyone be calm. Don't get him excited. Emerson, hold on to her. Ramses, can you . . ."

"I can try," said Ramses. He slipped out of his coat, raised it, and advanced cautiously on the cat.

"He won't hurt her," Nefret said. Still on her knees, she began edging forward, and addressed Horus in a soft cooing voice. "Come to Nefret, bad Horus. Did you miss me? I missed you. Come and say hello. Good boy, Horus . . ."

The wretched beast did not even turn his head. I became aware of another sound, loud enough to be heard over Nefret's murmured endearments. It was quite an unpleasant sound, like the rasp of a rusty file, but it was unquestionably Horus's best attempt at a purr.

"Good Gad," I said.

"Good God," Emerson corrected. "Peabody, do you think—"

Horus flopped over onto his back and waved his paws. He looked perfectly ridiculous.

"It's a ruse," Ramses muttered. "A trick, to lower our guard. Nefret, get out of the way."

"No, don't." She pushed his raised coat aside and reached for the cat. Horus remained as unresponsive and as heavy as a rock when she lifted him up, only twisting his head round at an impossible angle so he could continue to stare at Sennia. Nefret sat down next to Emerson, who edged away.

"He won't hurt her, I tell you. He wants to make friends."

"Ha!" said Emerson.

"I've got him," Nefret assured him, taking a firm grip on the cat's front legs. Then—for the first time—she looked directly at the child and smiled. "Hold out your hand, little bird. Pat the lion. Gently, gently."

It was a most touching moment, and would have been even more touching if the child, squeaking with delight, had not grabbed hold of one of Horus's prominent ears and tugged.

"Gently," said Nefret, while the rest of us remained petrified in horrified anticipation. She detached the small fingers and put them on the cat's motionless head. "So."

Watching the creature submit meekly to hard pats and prodding fingers, I felt kindly toward him for the first time since I had made his acquaintance. As she attempted to guide the little hands Nefret was explaining to Emerson that Horus was only vicious with adult animals, including (I would have said especially) humans. He had never put a claw or a tooth into one of the kittens, even when they chewed his tail and jumped onto his back.

I turned to Ramses, who stood watching with his usual absence of expression. "You are dripping blood on the carpet," I remarked. "And I suppose you have got it all over your coat."

He had.

Horus had not only broken the ice, he had melted it. His unaccountable behavior formed the primary topic of conversation. Sennia had been with difficulty removed to the nursery, and Horus had been, with even greater difficulty, prevented from following her into the room. We left him lying across the threshold, since he growled and spat even at Nefret when she tried to remove him.

"I will have to acquire another cat, it seems," she remarked. "Horus is lost to me."

"In all honesty I cannot say I regret that," Geoffrey said, laughing. "You know, my darling, I would not deprive you of anything you desired, but I had not looked forward to sharing quarters with Horus. He hates me."

"He hates everyone," said Ramses, shifting his soup spoon to his left hand. Horus had bit his right thumb to the bone; I had had to bandage it so heavily it stuck out at a somewhat awkward angle. I knew Ramses would have the bandage off as soon as he was out of my sight, but at least I had done my duty. "Almost everyone," he went on. "There's no need for you to give him up, Nefret; you and Geoffrey will be living here, won't you?"

"I hadn't thought," she said.

"Well, you had better," Emerson declared. "I need you back on the dig, Nefret. We've found quite a lot of bones for you, and we are days behind with photographing."

"Lia and I will take over the photography," David said. "And we are ready to start as soon as you like. I feel guilty at staying away so long."

"Tomorrow, then," Emerson began.

"Emerson, don't be absurd," I exclaimed. "They just got here."

The fantasia is the following evening; Selim and the others have been planning it for weeks."

"I'm looking forward to it," Cyrus declared. "I've attended a few fantasias in Luxor, but this should be a bang-up affair."

"No champagne, Cyrus," I reminded him.

"Well, I know that. But there's nothing to stop us having a few glasses beforehand, is there?" His eyes twinkled.

We parted earlier than Emerson would have liked; he was anxious to show David the photographic studio and would have detained him for hours going over plans of the site, had I not pointed out that it had been a long day for David and Lia. Nefret and Geoffrey left at the same time. We stood in the doorway (with Narmer barking like a maniac) watching them walking arm in arm along the dusty road, Lia with Nefret, the two young men following. It gave me an odd feeling to see someone other than Ramses making part of that group.

He had not gone with us to the door. Emerson shouted at Narmer, who barked joyously back at him, and put his arm round my waist. "It is still early, Peabody. What about a final whiskey and soda?"

"You feel the need of it, do you?"

"Need? Certainly not! Though," Emerson said morosely, as he drew me inside, "it gave me an odd feeling, seeing them go. They are leaving the nest, Peabody. I suppose Ramses will be next. I want to talk to you about him, Peabody. Do you think he—Ah, er, hmph, there you are, my boy. I thought you had retired."

"No, sir. Did you say you wanted to talk to me?"

"Don't stand at attention like some cursed military moron," Emerson said. "Sit down. That is an order," he added irritably.

Ramses smiled and obeyed. He had already removed his coat and tie; Emerson followed suit as he strode toward the sideboard, tossing his nice coat in the general direction of a chair. He missed, of course.

Emerson came back with three whiskeys. "I did want to talk to you," he said. "Have you and Nefret patched it up?"

"Why . . . yes, sir, certainly. You know that hasty temper of hers. She apologized very nicely."

"Oh? When was that?"

"Just after dinner, when I offered my official congratulations to Geoffrey. I had not had the opportunity of doing so before. She was charming to Sennia, didn't you think?"

Emerson's brows drew together. He is not the most sensitive of men (except with regard to me), but even he heard something chilling in that even, unemotional voice. "Don't get me off the track," he growled. "You would not mind, then, if they came here to stay?"

"Why should I? You heard me make the same suggestion at dinner. I repeated it later to Geoffrey. The suite Nefret decorated so prettily will be ideal for them. He accepted with thanks—subject, of course, to your approval."

"What about Nefret's approval?" I inquired.

"She did not object. In fact, I had intended to begin moving my things back to my old room tonight, so if you will excuse me—"

"One more thing," said Emerson. "You haven't found her yet?"

Ramses had drunk very little of his whiskey. He reached for the glass again; it tipped and spilled. "Damn it," said Ramses, glaring at his thumb. "I beg your pardon, Mother. But it's not just one thing, Father, it's too damned—"

"Don't apologize again," I said wearily. "It's too damned many things, isn't it? Have you spoken to David about the forgeries?"

"We've both spoken to him, but neither of us has given *him* a chance to offer an opinion! Then there's Maude's death, and Mr. Vandergelt's theory about the accidents, and my visit to Wardani—David isn't going to like my interfering, not one damned bit, but I'll have to tell him—and my futile search for Rashida . . . She's gone, Mother. I'd have located her by now if she were anywhere in Cairo—and alive."

"If she were dead, her body would have been found," I said.

"No. Deaths like hers aren't reported. She'd have been swept up and thrown out with the other refuse of the streets."

Over his bowed head I met Emerson's eyes, and in their icy blue depths I saw confirmation of Ramses's bitter words.

"What about Kalaan?" he asked.

"I found out where he lives. It wasn't easy. None of his women knew—they wouldn't—and he doesn't advertise his whereabouts. The house is in Heliopolis—quite an elegant establishment. No one was there. The place was shut up and swept clean."

"What did you do, break in?" Emerson inquired.

"Well, yes, you might call it that. From the amount of dust I would say he'd been gone for at least a week, and from the absence of everything except a few sticks of furniture I would say he isn't coming back in a hurry."

Emerson put his hand on Ramses's shoulder.

"We'll find him. We've never been defeated yet, and we won't be this time. How can we lose with your Mother and her deadly parasol on our side?"

"Quite right," I said briskly, and patted Ramses's other shoulder. "Go to bed now. Things will look better in the morning. It is always darkest before the dawn."

Ramses let out a choked sound that might have been a laugh or a muffled swear word, and got heavily to his feet. "Yes, Mother."

"I wonder how much Nefret has told Geoffrey," I said. "He will have to be taken into our confidence."

"Of course," Ramses said. "He's one of the family now, isn't he?"

Ramses brought Sennia down to breakfast next morning, without bothering to consult me. The sight of the child roused Emerson from his habitual grouchiness and reduced him to a state of fatuous amiability I hadn't seen in him at that hour for many years. Horus came with them. He squatted on the floor as close to the child as he could get and never took his eyes off her. Before long we were joined by Lia and David, who had, as Lia declared, been unable to stay away. It was almost like old times, with everyone laughing and talking at once, for David wanted to tell Emerson all about Crete and Lia demanded a tour of the house, and both of them kept offering tidbits to Sennia, while Fatima hovered over the table like a benevolent genie and the new nursemaid stood shyly in the doorway, afraid to come closer and unwilling to leave her charge entirely to others. Finally Sennia became so sticky with jam that even Emerson did not protest when I ordered that she be removed. She was borne off in triumph by the nurse. Horus got up and went after them.

"You needn't worry, Mother," said Ramses, reading my expression accurately. "I had to rescue *him* this morning; she had hold of his tail with both hands and was trying to eat it. He didn't even scratch me when I detached her."

"How long did you wait before you detached her?" David asked. He had never been fond of Horus either.

"A bit longer than was strictly necessary." Ramses smiled. I
was relieved to see that he looked tanned and rested and not so
tense. Having David back was good for him.

Emerson had been scrubbing ineffectually at the jelly spots on
his shirt. They looked unpleasantly like fresh blood.

"You had better change it," I said.

"Never mind that," Emerson grunted. "I thought we might
just take a little ride and—er—"

"Have a quick look at the site? Emerson, I told you—"

"A ride would be enjoyable," David said. "I haven't said hello
to Asfur and Risha. What do you say, Lia?"

It was obvious that she had anticipated something of the sort,
for she was dressed for riding—not in the absurd garments that
had once been de rigeur for lady equestriennes, but in the short
divided skirt and neat boots both girls wore on the dig—and her
ready acquiescence assured me she was anxious to return to the
busy life she had learned to love as dearly as the rest of us did.

"Did Nefret—and Geoffrey—say anything about coming
round today?" I asked, as we made our way through the garden
toward the stable.

"I believe they plan to," Lia replied. "Are they really . . . Is it
true that they will be moving in with you?"

"Good gracious, Lia, you sound as if you don't approve."

"No, not at all, Aunt Amelia. I mean, no, I don't mean to
sound that way. Are these the stables? How nice the garden looks!
It will be good to see the horses again."

"Selim has taken excellent care of them," Ramses said, as David flung both arms round Asfur's neck and she nuzzled his shirt.
"Shall we take them out, then? Mother, perhaps you would rather
not—"

"If you are all going, I am going too," I declared. "The mare
Selim hired for me in place of that other wretched animal does
very well."

From the open door at the far end of the stable came a murmur of sounds—squeaks, squawks and the rustle of straw. "I see
Nefret has her usual collection of animal patients," Lia said, looking in. "What on earth is in that large cage, and why is it covered?"

"Oh, dear," I said. "I had forgot about him. I hope Mohammed . . ."

"He's all right," said Ramses, behind me. "He has to be
hooded or covered so he won't hurt himself trying to fly."

He lifted the cloth covering the cage and Lia let out a cry of sympathy and admiration. The bird was a young male peregrine falcon, the same species depicted in the hieroglyph for the name of the god Horus. He sat hunched and unmoving, his great talons gripping the perch.

"Who has been feeding him?" I asked guiltily. I hadn't given much thought to Nefret's pets; I knew I could count on Mohammed to care for the others, but he had a superstitious fear of the great bird of prey. I knew the answer, though. Like Nefret, Ramses had a well-nigh uncanny rapprochement with animals, even feral beasts few people would have cared to approach. He opened the cage and reached inside. The bird stirred uneasily but did not struggle as his long brown fingers closed round its body and moved gently along the wings.

"The wing has healed," he explained. "She wanted to give him a few more days' rest before she freed him."

"She always hates to let them go," Lia said softly. "I suppose she has given him a name?"

"Harakhte," Ramses replied. "She couldn't call him Horus, since that repellent cat had already preempted the name."

"It means Horus of the Horizon," I explained. "Horus was a solar deity as well as the son of Osiris. After passing through the perils of the underworld, he emerged from the portal of dawn into a new day."

"Thank you, Aunt Amelia," Lia said.

The windows were always shuttered at night, to keep predators out. Ramses unlatched the nearest shutter and pulled it back. The hawk let out a strange little mewing cry and stirred, raising shoulders and wings slightly before letting them fall again. The sunlight brought out the delicate tracery of black feathers and the fierce curved beak. Ramses reached into his pocket. He must have stopped by the kitchen before joining us, since the bundle he withdrew squelched and—despite the oiled paper— began to drip darkly.

"Not a pretty sight, I'm afraid," he said to Lia as he unfolded the oiled paper. "Falcons like their food fresh and bloody. I hope I can coax him to eat. He's—"

He broke off, and I turned, following the direction of his gaze, to see Nefret standing in the doorway.

"Good morning," she said. "How is he?"

"As you see. Would you care to do it?" Ramses held out his

hand. The nasty objects, now fully exposed, reeked with the smell of fresh blood.

They faced one another across the cage, and I could not help thinking (for I am a connoisseur of the fine arts) that the tableau would have made a splendid subject for one of the pre-Raphaelite painters like Holman Hunt, or the great Dante Gabriel Rossetti. On one side the maiden, crowned with the coils of her golden hair; on the other the tall, dark-haired youth, his outstretched hand crimson with the blood of sacrifice; between them the god, the falcon of the dawn, caged in darkness. What rich symbolism, what evocative hints of myth and legend! Sunlight framed the figures like the gold gesso so lavishly employed by the school of painting to which I have referred. Rossetti would probably give the maiden robes of forest-green velvet . . .

Then the maiden said, "Throw the filthy stuff away."

"It would be a pity to waste it," Ramses murmured. He returned the mess to the paper and put it down on the table.

"Don't wipe your hand on your trousers, Ramses," I said, a moment too late.

The others had come to see what was going on. "Stay out," Nefret ordered.

Geoffrey, in the lead, gave her a look of hurt surprise. "What are you doing, sweetheart? Can I help?"

"I'm going to free him. Get out of my way. Ramses, open the back door."

He caught hold of her hands as she reached for the cage. "Not without the gloves."

The heavy gauntlets had seen hard usage and were streaked with droppings. She took them from him and drew them on. Once in the stableyard, she lifted the bird onto her forearm. He was not full grown and she was no fragile blossom of civilized leisure, but I did not see how she could manage the muscular effort necessary for what she contemplated doing. I thought for a moment that Ramses was going to offer to do it for her, or perhaps suggest a more practical, if less theatrical, method; but she turned her head to look at him and his parted lips closed.

She stood motionless for a moment, her free hand hovering over the feathered head, and I could have sworn she whispered to the creature. When she moved, the bird moved, at the same instant and with the same splendid strength. Its wings spread as she flung it up; it rose under its own power and soared, circling and climbing. She stood watching it, her head thrown back, until a great scream of triumph and release floated down from the morning sky. Then she turned and went back into the shed.

Geoffrey was standing next to me. "Magnificent," he whispered, his eyes shining. "She is like a goddess! What have I done to deserve a woman like that?"

"I am sure I have no idea," I replied, and then smiled as he bent a reproachful look on me. "Just one of my little jokes, Geoffrey. You will become accustomed to them in time. No, don't follow her yet. It always hurts her to let them go."

We left shortly thereafter, and since everyone was keen on trying the horses anyhow, I could see no objection to visiting the site. The fine animals made nothing of the short distance.

The men were not at work that day. Daoud and Selim were preparing for the fantasia, which they had assured us would be the most magnificent ever held in Egypt, and the site lay barren and deserted under the rays of the midday sun. A dry little wind blew mists of sand across the plateau. Nefret had drawn a thin scarf across her face, like the veil of a Moslem lady.

After we had walked round the perimeter and inspected the steeply sloping entrance stairs, we retired to my little shelter and sipped the cold tea I had brought along. David did his best to express enthusiasm over our battered pyramid and rows of wretched graves, but I could tell he was not excited about it, and so could Emerson.

"We are spoiled, that is our trouble," he announced gloomily. "Never forget, David, that this is what Egyptology is all about. Painstaking, dull research, not gold and treasure."

"I don't wonder you are spoiled, after finding the tomb of Tetisheri," Geoffrey remarked. "How I envy you the experience! We have come across some interesting things at Giza, but nothing to compare with that."

Since there were not enough chairs and stools for all of us, he was stretched gracefully at Nefret's feet. His coloring was even fairer than Lia's, his hair bleached almost to silver by the sun; the regularity of his features gave his face a look of remoteness unless it was warmed by animation, as it was now.

"I've been thinking," he went on, with a charming air of diffidence. "I hope you won't think me presumptuous for suggesting this, Professor—it is only a suggestion . . ."

"Well?" Emerson demanded.

"I do know a bit about this site, sir—enough, perhaps, to save you some time and trouble. I would like very much to join your staff."

"Now?" Emerson took his pipe from his mouth. "Naturally I would be glad to have you, but I don't think Reisner would forgive me for leaving him short-handed."

Geoffrey sat up and clasped his arms round his bent knees. "He would not only forgive you, sir, he would be forever in your debt if you allowed someone to replace me—someone whose qualifications are far greater than mine." He added, with a boyish grin, "He's not as scrupulous as you, Professor. Admit it, Ramses, Reisner has tried several times to persuade you to work with him."

Emerson's eyes flashed. "I suspected as much! Grrr! Curse it, excavators are all alike, not a moral among the lot of them. Ramses, is this true?"

"Yes, sir. I believe I mentioned last year, after my season with him at Samaria, that he had offered me a position on his Giza staff. He made no secret of it."

"Nor should he," I said, seeing Emerson's face redden. "You have always said, my dear, that Ramses is free to take any position he likes."

"Well, yes, but . . ." said Emerson. "Hmph."

"I have no interest in working for anyone else, sir," said Ramses.

"It's true that your talents are wasted here," Emerson muttered. "We're not likely to find much in the way of inscriptional material. Those Fourth Dynasty mastabas at Giza . . ."

Geoffrey looked from his crestfallen face to the expressionless countenance of Ramses. "I didn't mean to cause trouble," he said earnestly. "My decision has already been made. Leaving Mr. Reisner may be professionally wrong, but other considerations far outweigh that. Do you suppose, sir, that I am unaware of the dangers you face—I, who was present on the occasion Mrs. Emerson was attacked by an unknown gunman? I may not be of much use, but my place at a time of peril is at the side of my wife."

He reached for Nefret's hand and held it to his cheek.

"Hmmm," said Emerson. "So you told him, Nefret?"

"She didn't have to tell me," Geoffrey said indignantly. "Even if I were not familiar with your past history, I could not be fool enough to miss the signs. There have been too many suspicious accidents. Poor Maude's death was another such. I don't know what lies behind all this, and if you choose not to inform me I will not ask. All I ask is the privilege of helping you to the best of my poor abilities."

"A handsome offer," said Ramses. "I don't see how we can refuse."

So intense was the emotional atmosphere that when David cleared his throat, we all started and stared at him. He hardly ever spoke when we were all together; everyone else talked louder and faster than he did and his gentle nature prevented him from the rudeness of interrupting. Now he said quietly,

"I agree. The least we can do is tell Geoffrey what does lie behind this. Or have you already informed him about the forgeries, Nefret?"

"No. I thought . . . There hasn't been time."

Ramses, seated cross-legged on the rug, shifted position slightly. Nefret glanced at him and then looked away.

"You thought to spare me embarrassment," David said, with an affectionate smile. "That was good of you, dear, but it was not necessary."

I had told him most of the story that morning. He now repeated it to Geoffrey, who listened with astonishment writ large across his ingenuous countenance.

"But then," he stuttered. "Then—that explains the attacks on you. This person fears exposure. He will kill to prevent it!"

"It doesn't explain a damned thing," said Emerson. "Or, to be more accurate, it doesn't solve our problem. We've made no progress finding the swine. He could be anyone; he could be anywhere."

"Anywhere around Cairo," I corrected. "Unless the actual violence has been perpetrated by hired thugs, in which case, I agree, he might be elsewhere. If we can capture one of the villains next time he attacks us—"

David raised his hand. "Excuse me, Aunt Amelia. I know that waiting to be attacked is your preferred method of catching criminals, but I would rather try something less dangerous. You have been so tender of my feelings and my reputation that you've overlooked the step we must take next. Indeed, it is the only one a man of honor could consider."

"What do you mean?" I asked apprehensively. When men start talking about honor, there is sure to be trouble.

"I intend to write to every dealer who handled the forgeries, informing them that my grandfather had no collection of antiquities and that the individual who sold them the objects was an impostor. You can supply me with a list, I presume?"

For a time the only sounds that broke the silence were the hiss of windblown sand and the droning of flies. Ramses was—of course—the first to speak. "I have a list. It is not complete."

"It's a start," David said. "The word will spread. This may or may not lead to information that will help us identify the man we want, but that is not the important thing."

Emerson's pipe had gone out. Slowly and deliberately he removed it from his mouth, tapped out the ashes, and put it in his pocket. Then he rose and offered David his hand.

"I am," he remarked, "a damned idiot. It just goes to show that one should never allow sentiment to interfere with common sense. Shake hands, my boy, and accept my apologies."

"Not at all, sir. It was my fault, for getting married and distracting everyone."

He was laughing as he looked up at the impressive form towering over him. What a handsome, upstanding lad he was! Marriage had given him additional confidence and maturity; I fancied (for I have my moments of sentiment) that his grandfather must have looked like David when he had been the same age, long before I met him. Abdullah had been a fine-looking man till the day of his death. He had been so proud of David. He would have been even prouder if he had heard him that day.


In the villages the separation of the sexes which rouses the indignation of foreign visitors is not so strictly enforced. Separate harems or women's quarters are only found in the villas of the well-to-do, and only a wealthy man can afford to keep a woman who contributes nothing to the maintenance of the household. Such a woman is purely ornamental, a sign of his success. (I should not have to point out certain uncomfortable parallels with our own society; but in case the Reader be too obtuse or blinded by prejudice to see them, I will remind him or her of the upper-class ladies of England, who do little but dress richly and drive out in their carriages to pay calls on other richly dressed ladies.)

Egyptian women of the fellahin class work hard, and are, in my opinion, all the better for it. In many ways their position is invidious, but they have some rights Englishwomen still lack. Their property is their own and in the case of divorce or the death of their husband they are entitled by law to a portion of his estate.

Older women who have outlived several husbands are said to be among the wealthiest citizens of the country, lending money at usurious rates (and undoubtedly enjoying their power).

But I digress. The village of Atiyah, where our men and their families lived, was a model of its kind. Not only was it unusually clean, but it boasted a number of amenities not often found in such small places. Abdullah and his kin had commanded (and deserved) high wages, and I daresay their long acquaintance with us had modified some of their views of the world. Egypt was changing, slowly and not always for the better, but the younger men like Selim were far more open to new ideas than their fathers had been.

It had been almost five years since Abdullah left us, but whenever I went to the village my eyes automatically looked for the tall dignified form that had once been the first to greet us. Now it was Selim, his father's son and successor, who advanced to welcome our party. The village was draped with banners and bunting, and the noise was deafening—dogs barking, drums beating, children shouting, and rising over it all the shrill ululating cries of the women. A guard of honor escorted us to Selim's house, where a feast was to precede the fantasia.

Rugs and cushions covered the floor of the principal reception room, and we were invited to take our places upon them. I made a point of sitting next to Geoffrey, for I assumed he would appreciate a few tactful hints as to how to behave. To be sure, Egyptologists were less narrow-minded than other non-Egyptians, but few of them mingled socially with their workers, and some had never tasted Egyptian food.

Ignorant persons picture Egyptians as crouching round a platter of food and stuffing it into their mouths with both hands. In fact, the procedure is quite elegant and refined in its own way. After we had seated ourselves round the large copper tray that served as a table, servants poured water over our hands, into a basin with a pierced cover, and we dried them on the serviette (footah) that had been supplied. In a low, reverent voice Selim intoned the blessing—Bismillahi—in the name of God—inviting us to partake. Round flat loaves of bread are used as plates and as utensils, a piece being torn off, doubled, and used to scoop up bits of food. It takes some practice to do this neatly, but then, so does the use of a knife and fork! Knives were not necessary; the food was in the form of yakhnee, stewed meat with onions, or other edibles that could be daintily picked up with the thumb and the first and second fingers. One uses only the right hand, of course; when a roasted fowl must be dismembered it is sometimes necessary for two persons to cooperate, each using only the right hand.

I will not describe the dishes in detail; they included several of my favorites, including a large dish of bamiyeh, which is the pod of the hibiscus lightly cooked and sprinkled with lime juice. As platter followed heaping platter and the temperature rose higher, Geoffrey's pale face grew flushed and finally he fell back against the cushions with a subdued groan.

"I don't want to let the side down, Mrs. Emerson," he whispered. "But I don't think I can go on much longer. I've never eaten so much in my life!"

"You have done nobly," I assured him. "Just nibble."

We were all uncomfortably replete by the time we removed from the house to the village square, where the fantasia was to take place. Chairs had been placed for us (I saw Geoffrey brighten visibly when he realized he no longer had to kneel) and colored lanterns hung round the perimeter of the space.

The principal forms of entertainment at these celebrations are music and dancing. Egyptians are very fond of music; it is a tradition that goes back to ancient times. Modern Egyptian singing sounds strange to Western ears at first. I now found it very beautiful when it was well performed, as I expected would be the case that evening.

The drummers tuned their instruments—pottery jars of various sizes covered with animal skins drawn tight across the wide mouths—and began a soft beat. It was wonderful to watch the movements of their long fingers and supple wrists; even more wonderful to hear the variety of tone and volume their skill evoked. The beat quickened and grew louder, and other instruments joined in—pipes and flutes, lutes and dulcimers, and a kemengeh, an odd-looking stringed instrument which is played with a bow, like a viola.

The pièce de résistance was a performance by the most famous singer of the region, who had graciously consented to come out of retirement for this occasion. He was no longer young; but when he cupped his hand round his mouth and let his voice out, the tone was so beautiful the other musicians fell silent, so that not even the soft tap of a drum interrupted the golden notes.

Tumblers and jugglers, dancing by men and by women—though not together—a famed storyteller—it went on and on, for this was a celebration not only of a marriage but of the formalization of a relationship between two groups of people who were now united legally as well as by the bonds of affection. I would have said something to this effect had not Emerson warned me in advance that if I attempted to make a speech he would stop me by one means or another. He made a speech instead, in his most flowery Arabic, acknowledging both young couples and quoting several verses of poetry, which were not as vulgar as I had feared they would be. The speech was very well received, especially the poetry.

The evening ended with fireworks—purchased, as Selim proudly explained, at great expense. As we drove away, the spattering of firecrackers and the farewells of our friends faded into silence. The ride home in the open carriages was long but very beautiful, for the stars shone like jewels and the night breeze cooled faces flushed with pleasure and excitement. Emerson wrapped me tenderly in a shawl. If he had hoped to do more he was deterred by the presence of Ramses, who explained, with incontrovertible logic, that the other carriage would have been too crowded with five.

An Englishman who "goes native" betrays every other Englishman in the East. To learn something of the language is necessary in order to avoid being cheated; to wear native attire is sometimes convenient and comfortable; but acceptance of the corrupt moral standards of the Arab lowers our prestige. The women, for example . . .

**From Manuscript H**

Emerson had them out at dawn after their late night. He had always been able to go for days without any sleep to speak of, and he expected his associates to keep up with him. Ramses would rather have dropped in his tracks than admit he couldn't, but the combination of physical fatigue and mental confusion was taking its toll, and by the end of the day he could have cheered when his mother announced that they would stop work early. Another bit of good news was her decree that they would accept no social invitations for a few days—except, of course, with one another. They had a great deal of catching up to do, she said.

What she really meant was that she wanted Geoffrey and Nefret to herself for a while so that she could pry into the latter's feelings and get the former firmly under her thumb. He'd have plenty of company there.

When Lia asked Ramses to come to supper on the *Amelia*, just the three of them, adding that if they talked too late he should stay the night, it was as if someone had offered him a hand out of a fiery furnace. He was not managing as well as he had hoped.

After they got back from the fantasia, he had left the house, ostensibly for a walk, so he wouldn't have to watch Nefret and her husband go down the corridor to their rooms. Late as it was when he returned, he had not got much sleep.

There were several things he wanted to discuss with David anyhow, and he introduced the most pressing of them as soon as he decently could. They were sitting on the upper deck. It had been his mother's favorite place, and it was almost unchanged—the worn, comfortable wicker settees and low hassocks with their faded chintz covers, the awning flapping overhead, the tea-things set out on a low table. Lia had insisted he take off his coat and put his feet up. He hadn't realized how much of his fatigue was due to pure nerves until it began to drain out of him.

"You *are* rather a dear little thing," he said with a smile.

She put out her tongue at him. "And you are rather a dear yourself. For a man," she added, in his mother's very tone.

David beamed at both of them. "It's good to be back, and at work. You were right, though, Ramses; that is one confounded boring site! I felt as if I were photographing the same grave over and over—a few bones, a few broken pots, a few scraps of wood or stone. Only the Professor would insist on recording such rubbish."

"Geoffrey was a great help today," Lia said. "His Arabic isn't very good, but he's a first-rate excavator, even by the Professor's standards. Slow and meticulous. Ramses—what are you going to do about his idea that you should change places?"

"I wanted to consult both of you about that." She handed him a cup of tea and he took it with a nod of thanks. "It was a rather outrageous suggestion, and rather out of character for him. Not so much in itself, but that he should propose it without bothering to ask Father and Mr. Reisner—or me, come to that."

"Yes, but that's how one has to treat the Professor," David said, his eyes twinkling. "He is one of the most intimidating people I've ever met. If you don't stand up to him at the start, you're doomed to perpetual silence and servitude."

"Like you," his wife said with a fond look.

"Well, it took me a while," David admitted. "Quite a while. I agree, Ramses, that Geoffrey may have been a bit out of line, but it was a logical suggestion. One can't blame him for wanting to be with Nefret."

"Or wanting me out of the way?"

He hoped he wouldn't have to explain. Unless they saw it

too, he'd have to admit, if only to himself, that he had lost his sense of proportion. There was a long, nerve-racking pause before Lia spoke.

"He's still a suspect, isn't he? That hasn't changed. And—yes—if he's the one, and he's not given up his vendetta, he'd have a freer hand if you weren't there. You are a force to be reckoned with!"

"Only one of several, but the fewer the better, from the point of view of a potential enemy."

"The two of you make my blood run cold!" David exclaimed. "You'll be suspecting Nefret next! Look here, hasn't Geoffrey an alibi for one of the incidents? According to Aunt Amelia, he was with her when the shots were fired."

"That's true," Ramses said. "I'm only looking at the worst-possible scenario, as my dear mother taught me to do. Mr. Reisner won't be back from the Sudan until the end of the month, but Fisher is starting work shortly. I think I'll drop by Harvard Camp tomorrow and ask him if he'd like to take me on."

"Why did I know you were going to say that?" David demanded, running his hand through his hair. "And why did you bother asking our opinion if you'd already made up your mind?"

"I'm opposed," Lia said decidedly. "That would mean you'd be working with Jack Reynolds. For goodness' sake, Ramses, he threatened to shoot you!"

"That's one of the reasons," Ramses said, and laughed at her indignant look. "Not because he threatened to shoot me, dear—he was very drunk at the time and he seems to have settled down. But because he's also a suspect, and if I'm working with him I can play Sherlock Holmes, in my famous insinuating and clever fashion. There's another man working at Giza who is an even more logical suspect. Karl von Bork."

"Yes, Aunt Amelia mentioned him," David said. "But aside from the fact that his wife is an artist—"

"That's just one of Mother's little notions," Ramses said. "I can't imagine that he would involve Mary. The case against him is strong, though. He's been in Egypt a long time—not continually, but often enough to have struck up an acquaintance with a handy forger of antiquities. He's a good philologist. He's poor, and devoted to his extensive family. He's German. Our impostor sold objects to several dealers in that country, and he speaks the language. Von Bork knows us, and he knew Abdullah. Most damning of all is the fact that he once betrayed Mother and Father for money. His wife was dangerously ill and he didn't realize how serious the matter was, but it shows how far he might go if he believed his family was in need."

Lia drew a long breath. "That's damning, all right. I would rate him suspect number one."

"Which, in a work of fiction, would prove his innocence." Ramses smiled. "We haven't given him enough attention, though, and it's time we did."

The last steamer of the day let off a series of warning blasts, and Lia clapped her hands to her ears. "I'm going down to talk to Karima about dinner, and then rest for a while. That will give you two a chance to talk." Her light dress blew out around her graceful little figure as she walked to the head of the stairs, where she paused just long enough to say, "I'll tell Karima to make up the bed in your old room, Ramses. It's yours whenever and for as long as you want it."

Her bright head vanished below. Ramses turned an inimical look on his friend. David shook his head.

"No, my brother, I did not betray your confidence. But... well... you know women."

"I don't think I do."

"They are very romantic," David explained, with a worldly-wise air that would have amused Ramses under slightly different circumstances. "Inveterate matchmakers. We've been so close, the four of us, and you two seemed so ideally suited in every way... Lia talked about it, that's all. Just as something she would like to have happen."

"It didn't happen. Can we change the subject?"

"One thing more." David leaned forward. His soft brown eyes were warm with affection and concern. "I'll never mention the subject again until you bring it up—but for the love of God, don't push yourself too far. You have a bad habit of doing that. Do you think I can't tell? Come here to us if and when you like. Go to work for Reisner so you won't have to be with them all day every day. And when you're ready, talk to me."

𓅓

**I** thought Ramses had abandoned the search for Rashida until one afternoon when he asked if I would go to Nefret's clinic with him.

I was flattered that he should ask me, and said as much. "I have been wanting to visit the place, but your father put up such a fuss that I decided not to press the issue. He said that, much as he disliked her going, Nefret had a legitimate reason, but that idle curiosity was no excuse. Now you know, Ramses—"

"You are never inspired by idle curiosity," said my son gravely. "On this occasion your presence is necessary. Dr. Sophia knows me, but I am sure she would feel more comfortable about admitting me if I were with you. It is a forlorn hope, I am afraid, but one I feel I must make. If you will permit me, I will give you tea at Shepheard's afterward."

"Say no more," I exclaimed. "I am with you! Or will be, as soon as I put on my hat and find my parasol."

I have been in a number of the nastier sections of Cairo, but though el Was'a is in embarrassingly close proximity to Shepheard's, I had never gone there. I had heard about it, though. It proved to be even worse than my worst imaginings (which can be, as Emerson has often remarked, pretty bad). As evening approached, the houses were preparing to open for business. I am glad to say that my presence appeared to have a sobering effect on both the women and their prospective customers. Those who caught sight of me hastily withdrew behind curtains or around corners, and the raucous vulgarities being shouted by both parties were abruptly stilled.

"Perhaps I ought to come here every evening and walk about," I remarked, concealing my horror and disgust under a mask of levity.

"I keep forgetting how vile it is," Ramses muttered. "Father will murder me when he finds out I brought you here."

"Then we probably should not tell him."

Ramses had sent a message ahead, so we were expected. I was enormously impressed by the bright, cheerful interior of the house and the admirable state of cleanliness that prevailed. The doctor was Syrian Christian; the women of that region have more freedom than their Egyptian counterparts, and are taking the lead in the women's movement.

Sophia showed us to her office and Ramses plunged at once into his reason for coming. He must have planned in advance exactly what to say, for he gave only the necessary facts without entering into such details as the child's striking resemblance to me and the name of the presumed father. "It was an attempt at blackmail," he finished. "Which did not succeed. We have tried to find the girl, for I feel certain she was not a willing participant in the scheme, and it is possible Kalaan might vent his anger on her. In which case she might come here."

Though Sophia was courteous enough to pretend she knew nothing of the matter, it was clear to me that she had heard some version of it—the most malicious and insulting version, probably. I also understood why Ramses had asked me to accompany him. She had been rather stiff and formal with us; I had believed it to be her normal manner until her stern face relaxed. My presence supported his explanation, which she might not have accepted otherwise.

"I see. I cannot recall anyone of that description. I will notify you at once if she does come here, but I am afraid it is unlikely. We are able to help so few."

We chatted for a while. She had heard of Nefret's marriage and asked me to convey her good wishes, adding, with a smile and a twinkle, that they understood why Nefret had not been able to spend much time at the clinic. I expressed my admiration for the work she was doing, and she shook her head sadly.

"My medical training is limited to gynecology, Mrs. Emerson. We need a surgeon, but where are we to get one? Even if we could find a man who would be willing to donate his services, it might get us in trouble with the religious authorities. There are so few women being trained in that specialty."

We were about to take our leave when she said, "Perhaps I ought not ask; but you said the child's father is English. Would he be able to help you locate the young woman?"

"He was a tourist," I said. "It was not a long-lasting relationship, I believe."

"Expressed with your well-known irony, Mrs. Emerson. They will do it, the irresponsible creatures."

"I believe you are being ironic now," I said. "'Irresponsible' is certainly an understatement. Aside from the moral issues, they risk catching some singularly unpleasant diseases."

"How many men—and women—guide their actions according to safety and common sense?" was the inquiry. "The more sophisticated of them do take the usual precautions." She hesitated, her pleasant face hardening, and then added, "The *most* sophisticated use only girls who are . . . who had remained untouched."

When we were outside the house, Ramses drew my arm through his. "Mother, I'm sorry. I thought you knew."

"I know such things happen. I saw she was very young..."
I was unable to continue.

"I should never have taken you there. Forgive me."

I gave myself a little shake. "It is for you to forgive *me*. I do not often yield to weakness, I believe. But it is one thing to contemplate such a vile act in the abstract, quite another to think of its being committed by a man one knows—a man whose hand one has taken."

"Yes," Ramses said. "I understand."

Shepheard's terrace was crowded, as it always is at teatime, but I never have any difficulty in finding a place. Mr. Baehler now owned the hotel, and his successor as manager was just as obliging. I went to freshen up; by the time I returned, Freddy was waiting to show me to a choice table near the railing. Ramses was slow in joining me. I presumed he had encountered an acquaintance, so I amused myself by observing the passing crowds, one of whom, as I was soon to discover, had also observed me.

Percy was not in uniform, so I did not notice him until he was almost at my side. Taken by surprise, I was unable to conceal the shock and disgust I felt, even supposing I had been inclined to do so. He read my countenance and hastened to speak.

"Aunt Amelia! I have been haunting Shepheard's this past week in the hope of seeing you. May I offer you tea?"

"No. You had better take yourself off before I express my opinion of you loudly enough to be heard by everyone on the terrace."

"Ah." His face took on a look of quiet suffering. "Then the rumors I have heard—"

"I don't know what you have heard. If they accuse my son of one of the vilest crimes a man can commit, they are lies. Had you not lost all semblance of decency, you would clear Ramses and avoid the company of those who know the truth."

"But that is what I want to do!" Percy exclaimed vehemently. "To clear myself with you, at any rate. Won't you hear my side of it? You did not used to be unjust."

Ostentatiously I consulted my lapel watch. "You have sixty seconds."

He had remained standing. He did not venture now to sit down, but he put both hands on the back of a chair and leaned forward, lowering his voice.

"The child may be mine. I don't deny the possibility. No—please let me finish! I knew nothing of it, I swear! When I was last in Cairo I was young and foolish and easily led, but the—the act that led to the present difficulty was a single aberration, and one of which I am bitterly ashamed. I will do anything in my power to put things right. Money—any amount you think proper—"

He broke off with a strangled gasp and straightened, staring over my shoulder at something. I knew what it was, of course, even before I turned my head.

"The tables are very close together, Ramses," I said. "If you strike him he will fall over and injure some innocent people. Percy, I warned you you had only a minute. You ought to have heeded my advice."

Ramses's fists uncurled, but I thought I had better take hold of his arm just to be on the safe side. Percy had backed away as far as he could—only a step or two—but he had apparently decided he could risk a few more words.

"I meant what I said, Aunt Amelia. Do you believe I spoke the truth?"

"I don't care whether you spoke the truth or not," I said. "What you did is indefensible, and your attempts to excuse yourself only make it worse. I really don't think I can restrain Ramses much longer, Percy, and I am not at all certain I care to. Go away and never darken my door again."

"Very well." He bowed and backed up another few steps, glancing behind him in order to avoid running into a tourist. "I had meant to call on Nefret to offer my felicitations, but . . ."

I almost lost hold of Ramses. Percy beat a hasty retreat, weaving a path among the closely crowded tables with an agility born of a strong sense of self-preservation.

"Sit down," I said. "A public scene would only fuel the gossip. I remember once you asked me for permission to pound Percy. I am sorry now I didn't let you."

"I shouldn't have given myself away," Ramses muttered. "He only suspected before. Now he knows."

"Oh, I'm sure he already knew how thoroughly you detest him."

"What did he say before I arrived on the scene?" The angry color began to fade from Ramses's cheeks.

"He admitted the child might be his. It was a single aberration that occurred when he was young and easily led."

"He's good," Ramses said with grudging admiration. "He admits the truth only when he's backed into a corner, and then twists it to the best advantage."

"Well, my dear, we can be sure he will avoid us in future. I believe I made my feelings clear. Shall we order now? I could do with a nice hot cup of tea."

Two days later the body of a young woman was found caught in the reeds along the riverbank just above the barrage. We would probably not have heard of it had not Ramses's persistent inquiries made the Cairo police aware of our interest in any such discovery. It was Mr. Russell, the assistant commissioner, who informed us—or Ramses, to be precise. Ramses did not tell us until after he had seen the remains. A certain identification was impossible, since the body had been in the water for several days, but the general description matched that of Rashida, and twisted round the neck was a string of cheap beads like one she had owned. She had been stabbed a number of times. The police attributed the killing to a hashshaheen, for similar cases were known; excessive use of the drug may induce a homicidal frenzy.

We were unable to find any trace of Kalaan. Emerson believed he had left Cairo and was lying low. Ramses appeared to have lost interest in him. "There are too many others like him," he said with a shrug.

The next few weeks were without incident. I found this very alarming. Emerson scoffed at me when I expressed my forebodings (he always scoffs at my forebodings) but as I pointed out to him, an enemy who has already perpetrated several violent attacks, and a murder, is not likely to change his skin. This prompted another rude remark from Emerson on the subject of mixed metaphors, but I knew what I meant, and so did he.

When I say all was quiet I do not mean that a great many things were not going on. We dined with the Vandergelts and they dined with us; I gave a series of quiet but elegant dinner parties to welcome David and Lia and to honor the other young couple. All four of them, not to mention Emerson, had argued against my original idea of a large reception at one of the hotels, so I had been forced to give in. I do not enjoy such large social events, but I had wanted to outface the gossips. All in all, we had provided the narrow little world of Cairo society with a good deal of gossip that season, and I felt sure "they" were now engaged in malicious speculation on the suddenness of Nefret's marriage. When I mentioned this to Emerson he gave me one of the coldest looks I had ever received from that quarter.

"What sort of speculation?" he demanded.

"You know, Emerson. They will be counting the days."

"Until what?"

"Don't glower at me that way and don't pretend you don't understand."

"I do understand," Emerson snarled. "Confound it, Peabody, are all women so prurient and judgmental?"

"Yes, I think so. They were happy to believe 'the worst,' as the saying has it, of poor Maude Reynolds, and in their narrow little minds there is only one reason why a young woman would give up an elaborate church wedding with all the attendant fuss and ceremony. You know I don't believe it, Emerson, I only wanted . . ."

"I know." His stern face softened. "You wanted to indicate your love and support for Nefret and tell the gossips to go to the devil. Never mind, Peabody. She doesn't give a curse about the opinions of such people and neither should we."

So I sent out my invitations and in succeeding days we entertained practically every archaeologist in the Cairo area, and some from farther away. The Petries were not among them. The fact is, I did not get on with Mrs. Petrie any better than Emerson got on with her husband. Since women are more courteous than men (or greater hypocrites, according to a source I need not name), Hilda Petrie and I expressed our antipathy by being frigidly polite when we were forced to meet and by offering specious excuses for meeting as seldom as possible. I invited her, she wrote back to say she had a touch of catarrh or a slight sprain or nothing suitable to wear. Thus the civilities were maintained to the benefit of all.

M. Maspero also declined my invitation. I knew why *he* avoided us. It was shame, pure and simple! To see Emerson's superb talents wasted on a site as dreary as Zawaiet, while selfishly retaining the pyramids and cemeteries of Dahshur for lesser men, might have shaken even Maspero's superb French sangfroid.

To make matters worse, the disposition of the vast cemetery field of Giza was still in debate. Originally it had been broken up into three sections which were allotted to the Germans, the Italians and Mr. Reisner, but a few years later Signor Schiaparelli of the Turin Museum had abandoned the Italian concession. In theory this was divided between the other two, but they were still arguing about precisely who got what. The obvious solution—to hand over at least part of the Italian area to the most distinguished excavator of this or any other century—I believe I need not name names—was ignored by all those concerned. Emerson flatly refused even to mention the matter to Maspero and threatened me with divorce if I did so. This was, of course, just one of his little jokes. However, I decided not to speak to M. Maspero.

The temporary loss of his son had not improved Emerson's disposition. For the past fortnight Ramses had been working at Giza in place of Geoffrey. He had very properly announced his intentions to Emerson, whose noble nature had prevented him from objecting. There may have been just a slight touch of ignoble pride involved as well; it would not have been in character for Emerson to admit he would miss not only Ramses's professional skills but Ramses himself. Secretly, Emerson had hoped that Mr. Fisher, who was in charge at Giza until Mr. Reisner returned, would refuse to countenance this somewhat unorthodox arrangement without consulting his superior. Unfortunately, Fisher knew Reisner's high opinion of my son and fell upon the scheme with shameless enthusiasm. He wrote at once to Reisner, who was messing about in Middle Egypt, and eventually received approval, but not until after Ramses had already been at Giza for over a week.

It did not comfort Emerson to know, as he did, that the Harvard-Boston expedition was working in an area where they had already discovered wonderful things. Shortly after Ramses began, the Americans came upon a new tomb containing beautifully painted and carved scenes, a fine limestone statue, and other interesting items. It was enough to make Emerson's mouth water, especially when he returned each morning to scattered bones and broken pots. He knew Ramses's motives for abandoning us were not selfish; he knew it, but he envied him all the same.

One useful result of this arrangement was the reestablishment of relations with Jack Reynolds. Though he had straightened himself out (with a little help from me), he had rather avoided us. It is difficult to work in close proximity to a man who has accused you of murdering his sister; I had no fear for Ramses's safety, since I knew he was quite capable of looking after himself, but I took the earliest possible opportunity of asking him how he and Jack were getting on. He assured me Jack had been perfectly civil and helpful. I therefore invited Jack to one of our little dinner parties so I could see for myself.

Jack was on time, suitably dressed, and apparently sober. He had brought two large bouquets, one for each of the brides, which he presented with appropriately flowery speeches. As usual there were more men than ladies present; Howard Carter was in town, and young Mr. Lawrence, who had been working with Mr. Petrie, and who was loud in his praises. I must say that tact was not one of the young man's strong points. Fulsome praise of one's host's chief rival does not endear one to the said host, and he committed another faux pas by insulting the Egyptian workmen he had encountered. I heard a few words: "... horribly ugly, dull, low-spirited, foul-mouthed and fawning ..." before Ramses interrupted with a polite inquiry about Mr. Petrie's health.

Jack, whom I had placed across the table from me so I could watch him, had also overheard. "That is certainly not true of our people," he announced. "Perhaps it has something to do with the attitude of the man in charge. Mr. Reisner has always been on the best of terms with his workmen."

I gave him an approving smile. "Quite true. There have been no problems with the theft of antiquities, have there?"

"There are always problems with theft," Emerson grumbled. "Especially with Maspero refusing to heed accusations against his favorites. That disgraceful business at Sakkara—"

I was unable to administer a little kick to Emerson, since he was at the other end of the table, so I raised my voice to a particularly penetrating pitch and dragged the conversation back onto the track—with, I admit, something of a jolt.

"I suppose you have all also heard about the sales of antiquities this past summer purporting to have come from the collection of our late reis Abdullah? Some of you may not know that these objects are fakes, and that they were sold by a man who had assumed the name and identity of David here."

The first time I made this announcement at a dinner party Emerson had choked on a morsel of food and I had had to trot quickly round the table and pound him on the back. When he complained later that I ought to have warned him, I replied that I would have done so had I known in advance what I was going to do. In fact the idea came to me all of a sudden, as clever ideas often do, and I had seized the moment, so to speak.

David's decision to bring the matter of the forgeries out into the open had cut the Gordian knot: how to pursue our inquiries without admitting what we were inquiring about. It would be some time before he could expect to receive replies to the letters he had written, but now there was no reason for us to maintain reticence with our professional acquaintances. Some of them might be able to contribute useful information; one, caught off guard by my unexpected candor, might betray himself by a start of surprise or a look of guilt.

Thus far no one had. On this occasion there was a good deal of surprise, but nothing I could view as guilt. The surprise stemmed in part from my assertion that Abdullah had not collected antiquities. The truth is, some of them were sorry he had not. A good many of our acquaintances were enthusiastic collectors, for themselves or for various institutions. They agreed in theory that illegal excavations ought to be stopped, but took a pessimistic view of the chances of doing it.

Mr. Lawrence, continuing his exercise in tactlessness, was the first to voice aloud a view held by many. "The chap can't have been English! He must be an Egyptian—educated abroad, perhaps, with some superficial knowledge of the antiquities business. There aren't that many such persons. He should be easy to identify!"

"He might be if your assumptions were correct," I replied. "They are not. You must learn not to leap to conclusions, Mr. Lawrence, if you wish to succeed in your profession."


Work on our cemeteries continued. The tombs were small and poor in grave goods, but even they had been robbed and the bones of their occupants scattered. It was extremely boring. Cyrus grew bored too; eventually he announced that since nothing untoward had occurred for some time, he and Katherine thought they could risk leaving us long enough to make a quick trip to Luxor. Emerson encouraged this decision, since he had not believed he needed Cyrus's protection anyhow. So we saw them off and went back to our rubbish heaps.

One afternoon as we were packing the scraps for removal to the house, I allowed myself to express my increasing frustration.

"Emerson, if I have to put together one more early dynastic beer jar I will scream. Why can't we investigate the substructure of the pyramid?"

Geoffrey looked up from the box in which he was packing potsherds. His fair hair was wet with perspiration. Pushing it back under his pith helmet, he said, with a smile, "Your penchant for the interiors of pyramids is well known, Mrs. Emerson, but exploring this one would certainly be a waste of time."

"I will determine what is a waste of time," Emerson grunted. He sat down on a rock and took out his pipe. As usual he had misplaced his hat, and the sun beat down on his bare black head.

"Come back to the shelter and have something to drink," I said. "The rest of you had better do the same; you are looking very warm."

We withdrew to the shade, therefore, leaving Selim to finish packing the objects, and I made everyone take a glass of tea.

Nefret removed her hat and wiped her wet forehead. "I agree," she declared.

"What with?" Emerson's mind was already on something else.

"That we ought to shift to another location. Haven't you taught us that we must leave something to be excavated by future archaeologists, who may have developed more advanced techniques? We've done enough to know that this cemetery is purely early dynastic. There are later graves elsewhere; they might give us a clue as to the identity of the builder of the pyramid."

"We already know that, darling," Geoffrey said. "The vases in the mastaba we found last year have the name of a King Khaba."

"Whoever *he* was," Nefret said dismissively. "He's not mentioned in any of the king lists. Anyhow, you can't attribute a pyramid to a particular king by means of objects found in a nearby tomb."

"Sometimes it's the only indication, sweetheart," Geoffrey said mildly. "Third and Fourth Dynasty pyramids aren't inscribed. This one is probably even earlier. Mr. Reisner believes—"

"But you only excavated one mastaba. There are others on the north side."

Geoffrey sat up and clasped his arms around his bent knees. A few weeks working with Emerson had toughened the lad; his bare forearms were evenly tanned and his wet shirt molded well-shaped shoulders. "Your point is well taken, dearest. So long as there aren't any more accidents like the one that came close to injuring Ramses. When I think that it might have been you down there, my blood runs cold."

Nefret's lips tightened. Geoffrey's concern was natural for a bridegroom, but he would have to learn that she would not tolerate being treated like a fragile blossom. I could see a quarrel building, so I intervened.

"I assure you, Geoffrey, that Emerson does not take unnecessary risks or allow his people to do so. That was an unfortunate accident. I still cannot account for it."

Emerson brushed this distraction aside. "I would like to settle the question of the ownership once and for all," he admitted. "And perhaps get some clue as to why there are no signs of a burial in the pyramid. They must have buried the rascal somewhere, you know; if not in the pyramid, where? And why not in the pyramid?"

"Well, sir . . ." Geoffrey began.

Emerson bent a hard blue gaze upon him and he closed his mouth. The rest of us had known the questions were purely rhetorical. Emerson was about to lecture. He does not care to be interrupted when he is lecturing.

"The other so-called pyramid here at Zawaiet el 'Aryan was also empty. Admittedly it was never finished; there's no sign of a cursed superstructure. There was a burial chamber, though, with a sarcophagus in place at the bottom of a pit that had been painstakingly filled with huge stone blocks. The lid of the sarcophagus was still in place, and there wasn't a scrap inside it. Which leaves us with the same question: Where did they put the bas—er—the king's mummy?"

"What is your theory, my dear?" I inquired, knowing that he was going to tell us anyhow.

"I haven't got a theory," said Emerson aggravatingly. "But I will tell you one thing, Peabody: I am not finished with the pyramid yet."

"Oh, Emerson," I exclaimed, clasping my hands to my breast. "You believe that the burial chamber may be a blind—that there are passages and chambers as yet undiscovered?"

"Control yourself, Peabody," said my affectionate husband. "You are always hoping for unknown passages and chambers; it comes of reading sensational fiction. Such devices are singularly lacking in real life." He turned to Geoffrey, who started nervously. "You weren't one of the ones who entered the place last year?"

"I had a look. We all did. I was in charge of the cemetery, though. It was Mr. Reisner and Jack who investigated the pyramid."

"Hmph," said Emerson. "We'll go on with the excavation of

the private tombs. I also want a closer look at the outside of the structure. I cannot believe there was not a casing of some sort, though you say you found no traces of such a thing. There is a slight overhang on the face of the seventh layer . . ."

The young men listened with a convincing appearance of interest as Emerson continued to expound on construction techniques. Lia's blue eyes were fixed on David with that look of tenderness one likes to observe on the face of a young bride. Nefret was not looking at anyone. Head bent, brow frowning, she stared at the toes of her scuffed little boots. I wondered if she was thinking of those other little boots and the girl who had worn them. Though Emerson would never have admitted it, since he does not like to be considered sentimental, I knew that one of the reasons why he had postponed returning to the interior of the pyramid was his reluctance to return to a scene that held painful memories. How difficult would it be for Nefret?

I reminded myself to ask Emerson whether all evidence of the tragedy had been cleared away. Ramses had said there had not been much blood. He had not mentioned other things.


**From Manuscript H**

Ramses had told David about his meetings with Wardani. David hadn't liked it one damn bit.

They were sitting on the upper deck of the *Amelia* when the conversation took place. It was not late, but Lia had gone to bed, and the last of the tourists had left long ago. Only the stars and a slim crescent moon, and the crimson glow of David's pipe broke the darkness.

"I grant you your right to a certain interest in my affairs," David said, after he had cooled down. "But I don't need you to look after me, Ramses. Not in this, at any rate."

"I know you don't need me to look after you, but couldn't you consider lending your support to one of the more moderate organizations? You have a wife—"

"Don't bring her into this. Would you allow a woman—or a man—to keep you from what you consider your duty?"

Ramses sighed. "David, I know how you feel—"

"No, you don't. You try, but you can't know! You've never been in danger of being imprisoned or beaten half to death because you expressed unpopular opinions. You are sacrosanct because of your nationality and your class. Have you ever seen a man flogged, as they were at Denshawai?"

"Once."

The silence lengthened uncomfortably. "In case you wonder why I didn't stop it," Ramses said, biting the words off, "it is because I was tied to a post waiting my turn."

David didn't make the mistake of apologizing. "You never told me. What happened?"

Ramses took out a cigarette and lit it. "Oh, Father arrived, hurling thunderbolts. He always does, you know." Even in the dark he could sense David's distress. In a gentler voice he went on, "You were in Paris that summer. The business was hushed up. It was, as the diplomatists say, a matter of some delicacy."

"You were in Palestine. So that's why you—"

"No, that's not why I was ill last year. I told you, Father appeared before they'd got well started. However, the incident did rather lessen my tolerance for the Ottoman Empire. Wardani is soft on the Turks. It's understandable—co-religionists and all that—but there's an awful lesson to be learned from the Young Turks. They started out as reformers and revolutionaries too. Now they've been in power awhile, they are becoming as corrupt as the old regime, and the penal system in the provinces is unchanged. It's still the kurbash, and execution without trial, and absolute power for the local magistrates, some of whom have extremely ugly habits. I won't see that happen here, David, not if I can prevent it. Britain has a lot to answer for, but not as much as the Sultan."

There was another thing the experience had taught him, but he couldn't admit it even to David. Watching a man beaten to death by an expert who carried out his duties with cold-blooded skill had been a new experience. The business had taken quite a long time, and they had made sure he saw every stroke of the kurbash and heard every scream. By the time they removed the bloody remains and fastened him up in their place, he had been ready to scream or beg for mercy, and he'd have done it too, if his father hadn't arrived. To say the kurbash was the only thing he feared would have been a lie; he was afraid of a lot of things. But it was the only thing he feared more than death.

David began, "There's surely no danger of—"

"Egypt becoming an Ottoman province again? Legally it still is, you know. Why do you suppose they call it the *Veiled* Protectorate? Britain has never formally annexed the country; Cromer's titles were Consular Agent and Minister Plenipotentiary even though he was the ultimate power in Egypt for thirty years. Now Kitchener is in the same position. He's out to crush the Nationalists, and he's done a damned thorough job of it. Wardani is the only leader who isn't in prison or in exile, and he can't elude the authorities much longer. If he succumbs to the temptation to assassinate someone, he won't go to prison, he'll be executed. And so may you be, if you are known to be one of his lieutenants."

His voice had risen and he had talked himself breathless. He stopped, struggling to regain control.

"I hadn't thought of it that way," David said in his quiet, gentle voice. "I know it was your concern for me that prompted you to seek out Wardani—"

"Not entirely. We are hoping to use one another for our own selfish ends." Ramses smiled cynically. "He wasn't able to help with the business of the forgeries, except in a negative way—but even that is something."

He knew what the next question would be, and put an end to the conversation by yawning and getting to his feet. "Lia won't thank me for detaining you any longer, and I have some notes to write up before I get to sleep. Good night."

The notes were not written up that night. He had other business and it was almost morning before he returned to his room through the window he had left open.

He had been at it for over a week before Nemesis, in the shape of Wardani, caught up with him. Returning from Giza that afternoon, he found a charming little note from Lia inviting him to supper. "David says if you don't turn up he will come and fetch you."

He'd hoped he could snatch a few hours' sleep before going out again, but he knew better than to refuse the invitation. The message was clear. The only thing he didn't know was what particular piece of bad news David wanted to discuss with him.

David didn't leave him in doubt for long. Ramses had asked for coffee instead of tea, hoping it would keep him from falling asleep, and Lia had gone down to tell Karima, leaving them alone on the upper deck. The sun was low in the west, and the shapes of the Giza pyramids were framed in gold.

"I've had a message from my friend," David said. "We're to meet him at eleven at the Café Orientale."

"We?"

"He said I must bring you."

"That sounds like him."

"Will you go?"

"I suppose I *must*. What have you told Lia?"

"As much as I know, which isn't a great deal. He didn't say why he wanted to see us, only that it was important. She's not happy about it, but she said she'd worry less if you were with me."

"Trusting little soul," Ramses said. "Doesn't she know that most of the trouble you've got into was caused by me?"

Lia came up the stairs in time to hear this. "David's as bad as you are," she said. "But there won't be any trouble tonight, will there?"

She looked so sweet and troubled, Ramses wished he *were* brother to a few demons, so he could cast a spell that would send Wardani to Timbuktu and turn David into a sedentary, uxorious scholar.

"Not a chance of it," he said firmly. "Good heavens, Lia, the fellow isn't a killer, he's a—er—a friend of ours. The Café Orientale is perfectly respectable. We won't have to go down any dark streets or alleyways to get there."

The last two sentences were accurate, anyhow. The café was on the Muski, in the European Quarter. They had been told to sit in the inner room in as dark a corner as they could find. The whole room was dark, lit only by a few hanging lamps, and the air was close and hot and foggy with smoke. By the time they had been waiting for almost an hour, the innumerable cups of coffee Ramses had drunk weren't doing the job; his head felt as if it were coming loose from his body, and his stomach was churning. He should have known the bastard would keep them waiting.

The man who approached them wore the uniform of an Egyptian Army sergeant. He wore it with a swagger, his tarboosh set squarely on the top of his head, his boots gleaming.

"Overdoing it a bit, aren't you?" Ramses asked.

"The panache?" Wardani lowered himself into a chair. "If you read my insignia you will observe I am a long way from my regiment. On leave, of course."

He offered his hands to David. "Accept my felicitations and welcome, my brother. If it had been up to your friend here, we might not have met again."

"He told me," David said.

"He did?" Wardani sounded surprised, and Ramses smiled to himself.

"We too are brothers," David said.

"Then you will be pleased to hear that it was for your brother's sake I summoned you here." He snapped his fingers and ordered coffee from the waiter.

Ramses remained silent. It was David who asked, "What do you mean?"

Wardani waited until the waiter had painstakingly unloaded three glasses of water and three small cups of Turkish coffee. Then he looked directly at Ramses.

"You were seen recently with Thomas Russell."

"No doubt you've already collected the firing squad," Ramses said, trying to conceal his chagrin. He hadn't noticed he was being followed that day. "Why shouldn't I see him? He's a friend of the family."

"A slight acquaintance," Wardani corrected. "And a policeman."

"But Russell's stationed in Alexandria," David said.

"He's been transferred to Cairo—assistant commissioner."

"And you can thank God for it," Ramses said. He took a sip of the coffee and wished he hadn't. "He's an honest man and a good policeman, unlike his present superior. Harvey Pasha is a pompous fool. I knew there was no use going to him with the story you told me. He'd scoff at the idea that a sahib was involved in the drug business. Russell didn't scoff. Mother said he'd offered me a job. She thought he was joking. He wasn't. It's nice to be in such demand. Everybody wants me. Reisner, Fisher, Father, Russell . . . Almost everybody."

David put a hand on his shoulder and shook him. "Get hold of yourself. Are you telling me you are working for Russell—as a police spy?"

"Call it what you like. I'll do whatever I must to find the swine and stop him." David's hand was oddly steadying. He took a deep breath and tried to focus on the narrow dark face under the tarboosh. "If you know I saw Russell, you know why. If I succeed you'll hear about it. Why the devil did you drag me here tonight when I could have been more usefully employed?"

"Well, I thought that was the reason," Wardani said calmly. "But some of my people had certain doubts. Watch yourself, Ramses. I believe I've convinced my friends that you mean us no harm, but a few of the lads are a bit hot-headed, and there are others in Cairo who wouldn't mind seeing you out of the way."

"You astonish me," Ramses said. "Now can we go home?"

"No!" David kept his voice low. "Not until I know more about this. What others?"

"The man he's looking for, to mention only one." Wardani lit another cigarette. "He's an effendi and a member of your own superior caste. He may be someone you know. If that's the case, he also knows you, Ramses. I presume you're trying to infiltrate one of the gangs in some disguise or other. All I'm saying is that it had better be a damned good disguise."

"What others?" David repeated inflexibly.

"The man who killed that girl—or perhaps I should say the men who killed those girls." Wardani grinned unpleasantly. "Even mentioning them in the same breath would offend a lot of people, wouldn't it? The whore may have been killed by her pimp or one of her customers, but the American girl didn't jump down that shaft of her own accord. If you weren't—"

"That's enough," David said.

"My dear chap, I'm only trying to help!" Wardani opened his eyes very wide. "But I'd best be on my way. You'll hear from me soon again, David. My respectful salutations to your wife. And to the lovely Miss Forth—who is now, I believe, no longer a miss? Her husband is a fortunate man."

David's hand pressed down on Ramses's shoulder. "We will convey your good wishes."

"Oh, absolutely," Ramses agreed.

"Not to the Honorable Mr. Godwin, though," Wardani said. He looked very pleased with himself, like a student who has come up with the right answer against all the teacher's expectations. "He's a sahib of sorts, isn't he? He'd be shocked to learn you were acquainted with a reprobate like me." He rose and brushed fastidiously at his tunic. "We mustn't leave together. Stay here for another half hour; drink coffee."

"If I drink any more coffee I'll be sick," Ramses muttered, as the slender, upright figure sauntered toward the door. "Damn the fellow and his insinuations and his arrogance and his—"

"Have tea then, or a narghileh." David snapped his fingers.

"Or a little hashish. It's quite tasty when it's made into sweet-meats. What you do is, you take a quantity of honey—"

"Stop it!" David's voice was soft but it cracked like a whip. "Why didn't you tell me?"

"Tell you what? Wardani covered a number of subjects in a remarkably short period of time. He's usually more verbose. I *am* going to be sick," he added, and lowered his head onto his folded arms.

"Drink your tea," David said. "Then I'll take you home to Lia and we'll put you to bed."

"Yes, fine," Ramses said vaguely. A hand slipped under his forehead and lifted his head.

"You're not drunk," David said, inspecting him. "Or feverish. You're dead-tired, that's all that's wrong with you. No wonder, working all day and prowling the streets all night—or is it the wharves or the desert roads? Talk about arrogance! How long did you think you could keep this up? Here, drink it."

The tea was so hot he could feel blisters rising on his tongue, but he choked some of it down. "That's better," he said in mild surprise.

"Let's get out of here." David put a hand under his arm and hauled him to his feet. "Maybe what you need is a drink. We'll stop at Shepheard's and get a cab from there. And on the way back to the *Amelia* you will tell me exactly what you've done so that *we* can decide what *we* are going to do next."

The night life of Cairo went on till all hours, and the streets of the European section were bright and busy. Lights twinkled in the dark groves of the Ezbekieh Gardens.

"I don't want a drink," Ramses said. "Let's go home."

"All right." David hailed one of the open barouches and they got in. "Well?"

"Well what?"

David slapped him across the face, just hard enough to sting. "Wake up! I'm not angry yet, Ramses, but I soon will be if you continue to hide things from me. Why did you agree to work for Russell? A girl has been murdered, your mother has been attacked, the family may be in danger, and you are killing yourself trying to track down a man who has nothing to do with ... Oh, good Lord! He does, doesn't he? I ought to have known. Talk to me, damn it!"

"Don't hit me again," Ramses mumbled. "I'll talk. I was going to, but you kept yelling at me. Yes. I mean, yes, he does. It's the same man, David. The 'sahib' is using your name too."

In the East an Englishman must be willing to die rather than show a streak of yellow. The courage of a single individual raises the prestige of all; the cowardice of one man reflects on all his peers. I endeavored, in my own humble way, to live up to this standard . . .

I sat in the little room I had fitted up as an office, looking out over the garden, now being brought back to its former beauty; and I could not help thinking, with pardonable complacency, of how well our new living arrangements were working. Initially Emerson had objected to the size of the house, but as it turned out we needed all the space at our disposal. Our infantile charge required (in my expert opinion) several rooms, including one for her nurse. The lower areas, which I used for storage of artifacts, were rapidly filling up—not, alas, with statues and stelae like the ones Mr. Reisner had been finding, but with bones and broken vessels of stone and pottery.

Nefret and Geoffrey occupied the entire wing that had once been the harem. They had all the privacy they desired, and so did the other young couple—though Ramses had taken to spending a great deal of time with them. Lately he had spent more nights on the dahabeeyah than at the house. It was none of my business, of course, if they preferred it that way.

I had left my door ajar, and since the room opened onto the main corridor, I heard the tap of heels and was thus able to call out to Nefret when she came along. She had not meant to stop, I believe. Looking in, she began, "I don't want to disturb you, Aunt Amelia."

"Come in." I leaned back in my chair.

"It is almost teatime. I was just going—"

"If you will wait a bit, I will go with you. Where is Geoffrey?"

Realizing that I had caught her fairly, she wandered to the window and stood looking out. There were no mashrabiya screens on this side of the house; the wooden shutters stood open to the warm afternoon air. Her back to me, she said, "He went to see Jack. He is worried about him."

"Why? Ramses says he is behaving normally."

Nefret turned. "Ramses is a damned liar."

"Ramses never lies. However," I admitted, "he is an expert at equivocation. What makes you think he is—er—misleading us about Jack?"

"Jack is behaving oddly again. He refused your last invitation, and he's avoiding other people. Geoffrey says he spends most of his free time prowling the hills with a gun. When he can't find anything else, he shoots jackals."

"Is he drinking?"

Her slim shoulders lifted in a shrug.

"I had better go and see for myself," I said, putting my papers into a neat pile and rising from my chair.

"I was afraid you would say that. Please, Aunt Amelia, don't go rushing off. Geoffrey said he would try to bring Jack here for tea today."

"Very well, I will wait and see if he comes."

Nefret came and stood by my desk. She picked up a sheet of paper and examined it. "Will Ramses be here?"

"I don't know. He's got in the habit of having tea with David and Lia. In fact, I believe he went to the dahabeeyah earlier, as soon as he got back from Giza."

"We haven't seen a great deal of them lately."

"You see them every day at the site," I pointed out. "No doubt they appreciate their time alone together. You know, Nefret, that if you and Geoffrey would prefer to take tea, or any other meals, in your rooms, I would understand perfectly."

"Thank you, but we are both quite happy with things the way they are."

"Nefret . . ."

"Yes?" She looked directly at me, and the words that had

risen to my lips died there. It was as if a door had slammed shut behind her eyes.

"I have been revising my little fairy tale," I said, indicating the paper she held. "What do you think?"

"I'm no expert, Aunt Amelia." She glanced at the page. I had the feeling she had not really looked at it until then.

"On the language? No more am I. What is wanted here is an examination of Sinuhe's motives, and for that one needs not only a profound understanding of human nature but a familiarity with the sometimes oblique terms in which the ancient Egyptians expressed it.

"Everyone assumes that Sinuhe was a member of the conspiracy directed against the rightful heir, and indeed it is hard to conceive of another explanation for his flight and his fear of returning to Egypt. But Sinuhe claims he only learned of the plot by overhearing one of the conspirators talking—at least that is how I interpret a rather enigmatic passage—and that he was so terrified and dismayed, he fled. If that version is correct, he would be guilty of nothing worse than cowardice."

"Obviously it isn't correct," Nefret said. "It's the official version—the diplomatic lie. I think he was in the conspiracy up to his neck, and that what he overheard was a statement by one of Senusert's supporters, to the effect that the new pharaoh was already on his way to claim the throne, that he knew all about the plot, and that the loyalists in the army were about to arrest the guilty parties."

"Hmmm," I said. "Yes, that is also my interpretation. And when, after many years, he begged forgiveness—"

"*She* forgave him," Nefret said. She picked up the drawing that I knew was her favorite—the old man sitting at peace in his garden, looking out at the symbols of eternal life. "He had been in the service of the princess, hadn't he? She was now queen. She forgave him because she had loved him, and because she knew how badly he wanted to come home."

The silence that followed was broken only by the soft chirping of sparrows in the tamarisk tree outside the window—until one of Narmer's sudden outrageous howls made Nefret laugh and me swear (under my breath, naturally).

I put my work away and we went to the courtyard. It was Geoffrey who had come in; he was the only one there except for Fatima, who was setting the table for tea.

"Weren't you able to bring him?" I asked.

"Bring who?" inquired Emerson, emerging.

I explained. Geoffrey admitted he had not been able to convince Jack to join us. "Von Bork dropped by while I was there," he added. "I suppose Jack felt he could not abandon a guest."

"You should have asked Karl too," I said.

"Oh, I couldn't presume to do that."

He had presumed to invite Jack, though. I reminded myself that the situation was entirely different, and gestured to Nefret to pour. Geoffrey jumped up, took the cup from her, and carried it to me. "Here you are, Mrs. Emerson."

"Thank you. I think perhaps you ought to start calling me Aunt Amelia, if you would care to."

"May I?" His face lit up. "I hoped I might, but I did not want—"

"To presume," said Emerson, around the stem of his pipe. He said it fairly pleasantly, however, and the dimple in Geoffrey's thin cheek deepened as he glanced from Emerson to me. I gathered he had been warned not to refer to Emerson as Uncle Radcliffe.

"So how is Jack?" I inquired. "Ought I to call on him, do you think?"

"He isn't drinking," Geoffrey said. "At least not to excess. One can't mistake the signs, you know. I would say he is still suffering from melancholia."

"Depression is the modern psychological term," I remarked.

"Peabody," said Emerson, in an ominous growl.

"Yes, my dear, I beg your pardon. I know how you feel about psychology. Call it what you will, Jack is not in a healthy state. We must shake him out of it!"

"I agree," Geoffrey said earnestly. "I tried to persuade him to come with us tonight to the reception at the Agency, but he said he had another engagement."

"I am not going to the Agency," said Emerson, in the same tone in which he would have announced that the sun was due to rise in the east next day.

"Oh, no, sir, I never supposed you would."

Nefret sat immobile, her cup in her hand. "Did you suppose I would?" she asked in a very gentle voice.

"But darling, you said you would!" Geoffrey turned impulsively to her. "Yesterday. Don't you remember? Sir John Maxwell will be there, and you know what influence he wields with the

Department of Antiquities. A word in his ear—especially from you—might do great things for the Professor."

"Oh." Nefret put her cup down on the table. "I'm afraid I wasn't paying attention. Are you sure you feel up to it?"

"What is wrong, Geoffrey?" I asked.

"Nothing at all, ma'am. Honestly. I told Nefret she mustn't fuss."

He gave his wife a look of gentle reproach. She flushed. "All right, then."

"Wear your new frock," Geoffrey urged. "The one that has all the colors of the sea off southern Greece. It makes your eyes sparkle like aquamarines. Er—would you care to go with us, Mrs.—er—Aunt Amelia?"

"I suppose you don't need a chaperone," I remarked dryly. "Did you tell Fatima you would not be dining at home?"

"Good heavens, I forgot," Geoffrey said apologetically.

Fatima, passing round a plate of little cucumber sandwiches, hastened to assure him it did not matter. Emerson had been grumbling to himself. "I don't want people fawning on the Department of Antiquities on my account," he announced loudly.

"Someone had better do it," I informed him. "Since you keep antagonizing M. Maspero and you won't let me—"

He interrupted me, of course, and we had a refreshing little discussion.

After tea Nefret and Geoffrey went to change, and Emerson and I proceeded to the nursery. I had been forced to forbid Sennia to join us for tea until Emerson learned to behave himself. Not only did he allow her to eat every biscuit on the plate but he smuggled sweets from the kitchen in his pockets. We had a very enjoyable little interlude, though Sennia kept demanding Ramses, and Emerson had to play lion before she was pacified.

Later we found ourselves à deux at the dining table. The situation was so unusual that at first all we could do was stare blankly at one another.

Emerson burst out laughing. "Alone at last! Good Gad, Peabody, has it come to this? What the devil are we going to do when they have all gone off and left us?"

"I'm sure you will think of something, Emerson."

"Quite right, my love." He blew me a kiss from the other end of the table. Fatima beamed sentimentally, and Emerson looked embarrassed. "Well, er, as I was about to say, it is a pleasure to have you to myself. We've got a number of things to discuss,

Peabody. I say, what's this?" He stared suspiciously at the plate Fatima had put in front of him.

"Deviled beef," I replied. "Rose gave Fatima some of her recipes, and she has been teaching Mahmud."

"Hmph," said Emerson.

Fatima lingered until he had expressed his approval, then trotted out to report success to Mahmud. "It's not bad at all," said Emerson, chewing. "A bit gamier than Rose's."

"A different variety of beef, I expect."

"One would suppose so." Emerson leaned back and fixed me with a solemn stare. "Things are in the deuce of a mess, Peabody."

"They usually are, Emerson."

"True. This time, however, there are too many unrelated things going on. I mean to settle one of them this evening." He took out his watch. "They won't be leaving for a while yet. Finish your dinner, my dear, and we will take coffee with them."

The hideous foreboding that filled me was so familiar it felt almost comfortable. "Good Gad," I exclaimed. "It is Ramses you mean, isn't it? Ramses and David. Leaving for where? What are they up to now? I should have known! Why haven't they told us?"

"I mean to learn the answers tonight," Emerson said placidly. "You must have suspected something yourself, or you wouldn't have leaped to the correct conclusion so quickly. Thank you, Fatima, that was excellent."

Having observed how these matters were managed in England, Fatima was training one of her nephews in the fine art of butling, but he had not yet attained the degree of skill she considered minimal. I doubted he ever would satisfy her; she enjoyed waiting on us herself, and listening to our conversation. When she served the next course I had to force myself to eat, I was in such a state of worried exasperation.

"Of course I was suspicious," I said. "Ramses has taken pains to avoid me, but I know the signs; he looks like an owl, or that falcon Nefret freed, with those dark lines under his eyes. David hasn't been his usual self, either. They are prowling again! At night, in the old city, in their disgusting disguises! Have they found some clue to the forger, do you suppose?"

Fatima had missed my first reference to David. Hearing this one, she let out a little hiss of alarm. I reassured her (not an easy task, since I was in considerable need of reassurance myself) and warned her not to mention the subject to anyone else.

"You do put things in such a melodramatic way," Emerson said critically. "I expect they are—it's not a bad word, actually—prowling again. That is why Ramses has taken to spending his nights on the dahabeeyah."

"Then Lia must know what they are doing."

"David probably swore her to secrecy. And someone else may have sworn him and Ramses to secrecy."

I stared at him in consternation. "Wardani?"

"It makes sense, doesn't it? I believe they would have told us if they were on the track of the forger."

"But Emerson, that could be disastrous! Russell warned me that the police were after Wardani, and that David is already on a list of—" I stopped myself, for Fatima was standing in the doorway, her eyes wide and the bowl she held quivering violently.

"Put it down before you drop it, Fatima," I said. "I told you there is nothing to worry about. We will see that David is safe. You trust us, don't you?"

"Aywa. Yes, Sitt Hakim."

She placed the bowl tenderly on the table. It appeared to be a somewhat exotic version of a trifle, wobbly with custard and cream and jelly. Bits of unidentified fruits stuck out from it.

"I don't think I can eat that, Emerson," I said out of the corner of my mouth.

"We'll take it with us," Emerson declared. "Parcel it up, Fatima."

"Parcel it—"

"Put it in a bag or a box or something," Emerson said. "The children will enjoy it."

I rather looked forward to seeing Emerson striding down the road toward the quay with a bowl of trifle tucked under one arm. He would have done it, too, but for Fatima; she turned pale with horror at the idea and insisted on sending Ali with us to carry the box in which she had wedged the bowl. The poor lad had to trot to keep up with Emerson's long strides, and we were followed all the way to the *Amelia* by little gasps and squawks as Ali juggled the awkward thing.

As Emerson says, one can always count on a touch of comic relief in our family.

There was no creeping up on the plotters unannounced, for we were observed approaching by an alert guard and hailed in a loud voice. When we got to the saloon, where they were finishing dinner, both young men were on their feet and all three faces wore insincere smiles of welcome. The unpacking of the trifle— a good deal of which had slopped over the sides of the bowl— occasioned some mirth. Karima scraped the remains onto plates, and in duty bound we all ate some of it.

Emerson soon began to fidget. He is not a patient man, and he had a great deal on his mind. Since I did not want Karima and the other servants to overhear, I managed, with little nudges and winks, to keep the conversation on casual subjects until after we had retired to the upper deck for coffee, and Karima had left us alone.

Lia had already expressed her pleasure at seeing us—"so unexpectedly"—and I had already apologized for breaking my own rule about dropping in uninvited. I did not doubt all three knew there was some purpose in our coming; the only question in my mind was whether Ramses would confess before his father accused him.

Emerson did not give him time, supposing he had intended to. "What the devil are you up to now?" he demanded.

The disadvantage of the ambience was that I could not make out their faces clearly. Candles in pottery bowls shone softly, but gave little light. I saw only Ramses's hands as he put his cup down on the nearest table. They were always scratched and scraped, for, like his father, he is forgetful about wearing gloves when he is digging.

"I suppose I should apologize for not confiding in you and Mother," he said. "I gave my word I would not."

"Be damned to that," said Emerson.

"Yes, sir."

"Was it Wardani who swore you to secrecy?"

"No, sir."

"We had better confess," David said, over the low rumble from Emerson that betokened an imminent explosion.

"I wish you would," Lia murmured. "I hate keeping secrets, especially from Aunt Amelia and the Professor."

"Ha!" said Emerson. "Well, Ramses?"

It was as if, having made up his mind to speak, Ramses was anxious to unburden himself (or possibly he was anxious to get it over so he could go about whatever business he had planned for that night).

"I have been working for Mr. Russell, who is attempting to

put an end to the traffic in drugs. One of the persons involved is rumored to be an Englishman. David and I have been trying to infiltrate one of the gangs in order to learn who this man is. Thus far—"

I could contain myself no longer. "Russell, did you say? Confound the man, I told him in the most decided terms that you were not to be a policeman!"

"Police spy," Ramses corrected. "Why mince words? Perhaps you now understand why I did not inform you. There's not much point in being a spy if everybody knows you are one."

"We are not everybody," said his father, unmoved by the bitterness in his voice—or so I believe, until Emerson added, "And there is no shame in spying if it is for a worthy cause. Where did you get the idea that an Englishman was involved?"

"Wardani. It occurred to me that he might have invented it, just to make mischief—he's quite capable of that—but the rumors are out there. We've heard them for ourselves." His head turned toward me and he added seriously, "Where there is smoke there is fire, you know."

There is no doubt that confession is good for the soul, depending, of course, on who is confessing and to whom. Ramses leaned back and lit a cigarette; his father took out his pipe; Lia poured coffee; and David let out a long breath. "I don't mind admitting I'm glad to have it off my chest," he said ingenuously.

"Hmmm," said Emerson, sucking on his pipe. "You still have some way to go. Tell me what steps you have taken."

Originally Mr. Russell had concentrated on the coast, trying to confiscate the cargoes as they were unloaded. As Ramses had mentioned earlier, this was a hopeless task, for the area was extensive. "It seemed to me," Ramses continued, "that it made better sense to try and intercept the stuff when it entered Cairo. It might come by water, up one of the arms of the Nile, or overland. In either case it would end up in a warehouse or shed or some other storage area, awaiting distribution to the dealers."

"More than one such storage place, surely," said Emerson, who was listening with keen interest. "Common sense would suggest they change the locale periodically."

"Not if they had no reason to believe it was suspected," Ramses argued. "Even so, pinning down a specific location would be difficult. So I started from the other end—the local distributors. I managed to get a position in one of the hashish dens—"

"How did you manage that?" Emerson asked curiously.

"I started a fight. It wasn't difficult; some of the lads become combative as the night wears on. After I had pitched my unfortunate victim out into the alley and expressed my regret for the disturbance, the owner offered me a job as lookout. It didn't take long to figure out the schedule of deliveries and identify the deliverers. To make a long story short, I worked my way up the ladder until I was taken on as one of the laborers who meet the incoming shipments."

"So you've located the warehouse?" Emerson inquired. He sounded a little envious, I thought.

"One of them. That wasn't what I wanted, though, and it finally occurred to my slow wits that I was never going to get past a certain point. There is a great gap between the people who handle the stuff and the people who finance the business, and only a few points of contact between them. I was racking my brain trying to think how to bridge the gap when David found out what I was doing."

"I owe Wardani a debt for enlightening me," David said. "You wouldn't have told me."

"There's no need to go into that," Ramses said. "It was David who came up with the brilliant idea of setting up a police ambush, so that we could save the shipment and become heroes. Russell approved the scheme; so David joined the group, on my recommendation, and when the attack occurred we gave our all for the cause. We'd planned exactly what we would do and it went off rather well; in all the pandemonium and in the dark nobody could really tell who was hitting whom. In the end David and I and our immediate superior were the only ones left standing, and we dashed off with the hashish. Bleeding copiously, of course, and covered with bruises."

Emerson chuckled. Ramses picked up one of the little pottery lamps and used it to light a cigarette. The glow illumined his face and David's; both had a look of reminiscent amusement that made me want to shake them. I wanted to shake Emerson too, for laughing. Men are incomprehensible to me at times.

"So," said Emerson, "what next?"

"Next comes a spot of eavesdropping," said his son. "We will never be admitted to the inner councils, but because of our extraordinary heroism we are considered trustworthy; people don't always guard their tongues when we are around. There is a meeting tonight we must attend. We haven't been invited, so we will have to hang about in the hope of hearing something interesting.

It will take a little time to get into position, so if you will excuse us—"

"Not quite yet," said Emerson, slowly and distinctly. "There is something more, isn't there? No, don't tell me; *I* will tell *you*. You and David wouldn't waste your time on police business unless it were connected with our other problems. It's the same man, isn't it? How did you make the connection? Is he also using David's name?"

After a moment Ramses said, "Yes, to both. Sir—"

"Confound you, Ramses, don't you see that attempting to keep me in the dark is not only a waste of time but devilish dangerous? It is for your sake that I insist on knowing the truth, my boy."

The speech that had begun in anger ended in appeal. That Ramses felt its effect I did not doubt; he bowed his head and murmured, "Yes, sir, I know. I apologize."

"Well, never mind," Emerson grunted. "This *is* an unpleasant state of affairs! The bastard seems determined to incriminate David one way or another. It cannot be a personal vendetta; David hasn't an enemy in the world. Er—have you, David?"

"No, sir. I think he got the idea of using my name when he sold the forgeries simply because it gave them a believable provenance. Why not continue to use it in his other business arrangements? I doubt the fellow holds a particular grudge against me; I was a convenient scapegoat because of my nationality and my background, that's all."

"As simple as that?" I exclaimed.

"As simple and as deadly," said Ramses. "We are accustomed to dealing with enemies who hate us for personal reasons. This is a motive we have never encountered and a kind of enmity we've never had to face. I think David is right; this bas—this man chose to victimize him not because of *who* he is but because of *what* he is—a member of an 'inferior' race who has, moreover, dared to demonstrate his intellectual superiority and violate the rules against intermarriage. What makes this mental aberration even more dangerous is that it is shared by those who will be David's judges—if it should come to that."

Emerson growled deep in his throat. "It won't come to that."

"I'm not worried," David said firmly. He took the hand Lia held out to him. "No suspect ever had a more impressive array of allies."

"Quite right," I said. "We'll find the bas—the villain, never fear."

"Well spoken, Mother," Ramses said. "Now that we've settled that—"

"One more thing." Emerson turned to David. "Have you heard from any of the European dealers to whom you wrote?"

"Yes, as a matter of fact. I had asked for a description of the artifacts in question, if you recall. I got a letter today from Monsieur Dubois in Paris. He was somewhat perturbed."

"I can well imagine," Emerson grunted. "I presume he insists that the article was genuine."

"Exactly. As he pointed out, the seller and the provenance may have been spurious, but that doesn't prove the artifact was. He sent a photograph."

"Oh? What was it?"

"You'd better see for yourself, sir. I had intended to show it to you tomorrow, but so long as you are here . . ."

David got to his feet. Emerson followed suit. "We'll go down to the saloon where the light is better. It's time we were getting along home, anyhow."

The saloon was not nearly so cluttered as it had been in my day, possibly because there was only one male person cluttering it up. The removal of all but two of the desks had actually left room for a dining table. Lia had replaced several of the rugs. When she saw me looking at them she said nervously, "I do hope you don't mind, Aunt Amelia. Some had rather large holes in them."

"From Emerson's pipe." I nodded. "My dear child, this is your home now. Make any changes you like."

David had found the photograph. Emerson snatched it up with a muffled expletive. "Let me see," I said, and tugged at his hand.

At first I could not make out what the objects were. There were four of them, their size indeterminable because no scale had been provided. Then Emerson said, "Carved animal legs—bulls' legs. Ivory?"

"So M. Dubois said. It's a little difficult to make out from the photograph."

"Inlaid," Emerson muttered, his finger tracing the outline of the oval base. "Curse it, this cannot be—"

"Gold and lapis lazuli. Have you ever seen anything like them?"

"Yes," said Emerson in an abstracted voice. "Oh, yes. May I take this along?"

"Certainly, sir."

Emerson straightened, the photograph in his hand. His eyes met those of Ramses. "Go on about your business, then," he said gruffly. "If you aren't here tomorrow morning I will just run into Cairo and ask a few questions of . . . whom?"

Ramses mentioned a name, which meant nothing to me. Emerson appeared to recognize it, however. He nodded. "So he's one of them. I'm not surprised. Good night. And good luck."

The night was overcast and a damp wind tugged at my skirts. Emerson did not appear to be in any hurry; his pipe in one hand, my hand in the other, he strolled in a leisurely fashion; and when we reached the house he gestured at the mastaba bench outside the door. "Sit down for a moment, Peabody. I want to discuss something with you."

"A fitting punishment for Mr. Thomas Russell? Honestly, Emerson, when I think of his going behind my back to—"

"Peabody, Peabody! Ramses does not need your permission to accept a position. Nor mine," Emerson added gloomily. "I don't like this any better than you do, but for pity's sake don't embarrass Ramses by scolding Russell as if they were naughty schoolboys and Russell had led him into mischief. That isn't what I want to discuss."

"The photograph."

"Yes. I've got a theory, Peabody."

"About the forgeries?"

"In a way."

"Really, Emerson, there are times when I would like to murder you," I exclaimed, so loudly that the grille in the door creaked open and the alarmed face of Ali peered out. At my urgent request he closed the grille again, and I returned to my grievance. "Are you going to tell me your theory, or are you just going to go on dropping enigmatic hints until I lose my temper?"

"Enigmatic hints, of course," said Emerson with a chuckle. "See what you can make of them, eh? I will play fair, though, and tell you what the objects in the photograph remind me of. Couches, both domestic and funerary, were often mounted on carved animal legs. Obviously only the well-to-do could afford such things, and the materials used in this set are rare and expensive. A set of such ivory legs was found at Abydos, in one of the Second Dynasty royal tombs."

He paused invitingly. I said nothing. An idea had come to me, too, but I was cursed if I was going to share it with him. Emerson always makes fun of my theories—until I am proved correct.

"Enigmatic hint number two," said Emerson. "I believe that Vandergelt had the right idea. There's something at Zawaiet we are not meant to find. Things have been suspiciously quiet lately—"

"Because we are digging in the wrong place!" The words popped into my head and straight out my mouth before I could stop them. I clapped my hand over my lips. Emerson let out a roar of laughter and put one arm round my shoulders.

"That is a possibility," he said. "Would you care to go on, or shall we have another of our little competitions in crime? Sealed envelopes and all the rest?"

"Are you telling me that you know the name of the person who is responsible for the accidents?"

"And for murdering Maude Reynolds? No, I don't. And if you have the confounded audacity to claim that you do—"

"No," I admitted. "I see a few rays of light I had not seen earlier; they explain some of what has happened, but I am still in the dark as to the identity of the criminal."

"All the same, Peabody, I think I will put a message in one of those little envelopes. Just in case."

I turned to him, taking hold of his coat. The lighted lamp beside the door cast enough illumination to show his smiling lips and firm chin. "In case something happens to you? What are you planning to do?"

"Why, I am going to dig at various other places all round the site, that's all."

"What, play hot and cold like the children's game, with a murderous attack as a sign you are getting warmer? You mustn't, Emerson, at least not until we have mustered our forces."

"Ramses, you mean? He has enough on his mind without worrying about me. What the devil, Peabody, we've always managed quite nicely by ourselves, you and I. Well—almost always."

"I do not doubt for a moment that we can manage," I said stoutly. "It is Ramses and David I am concerned about. Ramses is always taking foolish chances, and David cannot control him."

"Any more than I can control you." Emerson gave my shoulder a hearty squeeze. "People who live in glass houses, Peabody! The only way we can help the boys is to keep their activities strictly to ourselves. I want your word that you will not breathe a word about them to a living soul."

"Does that include Nefret?"

"There is nothing she can do. She would only worry."

It was true, but it was not the real reason. A young wife who has not learned better is likely to confide in her husband, and we did not know Geoffrey well enough to count on his discretion.

I woke before daylight and found I was unable to woo slumber again. The Reader may well imagine why. The boys (I could not help thinking of them that way still) had been involved in their perilous and disgusting quest for at least a week. Since I had not known of it, I had slept soundly; now that I did know of it, I did not see how I could sleep again until I knew they were safely back.

With the utmost caution I folded the thin sheet back, and was about to slip silently out of bed when an arm wrapped round me and pulled me back.

"If you intended to go haring off to the *Amelia*, I advise against it," Emerson said in my ear. "It is near dawn; if they had not returned Lia would have come to us."

"So you say," I retorted, wishing he had not done so in such close proximity to my aural orifice. Emerson's whispers are as penetrating as a shout.

"So I do." Another arm enclosed me, drawing me closer.

"I thought you were asleep."

"Obviously I am not."

Obviously he was not.

If he was trying to take my mind off the boys he succeeded, but only temporarily. By the time I rose and dressed, the dawn was breaking. As if in sympathy with my mood it was not the pearly pink of a normal sunrise, but a soggy gray. White mist veiled the windows. I knew the sun would probably dissolve the fog in a few hours, but the sight of it intensified the uneasiness that had returned following the conclusion of Emerson's engaging attentions. Like darkness, mist and fog are of great assistance to assassins.

When we went down to breakfast I was relieved to see Lia already there. So was Nefret, but in that first instant I had eyes only for my niece, whose greeting told me that my apprehensions had been needless.

"David will be along shortly. He and Ramses were up till all hours talking."

"Ah," I said. "Is Ramses coming with him?"

"He went straight to Harvard Camp." She smiled affectionately. "Don't worry, Aunt Amelia, I made Ramses eat something before he left."

"Hmph," said Emerson. He looked at Nefret, whose untouched breakfast had a congealed look about it. "What's wrong with you? Feeling ill?"

"No, sir." She would have left it at that, but Emerson's piercing blue stare is difficult to ignore. "I had trouble sleeping," she admitted.

"One of your dreams?" I inquired.

"Yes." She picked up her fork and took a bite of scrambled egg.

I knew she would say no more. She would never discuss those nightmares, which had troubled her for years. They were infrequent but very disturbing, and she claimed she could never remember the content. I had my doubts about that; but my efforts to induce her to discuss them, with me or with a qualified medical person, had come to naught.

The others soon joined us: first David, then Geoffrey a few minutes later. Fatima was in seventh heaven, with so many people to be stuffed with food. She kept pressing delicacies upon us and replacing people's plates with freshly cooked food. Everyone did his or her best to eat, but as I looked round the table I thought I had never seen so many haggard faces and drooping eyelids. The only ones who appeared normal were Geoffrey and Emerson. I wondered how the lad could have slept so well while his wife suffered the pangs of nightmare . . . And then I dismissed the rude speculation that had entered my mind.

As if feeling my gaze upon him Geoffrey looked up from his plate and gave me a cheerful smile. "You ought to have come with us last night, Aunt Amelia. I had a most interesting conversation with Sir John."

"I don't want to hear about it," Emerson declared. "It's time we were off."

I suggested we go by way of the Giza plateau but Emerson, misunderstanding my motives, vetoed the idea in terms that allowed no room for discussion. The pace he set allowed no room for discussion either. Upon our arrival he summoned all of us, including Selim and Daoud, to a conference.

"I have finished with the cemeteries for the time being," he announced. "Today we begin clearing the shaft. From the top."

This abrupt and arbitrary decision was accepted without comment by those who knew him well. Observing that Geoffrey's eyes had widened and that he was on the verge of speech, I intervened, to spare the lad the reprimand a question would undoubtedly have provoked.

"Far be it from me to question the dictatorial nature of your decrees, Emerson," I said, "but perhaps if you condescended to explain why you are taking this course and what you hope to accomplish—?"

Emerson drew a deep sigh, like a patient schoolmaster facing a particularly dull child. "I should think that would be obvious. However, if you insist. Where is that plan of Barsanti's?" He began throwing papers around. "Ah, here it is."

We all gathered round the table and Emerson began lecturing, using the stem of his pipe as a pointer. "The entrance to the substructure is this long descending stair and passageway. What then was the purpose of the shaft, which goes straight up to the surface from the end of the first passageway?"

"Perhaps it was made by tomb robbers?" Selim suggested.

Emerson snorted. "You know what tomb robbers' tunnels look like, Selim. This shaft was built by professional masons, not by robbers in haste and in secrecy. It may be a later construction. I want to see what, if anything, is in it. Does that answer your question, Peabody?"

"Only part of it. You mean to concentrate on the substructure then?"

"I intend to clear the place out." Emerson's handsome face took on a look of demonic pleasure. "I got Reisner to admit he didn't do a damn thing down there last year. Barsanti's excavations were inadequate. I am going to go about this slowly and methodically, taking all possible precautions. That is why I want the shaft completely clear before we enter the substructure."

Had I not been distracted by other considerations, I would have rejoiced at Emerson's new scheme. It was what I had wanted all along. He was absolutely correct in clearing the shaft before proceeding with his investigation of the substructure. If the filling gave way, several hundred tons of rock and sand would drop straight down into the corridors below.

The top of the shaft was marked by a shallow depression, no different in appearance from others that covered the uneven terrain, but of course we had plotted its precise location when we made our plan of the site. Emerson got the men to work, indicating an area we had already excavated as the location of the dump. Before long the sand was flying and the basketmen were trotting busily back and forth, accompanying their tedious labor with a crooning chant. Apparently they had got over the superstitious fear of the place that had followed the discovery of Maude's body.

However, when I expressed this optimistic sentiment to Emerson, he shook his head. "They are in the open air, some distance from the spot where her body was found. We may not be able to persuade them so easily to enter the place."

"Let us hope nothing else occurs."

Emerson's jaw tightened. "I will make certain it doesn't."

Hands on his hips, he stood looking on, his keen eyes intent on the men who were in the depression filling their baskets. He was watching, I knew, for the slightest sign of movement under their bare feet and busy hands, ready to leap to their rescue should a subsidence occur. Naturally I remained at his side, ready to leap to *his* rescue.

He and Selim saw the object at the same moment; their shouts caused the diggers to halt their activities. Before I could stop him, Emerson hastened to the spot. Naturally I followed him.

The object was a bone, too large to be human; others, half-buried by a layer of fine sand, lay around it, covering an area approximately a meter square. Emerson required no more than a glance to identify the strange deposit.

"Animal burials," he muttered. "They were mummified; that's a scrap of linen. All right, Selim, brush away the sand but don't move anything until we get photographs."

There were several layers of bones and horns—rams, goats, gazelles, oxen—separated from one another by layers of fine sand. Even with all of us concentrating on the area, progress was slow, owing to Emerson's insistence on proper procedures.

We were still uncovering bones when I decreed a halt. It was sometimes necessary for me to do this, since Emerson would have gone on until dark or until everyone else dropped in his or her tracks. That day it was David whose increasingly clumsy and slow movements aroused my concern. Geoffrey had teased him about his drowsy looks until a sharp glance from me put an end to little jokes about bridegrooms.

I hadn't been able to get any information out of anyone all

day. My attempts to get David to myself had been foiled by Lia, who stuck close to him and ignored my hints that she should go somewhere and do something else. It became clear to me that David knew something he did not want *me* to know and that Lia and Emerson were both in the conspiracy to keep me in ignorance.

That is a state of affairs I never allow. I therefore demanded Emerson's company on the way back to the house and held my horse to a walk. "What happened last night?" I demanded. "Were they able to learn the identity of the man they seek? What are they going to do next?"

"I don't know," said Emerson.

"Confound it, Emerson! I will not be kept in the dark. If you won't tell me—"

"Don't shout!" Emerson bellowed. Geoffrey, riding ahead with Nefret, turned his head to look at us.

"Now see what you've done," I said.

"I haven't done anything, curse it! He's accustomed to our shouting at one another, we do it all the time." But he moderated his voice. "I've not had an opportunity to speak with David at length. He said only that they had run up against a slight snag last night, but there was no harm done. They mean to give it one more try tonight, and if they are not successful we will discuss the matter further."

"I suppose I must be satisfied with that."

"You must, yes. And so must I." The tight set of his lips and the whitened knuckles of the hands that grasped the reins betrayed the same sense of frustration that affected me. After a moment he added, "Don't you suppose I want to go with them? I dare not; my presence would only increase the risk. There is nothing I can do to help them, except possibly to provide a distraction."

"So that is why you announced you would investigate the substructure."

"One of the reasons." Emerson grinned. "I want to see what's down there."

Lia and David would not stay for tea. Ramses was to meet them at the dahabeeyah and would, Lia said casually, probably spend the night. He had taken to keeping toilet articles and changes of clothing there.

"Bring him to breakfast tomorrow," I said.

It was an order, not a request; the only possible response was "yes," and Lia gave it.

They left the horses and went on on foot, arms entwined. The others went up to change, except for Nefret, who intercepted me. "Geoffrey wonders if Ramses is avoiding him," she said. "I promised him I would ask you."

"Now why would he wonder that?" I said in some confusion.

She did not reply, but stood looking at me with a singular lack of expression. I wondered if she had learned the trick from me; it is more likely to induce a response than repeated questions.

"He is enjoying David's company," I said at last. "You know how close they are. He—er—no doubt he also means it as a delicate attention to the two of you."

I hoped she would not ask me what I meant by that, since I did not know myself. Apparently she accepted it, for she nodded and left me.

The conversation at dinner was strictly archaeological and conducted almost entirely by Emerson and Geoffrey. The latter appeared to be very interested in our bones (the ones we had found, that is). "Were they, perhaps, sacrifices to the dead king?" he asked.

"The shaft was not dug to contain the animal burials," said Emerson. "They are later in date. You observed that the pit in which they lay was smaller in size than the shaft itself."

I am afraid I paid less attention than I ought to have done. The Reader need not doubt whither my thoughts had strayed.

After a restless (on my part) night we were up betimes. Again mist veiled the windows; again I hastened downstairs. Nefret and Geoffrey were already there, and Fatima had served the food before the others finally came. It was with inexpressible relief that I beheld them, but a second look at Ramses brought a quickly repressed exclamation to my lips.

It was repressed, to be precise, by Emerson, who placed his serviette firmly over my mouth. "A bit of butter on your chin, my dear," he said. "Let me remove it."

My dear Emerson and I communicate without words, nor had he missed the signs of exhaustion that marked his son's face. It was not long before his keen wits and amiable paternal concern had determined on a course of action.

"Pay attention, everyone," he said. "Certain changes in our schedule have become expedient. Ramses, I need to borrow you back from Reisner for a few days. He can have Geoffrey instead."

Geoffrey choked on a swallow of coffee and had to retreat behind his serviette.

"You can't trade people back and forth as if they were picks and shovels, Emerson," I exclaimed. "Have you spoken with Mr. Reisner about this?"

Geoffrey cleared his throat. "I'm afraid he won't agree, sir."

Emerson's fist came down on the table. "Reisner is not the Lord God Jehovah! He will have to agree because I have said so. I need Ramses to go over the proofs of the text volume of my history. I received another cursed letter from the cursed Oxford University Press yesterday saying they will have to delay publication for six months unless they receive the proofs by the end of February. I respect your acquaintance with the language, Geoffrey, but I trust I do not offend you when I point out it is not the equal of Ramses's. Besides, he is familiar with the material."

It was a suspiciously detailed explanation for Emerson, who does not often condescend to explain at all. I felt sure I understood his real motive, and I was filled with admiration for his ingenuity.

"No further objections?" Emerson inquired, glowering at each of us in turn. "Hmph. I will stop by Harvard Camp on the way to the dig and tell Reisner what I have decided. You had better ride with me, Geoffrey, and stay at Giza if you are wanted. Ramses, come up to my study and I will show you what needs to be done before I leave. The rest of you be ready to go."

"Yes, sir," said Ramses. He followed Emerson out of the room.

I gave them five minutes, and then followed. Emerson was just coming out of his study. Through the open doorway I saw that Ramses was already asleep on the sofa, motionless as an effigy of a knight on a tombstone and looking remarkably innocent with his hands limp at his sides and his lashes dark against his cheeks. Emerson closed the door.

"I couldn't wait," I explained. "Did they have any luck last night? Er . . . he is all right, isn't he?"

Emerson gave me a quick kiss. "Sleep is all he needs. This was the only way I could think of to explain his absence from work."

"And very clever it was, Emerson."

"Hmph." Emerson fingered the cleft, or dimple, in his chin, as he does when deep in thought. "I've never seen him drawn

quite so fine, Peabody. It is more than physical exhaustion, it is
nervous strain as well. Was he in love with that girl?"

"Maude? Oh, no."

"And you would know." He drew my arm through his and
led me toward the front of the house. "Good Gad, we sound like
a pair of society gossips. As for last night, you can and undoubtedly will quiz David once you've got him to yourself. I will arrange matters so that he gets a few hours' rest today."

"Are they going out again tonight?"

"I don't know. Ramses was asleep on his feet and I didn't
want to keep the others waiting."

The mist was lifting, but it still lay thick upon the Giza plateau;
after Geoffrey and Emerson had turned onto the side road their
forms were gradually enveloped in clinging white fog. The rest
of us went on along the main road, which was filled with the
usual morning traffic, from camels to bicyclists. Riding four
abreast would not have been courteous (or safe, given the disposition of a camel). I directed the girls to precede me and David,
and then I got to work squeezing information out of him. Direct
assault was the method I selected.

"What happened to Ramses's hands?"

"His hands?" David's look of surprise would not have deceived a child.

"They were green."

"Oh, Lord. I thought we'd got the stuff off!"

"I have seen Kadija's ointment often enough to recognize it,
even on a cloudy morning when the individual in question is
doing his best to hide his palms. It is not easy to remove with
soap and water. What happened?"

"Just rope burns," David said. "He was hanging on to the
rope and had to descend in something of a hurry."

"Because people were shooting at him?"

"Goodness no." David essayed to chuckle. "They were only—
um—about to cut the rope. It was rather a long drop, you see.
Onto a stone paving."

He was beginning to sound a little rattled, so I continued to
press him. "When was this?"

"Night before last."

"That is why he kept out of my way yesterday," I mused.
"Did they get a good look at him?"

"He doesn't think so."

"He doesn't think so," I repeated. "What about you?"

"No. I was down below."

"And what happened last night?"

"Nothing." David took out his handkerchief and mopped his brow. "Something went wrong. Oh, the deuce. I may as well tell you."

"You may as well."

"Well, you see, one of the things Ramses overheard before someone took a notion to approach the window was that Failani was to meet the—er—the effendi last night. Unfortunately the place of the meeting was not mentioned. The only thing we could do was trail Failani, which we did—for six bloody—excuse me, Aunt Amelia!—six hours. He visited a number of interesting places, but if a meeting took place we missed it. We might have done. We couldn't follow him into . . . into certain of the places."

I decided not to press him on that issue. "You said Ramses's presence was observed the previous night, even if he was not recognized. Has it occurred to you that Failani may have anticipated he would be followed? That he led you on a wild-goose chase instead of keeping his appointment? That he arranged to have someone follow *you?*"

"Yes, ma'am," David said wretchedly. "It did occur to us. Eventually."

"David, this has become too dangerous. You must stop it."

"It's not up to me," David said gently but firmly. "Where my brother goes, I go."

Emerson arrived at the site soon after us and looked surprised when I asked what Mr. Reisner had said. "He said nothing. What was there to say?" He inspected David from head to foot and back again, and scowled. "David, I won't need you for a few hours. Go round to the south side and get me a series of photographs of the area at the base of the pyramid. There's got to be some trace of a casing, curse it. Selim? Where the devil are . . . Oh. Let's get back to the shaft."

"Do you want me to help David with the photography?" Nefret asked.

"No, Lia can give him a hand." He avoided looking at her, and a wave of sadness washed over me. Emerson and I had sometimes kept the children in the dark about certain of our schemes, but never before had all of us treated Nefret like an outsider. In a sense she was, though. Her chief allegiance was now to another, and although I knew Geoffrey could not be the villain we sought, we could not be certain of his discretion or his understanding. The delicacy of the situation was particularly acute with regard to the activities of Ramses and David.

This realization brought home to me how closely knit and united our little band had grown over the years. In time Geoffrey might become part of it. No doubt he would. It took normal people a while to get used to us.

Lia and David went off, not to photograph but to snatch a few hours' sleep, and the rest of us returned to the shaft. The dimensions of the animal pit became more apparent as we went deeper. It was narrower than the shaft itself, and Emerson's assumption that it was considerably later in date was confirmed by the discovery of faience amulets and wooden animal figures mixed in with the bones. David and Lia joined us for luncheon; I was pleased to observe that the lad appeared greatly refreshed, and when we went back to work on the shaft he accompanied us. We were still digging up bones when the sudden disappearance of the declining sun behind a bank of cloud cast a shadow like twilight over the scene.

"Confound it!" said David, who had been about to make an exposure.

Emerson cast a malevolent look at the cloud bank. Rimmed by the rays of the sun it had concealed, it hung like a gold-trimmed purple curtain across the western sky. "Confound it," he repeated.

It was not the increased difficulty of photography that concerned him, but the possible consequences of a heavy rain. He began bawling out orders.

"Nefret, stop sorting those bones and pile them into baskets. Selim—Daoud—get the tarpaulin from the shelter and stretch it over the excavation. We'll need heavy stones to anchor the corners. David, pack up the cameras. Peabody—Lia—"

I was already on my way to the shelter, to gather up our notes and papers and pack the remains of the food. It was inspiring to see how quickly everyone scattered, each to his appointed task, all moving with the efficiency long experience had taught us. The rain held off, but the skies darkened and a brisk wind arose, tugging at the canvas so that we had the devil of a time getting it into place and keeping it there. The hired laborers had scampered away toward their village; only our loyal men remained, working as assiduously as we.

I lay flat across one section of canvas, holding it down until Daoud could fetch another stone, and admiring the unusual atmospheric manifestations. The eastern sky was clear, but the uncanny shadow cast an eerie light across the cultivation. Toward the north the shapes of the pyramids stood out black against an encrimsoned rent in the clouds. Another shape became apparent; it was that of a horse and rider, approaching at an easy pace. There was no mistaking the elegant outline of Risha, or, come to that, the outline of Ramses. Someone had once said Ramses rode like a centaur, and he looked like one just then, for the forms of man and horse blended into a featureless silhouette.

He was still some little distance away when a sharp cracking sound made me start and look up. A repetition of the sound told me what I ought to have known from the first. It was not thunder I had heard, it was a rifle shot. I jumped up in time to hear a third shot and see Ramses fall forward over the horse's neck.

He held on, though, and when Risha came to a stop he straightened and looked down with a particularly supercilious expression at the agitated group surrounding him and the horse. We had all run like fury, and so had Risha, straight to us. Having delivered his rider, he turned his head and snuffled inquiringly at Ramses's arm. The latter raised both eyebrows at me.

"Put your pistol away, Mother. May I ask what you intended to shoot at?"

Unaware of having removed the weapon from my pocket, I looked at it in surprise. Emerson snatched at my hand. "Don't point it at your face, Peabody, curse it! Ramses, are you hurt?"

"No."

"Then why did you appear to collapse?" I demanded angrily, as Emerson took the pistol from me.

"It seemed advisable to present a smaller target."

"There is blood on your shirt," said Nefret.

"Jam," said Ramses. "I took tea with Sennia."

**13**

My wounds were negligible, but the maiden insisted upon
binding them up with strips torn from her diaphanous garments . . .

**M**y suggestion, that we fan out in search of the hidden assassin, was unanimously rejected. Ramses claimed he could not tell
from which direction the shots had come; Nefret declared that
such a procedure would be foolhardy in the extreme; Lia pointed
out that the increasing darkness would render a search futile.
David did not get a chance to say anything, and Emerson's blis-
tering comments cannot be reproduced in these pages.

So we finished packing up and started for home. By the time
we reached the house, rain was falling heavily. It splashed into
the fountain and formed puddles on the tiled floor of the courtyard. Fatima had seen the storm approaching and moved all the
overstuffed furniture and cushions under cover.

As soon as Emerson had seen his precious boxes of bones and
scraps safely stowed away, he started across the courtyard toward
the front door. I had anticipated this, so I was able to intercept
him when he reached the takhtabosh, where the doorman had
taken shelter from the rain and was sitting on one of the benches.

"And where do you think you are going?" I demanded. "You
are soaked to the skin. Change your clothing at once."

"Why? I will be wet again immediately," said Emerson.

The door to the street opened, admitting Ramses and David, who had taken the horses to the stable. "What is the matter?" David asked.

I did not blame him for asking; Emerson's and my relative positions were somewhat combative. "I am attempting to prevent him from rushing off to Mr. Reynolds's house and accusing him of attempted murder," I explained, taking a firmer grip on my impulsive husband's shirtsleeve. "That is where you were going, wasn't it, Emerson?"

"I want to get to him before he has time to conceal the evidence," snarled Emerson. "Out of my way, Peabody."

"It is already too late for that," said Ramses. "Assuming there was any evidence to conceal."

"Quite right," I agreed. "Quiet, calm consideration is what we want now, not impulsive action. Go and change, all of you, and we will meet in the sitting room for a council of war!"

Since it was necessary for me to make certain Emerson did as he was told before I took care of my own needs, I was the last to join the group. The sitting room felt quite cozy with the lamps lighted and the soft murmur of falling rain outside the open windows. Nefret had supplied Lia with a change of clothing and David was wearing one of Ramses's galabeeyahs, and Geoffrey . . .

I had completely forgot about him! Guilt made my greeting warmer than the situation actually demanded. In response to my question he explained that he had returned to the house in the afternoon, meaning to rest for a few minutes, and had fallen sound asleep. At this point in his narrative a burst of coughing interrupted his speech.

"That cough is getting worse," I said. "You had better let me—er—let Nefret—"

"Perhaps he will let *you*," said Nefret, smiling at my inadvertent faux pas even as a frown wrinkled the smooth surface of her brow. "He refuses to see a physician or allow me to examine him."

"It's only the dust," Geoffrey protested.

"Have a whiskey and soda," said Emerson. He has very little patience with illness, his own or anyone else's. "And then we can get to business. Did Nefret tell you about your friend Reynolds's latest aberration?"

"Yes, sir," Geoffrey said in a low voice. "I had thought he was better."

"It seems to me," said Ramses, "that you are all ignoring one of the basic principles of British law. We have no proof whatever that Jack Reynolds fired those shots."

"I was attempting to get that proof when your mother prevented me," Emerson replied, giving me a whiskey and soda and an inimical look.

Ramses leaned forward, forearms resting on his knees and hands clasped. "That's all very well, sir, and I agree someone ought to pay Jack a visit; but first we must consider what it is we hope to learn. He had ample time to clean and replace the weapon. If he has an alibi for the critical time, well and good; if he has not, which is more likely, that is still not proof of guilt."

"Hmph," said Emerson. "It won't do any harm to ask, will it? Have I your permission to call on Reynolds and inquire, with the utmost tact and subtlety, where he was and what he was doing this afternoon at approximately . . . What time was it?"

Another brief and inconclusive discussion ensued. None of us had been keeping track of the time. Finally Emerson declared that we had talked long enough and that he meant to go at once. Alone.

Naturally I accompanied him. The rain had almost stopped, and the night air was refreshing. Emerson had his torch and I my parasol. He would not come under it with me or walk close by me, since he claimed the spokes kept hitting him in the face, so we splashed through puddles and patches of mud like two strangers who happened to be going in the same direction.

I was preoccupied with my own thoughts, as—I did not doubt—Emerson was with his. I had persuaded Lia and David to stay and dine with us, but I felt certain they would be off shortly after dinner, and Ramses with them—and that shortly after that, he and David would be on their way to Cairo to risk heaven only knew what terrible danger. I found myself wishing Ramses *had* been struck by a bullet—not in a vital organ, of course, but in a spot that would keep him immobile for a few days.

The little house which had once been filled with merriment and harmless (for the most part) pleasure looked desolate and forlorn. Few lights showed. Raindrops dripped in mournful melody from the surrounding trees. The doorman had retreated within. We had to pound and ring for several minutes before there was a response and that, when it came, was not welcoming.

"Go away," a voice shouted in Arabic. "The effendi is not at home."

Emerson shouted back. His voice is unmistakable; before he had got more than a few words out, the portal was flung open and the groveling servant ushered us into the house. We sent him off to announce us while I tried to persuade Emerson to wipe his feet.

"Why bother?" he inquired, with a critical look round the untidy entrance hallway.

We were kept waiting rather a long time, and Emerson was about to lose his patience when someone came. The Reader may conceive of my surprise when I recognized Karl von Bork. I ought not to have been surprised, in fact, since I remembered hearing that Karl had got in the habit of spending a great deal of time with his friend Jack, though what the two had in common aside from their interest in Egyptology I could not imagine. It was not until he bowed us into the sitting room that I got a good look at him.

Evidently he and Jack had been having one of those comfortable masculine evenings at home. A man's idea of comfort is to be as untidy as possible. Karl had reassumed his coat, in some haste, since it was buttoned askew; his attempt to smooth his hair with his hands had not been successful. His face was flushed, his eyes unfocused. He began to apologize for Jack, who, he explained, was unwell.

"Intoxicated, you mean?" I inquired. "I am sorry to see, Karl, that you have been encouraging his weakness by drinking with him."

"Not drinking," said Emerson. His nose wrinkled. In one long stride he reached the door of Jack's study and turned the knob.

Disheveled and coatless, Jack sat sprawled in an easy chair, staring blearily at the door. The sofa cushions were every which way, so I presumed Karl had been reclining on that article of furniture when the servant summoned him. On a nearby table were an ash receptacle, a pipe, and a plate of almond biscuits, one half-eaten. Jack held his pipe in one lax hand. The smoke that eddied about the room did not have the scent of ordinary tobacco. It was the same strange odor I had once taken for that of decay. There was no mistaking its origin now.

I turned to Karl. "Shame!" I cried. "Oh, Karl, how could you? What would Mary say?"

Tears filled his eyes. He flung his arm up to cover his face.

"I was so lonely for her," he gasped. "Und für die Kinder. Ach, Gott, ich habe myself disgraced—meine Geliebte betrayed . . ."

Sobs stifled his speech, which had become increasingly incoherent. I patted him absently on the shoulder. Emerson removed the pipe from Jack's hand and shook him vigorously. The only response was a faint smile.

"Too far gone," said Emerson. "It will take several hours for the effects to wear off. How long have you been here with him, von Bork?"

His curt tone recalled Karl to some semblance of manhood. He wiped his eyes on the back of his hand.

"Ich weiss nicht, Herr Professor," he muttered. "A long time."

I passed him my handkerchief. "Pull yourself together, Karl. It is vitally important that we extract a coherent statement from you."

"I doubt we can get it," said Emerson dryly.

By direct questioning we managed to extract a few scraps of information from Karl. He had been in Cairo at the Institut, not at Giza. The sun had been shining when he got to the house . . . At least he thought it had. Jack had arrived shortly after him. No, alas, he could not remember how long after. At some point it had begun to rain . . . He and Jack had been together ever since. As for the hashish, this was not the first time they had indulged. It was Jack who had provided the filthy stuff. He did not know where Jack had got it.

Depression so profound it forbade even the release of tears had gripped our friend. It soon became clear we would get no more from him that night—if ever.

Emerson abandoned his interrogation and went to the gun case. The key was in the lock; he turned it and opened the door. "I see only one of the famous Colts."

"Jack mentioned some days ago that a weapon had been stolen."

"That is what he would say if he intended to use it for purposes of homicide," Emerson remarked. "However, it was not a revolver that was employed this afternoon."

He removed each of the weapons from its place and examined it. "No," he said, replacing the last. "If one of them was used it has been cleaned and any remaining ammunition removed. At least he has sense enough not to leave a loaded weapon in the case. There's nothing more for us here, Peabody."

"Should we not question the servants, Emerson?"

"Useless," said Emerson. "They will say what they have been told to say or what they believe we want to hear. Von Bork, I will speak with you again tomorrow."

A barely audible murmur of "Ja, Herr Professor," came from the huddled form. Emerson's stern face softened slightly. "Don't do anything foolish," he said.

Emerging from that house was like coming out of a prison—a dungeon that held two men in fetters more difficult to break than any material chains. Emerson took a deep breath of the clean night air.

"Don't put up the cursed parasol, Peabody, it has stopped raining. Odd, isn't it, that once again our old friend von Bork has provided an alibi for a suspected killer?"

"I cannot believe he deliberately lied, Emerson. He was so repentant after that other occasion—so grateful that we had forgiven him. Is it possible that Jack misled him? The drug has strange effects."

"You are hopelessly soft-hearted, my dear. But you are right about the unpredictable effects of hashish. They depend on the constitution of the user and the purity of the substance. Euphoria is the commonest reaction, which is why people use the confounded stuff, but there are others, and most of them are easy to counterfeit."

The clouds were lifting; stars glimmered in the sky over Cairo. Emerson's steps slowed. He took out his pipe and I let go his arm so he could fill it, recognizing the need for his favorite aid to ratiocination.

"Are you implying that Karl's remorse was pretense, Emerson? That he was acting the whole time?"

"It is a possibility."

"But that would mean . . . Good Gad, that would mean that Karl is the man we are after! He supplied Jack with the drug, pretended to smoke it with him—took advantage of Jack's stupor to creep away and follow Ramses . . . It wasn't much of an alibi he gave Jack, you know. He was very vague about times."

A match flared. Emerson chuckled. "Jumping to conclusions again, Peabody. There are a number of holes in that scenario. We are gradually getting closer to the truth, but we are still a long way from understanding how they all fit together—our 'accidents' at Zawaiet el 'Aryan, the drug business, the forgeries, the murder of Maude Reynolds."

"You believe there is a common denominator?"

"There must be. It wouldn't be playing fair if there were not."

"God," I remarked, "does not always play fair."

"That is why I don't believe in him. A decent deity would have better manners than the creatures he created out of dirt."

I prefer to avoid theological discussions with Emerson. His opinions are distressingly unorthodox, and sometimes uncomfortably close to my own private musings.

We had reached our house; the doorman stood ready to admit us. I shivered. "Emerson, can't we keep the boys from going to Cairo tonight?"

"Having one of your dire forebodings, are you, Peabody?"

"I don't need a premonition to know they will be in danger. David told me what happened last night. It is highly suspicious."

"Everything strikes you as highly suspicious," Emerson said agreeably. "But I know what you mean. We will have another conference with the boys immediately after dinner."

We went straight in to dinner, since we were later than I had expected we would be, and Emerson proceeded to regale the others with a description of what we had found at Jack's. It was not the most appropriate conversation for a dinner table, but then most of our conversations are not.

Of all of us Geoffrey was the most disturbed. "Hashish! That is even worse than I feared. Where could Jack have got it?"

"Since it is illegal, he would have to exercise some discretion in obtaining it," Ramses replied. "But it is not difficult to find."

"Karl too," Nefret murmured. I knew she was thinking of Mary and the children.

"Let us not waste time in vain regrets," I said briskly. "Rather we should apply our collective intelligence to answering the questions that arise from this discovery."

Agreement was unanimous, but answers were few; part of the difficulty was the necessity of avoiding the other "hashish connection," as I called it to myself. I understood Ramses's insistence that Nefret not be told of that aspect of the case, but omitting any mention of the subject made discussion cursed difficult in the light of what we had learned that evening. Several times I found myself on the verge of a reference to it, and Ramses sat poised like a bird of prey, anticipating a slip and ready to pounce on the culprit.

Finally Emerson declared, "I promised von Bork I would have another little chat with him tomorrow. I will interview Reynolds at the same time. If I can do nothing more, I will at least put the fear of God into him."

"The fear of Emerson, rather," I said. "Can't you take his guns away from him?"

"Now there's a thought," Emerson admitted, stroking his chin. "That arsenal of his is too convenient—not only for Reynolds, but for anyone who chose to help himself. I understand there has already been one theft. Do you happen to know what was taken, Geoffrey?"

"No, sir." A look of distaste twisted the young man's delicate lips. "As I told you, I abhor firearms. I wouldn't know one from another."

"You mentioned the Colts," Ramses said. "There were two of them—new service revolvers, forty-five caliber. He also has—or had, when I saw the collection the day we first went to luncheon with the Reynolds's—a shotgun—a Winchester slide-action with a twenty-inch barrel—two rifles, a Springfield and a Mauser Gewehr, and a Luger pistol."

Observing Geoffrey's skeptical look, I explained, "Ramses's memory is seldom at fault, Geoffrey. Well, Emerson? Were any of them missing?"

"Only one of the Colts. Reynolds isn't the only man in Cairo who owns a rifle, but . . . Hmmm, yes. I will relieve him of his collection tomorrow."

The rain having ended, we went to the courtyard for coffee. I had no intention of allowing Ramses to get away from me without a private discussion—or, as he would have called it, a lecture—and was racking my brain to think of a way of accomplishing this when Nefret excused herself and Geoffrey. His cough had been troubling him all evening, and I could see she was worried about him. They went off arm in arm; as soon as the door had closed behind them, I turned to my son.

"After the failure of your plan last night and the attack on you this afternoon, I trust it has occurred to you that you had better not venture out tonight."

"Sssh!" said Emerson, glancing uneasily over his shoulder.

"Your whispers are louder than my ordinary speech," I retorted. "No one can overhear. Goodness gracious, how uncomfortable it is, having to keep things from our nearest and dearest! Ramses, I want your promise."

"You have it."

"It would be foolhardy in the extreme to . . . Oh."

Emerson leaned forward and David drew his chair closer. We must have looked like a band of conspirators, heads together, hissing at one another.

"What made you change your mind?" I demanded, nose to nose with Ramses. "For I do not suppose it was concern for your mother's feelings that moved you."

"Simple logic," said Ramses, refusing to take the bait. "We were under surveillance last night. It took me longer than it ought to realize that, and then we had something of a problem eluding the lads. How they became suspicious of us I don't know."

"Finding you dangling from a rope outside the window?" Emerson suggested sarcastically.

"That is one possibility. The point is that we can't use those personae again, and working our way into the organization from another direction would take a long time. Since we now know that the man we were after is also the forger, we may be able to employ other methods."

"He's been a busy little rascal," said Emerson in his normal tones. I immediately shushed him. He swore—softly—and leaned closer. "Dealing drugs, manufacturing forgeries, and excavating ancient sites. Not to mention committing a murder and arranging accidents for us. We still are not certain of the motive behind those."

"They must be designed to keep us away from the site," David murmured. "The attack on Ramses today cannot be the result of our investigation of the drug business. There's no way they could know who we really are."

"An informant in the police?" I asked.

Ramses shook his head. "Russell is the only one who knows our identities. He's too good a policeman to let that information slip. The attack today resembled the earlier accidents, and that suggests the motive is the one Mr. Vandergelt proposed."

"Yes, but what the—" Emerson caught himself. "Damn and blast!"

"Quite," said Ramses. "It's the very devil, isn't it, having to whisper and conspire? I think our friend is becoming a bit rattled, though. We've been pressing him from several different directions and we must continue to do so. Do you want me back at work tomorrow, Father? Under the circumstances I believe we should concentrate our forces."

"Mr. Reisner isn't going to like that," I remarked. "Especially if Geoffrey remains with us, as he has declared his intention of doing."

"Then he will have to lump it," said Emerson.

## From Manuscript H

The retreating footsteps must have been as light as a child's; it was the soft click of the closing latch that woke Ramses, and his sleep-fogged brain was slow to respond. It took him several seconds to realize that he was lying on the couch in his father's study. A drowsy smile curved his lips as he remembered. Emerson had ordered the others off to the dig and ordered him to rest. He must have slept heavily for hours. The light was that of late afternoon.

Rising, he stretched and yawned and went out. He found Sennia in the courtyard, with Basima in close attendance; the child was trotting back and forth from the fountain with a little pail with which she was watering the flowers, and the floor, and Horus. When she saw Ramses she dropped the pail and ran to him, squealing with pleasure.

"She is very wet," Basima warned him.

"So I see. It's all right, Basima," he added, laughing, as a pair of wet arms went round his neck and a dripping body soaked his shirt. "I need to change my clothing, anyhow."

"Not until you have eaten," said Fatima, appearing in the archway. "The Father of Curses said you were working and not to disturb you, but it is not good to go so long without food. I will bring soup and cold lamb and lettuces and bread and—"

"No, don't bother. We'll have an early tea, Sennia and I. Would you like that, little bird?"

"Jam," said Sennia.

She was picking up English rapidly, though her speech was still a bewildering mixture of both languages. Perched on his knee she explained to him that flowers needed much water, and that she was helping to make them look pretty.

"Do you think Horus looks pretty when he is watered?" Ramses asked. The cat gave him a sour look.

But as he responded to the child's chatter, part of his mind wandered back to the sound that had wakened him. If it wasn't Fatima who had looked in to see if he wanted food or drink, who was it? Or had he imagined that sly soft little sound?

When Fatima came back with tea and food and milk for Sennia, he said casually, "I suppose the others are still at the dig."

"All but Geoffrey Effendi. He said he did not feel well, and went to his room to rest. I hope it is not a bad sickness. He is not a strong man."

"He's stronger than he looks," Ramses said. "No, little bird, cats do not like jam. And don't eat it from the same spoon you put in Horus's mouth."

She was a distraction and a delight, the innocent cause of his misery and one of the few things that allowed him to forget it for a while. No doubt his mother could compose a pithy aphorism on the irony of that.

After Sennia had been carried off for a bath and a change of clothing he was too restless to sit still, so he went to the stable. With no particular goal in mind he headed up into the desert; the emptiness of sand and sky always helped him to think more clearly. This time he could have wished he wasn't thinking straight, that he was misled by anger and jealousy; but the evidence was mounting, and all of it pointed to the same man. He hoped he was wrong. Of all the solutions to his personal problems, this would be the worst.

He let Risha set his own pace, paying little attention to his surroundings until a cool wind lifted the hair on his forehead and a sudden twilight turned the air gray. Looking up, he saw the approaching storm; it was still some distance away, but it looked like a bad one. Undirected, Risha had headed for the same place they had been so often; they were less than a mile from Zawaiet el 'Aryan. He decided he might as well go on and lend a hand if they were still there. Knowing his father, he thought they probably were.

He was within sight of the little group when the first shot whistled past, so close he could have sworn he heard the wind of its passage. His hands tightened on the reins, but Risha, who had better sense than he, stretched out and broke into his long, smooth gallop. By the time his agitated family had done arguing and interrogating him and inspecting him for bullet holes, there was no sense in searching for the rifleman.

He and David took the horses to the stable and helped rub them down. He learned there what he had expected to learn. It still wasn't proof positive, he told himself. Apparently none of the others shared his suspicions; his father would have gone straight after Reynolds if his mother had not prevented him.

Obeying her orders, he and David went to his room to change their wet clothing.

"It must have been Jack Reynolds," David said, while Ramses rummaged through the wardrobe looking for dry garments.

"The rumors mention an Englishman."

"That means little or nothing. Wardani used the words sahib and effendi and Inglizi interchangeably; they indicate a social class rather than a particular nationality."

"I seem to be out of clean shirts," Ramses muttered.

"A lot of your things are at the *Amelia.*" David left his wet clothes lying on the floor and went to assist in the search. He pulled out a dresser drawer and reached in. "What's this?"

He had found the little statue of Horus. "Maude gave it to me," Ramses said. "It was a Christmas gift. She bought it in the suk, I suppose."

"Charming Western naïveté," David said.

"What do you mean?"

"Isn't that what Europeans say of Egyptian work? Primitive, naive? All that means is that they don't understand, or care to understand, that particular artistic tradition. No Egyptian made this."

Ramses tossed the galabeeyah he had removed from the wardrobe across a chair and went to David.

"How do you know?"

"Hard to put in words. The workmanship is rather good, really; but the musculature of the chest and arms, the cast of the features—well, they aren't Egyptian, that's all. They are in the Western tradition, even though the artist was trying to imitate the ancient style. She must have . . ."

His voice trailed off as a belated realization of the implication of his analysis came to him.

"Made it herself?" Ramses finished the sentence.

"Why didn't you show me this before?" David demanded.

"My gentlemanly instincts got in my way," Ramses said in disgust. "It seemed indecent to show the girl's gift, especially after Nefret ridiculed it so ruthlessly. Besides, the idea never occurred to me. I haven't your eye. And Maude never said anything about her hobby, or showed us examples of her work . . ."

"He'd make damned good and sure she didn't," David said. "Especially after he learned you were on his trail. Everything points to him, you know. He took alarm when Nefret made that pointed reference to fakes and the London dealer; how else could anyone have known that the Professor had the scarab? He had to kill Maude because she was about to tell you the truth."

"It fits," Ramses admitted. "She couldn't have understood his real motives or the seriousness of selling forgeries; she probably thought of it as a jolly little joke to be played on a group of solemn scholars. We're still missing something, though. Why did he have to retrieve the scarab?"

David had been turning the figure over and over in his hands. "Because she signed her work," he said. "Part of the joke. Look here. Are you sure this wasn't on the scarab?"

They were incised on the flat base of the statue—two small hieroglyphic signs. One was an owl, the ancient Egyptian M; the other, below it, was the alphabetic sign for the letter R. Together they were not only Maude's initials; they made up an Egyptian word.

Ramses had deliberately cultivated his visual memory, but he didn't even have to close his eyes and concentrate in order to remember that part of the inscription.

"Of course it was," he said. "It's a title—the word that means overseer or superintendent. That was one of the anomalies I noticed—the fact that the inscription *began* with the titles of the official who composed it. He practically rubbed my nose in it, the bastard, and I flat-out missed it!"

"There you go again, taking yourself to task because you aren't omniscient. How could you possibly have realized what it meant?" David slipped the galabeeyah over his head. "I think," he went on, after his head had emerged, "he panicked unnecessarily when he realized you might have the scarab. Breaking into the house was a risk."

"There was no risk to him. The men he hired knew nothing about him, and he left no trail that could lead back to him."

"We had better show this to the Professor," David said. "Are you ready?"

"Mother wouldn't think so." Attired only in trousers and boots, Ramses shut the bureau drawer and went back to the wardrobe. "There's got to be a confounded shirt around here someplace . . . Ah. They're on the top shelf."

His indignant tone made David laugh. "That's where they are supposed to be."

"Are they? Why do women button the damned things before they put them away? They only have to be unbuttoned again.

David, I don't want to mention this to Father—or Mother—tonight."

"This is the most damning evidence we've found yet, Ramses. We cannot keep it from them."

"The last nail in Jack Reynolds's coffin," Ramses muttered. "No, David. It's too easy."

David pushed a pile of papers off a chair and sat down. "Out with it, then. If it's not Jack, it must be Geoffrey you suspect. Look here, Ramses—"

"It's not what you think." He tucked his shirt in.

"I wasn't suggesting—"

"Yes, you were. You're wrong. Do you suppose I *want* him to be guilty? Think what that would do to Nefret! But it would be even worse to cover up his guilt on her account; if he's the man we're after he is totally unprincipled and as dangerous as a snake. He took one of the horses out this afternoon and didn't get back until just before it started raining—you heard what Mohammed said. He could have followed Mother that day solely in order to establish an alibi; why the devil else *would* he have followed her? It wouldn't be difficult to arrange a few firecrackers to go off after he had come gallantly to her rescue. He's had access to Jack's weapons, to Jack's poor naive mind, and to Jack's sister—"

A sharp catch of breath from David interrupted him. He shrugged. "Feel free to tell me if I've overlooked something. God knows I'd like to think so."

"It's all circumstantial," David muttered.

"I know. Give me another day before we break this latest bit of news. I'll stay here at the house tonight and keep an eye on him. He may do something—or refrain from doing something— that will settle the business."

What they learned from his parents at dinner that evening could be regarded as another nail in Reynolds's coffin. To Ramses it was a point in his favor. The top men in the drug business seldom used the stuff themselves. They had better sense.

So he spent the early hours of the night in the garden watching a particular window. It had been dark for quite a long time before a form emerged and crept through the shadows in the direction Ramses had expected. There was no objection from Narmer; Ramses had ordered the dog to be shut up at night when he began working for Russell.

Slowly Ramses approached the window of the room that had

once been his. He didn't suppose she would be there, but he made certain there was no sound of movement or breathing within before he climbed over the sill. It did not take long to find what he was looking for. He removed the bullets before he put the weapon back under the mattress.

Up to that point he had managed to think of nothing except the job at hand, but as he straightened, a series of remembered images flashed across his mind, so vividly and painfully that he closed his eyes, as if that could shut them out. How in God's name was he going to tell her?

As a rule I rise before Emerson, who is a heavy sleeper and not at his best in the morning. Conceive of my surprise, therefore, to open my eyes and behold a small circle of glowing red and a statuesque form silhouetted against the starlit window. It was Emerson—not only awake, but dressed and smoking his pipe.

I sat up with a start and a cry. "What has happened?"

"Nothing as yet," was the calm reply. "A number of things are about to happen, however. I must see Reynolds and von Bork, and pay a courtesy call on Reisner, before we begin work. Do you want to come with me?"

"Certainly."

"I felt sure you would say that. Do you need any help with your buttons?"

"No, thank you. I can probably dress more quickly without your assistance."

Emerson chuckled. "Fatima won't be up yet. I will go to the kitchen and make coffee for you, my dear."

If I had needed any encouragement to assume my attire without delay, that magnanimous offer would have done it. Emerson's intentions are of the best, but it would probably take Fatima an hour to clean up after him if he did not actually set the stove on fire.

Sure enough, I found him swearing and nursing a scalded hand. He had smashed a cup and overturned the coffeepot. There was a dead mouse in the middle of the table—one of Horus's offerings, I presumed.

I made the coffee and swept up the fragments of the broken

cup while Emerson disposed of the mouse. "Looks like a fine day," he remarked, joining me at the table.

"For what?" I demanded somewhat waspishly. (I had cut my finger on a bit of broken cup.)

"Among other things," said Emerson, "for excavating. One part of the plot is clear to me now. I know what is behind the forger's activities, and what it is we are not meant to find at Zawaiet."

"I suppose you aren't going to tell me."

"I will give you a hint. Two of the objects the forger sold were unusual—the little ivory statue and the legs of the couch. Both are early dynastic in date. By a strange coincidence, that is also the date of our pyramid. By another strange coincidence, someone is trying to keep us from excavating there." He paused invitingly.

"Good Gad," I breathed. "That is—I meant to say—yes, of course. The legs of a funeral couch, richly ornamented with gold; the image of a king, the father or grandfather of a king . . . A royal burial!"

"Or a cache," Emerson amended. "Let us suppose our friend found it last year and determined to keep the treasure for himself. How was he to dispose of it without arousing suspicion? By making the genuine artifacts appear to be part of a larger collection with a believable provenance."

"Brilliant, Emerson! And he cannot have cleared the entire burial or he wouldn't be trying to drive us away from the site. Some of the funerary goods must still be there!"

"It appears that that may be the case," said Emerson. "He would have believed there was no urgency about removing the objects last season; the site is part of Reisner's concession, and he had no intention of returning to it. No one could have anticipated he would offer it to me."

"And he—the forger—would not have found that out until recently. Reisner would have no reason to mention it to anyone except M. Maspero, and your habit of keeping your plans a secret until the last moment—"

"It must have come as a considerable shock to the bastard," Emerson agreed. "My heart bleeds for him."

The appearance of Fatima, openmouthed with surprise at seeing us, put an end to the conversation. I put an end to her apologies and apologized to her for the mess.

There was just enough light in the courtyard to allow us to see the shapeless outlines of furniture and fountain. The sky above was a pale shade, almost without color as yet, but I knew it would be a fine day. I took my parasol, however. Rain is not the only thing against which it is a protection.

"Shall we leave a message for the others?" I asked, as the sleepy doorman unbarred the portal.

"We will be back before they miss us," said Emerson. "It won't take long."

He was not correct in that assumption. When we reached Jack Reynolds's house we found the bird had flown.

One of them, at any rate. After ascertaining that Jack was not in the house, and that none of the servants admitted knowledge of his present whereabouts, Emerson burst into the guest chamber where Karl von Bork lay and shook him awake. The brusque awakening and the sight of Emerson's engorged countenance only a few inches away would have reduced a man with less on his conscience than Karl to incoherence. I had quite a time calming him enough to get a statement out of him, and it was not much use. He had stumbled off to bed after we took our departure, leaving Jack in the study. He had not seen him since. He had heard nothing, seen nothing, knew nothing—except that he was the lowest of worms, the most contemptible creature on the face of the earth, undeserving of our friendship and Mary's love.

This was true, but not of much help, so I left him wringing his hands and crying. Emerson had returned to Jack's study. When I joined him there, he had opened the gun case.

"One of the rifles is missing," he announced. Icy calm had replaced his fury and he went about his business with the terrifying efficiency that makes Emerson so formidable. Returning to the guest chamber, he searched that room and the shrinking form of Karl von Bork without finding any sign of a weapon. We then hastened to the stable, where we found, as we had expected, that Jack's horse was gone. The stableman was not to be seen; in fact, most of the servants, aroused by Emerson's initial shouts, had fled.

Emerson's penultimate act was to strip the gun case of all it contained. Pistols in his belt, the other weapons under his arm, he delayed only long enough to speak a final word to Karl.

"Go to work and say nothing to Junker or anyone else," he instructed. "If you are innocent we may be able to get you out of this yet. Guilty or innocent, running away would be the worst mistake you could make."

We hastened back to the house. The doorman's greeting

brought everyone rushing out of the breakfast room, including Lia and David, who had just arrived. Emerson apprised them of the situation in a few brief sentences.

"So finish your breakfasts," he concluded. "I could do with another cup of coffee myself. Peabody, you have not eaten; make haste, my dear, we must be off."

"Off?" Geoffrey exclaimed. "To the dig? But, sir, shouldn't we look for Jack? If he is out there somewhere with a rifle, he could be dangerous!"

"Where would we look?" Ramses asked, for Emerson's look of mild exasperation indicated he did not mean to waste time pointing out the obvious.

"At least you will go armed," Geoffrey persisted.

"Armed?" Emerson appeared to notice for the first time that he was carrying Jack's weapons. He dropped them with a clatter. "None of them is loaded."

"I know where he keeps the ammunition," Geoffrey said eagerly. "Let me go and—"

"In his desk," Emerson interrupted. "The damned fool didn't even lock the drawers. I do not carry firearms, Geoffrey. Mrs. Emerson does; I do not object, since to the best of my knowledge she has never hit anything yet. Kindly refrain from arguing with me and do as I say."

No one else had argued with him. They knew better. However, conversation cannot be restrained for long among us, and after we had taken our places at the table the inevitable speculation began.

"Perhaps he only went hunting," Lia suggested. "Don't sportsmen like to get out early?"

She looked so sweet and so worried, no one wanted to dispel this optimistic fantasy. Ramses, who had scarcely spoken since we returned, smiled at her. "That may well be the case."

Emerson put an end to the conversation by ordering us all to work. I was of course fully armed, for I pay no attention to Emerson's little foibles. Pistol, knife, belt of tools were all in their proper places, and as I went out the door I took my parasol from its hook.

When we reached Zawaiet the men were already there. Under Selim's direction several of them were removing the tarpaulin from over the shaft and Emerson dashed off to make sure no damage had been done. A little water had seeped in, but not much.

It cannot be said that my full attention was on the work. I had thought of the terrain as relatively flat, and so it was, compared with the broken cliffs and irregular contours of the Theban mountains where we had worked before; still, there were enough ridges to provide cover for any number of determined assassins. I took Selim aside. His young face lengthened and grew grim as he listened to what I told him. Before long there were men posted at various vantage points around the pyramid, and atop that structure.

By mid-morning another layer of animal bones had been photographed and removed. Mixed in with them were scraps of papyrus, on which Ramses pounced. "Demotic," he announced, after a brief look. "You were right about the late date of the deposits, Father. Here is the name of Amasis the Second."

The pit was by now over six feet deep and we had apparently reached the bottom of the deposit. No more bones appeared, only a thick layer of sand. Emerson, poised on the edge of the drop, suddenly called to the men below to stop digging and come up.

"What is wrong?" I asked, hastening to his side. "Is there evidence of imminent collapse?"

"One is seldom given warning of imminent collapse," said Emerson sarcastically. He rubbed his chin. "We've reached the bottom of the intrusive pit. If you look closely you can see the top of one of the original filling blocks. There cannot be more than a few layers of them; we've already gone down seven or eight feet and I calculated that the lowest part of the fill was less than twelve feet from the surface."

"We will need ropes," Selim said. "To pull the stones up."

"I want the men roped too," said Emerson. "No more than three down there at a time, Selim. Two men holding on to each rope, and tell them if they let go I will break their arms."

Emerson would have been one of the three in the pit had I not convinced him his strength and skill would be more useful elsewhere. So the task began, slowly and carefully. The stones were not the massive blocks employed at Giza, but each of them must have weighed several hundred pounds, and it took the men a long time to raise one of them far enough to pass a rope under it. Emerson ordered the men up before the stone was hauled to the surface and dragged away from the edge.

"It's going to take all day at this rate," I said, peering down into the cavity.

"A week, if need be," said Emerson, wiping his wet forehead with his sleeve.

"Of course. Shall we stop for a bite of lunch, since there is no hurry?"

Emerson grudgingly agreed, so we retired to the shelter and the men went off for a smoke and a rest. Before long I saw a horseman approaching from the north and called the attention of the others to him. No one reacted; aside from the fact that an assassin would not approach so openly, it would have been impossible to mistake the slim, graceful form of the rider for that of the burly American. It was Geoffrey, whom Emerson had sent off to Giza to ascertain whether Jack had reported for work.

"He's not there!" were the young man's first words, as he hurried toward us. "He never turned up this morning, and he hasn't been back to the house. I went there too."

Emerson said, "Hmph," and went on eating. I said, "Sit down, Geoffrey, and have a glass of tea. You look very warm."

Smiling and shaking his head, Geoffrey kissed his wife and sank down at her feet. "Your coolness amazes me, Mrs.—Aunt Amelia—though I ought to be accustomed to it by now."

"We are only demonstrating the qualities for which our superior caste is famous," Ramses drawled. "British phlegm, noblesse oblige, coolness under fire . . . What have I left out?"

"Don't be hateful," Nefret snapped.

"That's the part I left out," said Ramses. "Hatefulness. May I have another sandwich?"

"What did Mr. Reisner say?" I inquired.

"He wasn't very happy," Geoffrey admitted. "I told him there was trouble—"

"What?" Emerson exclaimed, in awful tones.

"Oh, I didn't go into detail, sir, I assure you. There was no need. He said trouble was your normal condition and that as soon as you'd settled the business he would appreciate having at least part of his staff returned to him."

Emerson chuckled, and Geoffrey said anxiously, "There's been no sign of Jack here, I suppose. Honestly, I don't mean to be an alarmist, but how can you go on working when you know he is out there somewhere, waiting and watching?"

"And lurking," Ramses suggested.

"I have never yet allowed a criminal to interfere with my excavations," Emerson declared. "We are on the verge of a great discovery here. This will come as a considerable surprise to . . . Oh, damnation! It won't, will it? Ramses!"

"I wasn't going to say anything," his son protested.

"I saw the way you and David looked at one another. So you've reasoned it out, have you?"

"The Third Dynasty royal burial? Yes, sir. It was a logical deduction, given the information we have collected. But," Ramses said hastily, "neither of us could come up with an idea as to where it might be. Do you think the shaft, sir?"

"No," said Emerson, somewhat appeased by this disingenuous admission of fallibility. "The place must be relatively easy of access or our friend couldn't have got at it without others knowing. The deposits in the shaft haven't been disturbed for millennia. There are only two possibilities. Either there is a hidden entrance to the real burial chamber down below, or the whole pyramid is a blind and the king was buried in a pit tomb in one of the cemeteries. I favor the former because—"

I felt obliged to interrupt. "Geoffrey, are you all right? That cough is quite nasty; sip a little tea if you can."

The young man straightened. "I am better now," he gasped, smiling at Nefret, whose arm was round his shoulders. "It was only . . . only surprise."

"Go on, Father," Ramses said. "Why do you think the hidden burial chamber is in the pyramid?"

"What? Oh. Well, for one thing, a burial in one of the cemeteries would be rather too accessible, to potential thieves as well as to us. The treasure must be inside the pyramid—under the floor of a corridor or storage chamber, or that of the false burial chamber itself—but I will not send our men down below until the shaft has been cleared. Agreed?" He did not wait for an answer but jumped up. "Back to work, then."

The others followed, leaving me alone with Geoffrey and Nefret. "Make him rest awhile," I said.

"Yes, Aunt Amelia." She spoke no more. Seeing her closed lips and remote expression I felt a pang, not of self-reproach but of loss. Would we ever be again what once we had been to one another?

As the day wore on my vigilance began to relax. There had been no sign of Jack. Perhaps, I thought hopefully, he had taken flight. When I expressed this possibility to Emerson, he only grunted. His full attention was bent on his work.

I am convinced Emerson has a sixth sense for archaeology, as I do for crime. He had read the signs few other excavators would have observed; when the catastrophe occurred, he was the only one of us who was prepared.

The men had removed four of the blocking stones, exposing another layer beneath. It was hard, slow work, and the ropes Emerson had insisted they fasten around their bodies kept getting tangled; a certain amount of cursing and complaining accompanied their activities. Finally a fifth stone was ready to be raised. The men in the pit were hauled up, and then the stone began to rise. It was halfway to the surface when the rope broke or the knots gave way—I could not see which, I only saw the thing fall. One corner of it struck the bottom, and the impact caused the whole understructure to give way, with a crash that echoed like a blast of dynamite. A cloud of sand and dust billowed up from the shaft, and Emerson threw himself across the body of one of the ropemen, who had slipped and was sliding inexorably toward the opening of the pit.

Everyone came running. When the dust settled Emerson sat up, counted heads, and let out a sigh of relief. "No harm done," he announced, wiping his mouth on the back of his hand, which did not improve matters greatly, since hand and face were equally dirty. A groan from the man he had saved drew his attention; he lifted the fellow up, inspected him, dusted him off, and handed him over to two of his friends. "No harm done," he repeated.

"That takes care of clearing the shaft," said Ramses, peering down into the depths.

"Get away from there, Ramses," I ordered. "You too, Geoffrey. Gracious, the depth must now be a good sixty feet."

"Hmmm, yes," said Emerson. "Just as well. Hauling the stones up by way of the stairs will take longer, but it won't be so dangerous. I'm afraid another of your windlasses has gone, Selim."

"So long as it was not a man, Father of Curses."

"Well said." Emerson clapped him on the back. "Let's have a look down there."

"Can't it wait until tomorrow?" I asked.

"Why wait? There are several hours of daylight left."

He had covered less than half the distance between the mouth of the shaft and the entrance to the descending stairs when he came to a stop—for an excellent reason. Jack Reynolds had not been lurking in the vicinity. He had been here all along, out of sight at the bottom of the rough-cut steps. Now he emerged, dusty and red-faced and wild-eyed, with a rifle raised to his shoulder. It was aimed at Emerson.

A sahib's born, not made. The code that governs our class is clear: uncompromising honesty, unflinching courage, respect for women and other helpless creatures, and that delicate sense of honor only the Anglo-Saxon races can fully understand.

"**D**on't do it, Emerson!" I shrieked—for I had seen the tensing of that splendid frame, and knew it betokened imminent attack. "See if you cannot reason with him!"

Emerson said something I could not hear—it was undoubtedly a swear word—but he obeyed Jack's gesture and backed slowly away as the younger man advanced toward him. Finally Jack stopped. "That will do, Professor. Close enough so we needn't shout at one another. Throat's dry. I finished the water a while back."

His voice rasped with thirst, but he sounded fairly rational. Taking heart, I said, "I have a canteen, Jack. If you will allow me—"

"No, thank you, ma'am. Not until after I have settled my account with Ramses."

"Ramses?" I repeated. "Jack, you are not being sensible. All of us know about the treasure, and your present illogical behavior substantiates our theory as to where it must be. It is futile to guard the substructure now. You cannot kill all of us."

"Kindly refrain from putting ideas into his head, Peabody," said Emerson.

Jack's forehead wrinkled. "I have no idea what you are talking about, Mrs. Emerson. Don't you come any closer—nor you, Nefret. It's Ramses I'm after. I don't want to hurt anyone else."

"None of us is going to stand quietly by while you shoot him, Jack," Nefret began. "Please—"

"Shoot?" His voice cracked. "D'you suppose I would shoot an unarmed man? I only want a square deal."

An inkling of the truth had begun to dawn on me, but it was so horrifying my brain refused to take it in. Emerson was the first to respond to Jack's statement. "If you don't intend to shoot anyone, why are you pointing that rifle at me? Put it down and we will talk."

"As soon as you promise you won't interfere. Make it a fair fight. Not everybody jumping me at once."

"Hold on a minute, Father," Ramses said, as Emerson, sputtering with fury, tried to articulate a reply. "What precisely do you have in mind, Reynolds? If this is a challenge, the choice of weapons is mine."

"Weapons be damned," Jack snarled. "Fists are good enough for me."

"And for me," Ramses said quickly.

"Jack, no!" Geoffrey cried. "You can't win. He doesn't fight like a gentleman!"

"Stay out of this, Geoff." Jack passed his sleeve across his sweating face. "He murdered Maude and wants to blame me for it, and I'll kill him if I can; but I'll do it with my bare hands in a fair fight. If he kills me . . . well, what have I got to live for now? Maude is gone, and you've got the woman I wanted, and he's manufactured enough evidence against me to send me to the gallows. But I won't shoot a man in cold blood."

Honesty—the honesty of a decent, rather stupid man—echoed in every word he had uttered. If he had spoken the truth, and I was certain he had, that meant that the evidence against him *had* been manufactured, and that his actions and beliefs had been subtly manipulated by another. The list of suspects had suddenly shrunk to one.

And now that individual knew his schemes had been thwarted by his failure to understand the limits to which a man of honor can be pushed. He could not allow the absurd exchange of fisticuffs to take place; Jack would lose, because Ramses did *not* fight like a gentleman, and under interrogation (especially of the variety Emerson employs) Jack would point the finger of blame at the real culprit.

He had to act instantly, and he did. His hands were in his pockets; he whipped the gun out and fired, with the cold calculation that had always guided him, at the only armed man present. The bullet struck poor gaping Jack in the thigh; he dropped the rifle and fell writhing to the sand. Ramses, who had sprung forward, jolted to a stop as the pistol turned, not toward him, but toward me.

"Don't bother fumbling for that little peashooter of yours, Aunt Amelia," Geoffrey said. "And don't any of the rest of you stir so much as an inch. I can kill at least three of you before you could reach me, and I will start with her."

"You will have to start with me," said Nefret in a clear, thin voice. "I am going to see what I can do for Jack."

"Please yourself," said her husband indifferently. "Just don't touch the rifle."

"She has better sense than that," said Ramses. "You could, and would, fire before she aimed the weapon. You have just demonstrated that you are an excellent shot, and that your squeamishness about guns was part of the facade you presented to us, and to the world. It was a masterful performance."

"Coming from you that is indeed a compliment," Geoffrey said. "I have heard a number of stories about your skill in the art of disguise. But you caught on to me before this, didn't you? Was it last night, while I was out of the house encouraging Jack to make himself scarce, that you removed the bullets from the Colt? Not a bad notion, but you underestimated me when you assumed I would not examine the weapon. I replaced the ammunition from Jack's supply when I went back to the house this morning."

I took stock of the situation. It was not encouraging. Nefret knelt beside Jack, who was halfway between us and the entrance to the substructure. Fists clenched and brow thunderous, Emerson was almost as far distant, a good ten feet away, with Lia and David behind him. The only one who was close enough to present a danger to Geoffrey was my son, and he dared not move because of the threat to me. Behind that mask of his I knew he was coolly calculating the odds and trying to think of ways of shifting them in our favor. He glanced at his father and then returned his gaze to Geoffrey.

"I did underestimate you," he admitted.

"It only goes to show how misleading physiognomy can be,"

Geoffrey said, with that sweet boyish smile. "I have the looks of an aesthete, don't I? When I was younger I tried to measure up to the family standards, but no matter how skilled I became at hunting and shooting and riding, the old man sneered at my accomplishments and my girlish face. So I decided to go my own way and use my defects to my advantage. I was doing rather well until you came along. You can understand why I will enjoy killing as many of you as possible before I am captured."

"That is foolish," I said disapprovingly. "Your doom is not certain at the present time; if you harm no one else, the possibilities of escaping justice—"

"Peabody, will you please refrain from making suggestions?" Emerson shouted.

"Emerson, will you please be quiet?"

Nefret got slowly to her feet. "Geoffrey, you know I will stand by you if you don't hurt anyone else. For better or worse, do you remember? Give Aunt Amelia . . . No, give Ramses the gun."

His face softened and his eyes turned to her.

Emerson had been waiting for just such a moment. With a shout of "Down, Peabody!" he leaped forward.

Not until later did I fully appreciate the heroic courage of that gesture. It was a deliberate, calculated attempt to draw Geoffrey's fire away from me and from his son. Emerson knew that Ramses would have risked an attack rather than see me shot down in cold blood, and at that range Geoffrey could not have missed him.

We all reacted precisely as my valiant spouse had known we would. The bullet whistled over me as I dropped to hands and knees. I heard a grunt from Emerson, and a scream from Nefret; I saw Ramses leap forward, striking the weapon from Geoffrey's hand and simultaneously hitting him very hard on the chin.

Geoffrey reeled back. He had been dangerously close to the edge of the shaft; the last step took him over. I had a flashing glimpse of a face, openmouthed in a silent scream of terror, and a pair of flailing arms. At the same instant Ramses flung himself flat onto the ground and reached out.

Time seemed to stop. As the cloud of dusty sand settled over Ramses's black head and sweat-soaked shirt, I saw that his arms and half his body, almost to the waist, were over the edge. His hands grasped Geoffrey's right wrist. That grip was the only thing between the miserable creature and a hideous death; the side of the shaft was too smooth to permit him to find a foothold.

He appeared to have fainted; his entire dead weight hung limp and his head was bowed.

I could hear Emerson swearing, which relieved my worst fear. Another was almost as acute, for it seemed to me that Ramses was too far off balance to pull himself back, much less himself and Geoffrey. I took hold of his belt and shouted for help.

It was there. Half-blinded by sand and in a considerable state of agitation, I had not seen David and Selim running toward me. With a cry of alarm, our young reis grasped Ramses round the legs and tried to pull him back. David lay flat and reached down. "Geoffrey! Give me your other hand," he called.

Geoffrey raised his head. He had not fainted; he was conscious and aware. Safety lay within his grasp. The man he had tried to murder held him fast, and the hand of the man he had traduced was held out to aid him.

His delicate lips curved in a smile. He raised his free arm; but instead of grasping David's hand he raked his nails viciously across Ramses's whitened knuckles and twisted himself free of Ramses's grasp. Like the throat of a monster the dark shaft swallowed him, and his scream ended in a hideous crunch.

Shuddering, I rose to my knees. Had I been a lesser woman I might have remained in that position to render thanks to the Almighty, but I do not waste time in prayer when there are more urgent matters to be attended to. I hastened to Emerson. Blood oozed from his side, but he was on his feet, with Nefret attempting to support him. He pushed her gently away.

"Only a scratch, Peabody. Knocked me down, though, curse it. Is Ramses—"

"Unharmed," Ramses replied. He and David had joined us. Both were pale, but not so pale as Nefret. She swayed, and would have fallen at Emerson's feet had he not caught her in his arms. "Fainted," he said, as her golden head came to rest against his breast. "Small wonder."

I glanced back at the scene of the tragedy and saw Selim running toward the entrance to the pyramid. I knew what he was doing, and blessed him for doing it on his own initiative, but someone must make additional arrangements for the disposal of the remains, and Jack was still unconscious, and Ramses looked as if he were about to be sick, and Emerson's shirt was sticky with blood, and—and in short, the situation was bad enough to tax even my powers. The only other person present who comprehended the nature of the latest emergency was Lia; bending over Nefret, she exclaimed, "Aunt Amelia! She—"

"Yes, Lia, I know. Daoud, carry Nefret back to the house, as quickly and as gently as possible. Lia, go with them. Find Kadija, she will know what to do. Emerson, remove your shirt and let me have a look at you."

But he would allow no other to take his daughter from him. The urgency in my voice had betrayed my concern for her; he knew there was something wrong. Without delaying to ask questions he strode away, the vigor of his movements assuring me that his injury was not serious.

"What do you want me to do, Aunt Amelia?" David asked.

"Go with them," Ramses said, before I could reply. "Tell Father to take Risha."

It was a sensible suggestion; the great stallion's strength and speed were the greatest and his gait the easiest. David hesitated, torn between conflicting duties. Ramses said impatiently, "Hurry, damn it. I'll bring Mother with me on Moonlight."

David ran off, with a last pleading look at me, which I did not at all need. I unhooked the flask of brandy from my belt.

"I don't want any brandy," said Ramses.

"I hadn't meant for you to drink it. Hold out your hands. There is nothing as dirty as human fingernails unless it is human teeth."

"Christ, Mother!"

"Swearing I must accept at times, but blasphemy I do not permit," I said sternly. "Hold out your hands."

"Father was hit," Ramses muttered. He did not flinch when the alcohol touched the raw lines across the backs of his hands. "I thought there was only one shot. What is wrong with Nefret?"

"Nothing that cannot be mended," I said, hoping I was right. "Let me speak a few words to Selim and Daoud, and then we must hurry on."

It came as no surprise when Selim told me Geoffrey was dead. I trust I will not be accused of callousness when I say I had hoped that was the case. I gave him the necessary instructions and then went to have a look at Jack, who had recovered consciousness. Nefret had done a neat job of bandaging the wound, but in my opinion he was too weak to mount a horse, so I gave him a little sip of brandy and told him to stay where he was until Selim could find some means of transportation. Hastening back to Ramses, I found him standing in the exact same spot where I had left him, staring blankly toward the north. For once he did as he was told without arguing, lifting me onto Moonlight and mounting Geoffrey's horse. We set out at the quickest possible pace for home.

When I came into the sitting room they were waiting—Emerson and Ramses and David. I was too tired and distressed to mince words, nor would it have been kind to keep them in suspense.

"She has miscarried," I said. "It is over. She is in no danger. Lia is with her, and Kadija."

Ramses sat down, rather in the manner of Queen Victoria, who never looked to see whether there was a chair to receive her. Fortunately he was standing in front of the sofa.

"Don't look like that," I exclaimed. "She is perfectly all right. This sort of thing is . . . is not uncommon."

"But it rather compounds my offense, don't you think?" Ramses inquired. "Not only her husband, but her—"

"That is morbid and self-indulgent," I said sharply. "The wretched man was a murderer and you risked yourself trying to save his life."

"Does she know that? My blow knocked him into the shaft. She didn't see what happened afterward."

"She must know. If she doesn't, I will tell her. As for . . . As for the other, it was not even . . . She was only. . . . I am speaking of weeks, not months."

Ramses pulled himself to his feet. "Excuse me. I will be in my room if I am wanted."

David started after him. Ramses turned on his friend with lowering brows and bared teeth. Never had he so closely resembled his father. "For God's sake, leave me alone!"

"Oh, dear," I said. "Oh, dear! David—"

"Never mind, Aunt Amelia. I understand. I'll be nearby if he should want me." He followed Ramses out.

Emerson took me by the hand. "Sit down, my dearest. You are certain Nefret is safe?"

"Oh yes," I said wearily. "She is young and strong; she will be herself again in a few days. It is Ramses I am concerned about. He seems to blame himself, and there is no need, Emerson, indeed there is not; it was Geoffrey's doing, all of it, from start to finish. I must go to Ramses, Emerson, and tell him—"

"No, sweetheart. Not now."

"Come and sit by me, Emerson, please. And you might just put your arm round me, if you wouldn't mind."

"My darling!" Holding me close, he rocked me gently as he would have rocked a child. "It's all right, Peabody. We'll weather this as we have weathered other troubles. It could be worse, you know."

"Could be, and has been," I agreed, taking heart from his closeness and strength. "Does your wound pain you, my dear? Perhaps I ought to have another look at it. I was in something of a hurry when—"

"No," Emerson said emphatically. "I feel half a mummy as it is."

"When I think what horrible harm that wretched man has done, I am sorry his death was so quick," I said fiercely. "It was money he wanted, wasn't it? No crime was too vile if it brought him wealth—dealing in drugs, robbing a tomb, selling forgeries—even marrying Nefret."

Emerson shook his head. "Her fortune was certainly an attraction, but as you know, Peabody, it is entirely under her control. I think he loved her as much as he was capable of loving anyone. In his own strange way."

"Strange indeed. How could we have been so obtuse, Emerson? All the evidence that made me suspect Jack applied equally well to Geoffrey, once I realized that the wretch had been poor Maude's lover. Why that possibility did not occur to me long ago I cannot imagine."

"Nor can I," said Emerson.

"Jack would never have had the imagination to think of manufacturing forgeries to cover up his sale of illegal antiquities," I went on. "He trusted Geoffrey; it would not have occurred to him that his friend would seduce his sister and use her for his own evil ends. She was putty in his hands, until she lost her heart to another and hoped to win his regard by betraying Geoffrey."

"Well, now, Peabody, that does seem extraordinary," Emerson remarked, in almost his normal voice. "She was a poor, silly little creature, but would she have been fool enough to believe a confession of that sort could win Ramses's affection? And how did Geoffrey get wind of her intention in time to stop her?"

"She warned him, of course," I said wearily. "To a silly, romantic girl, that would seem the honorable thing to do. She never realized how ruthless he was. Women can be perfect idiots where a man is concerned."

"Why, my dear, I believe that is the first time I have ever heard you make a rude generalization about your own gender."

"It is very good of you to make little jokes in an attempt to cheer me, Emerson." I drew away from him and smoothed my hair.

"That was not a joke." But his blue eyes shone with mingled amusement and tenderness, and he put his arm round my waist. "What is it, Peabody? What troubles you? We've come through another bad time relatively unscathed, and the ending, though dreadful enough, was at least . . . an ending."

"It was mercifully quick and final," I agreed. "Even the . . . the other business . . . Cruel as it may sound, one must regard the sad event as a blessing in disguise."

"Does she regard it as a blessing in disguise?"

"I didn't say that to her, Emerson! What sort of clumsy fool do you take me for? She wept very much. And oh, Emerson—" My tears could not be restrained. Mumbling incoherent words of affection, Emerson picked me up and took me onto his lap. "She didn't want me," I snuffled, against his shoulder. "Whenever she looked at me she started crying again."

A week later I met the morning train from Luxor and greeted my dear old friend Doctor Willoughby. My telegram had said only that he was needed; good man that he was, he had abandoned his patients and his clinic and come at once. As we proceeded by carriage to the house, I told him the entire story, holding nothing back, for I trusted his discretion as I trusted his expertise in nervous disorders.

"Physically she has fully recovered, Doctor, and she tries to eat and exercise and do all the other things I ask. It is heartbreaking to see how hard she tries—to see the effort it costs her to smile and pretend she is glad to see me. She doesn't want to see me, Dr. Willoughby! She doesn't want any of us. Most of the time she lies there without moving or speaking, and when she thinks we are not looking she starts to cry again."

"My dear Mrs. Emerson, it is not surprising," the good man said soothingly. "I have seldom heard such a tragic story. Wife and widow in the space of only a few weeks—learning that the young husband she had loved was a monster of villainy—seeing him die in such a horrible fashion—and then her hopes of motherhood destroyed! You cannot expect complete emotional recovery in so short a time. Don't apologize for summoning me; I would have been offended if you had not."

I had not told him the thing that worried me most. Try as she might to hide it, she shrank from me and from Emerson, the very sight of whom brought tears to her eyes; but Ramses she would not see at all, and he made no effort to see her. Surely, I told myself, she could not be so unjust as to blame him for what had happened. It was the only interpretation that occurred to me, however, and I dared not ask her point-blank while she was in her present state. Lia, from whom I had hoped to gain additional information, was unable or unwilling to give it. She claimed—and I had no reason to doubt her—that Nefret would not talk to her either. I would have worried about Lia too, if I had not had more pressing matters on my mind; she crept about the house like a little shadow of herself, finding solace only in the company of her husband. I thought I understood the cause of her distress; did we not all feel the same?

Dr. Willoughby stayed with us for two days. On three separate occasions he was alone with Nefret, but he would not discuss his diagnosis until after the final visit. We were all waiting for him in the courtyard that afternoon, and when he joined us Emerson jumped up and poured whiskey and soda for everyone, including Lia, who never drank whiskey and soda. Willoughby took his glass with a nod of thanks.

"I won't mince words, my friends," he said gravely. "The situation is more serious than I thought. I believe I have won her confidence, up to a point, but there is something preying on her mind she won't speak of even to me." His tired, kindly gray eyes—the eyes of a man who has seen too much sorrow—moved around the circle of anxious faces. "One thing you must understand; it may help to relieve you. She holds no one except herself accountable for what happened. The cause of her present illness is not grief, as I supposed, but guilt."

"Guilt!" I cried. "About what, in heaven's name? That is ridiculous, Dr. Willoughby. No one blames her; how could we? I will tell her so."

"If it were only that simple!" Dr. Willoughby sighed and shook his head. "I am not a follower of the new schools of psychological theory, Mrs. Emerson, but years of experience have taught me that the causes of mental illness cannot be countered by rational argument. You cannot cure an individual suffering from melancholia by pointing out that he has many reasons to be happy. You cannot remove Nefret's feelings of guilt by telling her they are groundless. She must come to terms with them herself."

My own experience told me he was right. "But if we could discover why she feels guilty?" I persisted.

"That is a task for an expert," Willoughby replied. "Not for me, or even for you—especially for you, Mrs. Emerson, if I may be so bold as to say so. The power of love is strong, but it can cloud the clinical detachment necessary for diagnosis and cure."

"In other words," said Emerson heavily, "you are telling us to keep out of it."

"I wouldn't have put it quite that way." Willoughby smiled. "Be of good heart, my friends, I gave you the bad news first. The good news is that I feel certain she will make a full recovery, in time."

"Have you any practical suggestions?" Emerson inquired.

"Originally I intended to suggest you bring her to Luxor, to my clinic. Now I think it would be advisable to remove her altogether from anything that reminds her of the tragedy."

"Including us?" Ramses asked. It was the first time he had spoken.

"I don't know," Willoughby admitted wearily. "We could hire a nurse to escort her; there is a private sanitarium in Switzerland that specializes in such cases."

"I will accompany them," I said firmly. "Without Nefret's knowledge, if you think it advisable."

Willoughby smiled at me. "I assumed you would say that. As soon as possible, then."

The arrangements were soon underway. With the doctor's concurrence, I told Nefret what had been planned.

It had been several days since I had ventured to visit her. I dreaded that interview and yet I yearned for it; the sympathetic Reader will understand those conflicting emotions. Nefret was sitting by the window wearing one of her pretty dressing gowns; Kadija, who had been with her, slipped out of the room when I entered, and I knew it was that silent, loving woman who had helped her to dress and brushed her hair. She looked better, I thought, and she summoned a faint smile of welcome.

"Dr. Willoughby told you we are sending you to Switzerland?" I inquired, taking the chair next to hers.

"Yes. I am sorry to cause so much trouble."

The listless voice struck straight to my heart, destroying my habitual self-control. I reached for her hand. "Don't you know that there is no trouble we would not take for you—you, who are as dear as a daughter?"

She flinched as if I had struck her. The fingers of the hand I held twisted, not in rejection, but in order to clasp mine more tightly. "You don't know what I have done."

"I don't know what you think you have done. It could not make me love you less."

Her eyes filled with tears, but she held them back. "I'll be better soon. I promise."

"I am sure you will. Do you want—will you let me come with you to Switzerland?"

She was silent for a moment. Then she murmured, as if to herself, "I must make a start. I am only hurting them more."

I ached with pity—and, yes, with curiosity—but I knew I dared not question her. So I waited, holding her hand in mine, until she nodded. "I would like you to come."

"Thank you," I said warmly. "What about . . . the others? Emerson has been so worried about you he isn't fit to live with. I don't believe I can stand his fits of temper much longer."

That brought another smile. "Bless him. Would he leave his work, though?"

"He would abandon the richest tomb in Egypt to be with you."

Her lips trembled. "If that is what he wants . . ."

I decided I had better not push my luck by asking about Ramses. I hastened to tell Emerson the good news, and came close to tears myself when I saw how his drawn face brightened.

For the past week Emerson had done nothing at the site, not even starting to remove the stones that blocked the passage. We had been busy enough, heaven knows, telegraphing Geoffrey's family and making the arrangements for a quiet private burial, talking with various government officials and Mr. Russell of the police. (I made it quite clear to him that Ramses was not to be a policeman.) Poor Jack Reynolds had to be consoled and nursed, Karl von Bork had to be lectured and set straight. The Vandergelts had rushed back to Cairo as soon as they learned of the tragedy, and Katherine was a great help to me with the last two; it was she who suggested that Karl be given the responsibility for Jack's care, and our German friend's response encouraged me to hope that this would be the saving of both of them.

Of Geoffrey's burial I will not speak. I was there because I felt I ought to be. The only member of the family who accompanied me was Ramses. I had told him he could not come, but he came anyhow.

I did not know what I was going to do about Ramses. "Leave him alone" was Emerson's advice; "leave me alone" was the unspoken message I received loud and clear from Ramses himself.

Now, with his mind more at ease about Nefret, Emerson declared his intention of investigating the substructure of the pyramid. Privately he explained to me that he was only doing it in the hope of "cheering Ramses up." I did not question his motives—not aloud, at any rate.

When we set out that morning for Zawaiet the weather was perfect; dawn spread across the eastern sky like a blush on a maiden's cheek. A soft breeze ruffled Lia's hair. We were all present—except Nefret, of course—and half a dozen of our most trusted men were waiting when we arrived. Nothing remained to testify to the tragedy that had occurred; even the bloodstains had been covered by blowing sand.

When Selim advanced to meet us, the look of suppressed excitement on the young man's ingenuous countenance told me that he had news for us.

"Well?" my spouse inquired.

"All is prepared, O Father of Curses. We have removed the rubble from the corridor and brought brooms."

"Emerson!" I exclaimed indignantly. "How could you?"

"Now, Peabody," Emerson began.

The others began talking very quickly. I was delighted to see that even Ramses had perked up a bit. He said, "What was it you saw, Father?" Lia said, "Brooms? Why brooms?" and David exclaimed, "I thought the passage was completely blocked."

Emerson glanced self-consciously at me. "It was all Selim's doing, really. He discovered that by shoving some of the fallen stones down into the lower part of the shaft he could crawl over them into the continuation of the entrance passage. I asked him to have a closer look at a section of the corridor outside the burial chamber. I had just—er—happened to notice the floor there was uneven. The surface was dusty and littered, and it was too dark to see clearly, and I—er—hmph."

"Why didn't you tell me?" I demanded indignantly.

"Because you would have gone haring down to see for yourself," Emerson snapped. "And been mashed by falling stones, or buried alive. I wanted the shaft empty before we continued, and then—well, you know what happened. I still don't know for certain that we've found the right place."

"Then let us ascertain whether it is so," I cried, starting for the stairs.

Emerson insisted on preceding me, of course. Selim had done a good deal more than move a few stones; the way was clear, and we proceeded without mishap into the corridor that ended in the soi-disant burial chamber. As soon as we reached the spot I saw what had caught Emerson's trained eye. It was more obvious now that the litter of millennia had been partially removed—a section of the floor that was slightly sunken and partially defined by patterns of suspiciously regular cracks.

"Give me a broom!" I cried, snatching it from Selim.

My first enthusiastic assault on the surface raised such a cloud of dust that the others retreated and I burst into a paroxysm of sneezing. Following my husband's profane advice, I moderated my efforts; and before long the truth of Emerson's assumption was confirmed. A section of the stone had been cut out and replaced by cunningly mortared blocks. Originally it would have been indistinguishable from the living stone itself, but the passage of time had crumbled the mortar in some sections.

"That's the one he had up," Ramses said, indicating one of the blocks. "He didn't bother replacing the mortar. Father, shall I . . . ?"

"Watch your fingers," Emerson grunted, handing him a small chisel.

At this demonstration of paternal affection tears came to my eyes—or perhaps I should say additional tears, since the irritation of the dusty air had caused all of us to weep like mourners at a funeral.

Ramses soon had the stone up. Emerson's superb—I might even say godlike—forbearance continued. Under ordinary circumstances he would have removed bodily anyone, myself included, to get the first look at such a discovery. On this occasion he handed Ramses the torch and stood back.

Lying flat, Ramses pointed the torch down.

"Well?" I cried.

Ramses looked up at me. Dust and perspiration had formed a sticky mask over his features. It cracked a little around his mouth. "See for yourself, Mother. There is just enough room for you next to me."

He held the torch steady as I stretched out prostrate upon the floor and peered into the cavity. At first I saw only a chaotic tumble of shapes, angular and rounded, rough and smooth. Then my astonished eyes and mind sorted them out. There were vessels of alabaster and granite inside a strange framework of crumbling wood and matting—a bed or couch, upside down and tilted to one side. Under it was another wooden surface—a coffin, I thought, though I could not be sure. All around were other scattered objects.

In silence, overwhelmed by what I had beheld, I let my noble spouse haul me to my feet and take my place. Everyone had a turn, including Selim; and then Emerson spoke. He was hoarse with emotion, or possibly with dust, but he spoke in the measured tones of a lecturer.

"You observed there are no small portable objects within arm's reach. Time was short and he did not dare remove more than one stone. He took as much as he could get his hands on, including the legs of the funerary couch, meaning to finish the job this season."

He avoided using Geoffrey's name. We had all got into that habit.

"He just grabbed and snatched, didn't he?" Lia said. "What a mess he's made of it."

"It wasn't particularly tidy anyhow," Ramses said. "It is obviously a reburial, and a hasty one. The thieves who attacked the original burial must have been caught before they finished their ghoulish task and the pious successor of King Khaba, if that was his name, decided to conceal what was left of the funerary equipment more securely. Er—do you agree, Father?"

"Quite, my boy, quite. And secure it remained, for over four thousand years, except for the natural processes of decay. They used cedar beams to roof the chamber and support the blocking stones, but the wood of the couch and coffin wasn't as tough. They and any other wooden objects that may be down there will crumble at a touch."

Lia began to cough, and David put his arm around her. "We are going out, Professor, if that is all right with you."

"We are all going," said Emerson. "Come along, Peabody."

When we emerged into the daylight I felt as if I had traversed not only several hundred meters of space but forty-five centuries of time. The find was unique; no other royal burial of that remote period had been found. This one, though unquestionably incomplete, would solve the question of the pyramid's owner, shed new light on the artistic and social attitudes of the time—and additional luster on the name of the greatest Egyptologist of this or any other era.

We tidied ourselves up a bit, for Selim, always efficient, had brought jars of water. Emerson gathered our men round. Even before he made his announcement I knew what he would say.

"I am leaving it to you, Selim, to replace the stone and conceal it. I know I can trust you to do the job as well as your father would have done, and that I can depend on all of you to say nothing of what we found today."

Selim's countenance betrayed the pride he felt at having such confidence reposed in him, but he said only, "Yes, Father of Curses. Your wish is our command. But it will be hard to wait."

"Hard for all of us," said Ramses, glancing at his father, who was chewing fiercely on the stem of his pipe. He spoke Arabic, as Emerson had done. "There is at least one season's work there, Selim, if it is carried out as the Father of Curses demands. We have less than a week."

"I understand. We will guard the secret and the burial will be here, safe and undisturbed, when you return."

So that was settled. I knew I could leave the closing of the house and the storage of our goods to Selim and Fatima. I did not suppose we would ever return to the villa. It held too many unhappy memories.

The question of what to do with Sennia had not occupied my mind for long. She would have to go with us, not only because I was too much of a coward to face the explosion that would ensue should I attempt to remove Ramses from her, but because Ramses had some notion she would not be entirely safe in Egypt, even in the devoted care of Daoud and Kadija. I doubted Kalaan would dare try to harm her—he was still in hiding, and he would not have risked the wrath of Emerson—but I did not try to dissuade Ramses. She was the only person who could make him laugh.

A few days before we were to leave for Port Said we gathered for the last time in the courtyard with Cyrus and Katherine, who had come to say good-bye. Emerson and David were smoking their pipes. Ramses sat on the rim of the fountain, looking down at the water.

"You sure you don't want me to have a crack at the pyramid?" Cyrus asked, without much hope.

"Bah," said Emerson amiably.

"I didn't suppose so. Oh, well, looks as if Maspero may give me part of Abusir next year, so if you folks are going to be at Zawaiet, we'll be neighbors again."

"We will drink to that," I proclaimed, and Emerson passed round the whiskey.

Why Ramses should have delayed his announcement until that particular evening I did not know. It could hardly have been delayed much longer.

"I won't be going back with you."

"What did you say?" I demanded, observing that Emerson was staring fixedly at a potted plant. The news was obviously not news to him.

"I am going to work with Mr. Reisner for another month or so," Ramses said. "He has been left shorthanded by the loss of two of his staff members."

"Nonsense," I exclaimed. "We owe him nothing. I strictly forbid—"

"It will be excellent experience," said Emerson, giving me a meaningful look.

We talked about it later when we were alone, and I was forced to agree that I could not change Ramses's mind. I never had been able to. Sennia would remain with him on the *Amelia*, attended, I did not doubt, by all the women in the family, and return with him and Basima in early April. By then ... Who knew what might have happened by then? For once not even I had the answer.

**From Manuscript H**

Ramses had not told David of his decision either. He had expected an argument, but he had not expected to lose it.

"There is no way you can prevent me from staying," David pointed out with infuriating calmness and even more infuriating accuracy. "What a pity you aren't the original Ramses the Great; you could have me bound in chains and carried on board ship by your royal guards."

They had retired to Ramses's room after dinner, supposedly to pack; clothes were strewn all over the place, and both of them were sitting on the floor glaring at one another.

"Marriage hasn't improved your manners," Ramses said rudely. "Or your sense of humor. What will Lia have to say about this?"

"She is staying too, of course. She agrees you should not be left alone."

"Oh, for God's sake! I am quite capable . . ." David's quizzical, affectionate, amused look made him break off with a half-hearted laugh. "I'm not, am I? You needn't remind me of how many times you've pulled me out of a sticky situation. But there's nobody trying to murder me just now, David."

"Are you sure?"

After a brief, breathless pause, Ramses said, "How much do you know? And how do you know?"

"About your cousin? It doesn't require great intelligence to deduce it was he who produced Sennia and her mother at a particularly strategic moment. He was trying to humiliate and hurt you, and he succeeded, didn't he?"

"Beyond his wildest dreams."

"You may as well tell me the rest of it. You have no idea," David added, "how much I enjoy saying that instead of hearing Aunt Amelia say it to me."

"If you saw it too, then it's not just my imagination. I began to wonder if I was going crazy. David, you cannot know how much I . . . I don't have to say it, do I?"

"No. You are too English," David said, smiling.

Ramses was silent for a time, trying to get his thoughts in order. There was a certain irony in the fact that his conclusions were based almost entirely on what his mother would have called intuition. In this case it was knowledge of a man's character, the way his mind worked. It left a track through the world. In Percy's case the track was like that of a snail, slimy and sticky.

"I don't know how Percy found out about Sennia, but he'd have gone back to the brothels as soon as he returned to Cairo. They are his natural habitat. The sight of her probably amused him a great deal—a little image of Mother, growing up in the slums of Cairo and destined for the same life as Rashida—"

An inarticulate murmur of revulsion from David interrupted him. His lips twisted. "He hates Mother almost as much as he does me. It was she who saw through his childish schemes all those years ago, and told him precisely what she thought of him. Percy arranged that meeting in the suk, I've no doubt of it. What happened after that was my own fault. I should have gone straight to Mother and Father. But I thought it would be better—"

"I would have done the same."

"No, you wouldn't. You aren't as stubborn and accustomed to going your own way. As it happened, I played straight into Percy's hands. At that time, of course, I hadn't the faintest inkling that he knew about Sennia, or any reason to anticipate what he would do with that knowledge. It was only hindsight that enabled me to put the pieces together. No one else knows, David; even Mother doesn't suspect, and I see no reason to tell her. There's no danger of his taking her in again, she despises him enough as it is."

David nodded gravely. "How did Kalaan come into it?"

"He owns those girls as a herder owns his cattle. If Rashida didn't tell him, one of the others did—about the Inglizi who had been coming round rather more often than usual. Kalaan would assume there was profit to be made from that; but if he tried to blackmail Percy he was sadly disappointed. They were brothers under the skin, the Cairo procurer and the fine English gentleman, and they struck up an alliance. Rashida would never have had the courage to approach Mother and Father on her own; Percy needed Kalaan for that, and Kalaan, of course, assumed he could get money from us."

"That was a serious miscalculation on his part."

"And perhaps on Percy's. Not that it mattered to him; he didn't care what happened to Sennia, his aim was to shame me in front of Mother and Father, and Nefret. He knew what she thought of men who use women like Rashida; the morning we ran into him in el Was'a she . . . You know about that, don't you? Nefret must have written Lia."

David nodded. He avoided his friend's eyes, though, and Ramses said, "What else did she tell Lia?"

"Well—uh—quite a number of things. Go on, Ramses, I'll stop you if you—uh—cover ground that is already familiar to me."

"Did Nefret mention to Lia that Percy had been after her? Yes, of course, she would. She never admitted it to *me*—she always thinks she can deal with everything single-handedly—but there must have been several encounters."

"She may not have told you about them because she was afraid of what you would do," David murmured.

"Possibly. Anyhow, what brought matters to a head was the

day I came home and found Percy with Nefret." He was watching David closely, and he knew his friend too well to miss the signs of self-consciousness. "Do stop me if this is familiar ground," he said gently.

David shook his head. He looked so miserable, Ramses took pity on him; divided loyalties were hellishly unpleasant, and David must have been sworn to secrecy by Lia. About what, though? Surely Nefret would not have confessed, even to her best friend, that she had given herself to a man she didn't love; surely Lia wouldn't repeat that painfully personal confidence, even to her husband . . .

At any rate *he* had no right to speak of it. Choosing his words with care, Ramses went on, "Well, there they were, you see. When I walked in he had hold of her and was trying to kiss her. It would have annoyed me a bit to see anyone forcing himself on any girl, but knowing what I knew about Percy's habits, I rather lost my head. I knocked him across the room, and then Nefret grabbed hold of me and hung on. It was the only way she could have stopped me from murdering the bastard, but he wouldn't have understood that. He assumed she and I were . . ."

David waited for him to go on. Then he said, "That would be a logical deduction, wouldn't it?"

"To Percy it would. He doesn't understand friendship or disinterested affection. You can imagine the effect of that touching scene on a man so blindly vain and self-centered. He must have gone raging back to Kalaan and set up the encounter for the following day. It's a pity you missed it; this family is good at melodrama, and that was a stellar performance by all concerned."

David was not deceived by the mocking tone. "Tell me. If you can bring yourself to do so."

"Mother didn't give you a word-for-word account?" He couldn't keep up the pretense; reaching for a cigarette, he was ashamed to see that his hand was shaking. "David, she was wonderful. So was Father. They believed me. How in God's name they could I don't know! I must have looked guilty as hell when I saw Sennia, and Kalaan blandly announced she was my daughter. The resemblance was strong enough to carry conviction in itself, and then the little thing ran to me, holding out her arms and calling me Father, and I . . ." He tossed the unlit cigarette aside and hid his face in his hands. "I know how poor old cowardly Saint Peter must have felt," he said in a muffled voice.

David put a comforting hand on his shoulder. "You denied she was your child? It was the truth."

"Yes, but she trusted me, you see, and I... At least I only denied her once." He passed his hand over his eyes and tried to smile. "Someday I may be able to forgive myself for that. Nefret never will. It was the denial, almost as much as the accusation, that made her despise me."

"But, my brother—"

"Just let me finish, please. I had to claim Sennia, to keep her from Kalaan; only a male relative could do that. Even then, Mother and Father never doubted me."

"But Nefret did. And you will never forgive *her* for that?"

Ramses did not reply. After a moment David said, "If she made a mistake she has paid dearly for it. There is a reason, perhaps, why it was harder for her than for your parents."

"I wouldn't know about that. She always told me I didn't understand women. There's no question of forgiveness; how could I blame her for anything when she's so unhappy? I'd tell her so if she would let me. I don't even blame her for not wanting to see me. In a way I was responsible for Geoffrey's death, and she loved him."

"I don't believe it," David said. "She was fond of him, she was sorry for him, she was furious with you. And Percy—"

"No, that's going too far." Ramses shook his head vehemently. "If Percy couldn't have her himself he might settle for the lesser satisfaction of keeping her from me, but there is no way he could have known Geoffrey had a chance with Nefret. None of us did."

"And what about Rashida's death?"

"You wondered too, did you?" Ramses got to his feet and began pacing. "I keep thinking I've plumbed the depths of Percy's swamp of a mind—sounds like Mother, doesn't it?—and I've been wrong every time. I didn't even realize he hated me so much, or that he would go to so much effort to damage me. The business with Sennia was weeks in the making; he must have begun planning it long before I found him with Nefret that afternoon. What put the idea into his head? Did something happen to set him off—something I don't know about?"

"Ramses. My brother..." David was on his feet, his hand outstretched, his face distorted by emotion.

"It's all right," Ramses said quickly. "Don't distress yourself. That was a rhetorical question; you cannot comprehend Percy's motives any more than I can." He went to the window and stood looking out. "The truth is, I'm afraid of him, David. He's got a mind so devious and dirty it's impossible for me to anticipate what he might do. However, I am taking no chances with Sennia. Kalaan wouldn't dare injure someone who is under Father's protection, but Percy . . ."

Her father. That word had a new and painful poignancy for him now, and not only because of the little girl who had given him the love her natural father didn't want or deserve. His mother's blunt announcement about Nefret's condition had literally knocked him off his feet. A blessing in disguise, she had called it. . . . I'll never know for certain, I suppose, Ramses thought. Perhaps it's better that way.

But he was glad David couldn't see his face.

**I** do not often trouble the Almighty with petitions, since I am sure there are others far more in need of supernatural assistance than I. I prayed that night, however, as I lay awake beside the sleeping form of my husband. His presence comforted me as it always does, but my aching heart demanded further reassurance—hope that the future would be brighter than the sad present.

There was no answer to my wordless request. But I soon fell asleep, and I dreamed.

"Well, Abdullah," I said. "You warned me of storms ahead. If I had known how bad they would be, I might not have been able to face them. I don't know that I can face them now."

The rising sun illuminated his handsome, hawklike features and the strong white teeth that shone in the blackness of his beard. "Do you remember the Snake, Sitt Hakim? He who stole Emerson away and kept him prisoner, so that we did not know whether he lived or not?"

"I remember. As I remember it was you who saved him, Abdullah."

"You did not lose heart then."

"Oh, but I did," I said, remembering the night I had wept uncontrollably, huddled on the floor with a towel pressed to my face so that no one would hear.

"And then you went to the window, and after your long night of weeping, you saw the dawn."

"So you know about that, too? Really, Abdullah, I am not sure I appreciate this omniscience of yours. Is there anything about me you don't know?"

"Very little." His black eyes shone with laughter.

"Hmmm. What can I do to help them?"

Abdullah shook his head. "How can a woman be so wise and yet so blind? It is well, perhaps, that you do not know everything. You would try to help, and you would blunder, Sitt. You are not always careful."

It was such a comfort to hear his old joking complaint and see the twinkle in his eyes. He took my hand in his; it was as warm and firm as that of a living man. "The worst of the storm is yet to come, Sitt. You will need all your courage to survive; but your heart will not fail you, and in the end the clouds will blow away and the falcon will fly through the portal of the dawn."